what was either a burst of inspiration or insanity,
mmed on the braking motors. The sled stopped
in mid-spin, flinging him sideways against his
-belts —

flinging the slavering jackal-dog off the back of
entirely, sending it flying into the pack, and
tumbling at least a dozen of them nose-over-tail.

Alex burned air back towards Tia; she dropped
open a cargo-bay, activated restraint-fields and hoped
he'd be able to brake in time to keep from hitting the
back wall. At the speed he was coming the restraint-
fields, meant to keep the sled from banging around in
rough flight, wouldn't do much.

He didn't even slow down as he hit the bay door,
which she slammed down behind him. Instead, he
killed the power and skidded to a halt on the sled's belly
in a shower of sparks. The sled skewed sideways and
crashed into the back wall — but between Alex's own
maneuver and the restraint-fields, the impact wasn't
bad enough to do more than dent her hold-wall. There
were a half-dozen impacts on the cargo door, indicating
the leaders of the pack hitting it, unable to stop.

Alex sat there for a moment, then sagged over the
steering wheel, breathing heavily. Nothing on Tia's
pickups made her think he was hurt, so she waited for
him to catch his breath.

When his breathing slowed, and he looked up, she
focused on his face. He was flushed, but showed no
shock, and no sign of pain.

"Well," she said, keeping her voice calm and light,
"you certainly know how to make an entrance."

He blinked — then leaned back in his seat, and
began laughing.

ANNE McCAFFREY
MERCEDES LACKEY

BAEN
BOOKS

A Baen Books Original

Baen Publishing Enterprises
P.O. Box 1403
Riverdale, NY 10471

ISBN: 0-671-72129-1

Cover art by Stephen Hickman

First Printing, August 1992

Printed in the United States of America

Distributed by Simon & Schuster
1230 Avenue of the Americas
New York, NY 10020

● CHAPTER ONE

The ruby light on the com unit was blinking when Hypatia Cade emerged from beneath the tutor's hood, with quadratic equations dancing before her seven-year-old eyes. Not the steady blink that meant a recorded message, nor the triple-beat that meant Mum or Dad had left her a note, but the double blink with a pause between each pair that meant there was someone Upstairs, waiting for her to open the channel.

Someone Upstairs meant an unscheduled ship — Tia knew very well when all the scheduled visits were; they were on the family calendar and were the first things reported by the AI when they all had breakfast. That made it Important for her to answer, quickly, and not take the time to suit up and run to the dig for Mum or Dad. It must not have been an emergency, though, or the AI would have interrupted her lesson.

She rubbed her eyes to rid them of the dancing variables, and pushed her stool over to the com-console so she could reach all the touch-pads when she stood on it. She would never have been able to reach things sitting in a chair, of course. With brisk efficiency that someone three times her age might have envied, she cleared the board, warmed up the relay, and opened the line.

"Exploratory Team Cee-One-Two-One," she enunciated carefully, for the microphone was old, and often lost anything not spoken clearly. "Exploratory Team Cee-One-Two-One, receiving. Come in, please. Over."

She counted out the four-second lag to orbit and

back, nervously. *One-hypotenuse, Two-hypotenuse, Three-hypotenuse, Four-hypotenuse.* Who could it be? They didn't get unscheduled ships very often, and it meant bad news as often as not. Planet pirates, plague, or slavers. Trouble with some of the colony-planets. Or worse — artifact thieves in the area. A tiny dig like this one was all too vulnerable to a hit-and-run raid. Of course, digs on the Salomon-Kildaire Entities rarely yielded anything a collector would lust after, but would thieves know that? Tia had her orders if raiders came and she was alone — to duck down the hidden escape tunnel that would blow the dome; to run to the dark little hidey away from the dig that was the first thing Mum and Dad put in once the dome was up. . . .

"This is courier TM Three-Seventy. Tia, dearest, is that you? Don't worry, love, we have a non-urgent message run and you're on the way, so we brought you your packets early. Over." The rich, contralto voice was a bit flattened by the poor speaker, but still welcome and familiar. Tia jumped up and down a bit on her stool in excitement.

"Moira! Yes, yes, it's me! But — " She frowned a little. The last time Moira had been here, her designation had been CM, not TM. "Moira, what happened to Charlie?" Her seven-year-old voice took on the half-scolding tones of someone much older. "Moira, did you scare away *another* brawn? Shame on you! Remember what they told you when you kicked Ari out your airlock! Uh — over."

Four seconds; an eternity. "I didn't scare him away, darling," Moira replied, though Tia thought she sounded just a little guilty. "He decided to get married, raise a brood of his own, and settle down as a dirtsider. Don't worry, this will be the last one, I'm sure of it. Tomas and I get along famously. Over."

"That's what you said about Charlie," Tia reminded her darkly. "And about Ari, and Lilian, and Jules, and — "

She was still reciting names when Moira interrupted her. "Turn on the landing beacon, Tia, please. We can talk when I'm not burning fuel in orbital adjustments." Her voice turned a little bit sly. "Besides, I brought you a birthday present. That's why I couldn't miss stopping here. Over."

As if a birthday present was going to distract her from the litany of Moira's failed attempts to settle on a brawn!

Well — maybe just a little.

She turned on the beacon, then feeling a little smug, activated the rest of the landing sequence, bringing up the pad lights and guidance monitors, then hooking in the AI and letting it know it needed to talk to Moira's navigational system. She hadn't known how to do all *that,* the last time Moira was here. Moira'd had to set down with no help at all.

She leaned forward for the benefit of the mike. "All clear and ready to engage landing sequence, Moira. Uh — what did you bring me? Over."

"Oh, you bright little penny!" Moira exclaimed, her voice brimming with delight. "You've got the whole system up! You *have* been learning things since I was here last! Thank you, dear — and you'll find out what I brought when I get down there. Over and out."

Oh well, she had tried. She jumped down from her stool, letting the AI that ran the house and external systems take over the job of bringing the brainship in. Or rather, giving the brainship the information she needed to bring *herself* in; Moira never handed over her helm to anyone if she had a choice in the matter. That was part of the problem she'd had with keeping brawns. She didn't trust them at the helm, and let them know that. Ari, in particular, had been less than amused with her attitude and had actually tried to disable her helm controls to prove *he* could pilot as well as she.

Now, the next decision: should she suit up and fetch Mum and Dad? It was no use trying to get them on the com; they probably had their suit-speakers off. Even though they weren't *supposed* to do that. And this wasn't an emergency; they would be decidedly annoyed if she buzzed in on them, and they found out it was just an unscheduled social call from a courier ship, even if it was Moira. They might be more than annoyed if they were in the middle of something important, like documenting a find or running an age-assay, and she joggled their elbows.

Moira didn't say it was important. She wouldn't have talked about errant brawns and birthday presents if what she carried was really, really earth-shaking.

Tia glanced at the clock; it wasn't more than a half hour until lunch break. If there was one thing that Pota Andropolous-Cade (Doctor of Science in Bio-Forensics, Doctor of Xenology, Doctor of Archeology), and her husband Braddon Maartens-Cade (Doctor of Science in Geology, Doctor of Physics in Cosmology, Associate Degree in Archeology, and licensed Astrogator) had in common — besides daughter Hypatia and their enduring, if absent-minded love for each other — it was punctuality. At precisely oh-seven-hundred every "morning," no matter where they were, the Cades had breakfast together. At precisely twelve-hundred, they arrived at the dome for lunch together. The AI saw that Hypatia had a snack at sixteen-hundred. And at precisely nineteen-hundred, the Cades returned from the dig for dinner together.

So in thirty minutes, *precisely*, Pota and Braddon would be here. Moira couldn't possibly land in less than twenty minutes. The visitor — or visitors; there was no telling if there was someone on board besides the brawn, the yet-unmet Tomas — would not have long to wait.

She trotted around the living room of the dome;

picking up her books and puzzles, straightening the pillows on the sofa, turning on lights and the holoscape of waving blue trees by a green lagoon on Mycon, where her parents had met. She told the kitchen to start coffee, overriding the lunch program to instruct it to make selection V-1, a setup program Braddon had logged for her for munchies for visitors. She decided on music on her own; the *Arkenstone Suite*, a lively synthesizer piece she thought matched the holo-mural.

There wasn't much else to do, so she sat down and waited — something she had learned how to do very early. She thought she did it very well, actually. There had certainly been enough of it in her life. The lot of an archeologists' child was full of waiting, usually alone, and required her to be mostly self-sufficient.

She had never had playmates or been around very many children of her own age. Usually Mum and Dad were alone on a dig, for they specialized in Class One Evaluation sites; when they weren't, it was usually on a Class Two dig, Exploratory. Never a Class Three Excavation dig, with hundreds of people and their families. It wasn't often that the other scientists her parents' age on a Class Two dig had children younger than their teens. And even those were usually away somewhere at school.

She knew that other people thought that the Cades were eccentric for bringing their daughter with them on every dig — especially so young a child. Most parents with a remote job to do left their offspring with relatives or sent them to boarding schools. Tia listened to the adults around her, who usually spoke as if she couldn't understand what they were talking about. She learned a great deal that way; probably more even than her Mum and Dad suspected.

One of the things she overheard — quite frequently, in fact — was that she seemed like something of an afterthought. Or perhaps an "accident" — she'd over-heard that before, too.

She knew very well what was meant by the "after-thought or accident" comment. The last time someone had said *that*, she'd decided that she'd heard it often enough.

It had been at a reception, following the reading of several scientific papers. She'd marched straight up to the lady in question and had informed her solemnly that she, Tia, had been planned very *carefully*, thank you. That Braddon and Pota had determined that their careers would be secure just about when Pota's biological clock had the last few seconds on it, and *that* was when they would have one, singular, female child. Herself. Hypatia. Planned from the beginning. From the leave-time to give birth to the way she had been brought on each assignment; from the pressure-bubble glove-box that had served as her cradle until she could crawl, to the pressure-tent that became a crib, to the kind of AI that would best perform the dual functions of tutor and guardian.

The lady in question, red-faced, hadn't known what to say. Her escort had tried to laugh it away, telling her that the "child" was just parroting what she'd over-heard and couldn't possibly understand any of it.

Whereupon Tia, well-versed in the ethnological habits — including courtship and mating — of four separate sapient species, including *homo sap.*, had proceeded to prove that he was wrong.

Then, while the escort was still spluttering, she had turned back to the original offender and informed her, with earnest sincerity, that *she* had better think about having *her* children soon, too, since it was ob-vious that *she* couldn't have much more time before menopause.

Tia had, quite literally, silenced that section of the room. When reproached later for her behavior by the host of the party, Tia had been completely unrepentant. "She was being rude and nasty," Tia had said. When the host protested that the remark hadn't been meant for her, Tia had replied, "Then she shouldn't have said it so loudly that everyone else laughed. And besides," she had continued with inexorable logic, "being rude *about* someone is worse than being rude *to* them."

Braddon, summoned to deal with his erring daughter, had shrugged casually and said only, "I warned you. And you didn't believe me."

Though exactly what it was Dad had warned Doctor Julius about, Tia never discovered.

The remarks about being "unplanned" or an "accident" stopped, at least in her presence — but people still seemed concerned that she was "too precocious," and that she had no one of her own age to socialize with.

But the fact was that Tia simply didn't care that she had no other children to play with. She had the best lessons in the known universe, via the database; she had the AI to talk to. She had plenty of things to play with and lots of freedom to do what she wanted once lessons were done. And most of all, she had Mum and Dad, who spent *hours* more with her than most people spent with their children. She knew that, because both the statistics in the books she had read on child-care and the Socrates, the AI that traveled with them everywhere, told her so. They were never boring, and they always talked to her as if she was grown up. If she didn't understand something, all she had to do was tell them and they would backtrack and explain until she did. When they weren't doing something that meant they needed all their concentration, they encouraged her to come out to the digs with them when her lessons were over. She hadn't ever heard of too many children who got to be with their parents at work.

If anything, sometimes Mum and Dad explained a little *too* much. She distinctly remembered the time that she started asking "Why?" to everything. Socrates told her that "Why?" was a stage all children went through — mostly to get attention. But Pota and Braddon had taken her literally. . . .

The AI told her not long ago that her "Why?" period might have been the shortest on record — because Mum and Dad answered every "Why?" in detail. *And* made sure she understood, so that she wouldn't ask that particular "Why?" again.

After a month, "Why?" wasn't fun anymore, and she went on to other things.

She really didn't miss other children at all. Most of the time when she'd encountered them, it had been with the wary feeling of an anthropologist approaching a new and potentially dangerous species. The feeling seemed to be mutual. And so far, other children had proven to be rather boring creatures. Their interests and their worlds were very narrow, their vocabulary a fraction of Tia's. Most of them hadn't the faintest idea of how to play chess, for instance.

Mum had a story she told at parties about how Tia, at the age of two, had stunned an overly effusive professorial spouse into absolute silence. There had been a chess set, a lovely antique, up on one of the tables just out of Tia's reach. She had stared longingly at it for nearly half an hour before the lady noticed what she was looking at.

Tia remembered that incident quite well, too. The lady had picked up an intricately carved knight and waggled it at her. "See the horsie?" she had gushed. "Isn't it a pretty horsie?"

Tia's sense of fitness had been outraged — and that wasn't all. Her intelligence had been insulted, and she was *very* well aware of it.

She had stood up, very straight, and looked the lady

right in the eye. "Is *not* a horsie," she had announced, coldly and clearly. "Is a *knight*. It moves like the letter L. And Mum says it is piece most often sacri— sacer— sacra—"

Mum had come up by then, as she grew red-faced, trying to remember how to say the word she wanted. "Sacrificed?" Mum had asked, helpfully. "It means 'given up.'"

Beaming with gratitude, Tia had nodded. "Most often *given up* after the pawn." Then she glared at the lady. "Which is *not* a little man!"

The lady had retired to a corner and did not emerge while Tia and her parents were there, although her Mum's superior had then taken down the set and challenged Tia to a game. He had won, of course, but she had at least shown she really knew how to play. He had been impressed and intrigued, and had taken her out on the porch to point out various species of birds at the feeders there.

She couldn't help but think that she affected grown-ups in only two ways. They were either delighted by her, or scandalized by her. Moira was among the "delighted" sort, though most of her brawns hadn't been. Charlie had, though, which was why she had thought that he just might be the one to stay with the brainship. He actually seemed to enjoy the fact that she could beat him at chess.

She sighed. Probably this new brawn would be of the other sort.

Not that it really mattered how she affected adults. She didn't see that many of them, and then it was never for very long. Though it was important to impress Mum's and Dad's superiors in a positive sense. She at least knew that much now.

"Your visitor is at the airlock," said the AI, breaking in on her thoughts. "His name is Tomas. While he is cycling, Moira would like you to have me turn on the ground-based radio link so that she can join the conversation."

"Go ahead, Socrates," she told the AI. That was the problem with AIs; if they didn't already have instructions, you had to tell them to do something before they would, where a shellperson would just do it if it made sense.

"Tomas has your birthday present," Moira said, a moment later. "I hope you like it."

"You mean, you hope I like *him*," she replied shrewdly. "You hope I don't scare him."

"Let's say I use you as a kind of litmus test, all right?" Moira admitted. "And, darling — Charlie really *did* fall in love with a ground-pounder. Even I could see he wanted to be with her more than he wanted space." She sighed. "It was really awfully romantic; you don't see old-style love at first sight anymore. Michiko is such a charming little thing — I really can't blame him. And it's partly your fault, dear. He was so taken with you that all he could talk about was how he wanted children just like you. Well, anyway, she persuaded Admin to find him a ground job, and they traded me Tomas for him, with no fine, because it wasn't my fault this time."

"It's going to take you *forever* to buy out those fines for bouncing brawns," Tia began, when the inner airlock door cycled, and a pressure-suited person came through, holding a box and his helmet.

Tia frowned at seeing the helmet; he'd taken it off in the lock, once the pressure was equalized. That wasn't a good idea, because locks had been known to blow, especially old ones like the Class One digs had. So already he was one in the minus column as far as Tia was concerned. But he had a nice face, with kind eyes, and that wasn't so bad; a round, tanned face, with curly black hair and bright brown eyes, and a wide mouth that didn't have those tense lines at the corners that

Ari'd had. So that was one in the plus column. He came out even so far.

"Hello, Tomas," she said, neutrally. "You shouldn't take your helmet off in the lock, you know — you should wait until the interior door cycles."

"She's right, Tomas," Moira piped up from the com console. "These Class One digs always get the last pick of equipment. All of it is old, and some of it isn't reliable. Door seals blow all the time."

"It blew last month, when I came in," Tia added helpfully. "It took Mum hours to install the new seal, and she's not altogether happy with it." Tomas' eyes were wide with surprise, and he was clearly taken aback. He had probably intended to ask her where her parents were. He had not expected to be greeted by a lecture on pressure-suit safety.

"Oh," was all he could say. "Ah, thank you. I will remember that in the future."

"You're welcome," she replied. "Mum and Dad are at the dig; I'm sorry they weren't here to meet you."

"I ought to make proper introductions," Moira said from the console. "Tomas, this is Hypatia Cade. Her mother is Doctor Pota Andropolous-Cade and her father is Doctor Braddon Maartens-Cade. Tia, this is Tomas Delacorte-Ibanez."

"I'm very pleased to meet you, Tomas," she replied with careful formality. "Mum and Dad will be here in — " she glanced at her wrist-chrono " — ten minutes. In the meantime, there is fresh coffee, and may I offer you anything to eat?"

Once again, he was taken aback. "Coffee, please," he replied after a moment. "If you would be so kind."

She fetched it from the kitchen; by the time she returned with the cup balanced in one hand and the refreshments in the other, he had removed his suit. She had to admit that he did look very handsome in the skintight ship-suit he wore beneath it. But then, all of Moira's brawns had been good-looking. That was part of the problem; she tended to pick brawns on the basis of looks first and personality second.

He accepted the coffee and food from her gravely, and a little warily, for all the world as if he had decided to treat her as some kind of new, unknown sentient. She tried not to giggle.

"That is a very unusual name that you were given," he said, after an awkward pause. "Hypatia, is it?"

"Yes," she said, "I was named for the first and only female librarian of the Great Library at Alexandria on Terra. She was also the last librarian there."

His eyes showed some recognition of the names at least. So he wasn't completely ignorant of history, the way Julio had been. "Ah. That would have been when the Romans burned it, in the time of Cleopatra — " he began. She interrupted him with a shake of her head.

"No, the library wasn't destroyed then, not at all, not even close. It persisted as a famous library into the day of Constantine," she continued, warming to her favorite story, reciting it exactly as Pota had told it to her, as it was written in the history database. "It was when Hypatia was the librarian that a pack of unwashed Christian fanatics stormed it — led by some people who called themselves prophets and holy men — intending to burn it to the ground because it contained 'pagan books, lies, and heresies.' When Hypatia tried to stop them, she was murdered, stoned to death, then trampled."

"Oh," Tomas said weakly, the wind taken quite out of his sails. He seemed to be searching for something to say, and evidently chose the first thing that sprang to mind. "Uh — why did you call them 'unwashed Christian fanatics?'"

"Because they *were*," she replied impatiently. "They were fanatics, and most of them were stylites and other hermits who made a point of not ever bathing because taking baths was Roman and pagan and not taking baths was Christian and mortifying the flesh." She sniffed. "I suppose it didn't matter to them that it was also giving them fleas and making them smell. I shan't even *mention* the disease!"

"I don't imagine that ever entered their minds," Tomas said carefully.

"Anyway, I think Hypatia was very brave, but she could have been a little smarter," Tia concluded. "I don't think I would have stood there to let them throw stones at me; I would have run away or locked the door or something."

Tomas smiled unexpectedly; he had a lovely smile, very white teeth in his darkly tanned face. "Well, maybe she didn't have much choice," he said. "I expect that by the time she realized she wasn't going to be able to stop those people, it was too late to get away."

Tia nodded, slowly, considering the ancient Alexandrian garments, how cumbersome they were and how difficult to run in. "I think you're right," she agreed. "I would hate to think that the librarian was stupid."

He laughed at that. "You mean you'd hate to think that the great lady you were named for was stupid," he teased. "And I don't blame you. It's much nicer to be named for someone who was brave and heroic on purpose than someone people *think* was a hero just because she was too dense to get out of the way of trouble!"

Tia had to laugh at that, and right then was when she decided that she was going to like Tomas. He hadn't quite known what to make of her at first, but he'd settled down nicely and was treating her quite like an intelligent sentient now.

Evidently Moira had decided the same thing, for when she spoke, her voice sounded much less anxious.

"Tomas, aren't you forgetting? You brought Tia her late birthday present."

"I certainly did forget!" he exclaimed. "I do beg your pardon, Tia!"

He handed her the box he had brought, and she controlled herself very well, taking it from him politely, and not grabbing like a little child would have. "Thank you, Moira," she said to the com-console. "I don't mind that it's late — it's kind of like getting my birthday all over again this way."

"*You* are just too civilized for your own good, dear," Moira giggled. "Well, go ahead, open it!"

She did, carefully undoing the fastenings of the rather plain box and exposing bright-colored wrapping beneath. The wrapped package within was odd-shaped, lumpy—

She couldn't stand it any longer; she tore into the present just like any other child.

"Oh!" she exclaimed when she revealed her prize, for once caught without a word, holding him up to the light.

"Do you like it?" Moira asked anxiously. "I mean, I know you asked, but you grow so fast, I was afraid you'd have outgrown him by now — "

"I *love* him!" Tia exclaimed, hugging the bright blue bear suddenly, reveling in the soft fur against her cheek. "Oh Moira, I just *love* him!"

"Well, it was quite a trick to find him, let me tell you," Moira replied, her voice sounding very relieved, as Tomas grinned even wider. "You people move around so much — I had to find a teddy bear that would take repeated decontam procedures, one that would stand up to about anything quarantine could hand out. And it's hard to *find* bears at all, they seem to have gone right out of style. You don't mind that he's blue?"

"I like blue," she said happily.

"And you like him fuzzy? That was Tomas' idea."

"Thank you, Tomas," she told the brawn, who beamed. "He feels *wonderful*."

"I had a fuzzy dog when I was your age," he replied. "When Moira told me that you wanted a bear like the one she had before she went into her shell, I thought this fellow felt better than the smooth bears."

He leaned down confidentially, and for a moment Tia was afraid that he was going to be patronizing just because she'd gone so enthusiastic over the toy.

"I have to tell you the truth, Tia, I really enjoyed digging into all those toy shops," he whispered. "A lot of that stuff is wasted on children. I found some logic puzzles you just wouldn't believe and a set of magic tricks I couldn't resist, and I'm afraid I spent far too much money on spaceship models."

She giggled. "I won't tell if you don't," she replied, in a conspiratorial whisper.

"Pota and Braddon are in the airlock," Socrates interrupted. "Shall I order the kitchen to make lunch now?"

"So why exactly *are* you here?" Tomas asked, after all the initial topics of conversation had been exhausted, and the subject turned, inevitably, to Pota and Braddon's work. He gestured at the landscape beyond the viewport; spectacular mountains, many times taller than anything found on Terra or any other inhabited planet. This little ball of rock with a thin skin of dirt was much like the wilder parts of Mars before it had been terraformed, and had a sky so dark at midday that the sun shared the sky with the stars. "I wouldn't expect to find much of anything out there for an archeologist — it's the next thing to airless, after all. The scenery is amazing, but that's no reason to stay here — "

Braddon chuckled, the generous mouth in his lantern-jawed face widening in a smile, and Tia hid a grin. Whether or not Tomas knew it, he had just triggered her Dad's lecture mechanism. Fortunately, Braddon had a gift for lecturing. He was always a popular speaker whenever he could be tempted to go to conferences.

"No one expected to find anything on planets like this one, Tomas," Braddon replied, leaning back against the supporting cushions of the sofa and tucking his hands behind his head. "That's why the Salomon-Kildaire culture is so intriguing. James Salomon and Tory Kildaire discovered the first buildings on the fourth moon of Beta Orianis Three — and there have never been *any* verifiable artifacts uncovered in what you and I would call 'normal' conditions. Virtually every find has been on airless or near-airless bodies. Pota and I have excavated over a dozen sites, doing the Class One studies, and they're all like this one."

Tomas glanced out the viewport again. "Surely that implies that they were —"

"Space-going, yes," Pota supplied, nodding her head so that her gray-brown curls vibrated. "I don't think there's any doubt of it. Although we've never found any trace of whatever it was they used to move them from colony to colony — but that isn't the real mystery."

Braddon gestured agreement. "The real mystery is that they never seem to have set up anything *permanent*. They never seem to have spent more than a few decades in any one place. No one knows why they left, or why they came here in the first place."

Tomas laughed. "They seem to have hopped planets as often as you two," he said. "Perhaps they were simply doing what *you* are doing — excavating an earlier culture and following *it* across the stars."

Braddon exclaimed in mock horror. "Please!" he said. "Don't even think that!"

Pota only laughed. "If they had been, we'd have

found signs of that," she told both of them, tapping Braddon's knee in playful admonition. "After all, as bleak as these places are, they preserve things wonderfully. If the EsKays had been archeologists, we'd have found the standard tools of the trade. We break and wear out brushes and digging tools all the time, and just leave them in our discard piles. They would have done the same. No matter how you try to alter it, there are only so many ways you can make a brush or a trowel —"

"There would be bad castings," Tia piped up. "You throw out bad castings all the time, Mum; if they were archeologists, we'd find a pile of bad castings somewhere."

"Bless me, Tia's right," Braddon nodded. "There you are, Tomas; irrefutable proof."

"Good enough for me," Tomas replied, good-naturedly.

"And if that idea was true, there also ought to be signs of the earlier culture, shouldn't there?" Moira asked. "And you've never found anything mixed in with the EsKay artifacts."

"Exactly so," Pota replied, and smiled. "And so, Tomas, you see how easily an archeologist's theories can be disposed of."

"Then I'm going to be thankful to be Moira's partner," Tomas said gracefully, "and leave all the theorizing to better heads than mine."

After a while, the talk turned to the doings of the Institute, and both professional and personal news of Pota and Braddon's friends and rivals. Tia glanced at the clock again; it was long past time when her parents would have gone back to the dig — they must have decided to take the rest of the day off.

But these weren't subjects that interested her, especially not when the talk went into politics, both of the Institute and the Central Worlds government. She took her bear, politely excused herself, and went back to her room.

She hadn't had a chance to really look him over when Tomas gave him to her. The last time Moira had come to visit, she'd told Tia some stories about what going into the shellperson program had been like, for unlike most shellpersons, she hadn't been popped into her shell until she'd been nearly four. Until that time, there had been some hope that there would have been a palliative for her particular congenital condition — premature aging that had caused her body to resemble a sixty-year-old woman at the age of three. But there was no cure, and at four, her family finally admitted it. Into the shell she went, and since there was *nothing* wrong with her very fine brain, she soon caught up and passed by many of her classmates that had been in their shells since birth.

But one of the toys she'd had — her very favorite, in fact — had been a stuffed teddy bear. She'd made up adventures for Ivan the Bearable, sending him in a troika across the windswept steppes of Novi Gagarin, and she'd told Tia some of those stories. That, and the *Zen of Pooh* book Moira brought her, had solidified a longing she hadn't anticipated.

For Tia had been entranced by the tales and by Pooh — and had wanted a bear like Moira's. A simple toy that did *nothing,* with no intel-chips; a toy that couldn't talk, or teach, or walk. Something that was just there to be hugged and cuddled; something to listen when she didn't want anything else to overhear. . . .

Moira had promised. Moira didn't forget.

Tia closed the door to her room and paged the AI. "Socrates, would you open a link to Moira in here for me, please?" she asked. Moira would be perfectly capable of following the conversation in the other room and still talk to her in here, too.

"Tia, do you really like your present?" Moira asked

anxiously, as soon as the link had been established.

"He's wonderful," Tia answered firmly. "I've even got a name for him. Theodore Edward Bear."

"Or Ted E. Bear for short?" Moira chuckled. "I like it. It fits him. He's such a solemn-faced little fellow. One would think he was a software executive. He looks like a bear with a great deal on his mind."

Tia studied Ted carefully. Moira was right; he was a sober little bear, with a very studious expression, as if he was listening very hard to whatever was being said. His bright blue coloration in no way contradicted the seriousness of his face, nor did the frivolous little red shirt he was wearing with the blue and yellow Courier Service circle-and-lightning-bolt on the front.

"Is there anything going on that I need to know, Moira?" she asked, giving over her careful examination of her new friend and hugging him to her chest instead.

"The results of your last batch of tests seems to have satisfied all the Psych people out there that you're a perfectly well-balanced and self-sufficient girl," Moira replied, knowing without Tia prompting her just what was on her mind. "So there's no more talk of making your parents send you to boarding school."

Tia sighed with relief; that had been a very real worry the last time Moira had been here. The ship had left with the results of a battery of tests and psych-profiles that had taken two days to complete.

"I have to tell you that I added to that," Moira said, slyly. "I told them what kind of a birthday present you had asked for from me."

"What did they say?" Tia asked, anxiously. Had they thought she was being immature — or worse yet, that it meant she harbored some kind of neurosis?

"Oh, it was funny. They were questioning me on open com, as if I was some kind of AI that wouldn't respond to anything that wasn't a direct question, so of course I could hear everything *they* said. There was silence for a moment, and then the worst of the lot finally blurted out, 'Good heavens, the child is *normal*,' as if he'd expected you to ask for a Singularity simulator or something." Moira chuckled.

"I know who it was, too," Tia said shrewdly. "It was Doctor Phelps-Pittman, wasn't it?"

"Dead on the target, wenchette," Moira replied, still chuckling. "I still don't think he's forgiven you for beating him in Battle Chess. By the way, what *is* your secret?"

"He moves the Queen too often," Tia said absently. "I think he likes to watch her hips wiggle when she walks. It's probably something Freudian."

A splutter of static was all that followed that pronouncement, as Moira lost control of the circuit briefly. "My, my," she replied, when she came back on-line. "You *are* a little terror. One might almost suspect you of having as much control as a shellperson!"

Tia took that in the spirit it was meant, as a compliment.

"I promise not to tell him *your* weakness," the ship continued, teasingly.

"What's that?" Tia was surprised; she hadn't known she had one.

"You hate to see the pawns sacrificed. I think you feel sorry for the little guys."

Tia digested this in silence for a moment, then nodded reluctant agreement. "I think you're right," she admitted. "It seems as if everybody can beat them up, and it doesn't seem fair."

"You don't have the problem with an ordinary holoboard game," Moira observed casually.

"That's because they're just little blobby pieces on a holoboard game," Tia explained. "In Battle Chess they're little pikemen. And they're cute." She giggled. "I really love it when Pawn takes Knight and he hits the Knight with the butt of his pike right in the — "

"And *that's* why you frighten old Phelps-Pittman," Moira said severely, though Tia could tell she didn't mean it. "He keeps thinking you're going to do the same to him."

"Well, I won't have to see old sour-face for another year and a half," she said comfortably. "Maybe I can figure out how to act like a *normal girl* by then."

"Maybe you can," Moira replied. "I wouldn't put even that past you. Now, how about a game of Battle Chess? Ted Bear can referee."

"Of course," she agreed. "You can use the practice. I'll even spot you a pawn."

"Oh come now! You haven't gotten *that* much better since I saw you last." At Tia's continued silence, the ship asked, tentatively, "Have you?"

Tia shrugged. "Check my record with Socrates," she suggested.

There was silence as Moira did just that. Then. "Oh, *decom* it," she said in mock disgust. "You really *are* exasperating. I should demand that you spot me two pawns."

"Not a chance," Tia replied, ordering the AI to set up the game, with a Battle Chess field in front of her. "You're taking advantage enough of a child as it is."

"Taking advantage of a child? Ha!" Moira said ironically. "You're not a child. I'm beginning to agree with Phelps-Pittman. You're an eighty-year-old midget in a little-girl costume."

"Oh, all right," Tia said, good-naturedly. "I won't give you another pawn, but I will let you have white."

"Good." Moira studied the analog of the board in her memory, as Tia studied the holoboard in front of her. "All right, unnatural child. Have at ye!"

Moira and Tomas couldn't stay long; by dinner the ship had lifted, and the pad was empty — and the Cade family was back on schedule.

Pota and Braddon spent the evening catching up with the message-packets Moira had brought them — mostly dispatches from friends at other digs, more scholarly papers in their various fields, and the latest in edicts from the Institute. Since Tia knew, thanks to Moira, that none of those edicts concerned *her*, she was free to watch one of the holos Moira had brought for her entertainment. All carefully screened by the teachers at the Institute, of course, who oversaw the education of every child that was on-site with its parents. But even the teachers didn't see anything wrong with history holos, provided they were properly educational and accurate. The fact that most of these holos had been intended for adult viewing didn't seem to bother them.

Perhaps it was just as well that the Psychs had no idea what she was watching. They would probably have gone into strong hysterics.

Moira had an uncanny ability to pick out the ones that had good scripts and actors — unlike whoever it was that picked out most of the holos for the Remote Educational Department.

This one, a four-part series on Alexander the Great, looked especially good, since it covered only the early parts of his life, before he became a great leader. Tia felt a certain kinship for anyone who'd been labeled "precocious"; and although she already knew that Alexander's childhood had been far from happy, she was looking forward to viewing this.

Having Ted beside her to whisper comments to made it even more fun.

At the end of the first part, even though she was fascinated, she virtuously told Socrates to shut everything down and went into the main room to say good-night to her Mum and Dad. The next courier wasn't due for a while, and she wanted to make her treats last as long as possible.

Both of them were so deep in their readers that she had to shake their elbows to get them to realize she was there, but once they came out of their preoccupied daze, they gave her big hugs and kisses, with no sign of annoyance at being interrupted.

"I have a really *good* Mum and Dad," she told Ted before drifting off to sleep. "I really, really do. Not like Alexander. . . . "

The next day, it was back to the usual schedule. Socrates woke her, and she got herself cleaned up and dressed, leaving Ted to reside on the carefully made bed until she returned. When she entered the main room, Pota and Braddon were already there, blinking sleepily over steaming cups of coffee.

"Hello, darling," Pota greeted her as she fetched her milk and cereal from the kitchen. "Did you enjoy Alexander?"

"We-ell, it was *interesting*," Tia said truthfully. "And I liked the actors and the story. The costumes and the horses were really stellar! But his mother and father were kind of — odd — weren't they?"

Braddon looked up from his coffee with his curly dark hair over one brown eye, and gave his daughter a wry grin. "They were certifiable crazy-cases by our standards, pumpkin," he replied. "But after all, there wasn't anyone around to apply those standards back then."

"And no Board of Mental Health to enforce them," Pota added, her thin, delicate face creasing with a puckish smile. "Remember, oh curious little chick, they were *not* the ones that had the most influence on Alexander. That was left to his tutors — Aristotle, of course, being the main one — and nurses. I think he succeeded in spite of his parents, personally, and not because of them."

Tia nodded sagely. "Can I come help at the dig

today?" she asked eagerly. This was one of the best things about the fact that her parents had picked the EsKays to specialize in. With next to no atmosphere, there were no indigent life-forms to worry about. By the time Tia was five, she had pressure-suit protocol down pat, and there was no reason why she couldn't come to the digs, or even wander about within specified limits on her own. "The biggest sandbox in the universe," Braddon called it; so long as she stayed within eye- and earshot, neither of them minded having her about outside.

"Not today, dearest," Pota said apologetically. "We've found some glassware, and we're making holos. As soon as we're done with that, we'll make the castings, and after that you can come run errands for us." In the thin atmosphere and chill of the site, castings were tricky to make; one reason why Pota discarded so many. But no artifact could be moved without first making a good casting of it, as well as holos from all possible angles — too many times the artifacts crumbled to nothing, despite the most careful handling, once they were moved.

She sighed; holos and castings meant she couldn't even come near the site, lest the vibrations she made walking interfere. "All right," she agreed. "Can I go outside, though? As long as I stay close to the airlock?"

"Stay close to the lock and keep the emergency cart nearby, and I don't see any reason why you can't play outside," Pota said after a moment. Then she smiled. "And how is your dig coming?"

"You mean really, or for pretend?" she asked.

"Pretend, of course," said Braddon. "Pretend is always more fun than really. That's why *we* became archeologists in the first place — because we get to play pretend for months at a time until we have to be serious and write papers!"

He gave her a conspiratorial grin, and she giggled.

"We-ell," she said, and drew her face down into a frown *just* like Doctor Heinz Marius-Llewellyn, when he was about to put everyone to sleep. "I've found the village site of a race of flint-using primitives who were used as slave labor by the EsKays at *your* site."

"Have you!" Pota fell right in with the pretense, as Braddon nodded seriously. "Well that certainly explains why we haven't found any servos. They must have used slaves to do all their manual labor!"

"Yes. And the Flint People worshipped them as gods from the sky," Tia continued. "That was why they didn't revolt; all the slave labor was a form of worship. They'd go back to their village and then they'd try to make flint tools just like the things that the sky-gods used. They probably made pottery things, too, but I haven't found anything but shards."

"Well, pottery doesn't hold up well in conditions like this," Pota agreed. "It goes brittle very quickly under the extremes of surface temperature. What have you got so far?"

"A flint disruptor-pistol, a flint wrist-com, a flint flashlight, and some more things," she said solemnly. "I haven't found any arrowheads or spear-points or things like that, but that's because there's nothing to hunt here. They were vegetarians, and they ate nothing but lichen."

Braddon made a face. "Awful. Worse than the food at the Institute cafeteria! No wonder they didn't survive — the food probably bored them to death!"

Pota rose and gathered up their plates and cups, stowing them neatly in the dishwasher. "Well, enjoy your lessons, pumpkin. We'll see you at lunch."

She smiled, hugged them both goodbye before they suited up, then went off to the schoolroom.

That afternoon, once lessons were done, she took down her own pressure-suit from the rack beside the

airlock inner door. Her suit was designed a little differently from her parents', with accordion folds at
wrists and elbows, ankles and knees, and at the waist, to
allow for the growth-spurts of a child. This was a brand
new suit, for she had been about to outgrow the last
one just before they went out on this dig. She liked it a
lot better than the old one; the manufacturer of the last
one had some kind of stupid idea that a child's suit
should have cavorting flowers with smiling faces all
over it. She had been ashamed to have anyone but her
parents *see* her in the awful thing. She thought it made
her look like a little clown.

It had come second-hand from a child on a Class
Three dig — like most of the things that the Cades got.
Evaluation digs simply didn't have that high a priority
when it came to getting anything other than the bare
essentials. But Tia'd had the bright idea when her
birthday came around to ask her parents' superiors at
the Institute for a new pressure-suit. And when it came
out that she was imitating her parents, by creating her
own little dig-site, she had so tickled them that they
actually sent her one. Brand new, good for three or
four years at least, and the *only* difference between it
and a grown-up suit was that hers had extra helmet
lights and a com that couldn't be turned off, a locator-
beacon that was always on, and bright fluorescent
stripes on the helmet and down the arms and legs. A
small price to pay for dignity.

The flowered suit had gone back to the Institute, to
be endured by some other unfortunate child.

And the price to be paid for her relative freedom to
roam was waiting in the airlock. A wagon, child-sized
and modified from the pull-wagon many children had
as toys — but this one had powered crawler-tracks and
was loaded with an auxiliary power unit and air-pack
and full face-mask. If her suit failed, she had been
drilled in what to do so many times she could easily

have saved herself when asleep. *One*, take a deep breath and pop the helmet. *Two*, pull the mask on, making sure the seals around her face were secure. *Three*, turn on the air and *Four*, plug into the APU, which would keep the suit heat up with the helmet off. Then walk — slowly, carefully, to the airlock, towing the wagon behind. There was no reason why she should suffer anything worse than a bit of frostbite.

It had never happened. That didn't mean it wouldn't. Tia had no intention of becoming a tragic tale in the newsbytes. Tragic tales were all very well in drama and history, but they were not what one wanted in real life.

So the wagon went with her, inconvenient as it was.

The filters in this suit were good ones; the last suit had always smelled a little musty, but the air in this one was fresh and clean. She trotted over the uneven surface, towing the cart behind, kicking up little puffs of dust and sand. Everything out here was very sharp-edged and clear; red and yellow desert, reddish-purple mountains, dark blue sky. The sun, Sigma Marinara, hung right above her head, so all the shadows were tiny pools of dark black at the bases of things. She hadn't been out to her "site" for several weeks, not since the last time Mum and Dad had asked her to stay away. That had been right at the beginning, when they first got here and uncovered enough to prove it was an EsKay site. Since that time there had been a couple of sandstorms, and Tia was a bit apprehensive that her "dig" had gotten buried. Unlike her parents' dig, *she* did not have force-shields protecting her trench from storms.

But when she reached her site, she discovered to her amazement that *more* was uncovered than she had left. Instead of burying her dig in sand, the storm had scoured the area clean —

There were several likely-looking lumps at the

farther end of the trench, all fused together into a bumpy whole. Wonderful! There would be hours of potential pretend here; freeing the lumps from the sandy matrix, cleaning them off, figuring out what the Flint People had been trying to copy. . . .

She took the tools her parents had discarded out of the wagon; the broken trowel that Braddon had mended for her, the worn brushes, the blunted probes, and set to work.

Several hours later, she sat back on her heels and looked at her first find, frowning. This wasn't a lump of flint after all. In fact, it seemed to be some kind of layered substance, with the layers fused together. Odd, it looked kind of wadded up. It certainly wasn't any kind of layered rock she'd ever seen before, and it didn't match any of the rocks she'd uncovered until now.

She chewed her lower lip in thought and stared at it, letting her mind just drift, to see if it could identify what kind of rock it was. It didn't look sedimentary.

Actually, it didn't look much like a rock at all. . . .

Not like a rock. What if it isn't a rock?

She blinked, and suddenly knew what it *did* look like. Layers of thin cloth or paper, wadded up, then discarded.

Finagle! Have I —

She gently — very gently — pried another lump off the outcropping, and carefully freed it of its gritty coating. And there was *no* doubt this time that what she had was the work of intelligent hands. Under the layer of half-fused sand and flaking, powdery dust, gleamed a spot of white porcelain, with the matte edge of a break showing why it had been discarded.

Oh, decom — I found the garbage dump!

Or, at least, she had found a little trash heap. That was *probably* it; likely there was just this lump of discards and no more. But anything the EsKays left behind was important, and it was equally important to stop digging *now*, mark the site in case another sandstorm came up and capriciously buried it as it had capriciously uncovered it, and bring some evidence to show Mum and Dad what she had found.

Except that she didn't have a holo-camera. Or anything to cast with.

Finally she gave up trying to think of what to do. There was only one thing for it. Bring her two finds inside and show them. The lump of fabric might not survive the touch of real air, but the porcelain thing surely would. Porcelain, unlike glass, was more resilient to the stresses of repeated temperature changes and was not likely to go to powder at the first touch of air.

She went back inside the dome and rummaged around for a bit before returning with a plastic food container for the artifacts, and a length of plastic pipe and the plastic tail from a kite-kit she'd never had a chance to use. Another well-meant but stupid gift from someone Dad worked with; someone who never once thought that on a Mars-type world there weren't very many opportunities to fly kites. . . .

With the site marked as securely as she could manage, and the two artifacts sealed into the plastic tub, she returned to the dome again, waiting impatiently for her parents to get back.

She had hoped that the seal on the plastic tub would be good enough to keep the artifacts safely protected from the air of the dome. She knew as soon as the airlock pressurized, though, that her attempt to keep them safe had failed. Even before she pulled off her helmet, the external suit-mike picked up the *hiss* of air leaking into the container. And when she held the plastic tub up to the light, it was easy enough to see that one of the lumps had begun to disintegrate. She pried the lid off for a quick peek, and sneezed at the dust. The wadded lump was not going to look like much when her parents got home.

Decom it, she thought resentfully. *That's not fair!*

She put it down carefully on the countop; if she didn't jar it, there might still be enough left when Mum and Dad got back in that they would at least be able to tell what it *had* been.

She stripped out of her suit and sat down to wait. She tried to read a book, but she just couldn't get interested. Mum and Dad were going to be *so* surprised — and even better, now the Psychs at the Institute would have no reason to keep her away from the Class Two sites anymore — because *this* would surely prove that she knew what to do when she accidentally found something. The numbers on the clock moved with agonizing slowness, as she waited for the moment when they would finally return.

The sky outside the viewport couldn't get much darker, but the shadows lengthened, and the light faded. Soon now, soon —

Finally she heard them in the outer lock, and her heart began to beat faster. Suddenly she was no longer so certain that she had done the right thing. What if they were angry that she dissected the first two artifacts? What if she had done the wrong thing in moving them?

The "what ifs" piled up in her head as she waited for the lock to cycle.

Finally the inner door hissed, and Braddon and Pota came through, already pulling off their helmets and continuing a high-speed conversation that must have begun back at the dig.

" — but the matrix is all wrong for it to be a food preparation area — "

" — yes, yes," Pota replied impatiently, " but what about the integument — "

"Mum!" Tia said, running up to them and tugging at her mother's elbow. "I've found something!"

"Hello, pumpkin, that's very nice," her mother replied absently, hugging her, and going right on with her conversation. Her intense expression showed that she was thinking while she spoke, and her eyes never wandered from her husband's face — and as for Braddon, the rest of the world simply did not exist.

"*Mum!*" Tia persisted. "I've found an artifact!"

"In a moment, dear," Pota replied. "But what about — "

"*MUM!*" Tia shouted, disobeying *every* rule of not interrupting grown-ups in desperation, knowing from all the signs that she would *never* get their attention otherwise. Conversations like *this* one could go on for hours. "*I've found an artifact!*"

Both her parents stopped their argument in mid-sentence and stared at her. Silence enveloped the room; an ominous silence. Tia gulped nervously.

"Tia," Braddon finally said, disapproval creeping into his voice. "Your mother and I are in the middle of a very important conversation. This is *not* the time for pretend."

"Dad, it's *not* pretend!" she said insistently, pointing to her plastic box. "It's not! I found an artifact, and there's more — "

Pota raised an eyebrow at her husband and shrugged. Braddon picked up the box, carelessly, and Tia winced as the first lump inside visibly disintegrated more.

"I am going to respect your intelligence and integrity enough to assume that you *think* you found an artifact," Braddon replied, prying the lid from the container. "But Tia, you know better than to — "

He glanced down inside — and his eyebrows arched upward in the greatest show of surprise that Tia had ever seen him make.

"I *told* you," Tia could not resist saying, triumphantly.

" — so they took the big lights out to the trench, and the extra field-generators," she told Ted E. Bear after she'd been put to bed for the night. "They were out there for *hours,* and they let me wait up to hear what it was. And it *was,* I *did* find a garbage dump! A big one, too! Mum made a special call to the Institute, 'cause this is the first really big EsKay dump anybody's ever found."

She hugged Ted closer, basking in the warmth of Pota's praise, a warmth that still lingered and made her feel happy right down to her toes. "You did everything *exactly* right with the equipment you had," Pota had told her. "I've had undergraduates that didn't do as well as you did, pumpkin! You remember what I told you, when you asked me about why I wanted to find garbage?"

"That we learn more from sentients' garbage than from anything other than their literature," she'd recited dutifully.

"Well," Pota had replied, sitting on the edge of her bed and touching her nose with one finger, playfully. "You, my curious little chick, have just upgraded this site from a Class One to a Class Three with four hours of work! That's more than Braddon and I have *ever* done!"

"Does that mean that we'll be leaving?" she'd asked in confusion.

"Eventually," Pota told her, a certain gloating glee in her voice. "But it takes time to put together a Class Three team, and *we* happen to be right here. Your father and I will be making gigabytes of important discoveries before the team gets here to replace us. And with that much already invested — they may *not* replace us!"

Tia had shaken her head, confused.

Pota had hugged her. "What I mean, pumpkin, is that there is a *very* good chance that we'll stay on here — as the dig supervisors! An instant promotion from Class One supervisor to Class Three supervisor! There'll be better equipment, a better dome to live in — you'll have some playmates — couriers will be by every week instead of every few months — not to mention the raises in pay and status! All the papers on this site will go out under *our* names! And all because *you* were my clever, bright, careful little girl, who knew what she saw and knew when to stop playing!"

"Mum and Dad are really, really happy," she told Ted, thinking about the glow of joy that had been on both their faces when they finished the expensive link to the nearest Institute supervisor. "I think we did a good thing. I think maybe you brought us luck, Ted." She yawned. "Except about the other kids coming. But we don't have to play with them if we don't want to, do we?"

Ted agreed silently, and she hugged him again. "I'd rather talk to you, anyway," she told him. "You never say anything dumb. Dad says that if you can't say something intelligent, you shouldn't say anything; and Mum says that people who know when to shut up are the smartest people of all, so I guess you must be pretty smart. Right?"

But she never got a chance to find out if Ted agreed with that statement, because at that point she fell right asleep.

Over the course of the next few days, it became evident that this was not just an ordinary garbage dump; this was one containing scientific or medical debris. That raised the status of the site from "important" to "priceless," and Pota and Braddon took to spending every waking moment either at the site or preserving and examining their finds, making copious notes, and any number of speculations. They hardly ever saw Tia anymore; they had changed their schedule so that they were awake long before she was and came in long after she went to bed.

Pota apologized — via a holo that she had left to play for Tia as soon as she came in to breakfast this morning.

"Pumpkin," her image said, while Tia sipped her juice. "I hope you can understand why we're doing this. The more we find out before the team gets sent out, the more we make ourselves essential to the dig, the better our chances for that promotion." Pota's image ran a hand through her hair; to Tia's critical eyes, she looked very tired, and a bit frazzled, but fairly satisfied. "It won't be more than a few weeks, I promise. Then things will go back to normal. Better than normal, in fact. I promise that we'll have a Family Day before the team gets here, all right? So start thinking what you'd like to do."

Well, *that* would be stellar! Tia knew exactly what she wanted to do — she wanted to go out to the mountains on the big sled, and she wanted to drive it herself on the way.

"So forgive us, all right? We don't love you any less, and we think about you all the time, and we miss you like anything." Pota blew a kiss toward the camera. "I know you can take care of yourself; in fact, we're counting on that. You're making a big difference to us. I want you to know that. Love you, baby."

Tia finished her juice as the holo flickered out, and a certain temptation raised its head. This could be a really unique opportunity to play hooky, just a little bit. Mum and Dad were not going to be checking the tutor to see how her lessons were going — and the Institute Psychs wouldn't care; they thought she was too advanced for her age anyway. She could even raid the library for the holos she wasn't precisely supposed to watch. . . .

"Oh, Finagle," she said, regretfully, after a moment. It might be fun — but it would be *guilty* fun. And besides, sooner or later Mum and Dad would find out what she'd done, and *ping!* there would go the Family Day and probably a lot of other privileges. She weighed the immediate pleasure of being lazy and watching forbidden holos against the future pleasure of being able to pilot the sled up the mountains, and the latter outranked the former. Piloting the sled was the closest *she* would get to piloting a ship, and she wouldn't be able to do that for years and years and years yet.

And if she fell on her nose *now*, right when Mum and Dad trusted her most — they'd probably restrict her to the dome for ever and ever.

"Not worth it," she sighed, jumping down from her stool. She frowned as she noticed that the pins-and-needles feeling in her toes still hadn't gone away. It had been there when she woke up this morning. It had been there yesterday too, and the day before, but by breakfast it had worn off.

Well, it didn't bother her that much, and it wouldn't take her mind off her Latin lesson. Too bad, too.

"Boring language," she muttered. *"Ick, ack, ock!"*

Well, the sooner she got it over with, the better off she'd be, and she could go back to nice logical quadratics.

The pins-and-needles feeling hadn't worn off by afternoon, and although she felt all right, she decided that since Mum and Dad were trusting her to do everything right, she probably ought to talk to the AI about it.

"Socrates, engage Medic Mode, please," she said, sitting down reluctantly in the tiny medic station. She *really* didn't like being in the medic-station; it smelled of disinfectant and felt like being in a too-small pressure suit. It was just about the size of a tiny lav, but something about it made it *feel* smaller. Maybe because it was dark inside. And of course, since it had been made for adults, the proportions were all wrong for her. In order to reach hand-plates she had to scoot to the edge of the seat, and in order to reach foot-plates she had to get right off the seat entirely. The screen in front of her lit up with the smiling holo of someone that was supposed to be a doctor. Privately, she doubted that the original had ever been any closer to medicine than wearing the jumpsuit. He just looked too — polished. *Too* trustworthy, *too* handsome, *too* competent. Any time there was anything official she had to interface with that seemed to scream *trust me* at her, she immediately distrusted it and went very wary. Probably the original for this holo had been an actor. Maybe he made adults feel calm, but he made her think about the Psychs and their too-hearty greetings, their nosy questions.

"Well, Tia," said the AI's voice — changed to that of the "doctor." "What brings you here?"

"My toes feel like they're asleep," she said dutifully. "They kind of tingle."

"Is that all?" the "doctor" asked, after a moment for the AI to access his library of symptoms. "Are they colder than normal? Put your hand on the hand-plate, and your foot on the foot-plate, Tia."

She obeyed, feeling very like a contortionist.

"Well, the circulation seems to be fine," the "doctor" said, after the AI had a chance to read temperature and blood pressure, both of which appeared in the upper right-hand corner of the screen. "Have you any other symptoms?"

"No," she replied. "Not really." The "doctor" froze for a moment, as the AI analyzed all the other readings it had taken from her during the past few days — what she'd eaten and how much, what she'd done, her sleep-patterns.

The "doctor" unfroze. "Sometimes when children start growing very fast, they get odd sensations in their bodies," the AI said. "A long time ago, those were called 'growing pains.' Now we know it's because sometimes different kinds of tissue grow at different rates. I think that's probably what your problem is, Tia, and I don't think you need to worry about it. I'll prescribe some vitamin supplements for you, and in a few days you should be just fine."

"Thank you," she said politely, and made her escape, relieved to have gotten off so lightly.

And in a few days, the pins-and-needles sensation *did* go away, and she thought no more about it. Thought no more, that is, until she went outside to her new "dig" and did something she hadn't done in a year — she fell down. Well, she didn't exactly fall; she *thought* she'd sidestepped a big rock, but she hadn't. She rammed her toes right into it and went heavily to her knees.

The suit was intact, she discovered to her relief — and she was quite ready to get up and keep going, until she realized that her foot didn't hurt.

And it should have, if she'd rammed it against the outcropping hard enough to throw her to the ground.

So instead of going on, she went back to the dome and pealed off suit and shoe and sock — and found her foot was completely numb, but black-and-blue where she had slammed it into the unyielding stone.

When she prodded it experimentally, she discovered that her whole foot was numb, from the toes back to the arch. She peeled off her other shoe and sock, and found that her left foot was as numb as her right.

"Decom it," she muttered. This surely meant another check-in with the medic.

Once again she climbed into the claustrophobic little closet at the back of the dome and called up the "doctor."

"Still got pins-and-needles, Tia?" he said cheerfully, as she wriggled on the hard seat.

"No," she replied, "But I've mashed my foot something awful. It's all black-and-blue."

"Put it on the foot-plate, and I'll scan it," the "doctor" replied. "I promise, it won't hurt a bit."

Of course it won't, it doesn't hurt now, she thought resentfully, but did as she was told.

"Well, no bones broken, but you certainly did bruise it!" the "doctor" said after a moment. Then he added archly, "What were you doing, kicking the tutor?"

"No," she muttered. She really *hated* it when the AI program made it get patronizing. "I stubbed it on a rock, outside."

"Does it hurt?" the "doctor" continued, oblivious to her resentment.

"No," she said shortly. "It's all numb."

"Well, if it does, I've authorized your bathroom to give you some pills," the "doctor" said with cloying cheer. "Just go right ahead and take them if you need them — you know how to get them."

The screen shut down before she had a chance to say anything else. *I guess it isn't anything to worry about,* she decided. *The AI would have said something otherwise. It'll probably go away.*

But it didn't go away, although the bruises healed. Before long she had other bruises, and the numbness of her feet extended to her ankles. But she told herself that the AI had said it would go away, eventually — and anyway, this wasn't so bad, at least when she mashed herself it didn't *hurt.*

She continued to play at her own little excavation, the new one — which she had decided was a grave-site. The primitives burned their dead though, and only buried the ashes with their flint-replicas of the sky-gods' wonderful things — hoping that the dearly departed would be reincarnated as sky-gods and return in wealth and triumph. . . .

It wasn't as much fun though, without Mum and Dad to talk to; and she was getting kind of tired of the way she kept tripping and falling over the uneven ground at the new "site." She hadn't damaged her new suit yet, but there were sharp rocks that could rip holes even in the tough suit fabric — and if her suit was torn, there would go the promised Family Day.

So, finally, she gave up on it and spent her afternoons inside.

A few nights later, Pota peeked in her room to see if she was still awake.

"I wanted you to know we were still flesh-and-blood and not holos, pumpkin," her mum said, sitting down on the side of her bed. "How are your excavations coming?"

Tia shook her head. "I kept tripping on things, and I didn't want to tear my suit," she explained. "I think that the Flint People must have put a curse on their grave-site. I don't think I should dig there anymore."

Pota chuckled, hugged her, and said, "That could very well be, dear. It never pays to underestimate the power of religion. When the others arrive we'll research their religion and take the curse off, all right?"

"Okay," she replied. She wondered for a moment if she should mention her feet —

But Pota kissed her and whisked out the door before she could make up her mind.

Nothing more happened for several days, and she got used to having numb feet. If she was careful to watch where she stepped, and careful never to go barefoot, there really wasn't anything to worry about. And the AI had *said* it was something that happened to other children.

Besides, now Mum and Dad were *really* finding important things. In a quick breakfast-holo, a tired but excited Braddon said that what they were uncovering now might mean a whole lot more than just a promotion. It might mean the establishment of a fieldwide reputation.

Just what that meant, exactly, Tia wasn't certain — but there was no doubt that it must be important or Braddon wouldn't have been so excited about it. So she decided that whatever was wrong with her could wait. It wouldn't be long now, and once Mum and Dad weren't involved in this day-and-night frenzy of activity, she could explain everything and they would see to it that the medics gave her the right shot or whatever it was that she needed.

The next morning when she woke up, her fingers were tingling.

Tia sighed and took her place inside the medic booth. This was getting very tiresome.

The AI ran her through the standard questions, which she answered as she had before. "So now you have that same tingling in your hands as you did in your feet, is that right?" the "doctor" asked.

"That's right," she said shortly.

"The same tingling that went away?" the "doctor" persisted.

"Yes," she replied. *Should I say something about how it doesn't tingle anymore, about how now it's numb?* But the AI was continuing.

"Tia, I can't really find anything wrong with you," it said. "Your circulation is fine, you don't have a fever, your appetite and weight are fine, you're sleeping right. But you *do* seem to have gotten very accident prone lately." The "doctor" took on a look of concern covering impatience. "Tia, I know that your parents are very busy right now, and they don't have time to talk to you or play with you. Is *that* what's really wrong? Are you angry with your parents for leaving you alone so much? Would you like to talk to a Counselor?"

"No!" she snapped. The idea! The *stupid* AI actually thought she was making this up to get attention!

"Well, you simply don't have any other symptoms," the "doctor" said, none too gently. "This hasn't got to the point where I'd have to insist that you talk to a Counselor, but really, without anything else to go on, I can't suggest anything else except that this is a phase you'll grow out of."

"This hasn't got to the point where I'd have to insist that you talk to a Counselor." Those were dangerous words. The AI's "Counselor" mode was only good for so much — and every single thing she said and did would be recorded the moment that she started "Counseling." Then all the Psychs back at the Institute would be sent the recordings via compressed-mode databurst — and they'd be all over them, looking for something wrong with her that needed Psyching. And if they found anything, anything at all, Mum and Dad would get orders from the Board of Mental Health that they couldn't ignore, and she'd be shipped back to a school on the next courier run.

Oh no. You don't catch me that easy.

"You're right," she said carefully. "But Mum and Dad trust me to tell you *everything* that's wrong, so I am."

"All right then." The "doctor's" face lost that stern look. "So long as you're just being conscientious. Keep taking those vitamin supplements, Tia, and everything will be fine."

But everything wasn't fine. Within days, the tingling had stopped, to be replaced by numbness. Just like her feet. She began having trouble holding things, and her lessons took twice as long now, since she couldn't touch-type anymore and had to watch where her fingers went.

She completely gave up on doing anything that required a lot of manual dexterity. Instead, she watched a lot of holos, even boring ones, and played a great deal of holo-chess. She read a lot too, from the screen, so that she could give one-key page-turning commands rather than trying to turn paper pages herself. The numbness stopped at her wrists, and for a few days she was so busy getting used to doing things without feeling her hands, that she didn't notice that the numbness in her legs had spread from her ankles to her knees. . . .

Now she was afraid to go to the AI "doctor" program, knowing that it would put her in for Counseling. She tried looking things up herself in the database, but knew that she was going to have to be very sneaky to avoid triggering flags in the AI. As the numbness stopped at the knees, then began to spread up her arms, she kept telling herself that it wouldn't, couldn't be much longer now. Soon Mum and Dad would be done, and they would know she wasn't making this up to get attention. Soon she would be able to tell them herself, and they'd make the stupid medic work right. Soon.

She woke up, as usual, to hands and feet that acted like wooden blocks at the ends of her limbs. She got a shower — easy enough, since the controls were push-button, then struggled into her clothing by wriggling and using teeth and fingers that didn't really want to move. She didn't bother too much with hair and teeth, it was just too hard. Shoving her feet into slippers, since she hadn't been able to tie her shoes for the past couple of days, she stumped out into the main room of the dome —

Only to find Pota and Braddon waiting there for her, smiling over their coffee.

"Surprise!" Pota said cheerfully. "We've done just about everything we can on our own, and we zipped the findings off to the Institute last night. *Now* things can get back to normal!"

"Oh *Mum*!" She couldn't help herself, she was so overwhelmed by relief and joy that she started to run across the room to fling herself into their arms —

Started to. Halfway there, she tripped, as usual, and went flying through the air, crashing into the table and spilling the hot coffee all over her arms and legs.

They picked her up, as she babbled apologies about her clumsiness. She didn't even notice what the coffee had done to her, didn't even think about it until her parents' expressions of horror alerted her to the fact that there were burns and blisters already rising on her lower arms.

"It doesn't hurt," she said, dazedly, without thinking, just saying the first thing that came into her mind. "It's okay, really, I've been kind of numb for a while so it doesn't hurt, honest —"

Pota and Braddon both froze. Something about their expressions startled her into silence.

"You don't feel anything?" Pota said, carefully. "No pain, nothing at all?"

She shook her head. "My hands and feet were tingling for a while, and then they stopped and went numb. I thought if I just waited you could take care of it when you weren't so busy —"

They wouldn't let her say anything else. Within moments they had established through careful prodding and tests with the end of a sharp probe that the numb area now ended at mid-thigh and mid-shoulder.

"How long has this been going on?" Braddon asked, while Pota flew to the AI console to call up the medical program the adults used.

"Oh, a few weeks," she said vaguely. "Socrates said it wasn't anything, that I'd grow out of it. *Then* he acted like I was making it up, and I didn't want him to get the Psychs on me. So I figured I would. . . . "

Pota returned at that moment, her mouth set in a grim line. "You are going straight to bed, pumpkin," she said, with what Tia could tell was forced lightness. "Socrates thinks you have pinched nerves; possibly a spinal defect that he can't scan for. So you are going to bed, and we are calling for a courier to come get you. All right?"

Braddon and Pota exchanged one of *those* looks, the kind Tia couldn't read, and Tia's heart sank. "Okay," she sighed with resignation. "I didn't mean to be such a bother, honest, I didn't —"

Braddon scooped her up in his arms and carried her off to her room. "Don't even *think* that you're being a bother," he said fiercely. "We love you, pumpkin. And we're going to see that you get better as quickly as we can."

He tucked her into bed, with Ted beside her, and called up a holo from the almost-forbidden collection. "Here," he said, kissing her tenderly. "Your Mum is going to be in here in a minute to put something on those burns. Then we're going to spend all our time making you the most disgustingly spoiled little brat in known space! What *you* have to do is lie there and think really hard about getting better. Is it a deal?"

"Sure, Dad," she replied, managing to find a grin for him somewhere. "It's a deal."

• CHAPTER TWO

Because Tia was in no danger of dying — and because there was no craft available to come fetch her capable of Singularity Drive — the AI-drone that had been sent to take her to a Central Worlds hospital took two more weeks to arrive. Two more long, interminable weeks, during which the faces of her Mum and Dad grew drawn and frightened — and in which her condition not only did not improve, it deteriorated.

By the end of that two weeks, she was in much worse shape; she had not only lost all feeling in her limbs, she had lost use of them as well. The clumsiness that had begun when she had trouble with buttons and zippers had turned into paralysis. If she hadn't felt the need to keep her parents' spirits up, she'd have cried. She couldn't even hold Ted anymore.

She joked about it to her Mum, pretending that she had always wanted to be waited on hand and foot. She *had* to joke about it; although she was terrified, the look of fear in her parents' eyes drove her own terrors away. She was determined, absolutely determined, not to let them know how frightened she was. They were already scared enough — if she lost her courage, they might panic.

The time crawled by, as she watched holo after holo and played endless games of chess against Braddon, and kept telling herself that once she got to the hospital everything would be fine. Of course it would be fine. There wasn't anything that a Central Worlds hospital couldn't cure. Everyone knew that! Only congenital defects couldn't be cured. But she had been fine, right up until the day this started. It was probably something stupid.

"Socrates says it has to be pinched nerves," Pota repeated, for the hundredth time, the day the ship was due. "Once they get you to the hospital, you'll have to be really brave, pumpkin. They're probably going to have to operate on you, and it's probably going to take several months before you're back to normal—"

She brushed Tia's hair and tied it in back in a neat tail, the way Tia liked it. "I won't be able to do any lessons, then, will I?" she asked, mostly to keep her mother's mind busy with something trivial. *Mum doesn't handle reality and real-time very well . . . Dad doesn't either.* "They're probably going to have me in a cast or something, and all dopey with pain-pills. I'm going to fall behind, aren't I?"

"Well," Pota said, with false cheer, "yes, I'm afraid so. But that will probably make the Psychs all very happy, you know, they think that you're too far ahead as it is. But just think — you'll have the whole library at the hospital to dig into any time you want it!"

That was enough even to divert her for a minute. The entire library at the hospital — magnitudes bigger than any library they could carry with them. All the holos she wanted to watch — and proper reading screens set up, instead of the jury-rig Dad had put together—

"They're here—" Braddon called from the outer room. Pota compressed her lips into a line again and lifted Tia out of the bed. And for the first time in weeks, Tia was bundled into her pressure-suit, put inside as if Pota was dressing a giant doll. Braddon came in to help in a moment, as she tried to cooperate as much as she could. She would be going outside again. This time, though, she probably wouldn't be coming back. Not to this dome, anyway.

"Wait!" she called, just before Pota sealed her in. "Wait, I want my bear!" And at the look of doubt her parents exchanged, she put on the most pleading expression she could manage. "Please?" She couldn't stand the idea that she'd be going off to a strange place with nothing familiar or warm in it. Even if she couldn't hold him, she could still talk to him and feel his fur against her cheek. *"Please?"*

"All right, pumpkin," Pota said, relenting. "I think there's just room for him in there with you." Fortunately Ted was very squashable, and Tia herself was slender. There *was* room for him in the body of the suit, and Tia took comfort in the feel of his warm little bulk against her waist.

She didn't have any time to think of anything else — for at that moment, two strangers dressed in the white pressure-suits of CenCom Medical came in. There was a strange hiss at the back of her air-pack, and the room went away.

She woke again in a strange white room, dressed in a white paper gown. The only spot of color in the whole place was Ted. *He* was propped beside her, in the crook of her arm, his head peeking out from beneath the white blanket.

She blinked, trying to orient herself, and the cold hand of fear clamped down on her throat. Where was she? A hospital room, probably, but where were Mum and Dad? How did she get here so *fast*? What had those two strangers done to her?

And why wasn't she feeling better? Why couldn't she feel *anything*?

"She's awake," said a voice she didn't recognize. She turned her head, which was all she could move, to see someone in another white pressure-suit standing beside her, anonymous behind a dark faceplate. The red cross of Medical was on one shoulder, and there was a name-tag over the breast, but she couldn't read it from this angle. She couldn't even tell if the person in the suit was male or female, or even human or humanoid.

The faceplate bent over her; she would have shrunk away if she could, feeling scared in spite of herself — the plate was so blank, so impersonal. But then she realized that the person in the suit had bent down so that she could see the face inside, past the glare of lights on the plexi surface, and she relaxed a little.

"Hello, Hypatia," said the person — a lady, actually, a very nice lady from her face. Her voice sounded kind of tinny, coming through the suit speaker; a little like Moira's over the ancient com. The comparison made her feel a little calmer. At least the lady knew her name and pronounced it right.

"Hello," she said cautiously. "This is the hospital, isn't it? How come I don't remember the ship?"

"Well, Hypatia — may I call you Tia?" At Tia's nod, the lady continued. "Tia, our first thought was that you might have some kind of plague, even though your parents were all right. The doctor and medic we sent on the ship decided that it was better to be completely safe and keep you and your parents in isolation. The easiest way to do that was to put all three of you in cold sleep and keep you in your suits until we got you here. We didn't want to frighten you, so we asked your parents not to tell you what we were going to do."

Tia digested that. "All right," she said, trying to be agreeable, since there wasn't anything she could have done about it anyway. "It probably would have gotten really boring on the ship. There probably wasn't much to watch or read, and they would have gotten tired of playing chess with me."

The lady laughed. "Given that you would have beaten the pants off both of them, quite probably," she agreed, straightening up a little. Now that Tia knew there was a person behind the faceplate, it didn't seem quite so threatening. "Now, we're going to keep you in isolation for a while longer, while we see what it is that bit you. You'll be seeing a lot of me — I'm one of your two doctors. My name is Anna Jorgenson-Kepal, and you can call me Anna, or Doctor Anna if you like, but I don't think we need to be that formal. Your other doctor is Kennet Uhua-Sorg. You *won't* be seeing much of him until you're out of isolation, because he's a paraplegic and he's in a Moto-Chair. Can't fit one of *them* into a pressure-suit."

The holo-screen above the bed flickered into life, and the head and shoulders of a thin, ascetic-looking young man appeared there. "Call me Kenny, Tia," the young man said. "I absolutely refuse to be stuffy with you. I'm sorry I can't meet you in person, but it takes *forever* to decontam one of these fardling chairs, so Anna gets to be my hands."

"That's — your chair — it's kind of like a modified shell, isn't it?" she asked curiously, deciding that if they were going to bring the subject up, *she* wasn't going to be polite and avoid it. "I know a shellperson. Moira, she's a brainship."

"Dead on!" Kenny said cheerfully. "Medico on the half-shell, that's me! I just had a stupid accident when I was a tweenie, not like you, getting bit by alien bugs!"

She smiled tentatively. *I think I'm going to like him.* "Did anyone ever tell you that you look *just* like Amenemhat the Third?"

His large eyes widened even more. "Well, no — that is definitely a new one. I hope it's a compliment! One of my patients said I looked like Largo Delecron, the synthcom star, but I didn't know she thought Largo looked like a refugee from a slaver camp!"

"It is," she assured him hastily. "He's one of my favorite Pharaohs."

"I'll have to see if I can't cultivate the proper Pharaonic majesty, then," Kenny replied with a grin.

"It might do me some good when I have to drum some sense into the heads of some of the Psychs around here! They've been trying to get at you ever since we admitted you."

If she could have shivered with apprehension, she would have. "I don't have to see them, do I?" she asked in a small voice. "They never stop asking stupid questions!"

"Absolutely not," Anna said firmly. "I have a double-doctorate; one of them is in headshrinking. I am *quite* capable of assessing you all by myself."

Tia's heart sank when Anna mentioned her degree in Psych — but it rose the moment she referred to Psych as "headshrinking." None of the Psychs who had plagued her life until now *ever* called their profession by something as frivolous as "headshrinking."

She patted Tia's shoulder. "Don't worry, Tia. It's my opinion that you are a very brave young lady — a little *too* responsible, but otherwise just fine. *They* spend too much time analyzing children and not enough time actually seeing them or paying attention to them." She smiled inside her helmet, and a curl of hair escaped down to dangle above her left eyebrow, making her look a lot more human.

"Listen, Tia, there's a little bit of fur missing from your bear, and a scrap of stuffing," Kenny said. "Anna says you wouldn't notice, but I thought we ought to tell you anyway. We checked him over for alien bugs and neurotoxins, and he's got a clean bill of health. When you come out of Coventry, we'll decontam him again to be sure, but we *know* he wasn't the problem, in case you were wondering."

She had wondered. . . . Moira wouldn't have done anything on purpose, of course, but it would have been horrible if her sickness had been due to Ted. Moira would have felt awful, not to mention how Tomas would feel.

"What's his name?" Anna asked, busying herself with something at the head of the bed. Tia couldn't turn her head far enough to see what it was.

"Theodore Edward Bear," she replied, surreptitiously rubbing her cheek against his soft fur. "Moira gave him to me, because she used to have a bear named Ivan the Bearable."

"Excellent name, Theodore. It suits him," Anna said. "You know, I think your Moira and I must be about the same age — there was a kind of fad for bears when I was little. I had a really nice bear in a flying suit called Amelia Bearhart." She chuckled. "I still have her, actually, but she mostly sits on the bureau in my guest room. She's gotten to be a very venerable matriarch in her old age."

But bears weren't really what she wanted to talk about. Now that she knew where she was, and that she was in isolation. "How long am I going to be in here?" she asked in a small voice.

Kenny turned very serious, and Anna stopped fiddling with things. Kenny sucked on his lower lip for a moment before actually replying, and the hum of the machinery in her room seemed very loud. "The Psychs were trying to tell us that we should try and cushion you, but — Tia, we think that you are a very unusual girl. We think you would rather know the complete truth. Is that the case?"

Would she? Or would she rather pretend —

But this wasn't like making up stories at a dig. If she pretended, things would only seem worse when they finally told her the truth, if it was bad.

"Ye-es," she told them both, slowly. "Please."

"We don't know," Anna told her. "I wish we did. We haven't found anything in your blood, and we're only just now trying to isolate things in your nervous system. But — well, we're assuming it's a bug that got you, a proto-virus, maybe, but we don't know, and that's the truth. Until we know, we won't know if we can fix you again."

Not when. If.

The possibility that she might *stay* like this for the rest of her life chilled her.

"Your parents are in isolation, too," Kenny said, hastily, "but they are one hundred percent fine. There's nothing wrong with them at all. So that makes things harder."

"I understand, I think," she said in a small, nervous-sounding voice. She took a deep breath. "Am I getting worse?"

Anna went very still. Kenny's face darkened, and he bit his lower lip.

"Well," he said quietly. "Yes. We're having to think about mobility, and maybe even life-support for you. Something considerably more than my chair. I wish I could tell you differently, Tia."

"That's all right," she said, trying to ease his distress. "I'd rather know."

Anna leaned down to whisper something through her suit-mike. "Tia, if you're afraid of crying, don't be. If I were in your position, I'd cry. And if you would like to be alone, tell us, all right?"

"Okay," she replied, faintly. "Uh, can I be alone for a while, please?"

"Sure." She stopped pretending to fuss with equipment and nodded shortly at the holo-screen. Kenny brought up one hand to wave at her, and the screen blinked out. Anna left through what Tia now realized was a decontam-airlock a moment later. Leaving her alone with the hissing, humming equipment, and Ted.

She swallowed a lump in her throat and thought very hard about what they'd told her.

She wasn't getting any better, she was getting worse. They didn't know what was wrong. That was on the negative side. On the plus side, there was nothing wrong with Mum and Dad, and they hadn't said to give up all hope.

Therefore, she should continue to assume that they *would* find a cure.

She cleared her throat. "Hello?" she said.

As she had thought, there was an AI monitoring the room.

"Hello," it replied, in the curiously accentless voice only an AI could produce. "What is your need?"

"I'd like to watch a holo. History," she said, after a moment of thought. "There's a holo about Queen Hatshepsut of Egypt. It's called *Phoenix of Ra*, I think. Have you got that?"

That had been on the forbidden list at home; Tia knew why. There had been some pretty steamy scenes with the Pharaoh and her architect in there. Tia was fascinated by the only female to declare herself Pharaoh, however, and had been decidedly annoyed when a little sex kept her from viewing this one.

"Yes, I have access to that," the AI said after a moment. "Would you like to view it now?"

So they hadn't put any restrictions on her viewing privileges! "Yes," she replied; then, eager to strike while she had the chance, "And after that, I'd like to see the *Aten* trilogy, about Ahnkenaten and the heretics — that's *Aten Rising*, *Aten at Zenith*, and *Aten Descending*."

Those had more than a few steamy scenes; she'd overheard her mother saying that some of the theories that had been dramatized fairly explicitly in the trilogy, while they made comprehensible some otherwise inexplicable findings, would get the holos banned in some cultures. And Braddon had chuckled and replied that the costumes alone — or lack of them — while completely accurate, would do the same. Still — Tia figured she could handle it. And if it was that bad, it would *certainly* help keep her mind off her own troubles!

"Very well," the AI said agreeably. "Shall I begin?"

"Yes," she told it, with another caress of her cheek on Ted's soft fur. "Please."

Pota and Braddon watched their daughter with frozen faces, faces that Tia was convinced covered a complete welter of emotions that they didn't want her to see. She took a deep breath, enunciated "Chair forward, five feet," and her Moto-Chair glided forward and stopped before it touched them.

"Well, now I can get around at least," she said, with what she hoped sounded like cheer. "I was getting awfully tired of the same four walls!"

Whatever it was that she had — and now she heard the words "proto-virus" and "dystrophic sclerosis" bandied about more often than not — the medics had decided it wasn't contagious. They'd let Pota and Braddon out of isolation, and they'd moved Tia to another room, one that had a door right onto the corridor. Not that it made much difference, except that Anna didn't have to use a decontam airlock and pressure-suit anymore. And now Kenny came to see her in person. But four white walls were still four white walls, and there wasn't much variation in rooms.

Still — she was afraid to ask for things to personalize the room. Afraid that if she made it more her own — she'd be stuck in it. Forever.

Her numbness and paralysis extended to most of her body now, except for her facial muscles. And there it stopped. Just as inexplicably as it had begun.

They'd put her in the quadriplegic version of the Moto-Chair; just like Kenny's except that she controlled hers with a few commands and series of tongue-switches and eye movements. A command sent it forward, and the direction she looked would tell it where to go. And hers had mechanical "arms" that followed set patterns programmed in to respond to more commands. Any command had to be prefaced by "chair" or "arm." A clumsy system, but it was the best they could do without direct synaptic connections from the brainstem, like those of a shellperson.

Her brainstem was still intact, anyway. Whatever it was had gotten her spine, but not that.

Other than that, Mrs. Lincoln, she thought with bitter irony, *how was the play?*

"What do you think, pumpkin?" Braddon asked, his voice quivering only a little.

"Hey, this is stellar, Dad," she replied cheerfully. "It's just like piloting a ship! I think I'll challenge Doctor Kenny to a race!"

Pota swallowed very hard and managed a tremulous smile. "It won't be for too long," she said without conviction. "As soon as they find out what's set up housekeeping in there, they'll have you better in no time."

She bit her lip to keep from snapping back and dug up a fatuous grin from somewhere. The likelihood of finding a cure diminished more with every day, and she knew it. Neither Anna nor Kenny made any attempt to hide that from her.

But there was no point in making her parents unhappy. They already felt bad enough.

She tried out all the points of the chair for them, until not even they could stand it anymore. They left, making excuses and promising to come back — and they were succeeded immediately by a stream of interns and neurological specialists, each of whom had more variations on the same basic questions she had answered a thousand times, each of whom had his own pet theory about what was wrong.

"First my toes felt like they were asleep when I woke up one morning, but it wore off. Then it didn't wear off. Then instead of waking up with tingles, I woke up numb. No, sir, it never actually hurt. No, ma'am, it only went as far as my heel at first. Yes, sir, then after two days my fingers started. No ma'am, just the fingers not the whole hand. . . ."

Hours of it. But she knew that they weren't being nasty, they were trying to *help* her, and being able to help her depended on how cooperative she was.

But their questions didn't stop the questions of her own. So far it was just sensory nerves and voluntary muscles and nerves. What if it went to the involuntary ones, and she woke up unable to breathe? What then? What if she lost control of her facial muscles? Every little tingle made her break out in a sweat of panic, thinking it was going to happen. . . .

Nobody had answers for any questions. Not hers, and not theirs.

Finally, just before dinner, they went away. After about a half an hour, she mastered control of the arms enough to feed herself, saving herself the humiliation of having to call a nurse to do it. And the chair's own plumbing solved the humiliation of the natural result of eating and drinking. . . .

After supper, when the tray was taken away, she was left in the growing darkness of the room, quite alone. She would have slumped, if she could have. It was just as well that Pota and Braddon hadn't returned; having them there was a strain. It was harder to be brave in front of them than it was in front of strangers.

"Chair, turn seventy degrees right," she ordered. "Left arm, pick up bear."

With a soft whir, the chair obeyed her.

"Left arm, put bear — cancel. Left arm, bring bear to left of face." The arm moved a little. "Closer. Closer. Hold."

Now she cuddled Ted against her cheek, and she could pretend that it was her own arm holding him there.

With no one there to see, slow, hot tears formed in her eyes and trickled down her cheeks. She leaned her head to the left a little, so that they would soak into Ted's soft blue fur and not betray her.

"It's not fair," she whispered to Ted, who seemed to nod with sad agreement as she rubbed her cheek against him. "It's not fair. . . ."

I wanted to find the EsKay homeworld. I wanted to go out with Mum and Dad and be the one to find the homeworld. I wanted to write books. I wanted to stand up in front of people and make them laugh and get excited, and see how history and archeology aren't dead, they're just asleep. I wanted to do things they make holos out of. I wanted — I wanted —

I wanted to see things! I wanted to drive grav-sleds and swim in a real lagoon and feel a storm and —

— and I wanted —

Some of the scenes from the holos she'd been watching came back with force now, and memories of Pota and Braddon, when they thought she was engrossed in a book or a holo, giggling and cuddling like tweenies. . . .

I wanted to find out about boys. Boys and kisses and —

And now nobody's ever going to look at me and see me. All they're going to see is this big metal thing. That's all they see now. . . .

Even if a boy ever wanted to kiss me, he'd have to get past a half ton of machinery, and it would probably bleep an alarm.

The tears poured faster now, with the darkness of the room to hide them.

They wouldn't have put me in this thing if they thought I was going to get better. I'm never going to get better. I'm only going to get worse. I can't feel anything, I'm nothing but a head in a machine. And if I get worse, will I go deaf? Blind?

"Teddy, what's going to happen to me?" she sobbed. "Am I going to spend the rest of my life in a room?"

Ted didn't know, any more than she did.

"It's not fair, it's not fair, I never did anything," she wept, as Ted watched her tears with round, sad eyes, and soaked them up for her. "It's not fair. I wasn't finished. I hadn't even started yet. . . ."

*   *   *

Kenny grabbed a tissue with one hand and snapped off the camera-relay with the other. He scrubbed fiercely at his eyes and blew his nose with a combination of anger and grief. Anger, at his own impotence. Grief, for the vulnerable little girl alone in that cold, impersonal hospital room, a little girl who was doing her damnedest to put a brave face on everything.

In public. He was the only one to watch her in private, like this, when she thought there was no one to see that her whole pose of cheer was nothing more than a facade.

"I wasn't finished. I wasn't even started yet."

"Damn it," he swore, scrubbing at his eyes again and pounding the arm of his chair. *"Damn* it anyway!" What careless god had caused her to choose the very words *he* had used, fifteen years ago?

Fifteen years ago, when a stupid accident had left him paralyzed from the waist down and put an end — he thought — to his dreams for med school?

Fifteen years ago, when Doctor Harwat Kline-Bes was *his* doctor and had heard him weeping alone into his pillow?

He turned his chair and opened the viewport out into the stars, staring at them as they moved past in a panorama of perfect beauty that changed with the rotation of the station. He let the tears dry on his cheeks, let his mind empty.

Fifteen years ago, another neurologist had heard those stammered, heartbroken words, and had determined that they *would not* become a truth. He had taken a paraplegic young student, bullied the makers of an experimental Moto-Chair into giving the youngster one — then bullied the dean of the Meyasor State Medical College into admitting the boy. *Then* he had seen to it that once the boy graduated, he got an internship in this very hospital — a place where a neurologist in a Moto-Chair was no great curiosity, not with the sentients of a hundred worlds coming in as patients *and* doctors. . . .

A paraplegic, though. Not a quad. Not a child with a brilliant, flexible mind, trapped in an inert body.

Brilliant mind. Inert body. Brilliant —

An idea blinded him, it occurred so suddenly. He was *not* the only person watching Tia — there was one other. Someone who watched every patient here, every doctor, every nurse. . . . Someone he didn't consult too often, because Lars wasn't a medico, or a shrink —

But in this case, Lars' opinion was likely to be more accurate than anyone else's on this station. Including his own.

He thumbed a control. "Lars," he said shortly. "Got a minute, buddy?"

He had to wait for a moment. Lars was a busy guy — though hopefully at this hour there weren't too many demands on his conversational circuits. "Certainly, Kenny," Lars replied after a few seconds. "How can I help the neurological *wunderkind* of Central Worlds MedStation *Pride of Albion*? Hmm?" The voice was rich and ironic; Lars rather enjoyed teasing everyone on-board. He called it "therapeutic deflation of egos." He particularly liked deflating Kenny's — he had said more than once that everyone else was so afraid of being "unkind to the poor cripple" that they danced on eggs to avoid telling him when he was full of it.

"Can the sarcasm, Lars," Kenny replied. "I've got a serious problem that I want your opinion on."

"My opinion?" Lars sounded genuinely surprised. "This must be a personal opinion — I'm certainly not qualified to give you a medical one."

"Most definitely, a very personal opinion, one that you are the best suited to give. On Hypatia Cade."

"Ah." Kenny thought that Lars' tone softened considerably. "The little child in the Neuro unit, with the unchildlike taste in holos. She still thinks I'm the AI. I haven't dissuaded her."

"Good, I want her to be herself around you, for the gods of space know she won't be herself around the rest of us." He realized that his tone had gone savage and carefully regained control over himself before he continued. "You've got her records and you've watched the kid herself. I know she's old for it — but how would she do in the shell program?"

A long pause. Longer than Lars needed simply to access and analyze records. "Has her condition stabilized?" he asked, cautiously. "If it hasn't — if she goes brain-inert halfway into her schooling — it'd not only make problems for anyone else you'd want to bring in late, it'll traumatize the other shell-kids badly. They don't handle death well. I wouldn't be a party to frightening them, however inadvertently."

Kenny massaged his temple with the long, clever fingers that had worked so many surgical miracles for others and could do nothing for this little girl. "As far as we can tell anything about this — disease — yes, she's stable," he said finally. "Take a look in there and you'll see I ordered a shotgun approach while we were testing her. She's had a full course of every anti-viral neurological agent we've got a record of. *And* noninvasive things like a course of ultra — well, you can see it there. I think we killed it, whatever it was."

Too late to help her. Damn it.

"She's brilliant," Lars said cautiously. "She's flexible. She has the ability to multi-thread, to do several things at once. And she's had good, positive reactions to contact with shellpersons in the past."

"So?" Kenny asked, impatiently, as the stars passed by in their courses, indifferent to the fate of one little girl. "Your opinion."

"I think she can make the transition," Lars said, with more emphasis than Kenny had ever heard in his voice before. "I think she'll not only make the transition, she'll do *well*."

He let out the breath he'd been holding in a sigh.

"Physically, she is certainly no worse off than many in the shellperson program, including yours truly," Lars continued. "Frankly, Kenny, she's got so much potential it would be a crime to let her rot in a hospital room for the rest of her life."

The careful control Lars normally had over his voice was gone; there was passion in his words that Kenny had never heard him display until this moment. "Got to you, too, did she?" he said dryly.

"Yes," Lars said, biting off the word. "And I'm not ashamed of it. I don't mind telling you that she had me in — well, not tears, but certainly the equivalent."

"Good for you." He rubbed his hands together, warming cold fingers. "Because I'm going to need your connivance again."

"Going to pull another fast one, are you?" Lars asked with ironic amusement.

"Just a few strings. What good does being a stellar intellect do me, if I can't make use of the position?" he asked rhetorically. He shut the viewport and pivoted his chair to face his desk, keying on his terminal and linking it directly to Lars and a very personal database. One called "Favors." "All right, my friend, let's get to work. First, whose strings can you jerk? Then, who on the political side has influence in the program, of that set, who owes me the most, and of that subset, who's due here the soonest?"

A Sector Secretary-General did not grovel, nor did he gush, but to Kenny's immense satisfaction, when Quintan Waldheim-Querar y Chan came aboard the *Pride of Albion*, the very first thing he wanted, after all the official inspections and the like were over, was to meet with the brilliant neurologist whose work had saved his nephew from the same fate as Kenny himself. He already knew most of what there was to know about Kenny and his meteoric career.

And Quintan Waldheim-Querar y Chan was not the sort to avoid an uncomfortable topic.

"A little ironic, isn't it?" the Secretary-General said, after the firm handshake, with a glance at Kenny's Moto-Chair. He stood up and did *not* tug self-consciously at his conservative dark blue tunic.

Kenny did not smile, but he took a deep breath of satisfaction. *Doubly good. No more calls, we have a winner.*

"What, that my injury was virtually identical to Peregrine's?" he replied immediately. "Not ironic at all, sir. The fact that I found myself in this position was what prompted me to go into neurology in the first place. I won't try to claim that if I *hadn't* been injured, and *hadn't* worked so hard to find a remedy for the same injuries, someone else might not have come up with the same answer that I did. Medical research is a matter of building on what has come before, after all."

"But without your special interest, the solution might well have come too late to do Peregrine any good," the Secretary-General countered. "And it was not only your technique, it was your skill that pulled him through. There is no duplication of that — not in this sector, anyway. That's why I arranged for this visit. I wanted to thank you."

Kenny shrugged deprecatingly. This was the most perfect opening he'd ever seen in his life — and he had no intention of letting it get away from him. Not when he had the answer to Tia's prayers trapped in his office.

"I can't win them all, sir," he said flatly. "I'm not a god. Though there are times I wish most profoundly that I was, and right now is one of them."

The Great Man's expression sobered. The Secretary-General was not just a Great Man because he was an excellent administrator; he was one because he had a human side, and that human and humane side could be touched. "I take it you have a case that is troubling you?" Then, conscious of the fact that he Owed Kenny, he said the magic words. "Perhaps I can help?"

Kenny sighed, as if he were reluctant to continue the discussion. *Wouldn't do to seem too eager.* "Well — would you care to see some tape of the child?"

Child. Children were one of the Great Man's weaknesses. He had sponsored more child-oriented programs than any three of his predecessors combined. "Yes. If it would not be violating the child's privacy."

"Here — " Kenny flicked a switch, triggering the holo-record he already had keyed up. A record he and Anna had put together. Carefully edited, carefully selected, compiled from days of recordings with Lars' assistance and the psych-profile of the Great Man to guide them. "I promise I won't take more than fifteen minutes of your time."

The first seven and a half minutes of this recording were of Tia at her most attractive; being very brave and cheerful for the interns and her parents. "This is Hypatia Cade, the daughter of Pota Andropolous-Cade and Braddon Maartens-Cade," he explained, over the holo. Quickly he outlined her background and her pathetic little story, stressing her high intelligence, her flexibility, her responsibility. "The prognosis isn't very cheerful, I'm afraid," he said, watching his chrono carefully to time his speech with the end of that section of tape. "No matter what we do, she's doomed to spend the rest of her life in some institution or other. The only way she could be at all mobile would be through direct synaptic connections — well, we don't do that here — they can only link in that way at Lab Schools, the shellperson project — "

He stopped, as the holo flickered and darkened. Tia was alone.

The arm of her chair reached out and grasped the sad little blue bear, hidden until now by the tray table and a pillow. It brought the toy in close to her face, and she gently rubbed her cheek against its soft fur coat. The lightning-bolt of the Courier Service on its shirt stood out clearly in this shot ... one reason why Kenny had chosen it.

"They've gone, Ted," she whispered to her bear. "Mum and Dad — they've gone back to the Institute. There's nobody left here but you, now."

A single bright tear formed in one corner of her eye and slowly rolled down her cheek, catching what little light there was in the room.

"What? Oh, no, it's not their fault, Ted — they had to. The Institute said so, I saw the dispatch. It said — it said since I w-w-wasn't going to get any b-b-b-better there was no p-p-p-point in — in — wasting v-v-valuable t-t-time — "

She sobbed once, and buried her face in the teddy bear's fur.

After a moment, her voice came again, muffled. "Anyway, it hurts them so m-much. And it's s-s-so hard to be b-brave for them. But if I cried, th-they'd only feel w-worse. I think m-maybe it's b-better this way, don't you? Easier. F-for every-b-b-b-body. ... "

The holo flickered again; same time, nearly the same position, but a different day. This time she was crying openly, tears coursing down her cheeks as she sobbed into the bear's little shirt.

"We've given her the complete run of the library and the holo collection," Kenny said, very softly. "Normally, they keep her relatively amused and stimulated — but just before we filmed this, she picked out an episode of *The Stellar Explorers* — and — well — her parents said she had planned to be a pilot, you see — "

She continued to cry, sobbing helplessly, the only understandable words being " — Teddy — I wanted — to go — I wanted to see the *stars* — "

The holo flickered out, as Kenny turned the lights in his office back up. He reached for a tissue and wiped his eyes without shame. "I'm afraid she affects me rather profoundly," he said, and smiled weakly. "So much for my professional detachment."

The Great Man blinked rapidly to clear his own eyes. "Why isn't something being done for that child?" he demanded, his voice hoarse.

"We've done all we can — here," Kenny said. "The only possibility of giving that poor child any kind of a life is to get her into the shellperson program. But the Psychs at the Laboratory Schools seem to think she's too old. They wouldn't even send someone to come evaluate her, even though the parents petitioned them and we added our own recommendations. . . . "

He let the sentence trail off significantly. The Secretary-General gave him a sharp look. "And you don't agree with them, I take it?"

Kenny shrugged. "It isn't just *my* opinion," he said smoothly. "It's the opinion of the staff Psych assigned to her, the shellperson running this station, and a brain-ship friend of hers in the Courier Service. The one," he added delicately, "who gave her that little bear."

Mentioning the bear sold the deal; Kenny could see it in the Great Man's expression. "We'll just see about that," the Secretary-General said. "The people you talked to don't have all the answers — and they *certainly* don't have the final say." He stood up and offered Kenny his hand again. "I won't promise anything — but don't be surprised if there's someone from the Laboratory Schools here to see her in the next few days. How soon can you have her ready for transfer, if they take her?"

"Within twelve hours, sir," Kenny replied, secretly congratulating himself for getting her parents to sign a writ-of-consent before they left. Of course, they thought it was for experimental procedures.

Then again, Pota and Braddon had been the ones who'd broached the idea of the shellperson program to the people at the Laboratory Schools and been turned down because of Tia's age.

"Twelve hours?" The Great Man raised an eyebrow. Kenny returned him look for look.

"Her parents are under contract to the Archeological Institute," he explained. "The Institute called them back out into the field, because their parental emergency leave was up. They weren't happy, but it was obey or be fired. Hard to find another job in that field that isn't with the Institute." He coughed. "Well, they trusted my work, and made me Tia's full guardian before they left."

"So you have right-of-disposition and guardianship. Very tidy." The Secretary-General's wry smile showed that he knew he had been maneuvered into this — and that he was not annoyed. "All right. There'll be someone from the schools here within the week. Unless there's something you haven't told me about the girl, he should finish his evaluation in two days. At the end of those two days . . ." One eyebrow raised significantly. "Well, it would be very convenient if he could take the new recruit back with him, wouldn't it?"

"Yes, sir," Kenny said happily. "It would indeed, sir."

If it hadn't been for Doctor Uhua-Sorg's reputation and the pleas of his former pupil, Lars Mendoza, Philip Gryphon bint Brogen would have been only too happy to tell the committee where to stick the Secretary-General's request. *And* what to do with it after they put it there. One did *not* pull strings to get an unsuitable candidate into the shell program! Maybe the Secretary-General thought he could get away with that kind of politicking with Academy admissions, but he was going to find out differently *here*.

Philip was not inclined to be coaxed and *would not*

give in to bullying. So it was in a decidedly belligerent state of mind that he disembarked from his shuttle onto the docks of the *Pride of Albion*. Like every hospital station, this one affronted him with its sterile white walls and atmosphere of self-importance.

There was someone waiting — obviously for him — in the reception area. Someone in a Moto-Chair. A handsome young man with thick dark hair and a thin, ascetic face.

If they think they can soften me up by assigning me to someone they think I won't dare be rude to — he thought savagely, as the young man glided the Chair toward him. *Conniving beggars* —

"Professor Brogen?" said the ridiculously young, vulnerable-looking man, holding out his hand. "I'm Doctor Sorg."

"If you think I'm going to — " Brogen began, *not* reaching out to take it — then the name registered on him and he did a classic double-take. "*Doctor* Sorg? Doctor Uhua-Sorg?"

The young man nodded, just the barest trace of a smile showing on his lips.

"Doctor *Kennet* Uhua-Sorg?" Brogen asked, feeling as if he'd been set up, yet knowing he had set up himself for this particular fall.

"Yes indeed," the young man replied. "I take it that you weren't — ah — expecting me to meet you in person."

A chance for an out — not a graceful one, but an out — and Brogen took it. "Hardly," he replied brusquely. "The Chief of Neurosurgery and Neurological Research usually does not meet a simple professor on behalf of an ordinary child."

"Tia is far from ordinary, Professor," Doctor Sorg responded, never once losing that hint of smile. "Any more than you are a 'simple' professor. But, if you'll follow me, you'll find out about Tia for yourself."

*   *   *

Well, he's right about one thing, Brogen thought grudgingly, after an hour spent in Tia's company while hordes of interns and specialists pestered, poked and prodded her. *She's not ordinary. Any "ordinary" child would be having a screaming tantrum by now.* She was an extraordinarily attractive child as well as a patient one; her dark hair had been cropped short to keep it out of the way, but her thin, pixie-like face and big eyes made her look like the model for a Victorian fairy. A fairy trapped in a fist of metal . . . tormented and teased by a swarm of wasps.

"How much longer is this going to go on?" he asked Kennet Sorg in an irritated whisper.

Kennet raised one eyebrow. "That's for you to say," he replied. "You are here to evaluate her. If you want more time alone with her, you have only to say the word. This is her second session for the day, by the way," he added, and Brogen could have sworn there was a hint of — smugness? — in his voice. "She played host to another swarm this morning, between nine and noon."

Now Brogen was outraged, but on the child's behalf. Kennet Sorg must have read that in his expression, for he turned his chair towards the cluster of white-uniformed interns, cleared his throat, and got their instant attention.

"That will be all for today," he said quietly. "If you please, ladies and gentlemen. Professor Brogen would like to have some time with Tia alone."

There were looks of disappointment and some even of disgust cast Brogen's way, but he ignored them. The child, at least, looked relieved.

Before he could say anything to Kennet Sorg, he realized that the doctor had followed the others out the door, which was closing behind his chair, leaving Brogen alone with the child. He cleared his own throat awkwardly.

The little girl looked at him with a most peculiar expression in her eyes. Not fear, but wariness.

"You're not a Psych, are you?" she asked.

"Well — no," he said. "Not exactly. I'll probably ask some of the same questions, though."

She sighed, and closed her soft brown eyes for a moment. "I'm *very* tired of having my head shrunk," she replied forthrightly. "Very, *very* tired. And it isn't going to make any difference at all in the way I think, anyway. It isn't *fair,* but this — " she bobbed her chin at her chair " — isn't going to go away because it isn't fair. Right?"

"Sad, but true, my dear." He began to relax, and realized why. Kennet Sorg was right. This was no ordinary child; talking with her was not like talking to a child — but it *was* like talking to one of the kids in the shell program. "So — how about if we chat about something else entirely. Do you know any shellpersons?"

She gave him an odd look. "They must not have told you very much about me," she said. "Either that, or you didn't pay very much attention. One of my very best friends is a brainship — Moira Valentine-Maya. She gave me Theodore."

Theodore? Oh — right. The bear — He cast a quick glance over towards the bed — and there was the somber-looking little bear in a Courier Service shirt that he'd been told about.

"Did you ever think about what being in a shell must be like?" he asked, fishing for a way to explain the program to her without letting her know she was being evaluated.

"Of *course* I did!" she said, not bothering to hide her scorn. "I told Moira that I wanted to be just like her when I grew up, and she laughed at me and told me all about what the schools were like and everything — "

And then, before he could say anything, the

unchildlike child proceeded to tell *him* about his own program. The brainship side, at any rate.

Pros and cons. From having to be able to multi-task, to the thrill of experiencing a singularity and warp-space firsthand. From being locked forever in a metal skin, to the loneliness of knowing that you were going to outlive all your partners but the last. . . .

"I told her that I guessed I didn't want to go in when I figured out that you could never touch anybody again," she concluded, wearily. "I know you've got sensors to the skin and everything, but that was what I didn't like. Kind of funny, huh?"

"Why?" he asked without thinking.

"Because now — I can't touch anybody. And I won't ever again. So it's kind of funny. I can't touch anyone anymore, but I can't be a brainship either." The tired resignation in her voice galvanized him.

"I don't know why you couldn't," he said, aware that he had already made up his mind, and both aghast and amused at himself. "There's room in this year's class for another couple of new candidates; there's even room in the brainship category for one or two pupils."

She blinked at him, then blurted, "But they told me I was too old!"

He laughed. "My dear, *you* wouldn't be too old if you were your mother's age. You would have been a good shell-program candidate well past puberty." He still couldn't believe this child; responsible, articulate, flexible. . . . Lars and Kennet Sorg had been right. It made him wonder how many other children had been rejected out of hand, simply because of age — how many had been lost to a sterile existence in an institution, just because they had no one as persistent and as influential as Kennet Sorg to plead their cases.

Well, one thing at a time. Grab this one now. Put something in place to take care of the others later. "I'm going to have to go through the motions and file the paperwork — but Tia, if you want, you can consider yourself recruited this very instant."

"*Yes!*" she burst out "Oh, yes! Yes, yes, yes! Oh, please, thank you, thank you so much — " Her cheeks were wet with tears, but the joy on her face was so intense that it was blinding. Professor Brogen blinked and swallowed a lump in his throat.

"The advantage of recruiting someone your age," he said, ignoring her tears and his tickling eyes, "is that you can make your career path decision right away. Shellpersons don't all go into brainships — for instance, you *could* opt for a career with the Institute; they've been asking to hire a shellperson to head their home-base research section for the last twenty years. You could do original research on the findings of others — even your parents' discoveries. You could become a Spaceport Administrator, or a Station Administrator. You could go into law, or virtually any branch of science. Even medicine. With the synaptic links we have, there is no career you cannot consider."

"But I want to be a brainship," she said firmly.

Brogen took a deep breath. While he agreed with her emotionally — well, there were some serious drawbacks. "Tia, a lot of what a brainship does is — well, being a truck driver or a cabby. Ferrying people or things from one place to another. It isn't very glamorous work. It *is* quite dangerous, both physically and psychologically. You would be very valuable, and yet totally unarmed, unless you went into the military branch, which I don't think you're suited for, frankly. You would be a target for thieves and malcontents. And there is one other thing; the *ship* is very expensive. In my not-so-humble opinion, brainship service is just one short step from indentured slavery. You are literally paying for the use and upkeep of that ship by mortgaging yourself. There is very little chance of buying your contract out in any reasonable length of time unless you do something truly spectacular or take on very dangerous duties. The former isn't likely to happen in ordinary service — and you won't be able to exchange boring service for whatever your fancy is."

Tia looked stubborn for a moment, then thoughtful. "All of that is true," she said, finally. "But — Professor, Dad always said I had his astrogator genes, and I was already getting into tensor physics, so I *have* the head for starflight. And it's what I want."

Brogen turned up his hands. "I can't argue with that. There's no arguing with preferences, is there?" In a way, he was rather pleased. As self-possessed as Tia was, she would do very well in brainship service. And as stable as she seemed to be, there was very little chance of her having psychological problems, unless something completely unforeseen came up.

She smiled shyly. "Besides, I talked this over with Moira — you know, giving her ideas on how she could get some extra credits to help with all her fines for bouncing her brawns? Since she was with Archeology and Exploration as a courier, there were lots of chances for her to see things that the surveyors might not, and I kind of told her what to look for. I kind of figured that with my background, it wouldn't be too hard to get assigned to A and E myself, and I could do the same things, only better. I could get a *lot* of credits that way. And once I owned my ship — well, I could do whatever I wanted."

Brogen couldn't help himself; he started to laugh. "You are quite the young schemer, did you know that?"

She grinned, looking truly happy for the first time since he had seen her. Now that he had seen the real thing, he recognized all her earlier "smiles" for the shams that they had been.

Leaving her here would have been a crime. A sin.

"Well, you can consider yourself recruited," he said comfortably. "I'll fill out the paperwork tonight, databurst it to the schools as soon as I finish, and there should be a confirmation waiting for us when we wake up. Think you can be ready to ship out in the morning?"

"Yes, sir," she said happily.

He rose and started to leave — then paused for a moment.

"You know," he said, "you were right. I really didn't pay too much attention to the file they gave me on you, since I was so certain that — well, never mind. But I am terribly curious about your name. Why on earth did your parents call you 'Hypatia'?"

Tia laughed out loud, a peal of infectious joy.

"I think, Professor Brogen," she said, "that you'd better sit back down!"

● CHAPTER THREE

CenCom's softperson operator had a pleasant voice and an equally pleasant habit of *not* starting a call with a burst of static or an alert-beep. "XH One-Oh-Three-Three, you have an incoming transmission. Canned message beam."

Tia tore herself away from the latest papers on the Salomon-Kildaire Entities with a purely mental sigh of regret. Oh, she could take in a databurst *and* scan the papers at the same time, certainly, but she wanted to do more than simply scan the information. She wanted to absorb it, so that she could think about it later in detail. There were nuances to academic papers that simple scanning wouldn't reveal; places where you had to know the personality of the author in order to read between the lines. Places where what *wasn't* written were as important as what *was*.

"Go ahead, CenCom," she replied, wondering who on earth—or off it, for that matter—could be calling her.

Strange how we've been out of Terran subspace for so long, and yet we still use expressions like "how on earth" . . . there's probably a popular-science paper in that.

The central screen directly opposite the column she was housed in flickered for a moment, then filled with the image of a thin-faced man in an elaborate Moto-Chair. No — more than a Moto-Chair; this one was kind of a platform for something else. She saw what could only be an APU, and a short-beam broadcast unit of some kind. It looked like his legs and waist were encased in the bottom half of space armor!

But there was no mistaking who was in the strange exoskeleton. Doctor Kenny.

"Tia, my darling girl, congratulations on your graduation!" Kenny said, eyes twinkling. "You should — given the vagaries of the CenCom postal system — have gotten your graduation present from Lars and Anna and me. I hope you liked it — them — "

The graduation present *had* arrived on time, and Tia had been enthralled. She loved instrumental music, synthcom in particular, but these recordings had special meaning for any shellperson, for they had been composed and played by David Weber-Tcherkasky, a shellperson himself, and they were not meant for the limited ears of softpeople. The composer had made use of every note of the aural spectrum, with super-complexes of overtones and counterpoint that left softpersons squinting in bewilderment. They weren't for everyone — not even for some shellpersons — but Tia didn't think she would ever get tired of listening to them. Every time she played them, she heard something new.

" — anyway, I remembered you saying in your last transmission how much you liked Lanz Manhem's synthcom recordings, and Lars kept telling me that Tcherkasky's work was to Manhem's what a symphony was to birdsong." Kenny shrugged and grinned. "We figured that it would help to while away the in-transit hours for you, anyway. Anna said the graduation was stellar — I'm sorry I couldn't be there, but you're looking at the reason why."

He made a face and gestured down at the lower half of his body. "Moto-Prosthetics decided in their infinite wisdom that since I had benefited from their expertise in the past, I *owed* them. They convinced the hospital Admin Head that I was the only possible person to test this contraption of theirs. This is *supposed* to be something that will let me stroll around a room — or more

importantly, stand in an operating theater for as long
as I need to. When it's working, that is." He shook his
head. "Buggy as a new software system, let me tell you.
Yesterday the fardling thing locked up on me, with one
foot in the air. Wasn't *I* just a charming sight, posing in
the middle of the hall like a dancer in a Greek frieze!
Think I'm going to rely on my old Chair when I really
need to do something, at least for a while."

Tia chuckled at the mental image of Kenny frozen in
place and unable to move.

He shook his head and laughed. "Well, between this
piece of — ah — hardware, and my patients, I had to
send Anna as our official deputation. Hope you've forgiven Lars and me, sweetheart — "

A voice, warm and amused, interrupted Doctor
Kenny. "There was just a wee problem with *my* getting
leave, after all," Lars said, over the office speakers, as
Kenny grinned. "And they simply wouldn't let me
de-orbit the station and take it down to the schools for the
graduation ceremony. *Very* inconsiderate of them, *I* say."

Tia had to laugh at that.

"That just means you'll have to come visit *me*. Now
that you're one of the club, far-traveler, we'll have to
exchange softie-jokes. How many softies *does* it take to
change a lightbulb?"

Kenny made a rude noise. Although he looked tired,
Tia noted that he seemed to be in very good spirits.
There was only one thing that combination meant;
he'd pulled off another miracle. "I resemble that
remark," he said. "Anyway, Lars got your relay number, so you'll be hearing from us — probably more
often than you want! We love you, lady! Big Zen hugs
from both of us!"

The screen flickered and went blank; Tia sighed with
contentment. Lars had been the one to come up with
"Zen hugs" — "the hugs that you would get, if we were
there, if we could hug you, but we aren't, and we can't" —

and he and Kenny began using them in their weekly transmissions to Tia all through school. Before long her entire class began using the phrase, so pointedly apt for shellpeople, and now it was spreading across known space. Kenny had been amused, especially after one of his recovering patients got the phrase in a transmission from his stay-at-home, techno-phobic wife!

Well, the transmission put the cap on her day, that was certain. And the perfect climax to the beginning of her new life. Anna and her parents at the graduation ceremony, Professor Brogen handing out the special awards she'd gotten in Xenology, Diplomacy, and First Contact Studies, Moira showing up at the landing field the same day she was installed in her ship, still with Tomas, wonder of wonders. . . .

Having Moira there to figuratively hold her hand during the nasty process of partial anesthesia while the techs hooked her up in her column had been worth platinum.

She shuddered at the memory. Oh, they could *describe* the feelings (or rather, lack of them) to you, they could psych you up for experience, and you *thought* you were ready, but the moment of truth, when you lost everything but primitive com and the few sensors in the shell itself . . . was horrible. Something out of the worst of nightmares.

And she still remembered what it had been like to live with only softperson senses. She couldn't imagine what it was like for those who'd been popped into a shell at birth. It had brought back all the fear and feeling of helplessness of her time in the hospital.

It had been easier with Moira there. But if the transfer had been a journey through sensory-deprivation hell, waking up in the ship had been pure heaven.

No amount of simulator training conveyed what it *really* felt like, to have a living, breathing ship wrapped around you.

It was a moment that had given her back everything she had lost. Never mind that her "skin" was duralloy metal, her "legs" were engines, her "arms" the servos she used to maintain herself inside and out. That her "lungs" and "heart" were the life-support systems that would keep her brawn alive. That all of her senses were ship's sensors linked through brainstem relays. None of that mattered. She had a body again! That was a moment of ecstasy no one plugged into a shell at birth would ever understand. Moira did, though . . . and it had been wonderful to be able to share that moment of elation.

And Tomas understood, as only a brawn-partner of long-standing could. Tomas had arranged for Theodore Edward Bear to have his own little case built into the wall of the central cabin as *his* graduation present. "And decom anyone who doesn't understand," he said firmly, putting a newly cleaned Ted behind his plexi panel and closing the door. "A brawn is only a brawn, but a bear is a friend for life!"

So now the solemn little blue bear in his Courier Service shirt reigned as silent supervisor over the central cabin, and to perdition with whatever the brawns made of him. Well, let them think it was some kind of odd holo-art. Speaking of which, the next set of brawn-candidates was due shortly. *We'll see how they react to Ted.*

Tia returned to her papers, keeping a running statistical analysis and cross-tabulations on anything that seemed interesting. And there *were* things that seemed to be showing up, actually. Pockets of mineral depletions in the area around the EsKay sites; an astonishing similarity in the periodicity and seasonality of the planets and planetoids. Insofar as a Mars-type world could *have* seasons, that is. But the periodicity — identical to within an hour. Interesting. Had they been *that* dependent on natural sunlight? Come to think of it

— yes, solar distances were very similar. And they were all Sol-type stars.

She turned her attention to her parents' latest papers, letting the EsKay discoveries stew in the back of her mind. Pota and Braddon were the Schliemanns of modern archeology, but it wasn't the EsKays that brought them fame, at least, not directly. After Tia's illness, they couldn't bring themselves to return to their old dig, or even the EsKay project — and for once, the Institute committees acted like something other than AIs with chips instead of hearts. Pota and Braddon were reassigned to a normal atmosphere water-world of high volcanic activity and thousands of tiny islands with a good population of nomadic sentients, something as utterly unlike the EsKay planets as possible. And it had been there that they made their discovery. Tracing the legends of the natives, of a king who first defied the gods and then challenged them, they replicated Schliemann's famous discovery of ancient Troy, uncovering an entire city buried by a volcanic eruption. Perfectly preserved for all time. For this world and these people, it was the equivalent of an Atlantis and Pompeii combined, for the city was of Bronze Age technology while the latter-day sentients were still struggling along with flint, obsidian, and shell, living in villages of no more than two hundred. While the natives of the present day were amphibious, leaning towards the aquatic side, *these* ancients were almost entirely creatures of dry land. . . .

The discovery made Pota and Braddon's reputation; there was more than enough there to keep fifty archeologists busy for a hundred years. Ta'hianna became their life-project, and they rarely left the site anymore. They even established a permanent residence aboard a kind of glorified houseboat.

Tia enjoyed reading their papers — and the private speculations they had brought her, with some findings that weren't in the papers yet — but the Ta'hianna project simply didn't give her the thrill of mystery that the EsKays did.

And — there was one other thing. Years of analyzing every little nuance of those dreadful weeks had made her decide that what had happened to her could just as easily happen to some other unwitting archeologist. Or even — another child.

Only finding the homeworld of the EsKays would give the Institute and Central World's Medical the information they needed to prevent another tragedy like Tia's.

If Tia had anything at all to say about it, *that* would never happen again. The next person infected might not be so lucky. The next person, if an adult, or even a child unfortunate enough to be less flexible and less intelligent than she had been, would likely have no choice but to spend the remainder of a fairly miserable life in a Moto-Chair and a room. . . .

"XH One-Oh-Three-Three, your next set of brawn-candidates is ready," CenCom said, interrupting her brooding thoughts. "You *are* going to pick one of these, aren't you?" the operator added wearily.

"I don't know yet," she replied, levelly. "I haven't interviewed them." She had rejected the first set of six entirely. CenCom obviously thought she was being a prima donna. *She* simply thought she was being appropriately careful. After all, since she was officially assigned to A and E with special assignment to the Institute, she had gotten precisely what she expected — a ship *without* Singularity Drive. Those were top-of-the-line, expensive, and not the sort of thing that the Institute could afford to hire. So, like Moira, she would be spending a *lot* of time in transit. Unlike Moira, she did not intend to find herself bouncing brawns so often that her buy-out had doubled because of the fines.

Spending a lot of time in transit meant a lot of time

with only her brawn for company. She wanted someone who was bright, first of all. At least as bright as
Tomas and Charlie. She wanted someone who would
be willing to add her little crusade to the standard
agenda and give it equal weight with what they had
officially been assigned. She rather thought she would
like to have a male, although she hadn't rejected any of
the brawns just because they were female.

Most of all, she wanted someone who would *like* her;
someone who would be a real partner in every sense.
Someone who would willingly spend time with her
when he could be doing other things; a friend, like
Kenny and Anna, Moira and Lars.

And someone with some personality. Two of the last
batch — both females — had exhibited all the personality of a cube of tofu.

That might do for another ship, another brain that
didn't want to be bothered with softpersons outside of
duty, but she wanted someone she could *talk* to! After
all, she had been a softperson once.

"Who's first?" she asked CenCom, lowering her lift
so that he — or she — could come aboard without
having to climb the stairs.

"That'll be Donning Chang y Narhan," CenCom
replied after a moment. "Really high marks in the
Academy."

She scanned the databurst as Donning crossed the tarmac to the launch pad; he'd gotten high marks all right,
though not stellar. Much like her; in the top tenth of the
class, but not the top one percent. *Very* handsome, if the
holo was to be believed; wavy blond hair, bright blue eyes,
sculptured face with holo-star looks — sculptured body,
too. But Tia was wary of good looks by now. Two of the
first lot had been gorgeous; one had been one of the
blocks of tofu, with nothing between the ears but what
the Academy had put there, and the other had only
wanted to talk about himself.

Movement outside alerted her to Donning's arrival; to her annoyance, he operated the lift manually instead of letting her handle it.

To her further annoyance, he treated her like some kind of superior AI; he was obviously annoyed with having to go through an interview in the first place and wanted to be elsewhere.

"Donning Chang y Narhan, reporting," he said in a bored tone of voice. "As ordered." He proceeded to rattle off everything that had been in the short file, as if she couldn't access it herself. He did not sit down. He paid no attention to Ted.

"Have you any questions?" he asked, making it sound as if questions would only mean that she had not been paying attention.

"Only a few," she replied. "What is your favorite composer? Do you play chess?"

He answered her questions curtly, as if they were so completely irrelevant that he couldn't believe she was asking them.

She obliged him by suggesting that he could leave after only a handful of questions; he took it with bad grace and left in a hurry, an aroma of scorched ego in his wake.

"Garrison Lebrel," CenCom said, as Donning vacated the lift.

Well, Garrison was possible. Good academic marks, not as high as Donning's but not bad. Interest in archeology . . . she perked up when she saw *what* he was interested in. Nonhumans, especially presumed extinct space-going races, including the EsKays!

Garrison let her bring him in and proved to be talkative, if not precisely congenial. He was *very* intense.

"We'll be spending a lot of time in transit," he said. "I wasn't able to keep up with the current literature in archeology while I was in the Academy, and I planned to be doing a lot of reading."

Not exactly sociable. "Do you play chess?" she asked

hopefully. He shook his head. "But I do play sennet. That's an ancient Egyptian game — I have a very interesting software version I could install; I doubt it would take you long to learn it, though it takes a lifetime to master."

The last was said a bit smugly. And there had been no offer from him to learn *her* game. Still, she did have access to far more computing power than he did; it wouldn't take her more than an hour to learn the game, if that.

"I see that your special interest is in extinct spacegoing races," she ventured. "I have a very strong background in the Salomon-Kildaire Entities."

He looked skeptical. "I think Doctor Russell Gaines-Barklen has probably dealt with them as fully as they need to be, although we'll probably have some chances to catch things survey teams miss. That's the benefit of being trained to look for specifics."

She finally sent him back with mixed feelings. He was arrogant, no doubt about it. But he was also competent. He shared her interests, but his pet theories differed wildly from hers. He was possible, if there were no other choices, but he wasn't what she was looking for.

"Chria Chance is up next," CenCom said when she reported she was ready for the next. "But you won't like her."

"Why, because she's got a name that's obviously assumed?" Neither CenCom nor the Academy cared what you called yourself, provided they knew the identity you had been born with and the record that went with it. Every so often someone wanted to adopt a pseudonym. Often it was to cover a famous High Family name — either because the bearer was a black sheep, or because (rarely) he or she didn't want special treatment. But sometimes a youngster got a notion into his or her head to take on a holostar-type name.

"No," CenCom replied, not bothering to hide his amusement. "You won't like her because — well, you'll see."

Chria's records were good, about like Garrison's — with one odd note in the personality profile. *Nonconformist,* it said.

Well, there was nothing wrong with that. Pota and Braddon were certainly not conformists in any sense.

But the moment that Chria stepped into the central room, Tia knew that CenCom was right.

She wore her Academy uniform, all right — but it was a specially tailored one. Made entirely of leather; real leather, not synthetic. And she wore it entirely too well for Tia to feel comfortable around her. For the rest, she was rapier-thin, with a face like a clever fox and hair cut aggressively short. Tia already felt intimidated, and she hadn't even said anything yet!

Within a few minutes worth of questions, Chria shook her head. "You're a nice person, Tia," she said forthrightly, "and you and I would never partner well. I'd run right over you, and you'd sit there in your column, fuming and resentful, and you'd never say a word." She grinned with feral cheer. "I'm a carnivore, a hunter. I need someone who'll fight back! I enjoy a good fight!"

"You'd probably have us go chasing right after pirates," Tia said, a little resentful already. "If there were any in the neighborhood, you'd want us to look for them!"

"You bet I would," Chria responded without shame.

A few more minutes of exchange proved to Tia that Chria was right. It would never work. With a shade of regret, Tia bade her farewell. While she liked a good argument as well as the next person, she *didn't* like for arguments to turn into shouting matches, which was precisely what Chria enjoyed. She claimed it purged tensions.

Well, maybe it did. And maybe that was why her favorite form of music — to the exclusion of everything else — was opera. She was a fanatic, to put it simply, And Tia — well — wasn't.

But there was certainly a lot of emotion-purging and carrying on in those old operas. She had the feeling that Chria fancied herself as a kind of latter-day Valkyrie.

Hoy-yo to-ho.

She reported her rejection to CenCom, with the recommendation that *she* thought Chria Chance had the proper mental equipment to partner a ship in the Military Courier Service. "Between you, me, and the airwaves," CenCom replied, "that's my opinion, too. Bloodthirsty wench. Well, she'll get her chance. Military got your classmate Pol, and he's just as bloody-minded as she is. I'll see the recommendation goes in; meanwhile, next up is Harkonen Carl-Ulbright."

Carl was a disappointment. Average grades, and while he was congenial, Tia knew that *she* would run right over the top of *him.* He was shy, hardly ever ventured an opinion, and when he did, he could be induced to change it in an eye-blink. However — "Carl," she said, just before he went to the lift, making no effort to hide his discouragement. "My classmate Raul is the XR One-Oh-Two-Nine. I think you two would get along splendidly. I'm going to ask CenCom to set up your very next interview with him — he was just installed today and I *know* he hasn't got a brawn yet. Tell him I sent you."

That cheered up the young man considerably. He would be even more cheered when he learned that Raul had a Singularity Drive ship. And Tia would bet that his personality profile and Raul's matched to a hair. They'd make a great team, especially when their job included carrying VIP passengers. Neither of them would get in the way or resent it if the VIPs ignored them.

"I got all that, Tia," CenCom said as soon as the boy was gone. "Consider it logged. They ought to make you a Psych; a Counselor, at least. It was good of you to think of Raul; none of us could come up with a match for him, but we were trying to match him with females."

If she'd had hands, she would have thrown them up. "Become a Psych? Saints and agents of grace defend us!" she quipped. "I think *not*! Who's next?"

"Andrea Polo y De Gras," CenCom said. "You won't like her, either. She doesn't want you."

"With the Polo y De Gras name, I'm not surprised," Tia sighed. "Wants something with a little more zing to it than A and E, hmm? Would she be offended if I agreed with her before she bothered to come out here?"

"I doubt it," CenCom replied, "but let me check." A pause, and then he came back. "She's very pleased, actually. I think that she has something cooking with the Family, and the strings haven't had time to get pulled yet. Piff. High Families. I don't know *why* they send their children to Space Academy in the first place."

Tia felt moved to contradict him. "Because some of them do very well and become a credit to the Services," she replied, with just a hint of reproach.

"True, and I stand corrected. Well, your last brawn-candidate is the late Alexander Joli-Chanteu." The cheer in his voice told her that he was making a bad joke out of the situation.

"Late, hmm? That isn't going to earn *him* any gold stars in his Good-Bee Book," Tia said, a bit acidly. Her parents' fetish for punctuality had set a standard she expected those around her to match. *Especially* brawn-candidates.

Well, I can at least go over his records. She scanned them quickly and came up — confused. When Alexander was good, he was very, very, good. And when he was bad, he was abysmal. Often in the same subject. He would begin a class with the lowest marks possible, then suddenly catch fire, turn around, and pull a miraculous save at the end of the semester. *Erratic performances,* said his personality profile. Tia not only agreed, she thought that the evaluator was understating the case.

CenCom interrupted her confusion. "Whoop! He got right by me! Here he comes, Tia, ready or not!"

Alexander didn't bother with the lift, he ran up the stairs, arriving out of breath, with longish hair mussed and uniform rumpled.

That didn't earn him any points either, although it was better than Chria's leather.

He took a quick look around to orient himself, then turned immediately to face the central column where she was housed, a nicety that only Carl and Chria had observed. It didn't matter, really, and a lot of shell-persons didn't care, so long as the softpersons faced one set of "eyes" at least — but Tia felt, as Moira did, that it was more considerate of a brawn to face where you *were,* rather than empty cabin.

"Hypatia, dear lady, I am most humbly sorry to be late for this interview," he said, slowly catching his breath. "My *sensei* engaged me in a game of *Go,* and I completely lost all track of time."

He ran his blunt-fingered hand through his unruly dark hair and grinned ruefully, little smile-crinkles forming around his brown eyes. "And here I had a perfectly *wonderful* speech all memorized, about how fitting it is that the lady named for the last librarian at Alexandria and the brawn named for Alexander should become partners — and the run knocked it right out of my head!"

Well! He knows where my name came from! Or at least he had the courtesy and foresight to look it up. Hmm. She considered that for a moment, then put it in the "plus" column. He was not handsome, but he had a pleasant, blocky sort of face. He was short — well, so was the original Alexander, by both modern standards and those of his own time. She decided to put his general looks in the "plus" column too, along with his politeness. While she certainly wasn't going to choose her brawns on the basis of looks, it would be nice to have someone who provided a nice bit of landscape.

"Minus," of course, were for being late and very untidy when he finally did arrive.

"I think I can bring myself to forgive you," she said dryly. "Although I'm not certain just what exactly detained you."

"Ah — besides a hobby of ancient history, Terran history, that is, especially military history and strategy, I, ah — I cultivate certain kinds of martial arts." He ran his hand through his hair again, in what was plainly a nervous gesture. "Oriental martial arts. One soft form and one hard form. Tai Chi and Karate. I know most people don't think that's at all necessary, but, well, A and E Couriers *are* unarmed, and I don't like to think of myself as helpless. Anyway, my *sensei* — that's a martial arts Master — got me involved in a game of *Go*, and when you're playing against a Master there is *nothing* simple about *Go*." He bowed his head a moment and looked sheepish. "I lost all track of time, and they had to page me. I really am sorry about making you wait."

Tia wasn't quite sure what to make of that. "Sit down, will you?" she said absently, wondering why, with this fascination with things martial and military, he hadn't shown any interest in the Military Services. "Do you play chess as well?"

He nodded. "Chess, and Othello, and several computer games. And if you have any favorites that I don't know, I would be happy to learn them." He sat quietly, calmly, without any of Garrison's fidgeting. In fact, it was that very contrast with Garrison that made her decide resolutely *against* that young man. A few months of fidgeting, and she would be ready to trank him to keep him quiet.

"Why Terran history?" she asked, curiously. "That isn't the kind of fascination I'd expect to find in a — a space-jockey."

He grinned. It was a very engaging, lopsided grin. "What, haven't you interviewed my classmate Chria yet? Now there is someone with odd fascinations!" Behind the banter, Tia sensed a kind of affection, even though the tips of his ears went lightly red. "I started reading history because I was curious about *my* name, and got fascinated by Alexander's time period. One thing led to another, and the next thing *I* knew, every present I was getting was either a historical holotape or a bookdisk about history, and I was actually quite happy about the situation."

So he *did* know the origin of her name. "Then why military strategy?"

"Because all challenging games are games of strategy," he said. "I, ah — have a friend who's really a big games buff, my best friend when I was growing up, and I had to have some kind of edge on him. So I started studying strategy. *That* got me into *The Art of War* and that got me into Zen which got me into martial arts." He shrugged. "There you have it. One neat package. I think you'd really like Tai Chi, it's all about stress and energy flow and patterns, and it's a lot like Singularity mechanics and —"

"I'm sure," she interrupted, hauling him verbally back by the scruff of his neck. "But why didn't you opt for Military Service?"

"The same reason I studied martial arts — I don't like being helpless, but I don't want to *hurt* anyone," he replied, looking oddly distressed. "Both Tai Chi and Karate are about never using a bit more force than you need to, but Tai Chi is the essence of using greater force against itself, just like in *The Art of War,* and —"

Once again she had to haul him back to the question. He tended to go off on verbal tangents, she noticed. She continued to ask him questions, long after the time she had finished with the other brawns, and when she finally let him go, it was with a sense of dissatisfaction. He was the best choice so far, but although he was plainly both sensitive and intelligent, he showed no signs at all of any interest in *her* field. In fact, she had seen and heard nothing that would make her think he would be ready to help her in any way with her private quest.

As the sky darkened over the landing field, and the spaceport lights came on, glaring down on her smooth metal skin, she pondered all of her choices and couldn't come up with a clear winner. Alex was the best — but the rest were, for the most part, completely unsuitable. He was obviously absentminded, and his care for his person left a little to be desired. He wasn't exactly slovenly, but he did not wear his uniform with the air of distinction that Tia felt was required. In fact, on him it didn't look much like a uniform at all, more like a suit of comfortable, casual clothes. For the life of her, she couldn't imagine how he managed *that*.

His tendency to wander down conversational byways could be amusing in a social situation, but she could see where it could also be annoying to — oh — a Vegan, or someone like them. No telling what kind of trouble that could lead to, if they had to deal with AIs, who could be very literal-minded.

No, he wasn't perfect. In fact, he wasn't even close.

"XH One-Oh-Three-Three, you have an incoming transmission," CenCom broke in, disturbing her thoughts. "Hold onto your bustle, lady, it's the Wicked Witch of the West, and I think someone just dropped a house on her sister."

Whatever allusions the CenCom operator was making were lost on Tia, but the sharply impatient tone of her supervisor was not. "XH One-Oh-Three-

Three, have you selected a brawn *yet*?" the woman asked, her voice making it sound as if Tia had been taking weeks to settle on a partner, rather than less than a day.

"Not yet, Supervisor," she replied, cautiously. "So far, to be honest, I don't think I've found anyone I can tolerate for truly long stretches of time."

That wasn't exactly the problem, but Beta Gerold y Caspian wouldn't understand the real problem. *She* might just as well be Vegan. She made very few allowances for the human vagaries of brawns and none at all for shellpersons.

"Hypatia, you're wasting time," Beta said crisply. "You're sitting here on the pad, doing nothing, taking up a launch-cradle, when you could already be out on courier-supply runs."

"I'm doing my best," Tia responded sharply. "But neither you nor I will be particularly happy if I toss my brawn out after the first run!"

"You've rejected six brawns that all *our* analysis showed were good matches for your personality," Beta countered. "All you'd have to do is compromise a little."

Six of those were matches for me? she thought, aghast. *Which ones? The tofu-personalities? The Valkyrie warrior? Spirits of space help me — Garrison? I thought I was nicer and — more interesting than that!*

But Beta was continuing, her voice taking on the tones of a cross between a policeman and a professorial lecturer. "You know very well that it takes far too long between visits for these Class One digs. It leaves small parties alone for weeks and months at a time. Even when there's an emergency, our ships are so few and so scattered that it takes them days to reach people in trouble — and sometimes an *hour* can make all the difference, let alone a day! We needed you out there the *moment* you were commissioned!"

Tia winced inwardly.

She'd have suspected that Beta went straight for the sore spot deliberately, except that she knew that Beta did not have access to her records. So she didn't know Tia's background. The agency that oversaw the rights of shellpersons saw to that — to make it difficult for supervisors to use personal knowledge to manipulate the shellpersons under their control. In the old days, when supervisors had known everything about their shellpersons, they had sometimes deliberately created emotional dependencies in order to assure "loyalty" and fanatic service. It was far, far too easy to manipulate someone whose only contact to the real world was through sensors that could be disconnected.

Still, Beta was right. *If I'd had help earlier, I might not be here right now. I might be in college, getting my double-docs like Mum, thinking about what postgraduate work I wanted to do. . . .*

"I'll tell you what," she temporized. "Let me look over the records and the interviews again and sleep on it. One of the things that the schools told us over and over was to *never* make a choice of brawns feeling rushed or forced." She hardened her voice just a little. "You don't want another Moira, do you?"

"All right," Beta said grudgingly. "But I have to warn you that the supply of brawns is not unlimited. There aren't many more for you to interview in this batch, and if I have to boot you out of here without one, I will. The Institute can't afford to have you sitting on the pad for another six months until the next class graduates."

Go out without a brawn? Alone? The idea had very little appeal. Very little at all. In fact, the idea of six months alone in deep space was frightening. She'd never had to do without *some* human interaction, even on the digs with Mum and Dad.

So while CenCom signed off, she reran her tapes of the interviews and re-scanned information on the twelve she had rejected. And still could not come up with anyone she *knew,* without a shadow of a doubt, that she'd like to call "friend."

Someone was knocking — quietly — on the closed lift door. Tia, startled out of her brooding, activated the exterior sensors. Who could *that* be? It wasn't even dawn yet!

Her visitor's head jerked up and snapped around alertly to face the camera when he heard it swivel to center on him. The lights from the field were enough for her to "see" by, and she identified him immediately. "Hypatia, it's Alex," he whispered unnecessarily. "Can I talk to you?"

Since she *couldn't* reply to him without alerting the entire area to his clandestine and highly irregular visit, she lowered the lift for him, keeping it darkened. He slipped inside, and she brought him up.

"What are you *doing* here?" she demanded, once he was safely in her central cabin. "This is not appropriate behavior!"

"Hey," he said, "I'm unconventional. I like getting things done in unconventional ways. The *Art of War* says that the best way to win a war is never to do what they expect you to do — "

"I'm sure," she interrupted. "That may be all very well for someone in Military, but this is *not* a war, and I should be reporting you for this." Tia let a note of warning creep into her voice, wondering why she wasn't doing just that.

He ignored both the threat and the rebuke. "Your supervisor said you hadn't picked anyone yet," he said instead. "Why not?"

"Because I haven't," she retorted. "I don't like being rushed into things. Or pressured, either. Sit down."

He sat down rather abruptly, and his expression turned from challenging to wistful. "I didn't think you'd hold my being late against me," he said plaintively. "I thought we hit it off pretty well. When your supervisor said you'd spent more time with me than any of the other brawns, I thought for sure you'd choose me! What's wrong with me? There must be something! Maybe something I can change!"

"Well — I — " She was taken so aback by his bluntness, and caught unawares by his direct line of questioning, that she actually answered him. "I expect my brawns to be punctual — because they have to be precise, and not being punctual implies carelessness," she said. "I thought you looked sloppy, and I don't like sloppiness. You seemed absentminded, and I had to keep bringing you back to the original subject when we were talking. Both of those imply wavering attention, and that's not good either. I'll be alone out there with my brawn, and I need someone I can depend on to do his job."

"You didn't see me at my best," he pointed out. "I was distracted, and I was thrown completely off-center by the fact that I had messed up by being late. But that isn't all, is it?"

"What do you mean by that?" she asked, cautiously.

"It wasn't just that I was — less than perfect. *You* have a secret . . . something you really want to do, that you haven't even told your supervisor." He eyed the column speculatively, and she found herself taken completely by surprise by the accuracy of his guess. "I don't match the profile of someone who might be interested in helping you with that secret. Right?"

His expression turned coaxing. "Come on, Hypatia, you can tell me," he said. "I won't tattle on you. And I might be able to help! You don't know that much about me, just what you got in an hour of talking and what's in the short-file!"

"I don't know what you're talking about," she said lamely.

"Oh, sure you do. Come on, every brainship wants

to buy her contract out — no matter what they say. And every ship has a hobby-horse of her own, too. Barclay secretly wants to chase pirates all over known space like a holo-star, Leta wants to be the next big synthcom composer, even quiet old Jerry wants to buy himself a Singularity Drive *just* so he can set interstellar records for speed and distance!" He grinned. "So what's your little hidden secret?"

She only realized that she'd been manipulated when she found herself blurting out her plans for doing some amateur archeological sleuthing on the side, and both the fact that *she* wanted a bit of archeological glory for herself, and that she expected to eventually come up with something worth a fair number of credits toward her buy-out. She at least kept back the other wish; the one about finding the bug that had bitten her. By now, the three desires were equally strong, for reading of her parents' success had reawakened all the old dreams of following in Pota's footsteps, dealing with Beta had given her more than enough of being someone else's contract servant, and her studies of brainship chronicles had awakened a new fear — plague. And what would happen if the bug that paralyzed *her* got loose on a planetarywide scale?

As she tried to cover herself, she inadvertently revealed that the plans were a secret held successfully not only from her CenCom supervisors but from everyone she'd ever worked with except Moira.

"It was because I thought that they'd take my determination as something else entirely," she confessed. "I thought they'd take it as a fixation, and a sign of instability."

All through her confession, Alex stayed ominously silent. When she finished, she suddenly realized that she had just put him in a position to blackmail her into taking him. All he had to do was threaten to reveal her fixation, and she'd be decommissioned and put with a Counselor for the next six months.

But instead of saying anything, he began laughing. Howling with laughter, in fact. She waited in confusion for him to settle down and tell her what was going on.

"You didn't look far enough into my records, lovely lady," he said, calming down and wiping his eyes. "Oh, my. Call up my file, why don't you. Not the Academy file; the one with my application for a scholarship in it."

Puzzled, she linked into the CenCom net and accessed Alex's public records. "Look under 'hobbies,' " he suggested.

And there it was. Hobbies and other interests.

Archeology and Xenology.

She looked further, without invitation, to his class records. She soon saw that in lower schools, besides every available history class, he had taken every archeological course he could cram into a school day.

She wished that she had hands so that she could rub her temples; as it was, she had to increase her nutrients a tad, to rid herself of a beginning headache.

"See?" he said. "I wouldn't mind my name on a paper or two myself. Provided, of course, that there aren't any curses attached to our findings! And — well, who *couldn't* use a pile of credits? I would very much like to retire from the Service with enough credit to buy myself — oh, a small planetoid."

"But — why didn't you apply to the university?" she asked. "Why didn't you go after your degree?"

"Money," he replied succinctly, leaning back in his seat and steepling his fingers over his chest. "Dinero. Cash. Filthy lucre. My family didn't have any — or rather, they had just enough that I didn't qualify for scholarships. Oh, I could have gotten a Bachelor's degree, but those are hardly worth bothering about in archeology. Heck, Hypatia, *you* know that! You know how long it takes to get *one* Doctorate, too — four years to a Bachelor's, two to a Master's, and *then* years and years and *years* of field work before you have enough

material to do an original dissertation. And a working
archeologist, one getting to go out on Class One digs or
heading Class Two and Three, can't just have one
degree, he has to have a double-doc or a quad-doc." He
shook his head, sadly. "I've been an armchair hobbyist
for as long as I've been a history buff, dear lady, but that
was all that I could afford. Books and papers had to suf-
fice for me."

"Then why the Academy?" she asked, sorely puzzled.

"Good question. Has a complicated answer." He licked his lips for a moment, thinking, then continued.
"Say I got a Bachelor's in Archeology and History. I
could have gotten a bottom-of-the-heap clerking job at
the Institute with a Bachelor's — but if I did that, I
might as well go clerk anywhere else, too. Clerking jobs
are all the same wherever you go, only the jargon
changes, never the job. But I could have done that, and
gotten a work-study program to get a Master's. Then I
might have been able to wangle a research assistant
post to someone, but I'd be doing all of the dull stuff.
None of the exploration; certainly none of the puzzle-
solving. That would be as far as I could go; an RA job
takes too much time to study for a Doctorate. I'd have
been locked inside the Institute walls, even if my boss
went out on digs himself. Because when you need
someone to mind the store at home, you don't hire
someone extra, you leave your RA behind."

"Oh, I see why you didn't do that," she replied. "But
why the Academy?"

"Standards for scholarships to the Academy are — a
little different," he told her. "The Scholarship Committees aren't just looking for poor but brilliant people —
they're looking for competent people with a particular
bent, and if they find someone like that, they do what it
takes to get him. And the competition isn't as intense;
there are a lot more scholarships available to the
Academy than there are to any of the university

Archeology and History Departments I could reach. All two of them; I'd have *had* to go to a local university; I couldn't afford to go off-planet. Space Academy pays your way to Central; university History scholarships don't include a travel allowance. I figured if I couldn't go dig up old bones on faraway worlds, I'd at least *see* some of those faraway worlds. If I put in for A and E I'd even get to watch some of the experts at work. And while I was at it, I might as well put in for brawn training and see what it got me. Much to my surprise, my personality profile matched what they were looking for, and I actually found myself in brawn training, and once I was out, I asked to be assigned to A and E."

"So, why are you insisting on partnering me?" she asked, deciding that if he had manipulated her, she was going to be blunt with him, and if he couldn't take it, he wasn't cut out to partner her. No matter what he thought. Hmm, maybe frankness could scare him away....

He blinked. "You really don't know? Because you are you," he said. "It's really appallingly simple. You have a sparkling personality. You don't try to flatten your voice and sound like an AI, the way some of your classmates have. You aren't at all afraid to have an opinion. You have a teddy bear walled up in your central cabin like a piece of artwork, but you don't talk about it. That's a mystery, and I love mysteries, especially when they imply something as personable as a teddy bear. When you talk, I can hear you smiling, frowning, whatever. You're a shell*person*, Hypatia, with the emphasis on *person*. I like you. I had hoped that you would like me. I figured we could keep each other entertained for a long, long time."

Well, he'd out-blunted her, and that was a fact. And — startled her. She was surprised, not a little flattered, and getting to think that Alex might not be a bad choice as a brawn after all. "Well, I like you," she replied hesitantly, "but . . ."

"But what?" he asked, boldly. "What is it?"

"I don't like being manipulated," she replied. "And you've been doing just that: manipulating me, or trying."

He made a face. "Guilty as charged. Part of it is just something I do without thinking about it. I come from a low-middle-class neighborhood. Where I come from, you either charm your way out of something or fight your way out of it, and I prefer the former. I'll try not to do it again."

"That's not all," she warned. "I've got — certain plans — that might get in the way, if you don't help me." She paused for effect. "It's about *what* I want to hunt down. The homeworld of the Salomon-Kildaire Entities."

"The EsKays?" he replied, sitting up, ramrod-straight. "Oh, my — if this weren't real life I'd think you were telepathic or something! The EsKays are my favorite archeological mystery! I'm *dying* to find out why they'd set up shop, then vanish! And if we could find the homeworld — Hypatia, we'd be holo-stars! Stellar achievers!"

Her thoughts milled about for a moment. This was very strange. Very strange indeed.

"I assume that part of our time Out would be spent checking things out at the EsKay sites?" he said, his eyes warming. "Looking for things the archeologists may not find? Looking for more potential sites?"

"Something like that," she told him. "That's why I need your cooperation. Sometimes I'm going to need a mobile partner on this one."

He nodded, knowingly. "Lovely lady, you are looking at him," he replied. "And only too happy to. If there's one thing I'm a sucker for, it's a quest. And this is even better, a quest at the service of a lady!"

"A quest?" she chuckled a little. "What, do you want us to swear to find the Holy Grail now?"

"Why not?" he said lightly. "Here — I'll start." He stood up, faced not her column but Ted E. Bear in his illuminated case, and held his hand as if he were taking the Space Service Oath. "I, Alexander Joli-Chanteu, do solemnly swear that I shall join brainship Hypatia One-Oh-Three-Three in a continuing and ongoing search for the homeworld of the Salomon-Kildaire Entities. I swear that this will be a joint project for as long as we have a joint career. And I swear that I shall give her all the support and friendship she needs in this search, so help me. So let it be witnessed and sealed by yon bear."

Tia would have giggled, except that he looked so very solemn.

"All right," he said, when he sat down again. "What about you?"

What about her? She had virtually accepted him as her brawn, hadn't she? And hadn't he sworn himself into her service, like some kind of medieval knight?

"All right," she replied. "I, Hypatia One-Oh-Three-Three, do solemnly swear to take Alexander Joli-Chanteu into my service, to share with him my search for the EsKay homeworld, and to share with him those rewards both material and immaterial that come our way in this search. I pledge to keep him as my brawn unless we both agree mutually to sever the contract. I swear it by — by Theodore Edward Bear."

He grinned, so wide and infectiously, that she wished she could return it. "I guess we're a team, then," she said.

"Then here — " he lifted an invisible glass " — is to our joint career. May it be as long and fruitful as the Cades'."

He pretended to drink, then to smash the invisible glass in an invisible fireplace, little guessing that Tia's silence was due entirely to frozen shock.

The Cades? How could *he —*

But before she vocalized anything, she suddenly

realized that he could not possibly have known who and what she really was.

The literature on the Cades would never have mentioned their paralyzed daughter, nor the tragedy that caused her paralysis. That simply wasn't done in academic circles, a world in which only facts and speculations existed, and not sordid details of private lives. The Cades weren't stellar personalities, the kind people made docudramas out of. There was no way he could have known about Hypatia Cade.

And once someone went into the shellperson program, their last name was buried in a web of eyes-only and fail-safes, to ensure that their background remained private. It was better that way, easier to adjust to being shelled. The unscrupulous supervisor could take advantage of a shellperson's background for manipulation, and there were other problems as well. Brainships were, as Professor Brogen had pointed out, valuable commodities. So were their cargoes. The ugly possibilities of using familial hostages or family pressures against a brainship were very real. Or using family ties to lure a ship into ambush. . . .

But there was always the option for the shellperson to tell trusted friends about who they were. Trusted friends — and brawns.

She hesitated for a moment, as he saluted Ted. Should she tell him about herself and avoid a painful gaffe in the future?

No. No, I have to learn to live with it, if I'm going to keep chasing the EsKays. If he doesn't say anything, someone else will. Mum and Dad may have soured on the EsKay project because of me, but their names are still linked with it. And besides — it doesn't matter. The EsKays are mine, now. And I'm not a Cade anymore, even if I do find the homeworld. I won't be listed in the literature as Hypatia Cade, but as Hypatia One-Oh-Three-Three. A brainship. Part of the AH team —

She realized what their team designation looked like.

"Do you realize that together our initials are —"

"'Ah'?" he said, pronouncing it like the word. "Actually, I did, right off. I thought it was a good omen. Not quite 'eureka,' but close enough!"

"Hmm," she replied. "It sounds like something a professor says when he thinks you're full of lint but he can't come up with a refutation!"

"You have no romance in your soul," he chided mockingly. "And speaking of romance, what time is it?"

"Four thirty-two and twenty-seven point five nine seconds," she replied instantly. "In the morning, of course."

"Egads," he said, and shuddered. "Oh-dark-hundred. Let this be the measure of my devotion, my lady. I, who *never* see the sun rise if I can help it, actually *got up* at *four in the morning* to talk to you."

"Devotion, indeed," she replied with a laugh. "All right, Alex — I give in. You are hereby officially my brawn. I'm Tia, by the way, not Hypatia, not to you. But you'd better sneak back to your dormitory and pretend to be surprised when they tell you I picked you, or we'll both be in trouble."

"Your wish, dearest Tia, is my command," he said, rising and bowing. "Hopefully I can get past the gate-guard going out as easily as I got past going in."

"Don't get caught," she warned him. "I can't bail you out, not officially, and not yet. Right now, as my supervisor told me so succinctly, I am an expensive drain on Institute finances."

He saluted her column and trotted down the stair, ignoring the lift once again.

Well, at least he'll keep in shape.

She watched him as long as she could, but other ships and equipment intervened. It occurred to her then that she could listen in on the spaceport security net for bulletins about an intruder —

She opened the channel, but after a half an hour

passed, and she heard nothing, she concluded that he must have made it back safely.

The central cabin seemed very lonely without him. Unlike any of the others — except, perhaps, Chria Chance — he had filled the entire cabin with the sheer force of his personality.

He was certainly lively enough.

She waited until oh-six-hundred, and then opened her line to CenCom. There was a new operator on, one who seemed not at all curious about her or her doings; seemed, in fact, as impersonal as an AI. He brought up Beta's office without so much as a single comment.

As she halfway expected, Beta was present. And the very first words out of the woman's mouth were, "Well? Have you picked a brawn, or am I going to have to trot the rest of the Academy past you?"

Hypatia stopped herself from snapping only by an effort. "I made an *all-night* effort at considering the twelve candidates you presented, Supervisor," she said sharply. "I went to the considerable trouble of accessing records as far back as lower schools."

Only a little fib, she told herself. *I did check Alex, after all.*

"And?" Beta replied, not at all impressed.

"I have selected Alexander Joli-Chanteu. He can come aboard at any time. I completed all my test-flight sequences yesterday, and I can be ready to lift as soon as CenCom gives me clearance and you log my itinerary." *There,* she thought, smugly. *One in your eye, Madame Supervisor. I'll wager you never thought I'd be that efficient.*

"Very good, AH-One-Oh-Three-Three," Beta replied, showing no signs of being impressed at all. "I wouldn't have logged Alexander as brawn if I had been in your shell, though. He isn't as . . . professional as I would like. And his record is rather erratic."

"So are the records of most genius-class intellects, Supervisor," Tia retorted, feeling moved to defend her brawn. "As I am sure you are aware." *And you aren't in my shell, lady,* she thought, with resentment at Beta's superior tone smoldering in her, until she altered the chemical feed to damp it. *I will make my own decisions, and I will thank you to keep that firmly in mind.*

"So they say, AH-One-Oh-Three-Three," Beta replied impersonally. "I'll convey your selection to the Academy and have CenCom log in your flight plan and advise you when to be ready to lift immediately."

With that, she logged off. But before Tia could feel slighted or annoyed with her, the CenCom operator came back on.

"AH-One-Oh-Three-Three — congratulations!" he said, his formerly impersonal voice warming with friendliness. "I just wanted you to know before we got all tangled up in official things that the operators here all think you picked a fine brawn. Me, especially."

Tia was dumbfounded. "Why — thank you," she managed. "But why —"

The operator chuckled. "Oh, we handle all the cadets' training-flights. Some of them are real pains in the orifice — but Alex always has a good word and he never gripes when we have to put him in a holding pattern. And — well, that Donning character tried to get me in trouble over a near-miss when he ignored what I told him and came in anyway. Alex was in the pattern behind him — he saw and heard it all. He didn't *have* to log a report in my defense, but he did, and it kept me from getting demoted."

"Oh," Tia replied. Now, that was interesting. Witnesses to near misses weren't required to come forward with logs of the incident — and in fact, no one would have thought badly of Alex if he hadn't. His action might even have earned him some trouble with Donning. . . .

"Anyway, congratulations again. You won't regret your choice," the operator said. "And — stand by for compressed data transmission —"

As her orders and flight-plan came over the comlink, Tia felt oddly pleased and justified. Beta did *not* like her choice of brawns. The CenCom operators did.

Good recommendations, both.

She began her pre-flight check with rising spirits, and it seemed to her that even Ted was smiling. Just a little.

All right Universe, brace yourself. Here we come!

● CHAPTER FOUR

"All right, Tia-my-love, explain what's going on here, in words of one syllable," Alex said plaintively, when Tia got finished with tracing the maze of orders and counter-orders that had interrupted their routine round of deliveries to tiny two- to four-person Exploratory digs. "Who's on first?"

"And What's on second," she replied absentmindedly. Just before leaving she'd gotten a datahedron on old-Terran slang phrases and their derivation; toying with the idea of producing that popular-science article. If it got published on enough nets, it might well earn her a tidy little bit of credit — and no amount of credit, however small, was to be scorned. But one unexpected side-effect of scanning it was that she tended to respond with the punch lines of jokes so old they were mummified.

Though now, at least, she knew what the CenCom operator had meant by "hang onto your bustle" and that business about the wicked witch who'd had a house dropped on her sister.

"What?" Alex responded, perplexed. "No, never mind. I don't want to know. Just tell me whose orders we're supposed to be following. I got lost back there in the fifth or sixth dispatch."

"I've got it all straight now, and it's dual-duty," she replied. "Institute, with backup from Central, although they were countermanding each other in the first four or five sets of instructions. One of the Excavation digs hasn't been checking in. Went from their regular schedule to nothing, not even a chirp."

"You don't sound worried," Alex pointed out.

"Well, I am, and I'm not," she replied, already calculating the quickest route through hyperspace, and mentally cursing the fact that they didn't have Singularity Drive. But then again, there wasn't a Singularity point anywhere near where they wanted to go. So the drive *wasn't* the miracle of instantaneous transportation some people claimed it was. *Hmm, and some brainships too, naming no names.* All very well if there were Singularity points littering the stellarscape like stars in the Core, but out here, at this end of the galactic arm, stars were close, but points were few and far between. One reason why the Institute hadn't opted for a more expensive ship. "If it were an Exploratory dig like my — like we've been trotting supplies and mail to, I would worry a *lot*. They're horribly vulnerable. And an Evaluation dig is just as subject to disaster, since the maximum they can have is twenty people. But a Class Three — Alex, this one had a complement of two hundred! That's more that enough people to hold off any trouble!"

"Class Three Excavation sites get a lot of graduate students, don't they?" Alex said, while she locked things down in her holds for takeoff with help from the servos. Pity the cargo handlers hadn't had time to stow things properly.

"Exactly. They provide most of the coolie labor when there aren't any natives to provide a work force — that's why the Class Three digs have essentially the same setup as a military base. Most of the personnel are young, strong, *and* they get the best of the equipment. This one has — " she quickly checked her briefing " — one hundred seventy-eight people between the ages of twenty-five and thirty-five. That's plenty to set up perimeter guards."

Alex's fingers raced across the keypads in front of him, calling up data to her screens. "Hmm. No really nasty native beasties. Area declared safe. And — my. Fully armed, are we?" He glanced over at the column. "I had no idea archeologists were such dangerous beings! They never told me that back in secondary school!"

"Grrr," she responded. She flashed a close-up of the bared fangs of a dog on one of the screens he wasn't using. In the past several weeks she and Alex had spent a lot of time talking, getting to know each other. By virtue of her seven years spent mobile, she was a great deal more like a softperson than any of her classmates, and Alex was *fun* to be around. Neither of them particularly minded the standard issue beiges of her interior; what he had done, during the time spent in FTL, was to copy the minimalist style of his *sensei*'s home, taking a large brush and some pure black and red enamel, and copying one or two Zen ideographs on the walls that seemed barest. She thought they looked very handsome — and quietly elegant.

Of course, his cabin was a mess — but she didn't have to look in there, and she avoided doing so as much as possible.

In turn, he expressed delight over her "sparkling personality." No matter what the counselors said, she had long ago decided that she had feelings and emotions and had no guilt over showing them to those she trusted. Alex had risen in estimation from "partner" to "trusted" in the past few weeks; he had a lively sense of humor and enjoyed teasing her. She enjoyed teasing right back.

"Pull in your fangs, wench," he said. "I realize that the only reason they get those arms is because there are no sentients down there. So, what's on the list of Things That Get Well-Armed Archeologists? I have the sinking feeling there were a lot of things they didn't tell me about archeology back in secondary school!"

"Seriously? It's a short list, but a nasty one." She sobered. "Lock yourself in; I'm going to lift, and fast.

Things are likely to rattle around." With drives engaged, she pulled away from her launch cradle, acknowledged Traffic Control and continued her conversation, all at once. "Artifact thieves are high on that list — if you've got a big dig, you can bet that there are things being found that are going to be worth a lot to collectors. They'll come in, blast the base, land, kill everyone left over that gets in their way, grab the loot and lift, all within hours." *Which was why the hidey was so far from our dome, and why Mum and Dad told me to get in it and stay in it if trouble came.* "But *normally* they work an area, and *normally* they don't show up anyplace where Central has a lot of patrols. There haven't been any thieves in that area, and it *is* heavily patrolled."

"So — what's next on the list?" Alex asked, one screen dedicated to the stats on the dig, his own hands busy with post-lift chores that some brawns would have left to their brains. Double-checking to make sure all the servos had put themselves away, for instance. Keeping an eye on the weight-and-balance in the holds. Just another example, she thought happily, of what a good partner he was.

She was clear of the cradle and about to clear local airspace. Nearing time to accelerate "like a scalded cat." *Now that's a phrase that's still useful. . . .* "Next on the list is something we don't even have to consider, and that's a native uprising."

"Hmm, so I see." His eyes went from the secondary screen where the data on the dig was posted and back to the primary. "No living native sophonts on the continent. But I can see how it could be the Zulu wars all over again."

He nodded, acknowledging her logic, and she was grateful to *his* self-education in history.

"Precisely," she replied. "Throw enough warm bodies at the barricades, and any defense will go down. In a native uprising, there are generally hordes of fervent fanatics willing to die in the cause and go straight to Paradise. Accelerating, Alex."

He gave her a thumbs-up, and she threw him into his seat. He merely raised an eyebrow at her column and kept typing. "There must be several different variations on that theme. Let's see — you could have your Desecration of Holy Site Uprising, your Theft of Ancient Treasures Uprising, your Palace Coup Uprising, your Local Peasant Revolution Uprising. Uh-huh. I can see it. And when you've overrun the base, it's time to line everyone up as examples of alien exploitation. Five executioners, no waiting."

"They normally don't kill except by accident, actually, or in the heat of the moment," she told him. "Most native sophonts are bright enough to realize that two hundred of Central Systems' citizens, a whole herd of their finest minds *and* their dependents, make a much better bargaining chip as hostages than they do as casualties."

"Not much comfort to those killed in the heat of the moment," he countered. "So, what's the next culprit on the list?"

"The third, last, and most common," she said, a bit grimly, and making no effort to control her voice-output. "Disease."

"Whoa, wait a minute — I thought that these sites were declared free of hazard!" He stopped typing and paled a little, as well he might. Plague was the bane of the Courier Service existence. More than half the time of every CS ship was spent in ferrying vaccines across known space — and for every disease that was eradicated, three more sprang up out of nowhere. Nor were the brawns immune to the local plagues that just might choose to start at the moment *they* planeted. "I thought all these sites were sprayed down to a fare-thee-well before they let anyone move in!"

"Yes, but that's the one I'm seriously concerned

about." *And not just because it was a bug that got me.* "That, my dear Alex, is what they *don't* tell you bright-eyed young students when you consider a career in archeology. The number one killer of xeno-archeologists is disease." *And the number one crippler, for that matter.* "Viruses and proto-viruses are sneaky sons-of-singularities; they can hibernate in tombs for centuries, millennia, even in airless conditions." She flashed up some Institute statistics; the kind they *didn't* show the general public. There was a thirty percent chance that a xeno-archeologist would be permanently disabled by disease during his career; a twenty percent chance that he would *die*. And a one hundred percent chance that he would be seriously ill, requiring hospitalization, from something caught on a dig, at some point in his life.

"So the bug hibernates. Then when the intrepid explorer pops the top off — " Alex looked as grim as she felt.

"Right. Gotcha." She laughed, but it had a very flat sound. "Well, sometimes it's been known to be fortuitous. The Cades actually *met* when they were recovering from Henderson's Chorea — ah — or so their biographies in *Who's Who* say. There could be worse things than having the Institute cover your tropic vacation."

"But mostly it isn't." His voice was as flat as her laugh had been.

"Ye-es. One of my — close friends is Doctor Kennet on the *Pride of Albion*. He's gotten to be a specialist in diseases that get archeologists. He's seen a lot of nasty variations over the years — including some really odd opportunistic bugs that are not only short-lived after exposure to air, but require a developing nervous system in order to set up housekeeping."

"Developing — oh, I got it. A kid, or a fetus, provided it could cross the placental barrier." He shivered, and his expression was very troubled. "Brr, that's a really nasty one."

"Verily, White Knight." She decided not to elaborate on it. *Maybe later. To let him know I'm not only out for fortune and glory.* "I just wanted you to be prepared when we got there, which we will in — four days, sixteen hours, and thirty-five minutes. Not bad, for an old-fashioned FTL drive, I'd say." She'd eliminated the precise measurements that some of the other shellpersons used with their brawns in the first week — except when she was speaking to another shellperson, of course. Alex didn't need that kind of precision, most of the time; when he did, he asked her for it. She had worried at first that she might be getting sloppy —

No, I'm just accommodating myself to his world. I don't mind. And when he needs precision, he lets me know in advance.

"Well, let me see if I can think of some non-lethal reasons for the dig losing communications — " He grinned. "How about — 'the dinosaur ate my transmitter'?"

"Cute." Now that their acceleration had smoothed and they were out of the atmosphere, she sent servos snooping into his cabin, as was her habit whenever a week or so went by, and he was at his station, giving her non-invasive access. "Alex, don't you ever pick up your clothes?"

"Sometimes. Not when I'm sent hauling my behind up the stairs with my tail on fire and a directive from CS ordering me to report back to my ship *immediately*." He shrugged, completely unrepentant. "I wouldn't even have *changed* my clothes if that officious b— "

"Alex," she warned. "I'm recording, I have to. Regulations." Ever since the debacle involving the Nyota Five, *all* central cabin functions were recorded, whenever there was a softperson, even if only a brawn, present. That was regulation even on AI drones. The regs had been written for AI drones, in fact; and CS administration had decided that there was no reason to rewrite them for brainships — and every reason why they *shouldn't*. This way no one could claim "discrimination," or worse, "entrapment."

"If that officious *bully* hadn't insisted I change to uniform before lifting." He shook his head. "As if wearing a uniform was going to make any difference in how well *you* handled the lift. Which was, as always, excellent."

"Thank you." She debated chiding him on his untidy nature and decided against it. It hadn't made any difference before, it probably wouldn't now. She just had the servos pick up the tunic and trousers — wincing at the ultra-neon purple that was currently in vogue — and deposited them in the laundry receptacle.

And I'll probably have to put them away when they're clean, too. No wonder they wanted him to change. Hmm. Wonder if I dare "lose" them? Or have a dreadful accident that dyes them a nice sober plum?

That was a thought to tuck away for later. "Getting back to the dinosaur — com equipment breaks, and even a Class Three dig can end up with old equipment. If the only fellow on the dig qualified to fix it happens to be laid up with broken bones — in case you hadn't noticed, archeologists fall down shafts and off cliffs a lot — or double-pneumonia . . . "

"Good point." He finished his "housekeeping chores" with a flourish and settled back in his chair. "Say, Tia, they're all professorial types — do they ever just get so excited they forget to transmit?"

"Brace yourself for FTL — " The transition to FTL was nowhere near as distressing to softpersons as the dive into a Singularity, but it required some warning. Alex gripped the arms of the seat, and closed his eyes, as she made the jump into hyperspace.

She never experienced more than a brief shiver — *like ducking into a freezing-cold shower* — but Alex always looked a little green during transition. Fortunately, he had no trouble in hyper itself.

And if I can ever afford a Singularity Drive, his records say he takes those transitions pretty well. . . .

Well, right now, that was little more than a dream. She picked up the conversation where it had left off. "That has happened on Class One digs and even Class Two, but usually somebody realizes the report hasn't been made after a while when you're dealing with a big dig. Besides, logging reports constitutes publication, and grad students need all the publication they can get. Still, if they just uncovered the equivalent of Tutankhamen's tomb, they *might* all be so excited — and busy documenting finds and putting them into safe storage — that they've forgotten the rest of the universe exists."

He swallowed hard, controlling his nausea. It generally seemed to take his stomach a couple of minutes to settle down. *Maybe the reason it doesn't hit me is because there's no sensory nerves to my stomach anymore. . . .*

But that only brought back unpleasant memories; she ruthlessly shunted the thought aside.

"So — " he said finally, as his color began to return. "Tell me why you aren't in a panic because they haven't answered."

"Artifact thieves would probably have been spotted, there aren't any natives to revolt, and disease *usually* takes long enough to set in that *somebody* would have called for help," she said. "And that's why CS wasn't particularly worried, and why they kept countermanding the Institute's orders. But either this expedition has been out of touch for so long that even *they* think there's something wrong, or they've got some information they didn't give us. So we're going in."

"And we find out when we get there," Alex finished; and there wasn't a trace of a smile anywhere on his face.

Tia brought them out of hyper with a deft touch that rattled Alex's insides as little as possible. Once in orbit, she sent down a signal that should activate the team's transmitter if there was anything there to activate. As she had told Alex several days ago, com systems broke. She was fully expecting to get no echo back.

Instead —

You are linked to Excavation Team Que-Zee-Five-Five-Seven. The beacon's automatic response came instantly, in electronic mode. Then came the open carrier wave.

"Alex, I think we have a problem," she said, carefully.

"Echo?" He tensed.

"Full echo — " She sent the recognition signal that would turn on landing assistance beacons and alert the AI that there was someone Upstairs — the AI was supposed to open the voice-channel in the absence of humans capable of handling the com. The AI came on-line immediately, transmitting a *ready to receive instructions* signal.

"Worse, they've got full com. I just got the AI go-signal."

She blipped a compressed several megabytes of instructions to give her control of all external and internal recording devices, override any programs installed since the base was established, and give her control of all sensory devices still working.

"Get the AI to give me some pictures," he said, all business. "If it can."

"Coming up — ah, external cam three — this is right outside the mess hall and — *oh shellcrack* — "

"I'll second that," Alex replied, just as grimly.

The camera showed them — somewhat fuzzily — a scene that was anything but a pretty sight.

There were bodies lying in plain view of the camera; from the lack of movement they could not be live bodies. They seemed to be lying where they fell, and there was no sign of violence on them. Tia switched to the next camera the AI offered; a view inside the mess hall. Here, if anything, things were worse. Equipment and furniture lay toppled. More bodies were strewn about the room.

A chill that had nothing to do with the temperature in her shell held her in thrall. Fear, horror, helplessness—

Her own private nightmares—

Tia exerted control over her internal chemistry with an effort; told herself that this could *not* be the disease that had struck her. These people were taken down right where they stood or sat—

She started to switch to another view, when Alex leaned forward suddenly.

"Tia, wait a minute."

Obediently, she held the screen, sharpening the focus as well as the equipment, the four-second lag-to-orbit, and atmospheric interference would allow. She couldn't look at it herself.

"There's no food," he said, finally. "Look — there's plates and things all over the place, but there's not a scrap of food anywhere."

"Scavengers?" she suggested. "Or whatever—"

Whatever killed them? But there are no signs of an invasion, an attack from outside—

He shook his head. "I don't know. Let's try another camera."

This one was outside the supply building — and this was where they found their first survivors.

If that's what you can call them. Tia absorbed the incoming signal, too horrified to turn her attention away. There was a trio of folk within camera range: one adolescent, one young man, and one older woman. They paid no attention to each other, nor to the bodies at their feet, nor to their surroundings. The adolescent sat in the dirt of the compound, stared at a piece of brightly colored scrap paper in front of him, and rocked, back and forth. There was no sound pickup on these cameras, so there was no indication that he was doing anything other than rocking in silence, but Tia had the strange impression that he was humming tunelessly.

The young man stood two feet from a fence and shifted his weight back and forth from foot to foot, swaying, as if he wanted to get past the fence and had no idea how. And the older woman paced in an endless circle.

All three of them were filthy, dressed in clothes that were dirt-caked and covered with stains. Their faces were dirt-streaked, eyes vacant; their hair straggled into their eyes in ratty tangles. Tia was just grateful that the cameras were not equipped to transmit odor.

"Tia, get me another camera, please," Alex whispered, after a long moment.

Camera after camera showed the same view; either of bodies lying in the dust, or of bodies and a few survivors, aimlessly wandering. Only one showed anyone doing anything different; one young woman had found an emergency ration pouch and torn it open. She was single-mindedly stuffing the ration-cubes into her mouth with both hands, like —

"Like an animal," Alex supplied in a whisper. "She's eating like an animal."

Tia forced herself to be dispassionate. "Not like an animal," she corrected. "At least, not a healthy one." She analyzed the view as if she were dealing with an alien species. "No — she acts like an animal that's been brain-damaged — or maybe a drug addict that's been on something so long there isn't much left of his higher functions."

This wasn't "her" disease. It was something else — deadly — but not what had struck her down. What she felt was not exactly relief, but she was able to detach herself from the situation, to distance herself a little.

You knew, sooner or later, you'd see a plague. This one is a horror, but you knew this would happen.

"Zombies," Alex whispered, as another of the survivors plodded past without so much as a glance at the woman eating, who had given up eating with her hands and had shoved her face right down into the torn-open ration pouch.

"You've seen too many bad holos," she replied absently, sending the AI a high-speed string of instructions. She had to find out when this happened — and how long these people had been like this.

It was too bad that the cameras weren't set to record, because that would have told her a lot. How quickly the disease — for a plague of some kind would have had an incubation time — had set in, and what the initial symptoms were. Instead, all she had to go on were the dig's records, and when they had stopped making them.

"Alex, the last recorded entry into the AI's database was at about oh-two-hundred, local time, a week and a half ago," she said. "It was one of the graduate students logging in pottery shards. Then — nothing. No record of illness, nothing in the med records, no one even using a voice-activator to ask the AI for help. The mess hall computer programmed the synthesizer to produce food for a few meals, then something broke the synthesizer."

"One of them," Alex hazarded.

"Probably." She looked for anything else in the database and found nothing. "That's about all there is. The AI has been keeping things going, but there's been no interaction with it. So forget what I said about diseases taking several days to set in — it looks like this one infected and affected everyone on the base between — oh — some time during the night, and dawn."

If she'd had a head, she would have shaken it. "I can't imagine how something like that could happen to *everyone* at the same time without someone at least blurting a few words to a voice pickup!"

"Unless . . . Tia, what if they had to be asleep? I mean, there's things that happen during sleep, neuro transmitters that initiate dream-sleep — " Alex looked up from the screen, with lines of strain around his eyes. "If they had to be asleep to catch this thing — "

"Or if the first symptom *was* sleep . . . " She couldn't help herself; she wanted to shiver with fear. "Alex, I have to set down there. You can't do anything for those people from up here."

"No argument." He strapped himself in. "Okay, lady — get us down as fast as you can. There's one thing I *have* to do, quick, before we lose any more."

She broke orbit with a sudden acceleration that threw him into the back of his seat; he didn't bat an eye. His voice got a little more strained, but that was all.

"I'll have to put on a pressure-suit and get into the supplies; put out food and pans of water. They're starving and dehydrated. Spirits of space only know what they've been eating and drinking all this time — could be a lot of them died of dysentery, or from eating or drinking something that wasn't food." He was thinking out loud; waiting for Tia to put in her own thoughts, or warn him if he was planning to do something really stupid. "No matter what else we do, I *have* to do that."

"Open up emergency ration bags and leave pans of the cubes all over the compound," she suggested, as her outer skin heated up to a glowing red as she hit the upper atmosphere. "Do the same with the water. Like you were feeding animals."

"I am feeding animals," he said, and his voice and face were bleak. "I have to keep telling myself that. Or I'll do something really, really stupid. You get a line established to Kleinman Base, ASAP."

"Already in the works." A hyperwave comlink that far wasn't the easiest thing to establish and hold —

But that was why she was a brainship, not an AI drone.

"Hang on," she said, as she hit the first of the turbulence. "It's going to be a bumpy burn down!"

The camera and external mike on Alex's helmet gave her a much clearer view of the survivors than Tia really wanted. Of the complement of two hundred at this base, no more than fifty survived, most of them between the ages of fifteen and thirty.

They avoided Alex entirely, hiding whenever they saw him — but they came out to huddle around the pans of food and water he put out, stuffing food into their faces with both hands. Alex had gotten three of the bodies he'd found in their beds into the med-center, and the diagnosis was the same in all three cases; complete systemic collapse, which might have been stroke. The rest — the ones that had not simply dropped in their tracks — had died of dysentery and dehydration. Of the casualties, it looked as if half of the dead had keeled over with this collapse, all of them the oldest members of the team.

After the third, Alex called a halt to it; instead he loaded the bodies into the base freezer. Someone else would have to come get them and deal with them. Tia had recorded his efforts, but could not bring herself to actually watch the incoming video.

He completed his grisly work and returned to caring for the living. "Tia, as near as I can guess, this thing hits people in one of two ways. Either you get a stroke or something and die, or you turn into — that." She saw whatever he was looking at by virtue of the fact that the helmet-camera was mounted right over his forehead. And "that" was something that had once been a human boy, scrambling away out of sight.

"That seems like a good enough assumption for now," she agreed. "Can you tell what happened with the food situation? Are they so — far gone that they can't remember how to get into basic supplies?"

"That's about it," he agreed, wearily. "Believe it or not, they can't even remember how to pop ration packs — they seem to have a vague memory of where the food was stored, but they never even tried to open the door to the supply warehouse." He trudged across the compound to one of the pans he had set out. It was already empty, without even crumbs. He poured ration-cubes into it from a bag he carried under his arm. She caught furtive movement at the edge of the camera-view; presumably the survivors were waiting for him to go away so that they could empty the pan again. "When they found the emergency pouches they tore them open, like that woman we watched. But a lot of times, they don't even seem to realize that the pouch has food in it."

"There's two kinds of victims; the first lot, who got hit and died in their sleep or on the way to breakfast," he continued, making his way to the next pan. "Then the rest of them died of dehydration and dysentery because they were eating half-rotten food."

"Those would go hand-in-hand, here," she replied. "With nothing to stop the liquid loss through dysentery, dehydration comes on pretty quickly."

"That's what I figured." He paused to fill another pan. "There'd be more of them dead, of exposure and hypothermia, except that the temperature doesn't drop below twenty Celsius at night, or get above thirty in the daytime. Shirtsleeve weather. Tia — see when this balmy weather pattern started, would you?"

"Right." He must have had an idea — and it didn't take her more than a moment to interrogate the AI. "About a week before the last contact. Does that sound as suspicious to you as it does to me?"

"Yeah. Maybe something hatched." Alex scanned the area for her, and she noted that there were a fair number of insects in the air.

But native insects wouldn't bite humans — or would

they? "Or sprouted — this could be a violent allergic reaction, or some other kind of interaction with a mold spore or pollen." Farfetched, but not entirely impossible.

"But why wouldn't the Class One team have uncovered it?" he countered, filling another pan with ration-cubes. "Kibble," the brawns called it. The basic foodstuff of the Central System worlds; the monotonous ration-bars handed out by the PTA to client-planets cut up into bite-sized pieces. Tia had never eaten it; her parents had always insisted on real meals, but she had been told that while it looked, smelled, and tasted reasonable, its very sameness would drive you over the edge if you had to eat it for very long. But every base had emergency pouches of the stuff cached all over, and huge bags stockpiled in the warehouse, in case something happened to the food-synthesizers.

Those pouches must have been what kept the survivors going — until they ran out of pouches that were easy to find.

The dig records were, fortunately, quite clear. "Got the answer to your question — Class One dig was here for winter, only — they found what they needed to upgrade to Class Three within a couple of days of digging. They really hit a big find in the first test trench, and the Institute pushed the upgrade through to take advantage of the good weather coming."

"And initial Survey teams don't *live* here, they live on their ships." Alex had a little more life in his voice.

"They were only here in the fall," she said. "There's never been a human here during spring and summer."

"Tia, you put that together with an onset of this thing after dark, and what do you get?"

"An insect vector?" she hazarded. "Nocturnal? I must admit that the pattern for venomous and biting insects is to appear after sunset."

"Sounds right to me. As soon as I get done filling the

pans again, I'm going to go grab some bedding from one of the victims' beds, seal it in a crate, and freeze it. Maybe it's something like a flea. Can you see if there's anything in the AI med records about a rash of insect bites?"

"Can do," she responded, glad to finally have something, *anything,* concrete to do.

The sun was near the horizon when Alex finished boxing his selection of bedding and sealing it in a freezer container. He came back out again after loading the container into one of Tia's empty holds. She saw to the sealing of the hold, while he went back out to try and catch one of the Zombies — a name he had tagged the survivors with over her protests.

She finally established the comlink while he was still out in the compound, fruitlessly chasing one after another of the survivors and getting nowhere. He was weighted down with his pressure-suit; they were weighted down by nothing at all and had the impetus of fear. He seemed to terrify them, and they did not connect the arrival of food in the pans with him, for some reason.

"They act like I'm some kind of monster," he panted, leaning over to brace himself on his knees while he caught his breath. "Since they don't have that reaction to each other, it has to be this suit that they're afraid of. Maybe I should — "

"*Stay in the suit,*" she said, fiercely. "You make one move to take that suit off, and I'll sleepygas you!"

"Oh, Tia — " he protested.

"I'm not joking." She continued her conversation with the base brain in rapid, highly compressed databursts with *horribly* long pauses for the information to transmit across hyperspace. "You stay in that suit! We don't know what caused all this — "

Her tirade was interrupted by a dreadful howling and the external camera bounced as Alex moved violently. At first she thought that something awful had happened to Alex — but then she realized that the sound came from his *external* suit-mike, and that the movement of the camera had been caused by his own violent start of surprise.

"*What the* — " he blurted, then recovered. "Hang on, Tia. I need to see what this is, but it doesn't sound like an attack or anything."

"Be careful," she urged fearfully. "Please — "

But he showed no signs of foolhardy bravery; in fact, as the howling continued under the scarlet light of the descending sun, he sprinted from one bit of cover to another like a seasoned guerrilla-fighter.

"Fifty meters," Tia warned, taking her measurement from the strength of the howls. "They have to be on the other side of this building."

"Thanks." He literally crept on all fours to the edge of the building and peeked around the corner.

Tia saw exactly what he did, so she understood his sharp intake of breath.

She couldn't count them, for they milled about too much, but she had the impression that every survivor in the compound had crowded into the corner of the fence nearest the sunset. Those right at the fence clung to it as they howled their despair to the sun; the rest clung to the backs of those in front of them and did the same.

Their faces were contorted with the first emotion Tia had seen them display.

Fear.

"They're scared, Tia," Alex whispered, his voice thick with emotions that Tia couldn't decipher. "They're afraid. I think they're afraid that the sun isn't going to come back."

That might have been the case — but Tia couldn't help but wonder if their fear was due to something else entirely. Could they have a dim memory that something *terrible* had happened to them in the hours of darkness, something that took away their friends and changed their lives into a living hell? Was that why they howled and sobbed with fear?

When the last of the light had gone, they fell suddenly silent — then, like scurrying insects, they dropped to all fours and scuttled away, into whatever each, in the darkness of his or her mind, deemed to be shelter. In a moment, they were gone. All of them.

There was a strangled sob from Alex. And Tia shook within her shell, racked by too many emotions to effectively sort out.

"You have two problems."

Tia knew the name to put to the feeling she got when her next transmission from the base was not from some anonymous CS doctor but from Doctor Kenny.

Relief. Real, honest, relief.

It flooded her, making her relax, clearing her mind. Although she could not speak directly with him, if there was *anyone* who could help them pull this off, it would be Doctor Kenny. She settled all of her concentration on the incoming transmission.

"You'll have to catch the survivors and keep them alive — and you'll have to keep them from contaminating your brawn. After that, we can deal with symptoms and the rest."

All right, that made sense.

"We went at this analyzing your subjects' behavior. You were right in saying that they act in a very similar fashion to brain-damaged simians."

This was an audio-only transmission; the video portion of the signal was being used to carry a wealth of technical data. Tia wished she could see Doctor Kenny's face — but she heard the warmth and encouragement in his voice with no problem.

"We've compiled all the data available on *any* experiments where the subjects' behavior matched your survivors," Doctor Kenny continued. "Scan it and see if anything is relevant. Tia, I can't stress this enough — no matter *what* you think caused this disease, *don't let Alex get out of that suit.* I can't possibly say this too many times. Now that he's gone out there, he's got a contaminated surface. I want you to ask him to stay in the suit, sleep in the suit, eat through the suit-ports, use the suit-facilities. I would prefer that he stayed out in the compound or in your airlock even to sleep — every time he goes in and out of the suit, in and out of your lock, we have a chance for decontamination to fail. I know you understand me."

Only too well, she thought, grimly, remembering all that time in isolation.

"Now, we've come up with a general plan for you," Doctor Kenny continued. "We don't think that you'll be able to catch the survivors, given the way they're avoiding Alex. So you're going to have to trap them. My experts think you'll be able to rig drop-traps for them, using packing crates with field generators across the front and rations for bait. The technical specs are on the video-track, but I think you have the general idea. The big thing will be not to frighten the rest each time you trap one."

Doctor Kenny's voice echoed hollowly in the empty cabin; she damped the sound so that it didn't sound so lonely.

"We want one, two at most, per crate. We're afraid that, bunched together, they might hurt each other, fight over food — they're damaged, and we just don't know how aggressive they might get. That's why we want you to pack them in the hold in the crates. Once you get them trapped, we want you to put enough food and water in each crate to last the four days to base — and Tia, at that point, leave them there. Don't do anything with them. Leave them alone. I trust you to exercise your good sense and not give in to any temptation to intervene in their condition."

Doctor Kenny sighed, gustily. "We bandied around the idea of tranking them — but they *have* to eat and drink; four days knocked out might kill them. You don't have the facilities to cold-sleep fifty people. So — box them, hope the box matches their ideas of a good place to hide, leave them with food and water and shove them in the hold. That's it for now, Tia. Transmit everything you have, and we'll have answers for you as soon as we're able. These double-bounce comlinks aren't as fast as we'd like, but they beat the alternative. Our thoughts are with you."

The transmission ended, leaving her only with the carrier-wave.

Now what? Give Alex the bad news, I guess. And calculate how many packing crates I can pack into my holds.

"Alex?" she called. "Are you having any luck tracking down where the survivors are?"

"I've turned on all the exterior lights," Alex said. "I hoped that I'd be able to lure some of them out into the open, but it's no good." She activated his helmet-camera and watched his gloved hand typing override orders into the keyboard of the main AI console. Override orders had to be put in by hand, with a specific set of override codes, no matter how minor the change was — that was to keep someone from taking over an AI with a shout or two. "Right now I'm giving myself full access to everything — I may not need it, but who knows?"

"I've got our first set of orders," she told him. "Do you want to hear them?"

"Sure." Typing in a pressure-suit was no easy task, and Tia did not envy him. It took incredible patience to manage a normal keyboard in those stiff gloves.

She retransmitted Doctor Kenny's message and waited patiently for his response when she finished.

"So I have to stay in the suit." He sighed gustily. "Oh, well. It could be worse, I suppose. It could be two weeks to base, instead of four days." He typed the last few characters with a flourish and was rewarded by the "Full Access, Voice Commands accepted" legend. "No choice, right? Look, Tia, I know you're going to be lonely, but if I have to stay in this suit, I might just as well sleep out here."

"But — " she protested, " — what if they decide you're an enemy or something?"

"What, the Zombies?" He snorted. "Tia, right now they're all crammed into some of the darnedest nooks and crannies you ever saw in your life. I couldn't pry them out of there with a forklift. I know where they all are, but I'd have to break bones to get them. *Their* bones. They're terrified, even with all the floodlights on. No, they aren't going to come after me in the dark."

"All right," she agreed reluctantly. She knew he was right; he'd be much more comfortable out there — there was certainly more room available to him there.

"I'll be closer to the Zombies," he said wearily, "and I can barricade myself in one of the offices, get enough bedding from stores to make a reasonable nest. I'll plug the suit in to keep everything charged up, and you can monitor the mike and camera. I snore."

"I know," she said, in a weak attempt to tease him.

"You would." He turned, and the camera tracked what he was seeing. "Look, I'm here in the site supervisor's office. There's even a real nice couch in here and — " He leaned down and fiddled with the underside of the piece of furniture. "Ah hah. As I thought. There's a real bed in the couch. Bet the old man liked to sneak naps. Look — " He panned around the office. "No windows. One door. A full-access terminal. I'll be fine."

"All right, I believe you." She thought, quickly. "I'll look over those plans for traps and transmit them to the AI, and I'll find out where everything you'll need is stored. You can start collecting the team tomorrow."

What's left of them, she thought sadly. *What isn't already stored in the freezer.*

"See what you can do about adding some sleepygas to the equation," he suggested, yawning under his breath. "If we can knock them out once they're in the boxes, rather than trapping them with field generators, that should solve the problem of frightening the others."

That was a good suggestion. A much better one than Doctor Kenny's. *If* she had enough gas. . . .

But wait; this was a fully-stocked station. There might be another option. Crime *did* exist wherever there were people, and mental breakdowns — sometimes it was necessary to immobilize someone for his protection and the protection of others.

She interrogated the AI and discovered that, indeed, there were several special low-power needlers in the arms locker. And with them, full clips of anesthetic needles.

"Alex," she said, slowly, "how good a shot are you?"

"When this is over, I'm requisitioning an ethological tagging kit," she said fiercely, as Alex crouched on the roof of the mess hall and waited for his subject's hunger to overcome her timidity. She hesitated, just in front of the crate — she smelled the food, and she wanted it, but she was afraid to go inside after it. She swayed from side to side, like one of the first three survivors they'd seen; that swaying seemed to be the outward sign of inner conflict.

"Why?" he asked. The woman stopped swaying and was creeping, cautiously, into the crate. Alex wanted her to be all the way inside before he darted her, both to prevent the rest from seeing her collapse and to avoid having to haul her about and perhaps hurt her.

"Because they have full bio-monitor contact-buttons in them," she replied. "Skin adhesive ones. They're normally put inside ears, or on a shaved patch."

After a bit more consultation with Kleinman Base and Doctor Kenny, darting the survivors had been given full approval — and since they were going to be out, a modification in the setup had been arranged for. There would be shredded paper bedding in the crates as well as food and water — and each victim would wear a contact-button glued to the spine between the shoulder blades with surgical adhesive. With judicious reprogramming, a minimal amount of medical information could come from that — heart rate, respiration, skin temperature. Tia had reprogrammed the buttons; now it was her brawn's turn to live up to his title.

"I sure never thought my marksmanship would ever be an asset," he said absently. The woman had only a foot or so to go. . . .

"I never thought I was going to be packing my hold with canned archeologists." The packing crates would fit — but only if they were stacked two deep. Alex had already set up the site machine shop servos to drill air holes in all of the crates, and there would be an unbreakable bio-luminescent lightstick in each. They were rated for a week of use. Hopefully that much light would be enough to keep their captives from panicking.

"That's a good girl," Alex crooned to the reluctant Zombie. "Good girl. Smell the nice food? It's really good food. You're hungry, aren't you?" The woman took the last few steps in a rush and fell on the dish of ration-cubes. Alex darted her in the same moment.

The trank took effect within seconds, and she didn't even seem to realize that she'd been struck. She simply dropped over on her side, asleep.

Alex left the needler up on the roof where he'd rigged a sniper-post with a tripod to hold the gun steady. He trotted down the access steps to the first floor and hurried to get out where he could be seen before someone else smelled the food and came after it. As he burst out into the dusty courtyard, a hint of movement at the edge of the camera-field told Tia there *was* another Zombie lurking out there.

After many protests, she had begun calling the survivors "Zombies," too — it helped to think of them as something other than humans. She admitted to Doctor Kenny that without that distancing it was hard to keep working without strong feelings getting in the way of efficiency.

"That's all right, Tia," he soothed on his next transmission. "Even I have to stop thinking of my patients as people and start thinking of them as 'cases' or 'case studies' sometimes. That's the nature of this business, and we'll both do what we have to in order to get as many of these people back alive as we can."

She would have liked to ask him if he'd ever thought of *her* as a "case study," but she knew, in her heart of hearts, that he probably had. But then, look what he had done for her. . . .

No, calling these poor people "Zombies" wasn't going to hurt them, and it would keep her concentrating on what to do for them, and not on *them*.

Alex had been boxing Zombies all morning, and now he had it down to a system. Wheeling out of the warehouse, under the control of the AI, came a small parade of servos laden with the supplies that would keep the woman — hopefully — alive and healthy in her crate for the next five or six days. A bag of finely shredded paper, to make a thick nest on the bottom of the box. A whole bag of ration-cubes. A big squeeze-bottle of water. A tiny chemical toilet, on the off-chance she *might* remember how to use it. The bio-luminescent lightstick. Inside of fifteen minutes, Alex had his setup. The big bottle of water was strapped to one wall, the straps glue-bonded in place, the bottle bonded to the straps. The toilet was bonded to the floor in the corner of the six foot by six foot crate. The bag of ration-cubes was opened at the top, and strapped and bonded into the opposite corner. Paper was laid in a soft bed over the entire floor, and the unconscious woman rolled onto it, with the contact-button glued to her back. Lastly, the bio-luminescent tube was activated and glue-bonded to the roof of the crate, the side brought up and fastened in place, and the crate was ready for the loader.

That was Tia's job; she brought the servo-forklift in from the warehouse under her control rather than the AI's. Alex did not trust the AI to have the same fine control that Tia did. The lift bore the now-anonymous crate up her ramp, and she stored it with the rest, piled not two but three high and locked in place. Each crate was precisely eight inches from the ones next to it, to allow for proper ventilation on four sides. There were twelve crates in the hold now. They hoped to have twelve more before nightfall. If all went well.

Thirty minutes for each capture. . . .

They couldn't have done it if not for Tia's multi-tasking abilities and all the servos under her control. Right now, a set of servos were setting up crates all over the compound, near the hiding places of the Zombies. The Zombies seemed just as frightened of the servos as they were of Alex in his suit. By running the servos all over the compound, they managed to send every one of the Zombies into hiding. They ran servos around each hiding place until they were ready to move to that area for darting and capture. By now, the Zombies were getting hungry, which was all to the good, so far as Alex and Tia were concerned. One trap was being baited now — and Alex was on his way to the hidden sniper position above it. Meanwhile, the rest of the servos were patrolling the compound *except* in the area of that baited crate, keeping the Zombies pinned down.

A second hair-raising moment had occurred at dawn, bringing Alex up out of his bed with a scream of his own. The Zombies had gathered to greet the rising sun with another chorus of howls, although this time they seemed more — well, not joyous, but certainly there was no fear in the Zombie faces.

Once the first servo appeared, and frightened the Zombies into hiding again, the final key to their capture plan was in place.

They would catch as many of the Zombies as possible during the daylight hours. Alex had marked their favorite hiding places last night, and by now those patrolling servos had those that were not occupied blocked off. More crates would be left very near those blocked-off hiding holes. Would they be attractive enough for more of the Zombies to hide in them? Alex thought so. Tia hoped he was right — for every Zombie cowering in a crate meant one more they could dart and pack up — one more they would not have to catch tomorrow.

One less half-hour spent here. If they could keep up the pace — if the Zombies didn't get harder to catch.

Alex kept up a running dialogue with her, and she sensed that he was as frightened and lonely as she was, but was determined not to show it. He revealed a lot, over the course of the day; she built up a mental picture of a young man who had been just different enough that while he was mildly popular — or at least, not unpopular — he had few close friends. The only one who he really spoke about was someone called Jon — the chess and games player he had mentioned before. He spent a lot of time with Jon — who had helped him with his lessons when he was younger, so Tia assumed that Jon must have been older than Alex.

Older or not, Jon had been, and still was, a *friend*. There was no mistaking the warmth in Alex's voice when he talked about Jon; no mistaking the pleasure he felt when he talked about the message of congratulation Jon had sent when he graduated from the academy—

Or the laughter he'd gotten from the set of "brawn jokes" Jon had sent when Tia picked Alex as her partner.

Well, Doctor Kenny, Anna, and Lars were my friends — and still are. Sometimes age doesn't make much of a difference.

"Hey, Alex?" she called. He was waiting for another of the timid Zombies to give in to hunger. The clock was running.

"What?"

"What do you call a brawn who can count past ten?"

"I don't know," he said good-naturedly. "What?"

"Barefoot."

He made a rude noise, then sighted and pulled the trigger. One down, how many more to go?

They had fifty-two Zombies packed in the hold, and one casualty. One of the Zombies had not survived the darting; Alex had gone into acute depression over that death, and it had taken Tia more than an hour to talk him out of it. She didn't dare tell him then what those contact-buttons revealed; some of their passengers weren't thriving well. The heart rates were up, probably with fear, and she heard whimpering and wailing in the hold whenever there was no one else in it but the Zombies. The moment any of the servos or Alex entered the hold, the captives went utterly silent. Out of fear, Tia suspected.

The last Zombie was in the hold; the hold was sealed, and Tia had brought the temperature up to skin-heat. The ventilators were at full-strength. Alex had just entered the main cabin.

And he was reaching for his helmet-release.

"Don't crack your suit," she snapped. How could she have forgotten to tell him? Had she? Or had she told him, and *he* had forgotten?

"What?" he said — then — "Oh, *decom* it. I forgot."

She restrained herself from saying what she wanted to. "Doctor Kenny said you have to stay in the suit. Remember? He thinks that the chance we might have missed something in decontamination is too much to discount. He doesn't want you to crack your suit until you're at the base. All right?"

"What if something goes wrong for the Zombies?" he asked, quietly. "Tia, there isn't enough room in that hold for me to climb around in the suit."

"We'll worry about that if it happens," she replied firmly. "Right now, the important thing is for you to get strapped down, because *their* best chance is to get to Base as quickly as possible, and I'm going to leave scorch-marks on the ozone layer getting there."

He took the unsubtle hint and strapped himself in; Tia was better than her word, making a tail-standing takeoff and squirting out of the atmosphere with a blithe disregard for fuel consumption. The Zombies were going to have to deal with the constant acceleration to hyper as best they could — at least she knew that they were all sitting or lying down, because the crates simply weren't big enough for them to stand.

She had been relaying symptoms — observed and recorded — back to Doctor Kenny and the med staff at Kleinman Base all along. She had known that they weren't going to get a lot of answers, but every bit of data was valuable, and getting it there ahead of the victims was a plus.

But now that they were on the way, they were on their own, without the resources of the abandoned dig or the base they were en route to. The med staff might have answers — but *they* likely would not have the equipment to implement them.

Alex couldn't move while she was accelerating — but once they made the jump to FTL, he unsnapped his restraints and headed for the stairs.

"Where are you going?" she asked, nervously.

"The hold. I'm in my suit — there's nothing down there that can get me through the suit."

Tia listened to the moans and cries through her hold pickups; thought about the contact-buttons that showed fluttering hearts and unsteady breathing. She knew what would happen if he got down there.

"You can't do anything for them in the crates," she said. "You know that."

He turned toward her column. "What are you hiding from me?"

"N-nothing," she said. But she didn't say it firmly enough.

He turned around and flung himself back in his chair, hands speeding across the keyboard with agility caused by days of living in the suit. Within seconds he had called up every contact-button and had them displayed in rows across the screen.

"Tia, what's going on down there?" he demanded. "They weren't like this before we took off, were they?"

"I think — " She hesitated. "Alex, I'm not a doctor!"

"You've got a medical library. You've been talking to the doctors. *What* do you think?"

"I think — they aren't taking hyper well. Some of the data the base sent me on brain-damaged simians suggested that *some* kinds of damage did something to the parts of the brain that make you compensate for — for things that you know should be there, but aren't. Where you can see a whole letter out of just parts of it — identify things from split-second glimpses. Kind of like maintaining a mental balance. Anyway, when that's out of commission — " She felt horribly helpless. "I think for them it's like being in Singularity."

"For *four days*?" he shouted, hurting her sensors. "I'm going down there —"

"And do what?" she snapped back. "What are you going to do for them? They're afraid of you in that suit!"

"Then I'll —"

"You do, and I'll gas the ship," she said instantly. "I *mean* that, Alex! You put *one finger* on a release and I'll gas the whole ship!"

He sat back down, collapsing into his chair. "What can we do?" he said weakly. "There has to be something."

"We've got some medical supplies," she pointed out. "A couple of them can be adapted to add to the air supply down there. *Help* me, Alex. Help me find something we can do for them. Without you cracking your suit."

"I'll try," he said, unhappily. But his fingers were already on the keyboard, typing in commands to the med library, and not sneaking towards his suit-releases. She blanked for a microsecond with relief—

Then went to work.

Three more times there were signs of crisis in the hold. Three more times she had to threaten him to keep him from diving in and trying to save one of the Zombies by risking his own life. They lost one more, to a combination of anti-viral agent and watered-down sleepygas that they *hoped* would act as a tranquilizer rather than an anesthetic. Zombie number twenty-seven might have been allergic to one or the other, although there was no such indication in his med records; his contact-button gave all the symptoms of allergic shock before he died.

Alex stopped talking to her for four hours after that — twenty-seven had been in the bottom rank, and a shot of adrenaline would have brought him out — *if* it had been allergic shock. But his crate was also buried deep in the stacks, and Alex would have had to peel the whole suit off to get to him. Which Tia wouldn't permit. They had no way of knowing if this was really an allergic reaction, or if it was another development of the Zombie Bug. Twenty-seven had been an older man, showing some of the worst symptoms.

Although Alex wasn't talking to her, Tia kept talking at him, until he finally gave in. Just as well. His silence had her convinced that he was going to ask for a transfer, and that he hated her — if a shellperson could be in tears, she was near that state when he finally answered.

"You're right," was all he said. "Tia, you were right. There are fifty more people there depending on both of us, and if I got sick, that's the mobile half of the team out." And he sighed. But it was enough. Things went back to normal for them. Just in time for the transition to norm space.

Kleinman Base kept them in orbit, sending a full decontamination team to fetch Alex as well as the Zombies, leaving Tia all alone for about an hour. It was a very lonely hour. . . .

But then another decontamination team came aboard, and when they left again, two days later, there was nothing left of her original fittings. She had been fogged, gassed, stripped, polished, and refitted in that time. All that was left — besides the electronic components — were the ideographs painted on the walls. It still looked the same, however, because everything was replaced with the same standard-issue, psychologically approved beige. . . .

Only then was she permitted to de-orbit and land at Kleinman Base so that the decontamination team could leave.

No sooner had the decontamination team left, when there was a welcome hail at the airlock.

"Tia! Permission to come aboard, ma'am!"

She activated her lock so quickly that it must have flown open in his face, and brought him up in the lift rather than waiting for him to climb the stairs. He sauntered in sans pressure-suit, gave her column a jaunty salute, and put down his bags.

"I have good news and better news," he said, flinging

himself into his chair. "Which do you want to hear first?"

"The good news," she replied promptly, and did *not* scold him for putting his feet up on the console.

"The good news is all personal. I have been granted a clean bill of health, and so have you. In addition, since the decontamination team so rudely destroyed my clothing and anything else that they couldn't be sure of, I have just been having a *glorious* spending-spree down there at the Base, using a CS unlimited credit account!"

Tia groaned, picturing more neon-purple, or worse. "Don't open the bags, or they'll think I've had a radiation leak."

He mock-pouted. "My dear lady, your taste is somewhere back in the last decade."

"Never mind my taste," she said. "What's the better news?"

"Our patients are on their way to full recovery." At her exclamation, he held up a cautionary hand. "It's going to take them several months, maybe even a year. Here's the story — and the reason why they stripped you of everything that could be considered a fabric. Access your Terran entomology, if you would. Call up something called a 'dust mite' and another something called a 'sand flea.' "

Puzzled, she did so, laying the pictures side by side on the central screen.

"As we guessed, this was indeed a virus, with an insect vector. The culprit was something like a sand flea, which, you will note, has a taste for warm-blooded critters. But it was about the *size* of a dust mite. The fardling things don't hatch until the temperature is right, the days are long enough, and there's been a rainstorm. Once they hatch, the only thing that kills them is really intense insecticide or freezing cold for several weeks. They live in the dust, like sand fleas. Those archeologists had been tracking in dust ever since the rainstorm, and since there'd been no sign of any problems, they hadn't been very careful about their decontamination protocols. The bugs all hatched within an hour, or so the entomologists think. They bit everything in sight, since they always wake up hungry. *But* — here's the catch — since they were so small, they didn't leave a bite mark, so there was nothing to show that anyone had been bitten." He nodded at the screen. "Every one of the little beggars carries the virus. It's like *E. coli,* the human bacillus, living in their guts the way it does in ours."

"I assume that everyone got bitten about the same time?" she hazarded.

"Exactly," he said. "Which meant that everyone came down with the virus within hours of each other. Mostly, purely by coincidence, in their sleep. The virus itself invokes allergic shock in most people it infects. Which can look a lot like a stroke, under the right circumstances."

"So we didn't — " She stopped herself before she went any further, but he finished the statement for her.

"No, we didn't kill anyone. It was the Zombie Bug. And the best news of all is that the Zombie state is caused by interference with the production of neurotransmitters. Clean out the virus, and eventually everyone gets back to normal."

"Oh *Alex* — " she said, and he interrupted her.

"A little more excellent news — first, that we get a bonus for this one. And second, my very dear, you saved my life."

"I did?" she replied, dumbfounded.

"If I had cracked my suit even once, the bugs would have gotten in. They were everywhere, in your carpet, the upholstery; either they got in the first time we cracked the lock, or the standard decontamination didn't wash them all off the suit or kill them. And I am one of those seventy-five percent of the population so violently allergic to them that — " He let her fill in the rest.

"Alex — I'd rather have you as my brawn than all the bonuses in the world," she said, after a long pause.

"Good," he said, rising, and patting her column gently. "I feel the same way."

Before the moment could get maudlin, he cleared his throat, and continued. "Now the bad news: we're so far behind on our deliveries that they want us out of here yesterday. So, are you ready to fly, bright lady?"

She laughed. "Strap on your chair, hotshot. Let's show 'em how to burn on out of here!"

• CHAPTER FIVE

"Well, Tia," Doctor Kenny said genially, from his vantage point in front of her main screen. "I have to say that it's a lot more fun talking to you face-to-column than by messages or double-bounce comlink. Waiting for four hours for the punchline to a joke is a bit much."

He faced her column, not the screen, showing the same courtesy Alex always did. Alex was not aboard at the moment; he was down on the base spending his bonus while Tia was in the refit docks in orbit. But since the *Pride of Albion* was so close, Doctor Kenny had decided that he couldn't resist making a visit to his most successful patient.

The new version of his chair had been perfected, and he was wearing it now. The platform and seat hid the main power-supply, a shiny exoskeleton covered his legs up to his waist, and Tia thought he looked like some kind of ancient warrior-king on a throne.

"Most of my classmates don't get the point of jokes," she said, with a chuckle. "They just don't seem to have much of a sense of humor. I have to share them with you softies."

"Most of your classmates are as stiff as AIs," he countered. "Don't worry, they'll loosen up in a decade or two — that's what Lars tells me, anyway. He says that living around softies will contaminate even the most rule-bound shellperson. So, how's life with a partner? As I recall, that was one of your worst worries, that you'd end up with a double-debt like Moira for playing brawn-basketball."

"I really like Alex, Kenny," she said slowly. "Especial-ly after the Zombie Bug run. I hate to admit this, but — I even like him more than you, or Anna, or Lars. And that's what I wanted to talk to you about when you called the other day. I really — trust your judgment."

He nodded, sagely. "And since I'm not in the brain-brawn program, *I* am not bound by regs to report you when you tell me how much you are attracted to your brawn." He sent an ironic wink toward her column.

She let herself relax a little. "Something like that," she admitted. "Kenny, I just don't know what to think. He's sloppy, he's forgetful, he's a little impulsive — he has the *worst* taste in clothes — and I'd rather have him as a partner than anyone else in the galaxy. I'd rather talk to *him* than my classmates, and being classmates is supposed to be the strongest bond a shellperson can have!" Supposed to be — that was the trick, wasn't it? There was very little in her life that had happened the way it was supposed to. At this point, she should have been entering advanced studies under the auspices of the Institute — not working for it. She should have been a softie — not a shellperson.

But you didn't deal with life by dwelling on what "should" have happened. You handled it by making the best out of what *had* happened.

"Well, Tia, you spent the first seven of your most for-mative years as a softperson," Kenny pointed out gently. His next words echoed her own earlier thoughts. "You never thought you'd wind up in a shell, where your classmates never knew anything but their shells and their teachers. Just like when a chick hatches — what it imprints on is what it's going to fall in love with."

"I — I didn't say I was in love," she stammered, sud-denly alarmed.

Kenny held his peace. He simply stared at her column with a look she remembered all too well. The one that said she wasn't entirely telling the truth, and he knew it.

"Well — maybe a little," she admitted, in a very soft voice. "But — it's not like I was another softie — "

"You can love a friend, you know," Kenny pointed out. "That's been acknowledged for centuries — even among stuffy shellperson Counselors. Remember your Greek philosophers — they felt there were three kinds of love, and only one of them had anything to do with the body. *Eros, filios,* and *agape.*"

"Sexual, brotherly, and religious," she translated, feeling a little better. "Well, okay. *Filios,* then."

"Lars translates them as 'love involving the body,' 'love involving the mind,' and 'love involving the soul.' That's even more apt in your case," Kenny said comfortably. "Both *filios* and *agape* apply here."

"I guess you're right," she said, feeling sheepish.

"Tia, my dear," Kenny said, without a hint of patronization, "there is nothing wrong with saying that you love your brawn — the first words you transmitted to me from your new shell, in case you've forgotten, were 'Doctor Kenny, I love you.' Frankly, I'm a lot happier hearing *this* from you than something 'appropriate.' "

"Like what?" she asked curiously.

"Hmm. Like this." He raised his voice an octave. "Well, Doctor Kennet," he said primly, "I'm quite pleased with the performance of my brawn Alexander. I believe we can work well together. Our teamwork was quite acceptable on this last assignment."

"You sound like Kari, exactly like Kari." She laughed. "Yes, but imagine trying to have this conversation with one of my BB Counselors!"

He screwed up his face and flung up his hands. "Oh, *horrors!*" he exclaimed, his expression matching the outrage in his voice. "How *could* you confess to feeling *anything?* AH-One-Oh-Three-Three, I am going to *have* to report you for *instability!*"

"Precisely," she replied, sobering. "Sometimes I think they just want us to be superior sorts of AIs. Self-aware and self-motivating, but someone get out a scalpel and excise the *feeling* part before you pop them in their shells."

"There's a fine line they have to tread, dear," he told her, just as soberly. "Your classmates lack something you had — the physical nurturing of a parent. They never touched anything; they've never known anything but a very artificial environment. They don't really under-stand emotions, because they've never been allowed to experience them or even see them near at hand. I don't think there's any question in *my* mind what that means, when they first come out into the real world of us softies. It means they literally enter a world as foreign and incomprehensible as any alien culture. In some ways, it would be better if they all entered professions where they never had to deal with humans one-on-one."

"Then why — " She picked her words with care. "Why don't they put adults into shells?"

"Because adults — even children — often can't adapt to the fact that their bodies don't work anymore, and that — as you pointed out yourself — they will never have that human *touch* again." He sighed. "I've seen plenty of that in my time, too. You are an excep-tion, my love. But you always have been special. Outstandingly flexible, adaptable." He sat back in his chair and thought; she didn't interrupt him. "Tia, there are things that I don't agree with in the way the shellperson training program is run. But you're out of the training area now and into the real world. You'll find that even the Counselors can have an entirely dif-ferent attitude out here. They're ready to accept what works, not just what's in the rule books."

She paused a moment before replying. "Kenny, what do I do if — things creep over into *eros*? I mean, I'm not going to crack my column or anything, but . . ."

"Helva," Kenny said succinctly. "Think of Helva. She and her brawn had a romance that still has power over the rest of known space. If it happens, Tia, let it happen. If it *doesn't*, don't mourn over it. Enjoy the fact that your brawn is your very best friend; that's the way it's supposed to be, after all. I have faith in your sense and sensibility; I always have. You'll be fine." He coughed a little. "As it — ah — happens, I have a bit of fellow-feeling for you. Anna and I have gotten to be something of an item."

"Really?" She didn't even try to modulate the glee out of her voice. "It's about time! What did she do, tip your chair over to slow you down and seduce you on the spot?"

"That's just about word for word what Lars said," Kenny replied, blushing furiously. "Except that he added a few other pointed remarks."

"I can imagine." She giggled. Lars was over two centuries old, and he had seen a great deal in that time. Every kind of drama a sentient was capable of, in fact — he was the chief overseer of one of the largest hospital stations in Central Systems. If there was ever a place for life-and-death drama, a hospital station was it — as holo-makers across the galaxy knew. From the smallest incident to the gravest, Lars had witnessed — and sometimes participated in — all of it.

He had been in charge of the *Pride of Albion* since it was built — he had been built into it. He would never leave, and never wanted to. Cynical, brilliant — with an unexpectedly kind heart. That was Lars. . . .

He could be the gentlest person, soft- or shell-, that Tia had ever met. Though he never missed an opportunity to jab one of his softperson colleagues with his sharp wit.

"But Kenny — " She hesitated, eaten alive with curiosity, but unsure how far she could push. "Kenny, how nosy can I be about you and Anna?"

"Tia, I know everything there is to know about you, from your normal heart rate to the exact composition of the chemicals in your blood when you're under stress. *My* doctor knows the same about me. We're both used to being poked and prodded — " he paused " — and you are my very dear friend. If there is something you are really curious about, please, go ahead and ask." His eyes twinkled. "But don't expect me to tell you about the birds and the bees."

"You're — when we first met, you called yourself a 'medico on the half-shell.' You're half machine. How does Anna — feel about that?" If she could have blushed, she would have, she felt so intrusive.

He didn't seem to feel that she was intruding, however. "Hmm, good questions. The answer, my dear, is one that I am afraid can't apply to you. I'm only 'half machine' when I'm strapped in. When I'm not in my chair, I'm — an imperfect, but entirely human creature." He smiled.

"So it's like comparing rocks to bonbons." That was something she hadn't anticipated. "Or water to sheet-metal."

"Good comparisons. You're not the first to ask these questions, by the way. So don't think you're unique in being curious." He stretched and grinned. "Anna and I are doing a lot of — hmm — personal-relations counseling of my other handicapped patients."

"At least I'm not some kind of — would-be voyeur." That was nice to know.

"You, however, were and are in an entirely different boat than my other patients," he warned. "What applies to them does not apply to you." He shook his head. "I'm going to give this to you straight and without softening. You have no working nerves, sensory or motor control, below your neck. And from what I've seen, there was some further damage to the autonomic system as well before we stabilized you.

What with the mods they made to you when you went into the shell, you're dependent on life-support now. I don't think you could survive outside your shell — I know you wouldn't be happy."

"Oh. All right." In a way, she was both disappointed and relieved. Relieved that it was one more factor she wouldn't have to consider in her ongoing partnership. Disappointed — well, not that much. She hadn't really thought there would ever be any way to reverse the path that had brought her into her column.

"I did bring some records of the things I've been working on to show you — devices that are helping out some of our involuntary amputees. I thought you'd be interested, just on an academic basis." He slipped a datahedron into her reader, and she brought up the display on her central screen. "This young lady was a professional dancer — she was trapped under several tons of masonry after an earthquake. By the time medics got to her, the entire limb had suffered cell-death. There was no saving it."

The video portion of the clip showed a lovely young lady in leotards and tights trying out what looked like a normal leg — except that it moved very stiffly.

"The problem with the artificial limbs we've been giving amputees is that while we've fixed most of the weight and movement problems, they're still completely useless for someone like a dancer, who relies on sensory input to tell her whether or nor her foot is in the right position." Kenny smiled fondly as he watched the girl on the screen. "That's Lila within a few minutes of having the leg installed. At the hip, may I add. The next clip will be three weeks later, then three months."

The screen flickered as Tia found her attention absorbed by the girl. Now she was working out in what were obviously ballet exercises, and doing very well, so far as Tia could tell. Then the screen flickered a third time —

And the girl was on stage, partnered in some kind of classic ballet piece — and if Tia had not known her left leg was cyborged, she would never have guessed it.

"Here's a speed-keyer who lost his hand," Kenny continued, but he turned towards the column. "Between my work and Moto-Prosthetics, we've beaten the sensory input problem, Tia," he said proudly. "Lila tells me she's changed the choreography so that she can perform some of the more difficult moves on her left foot instead of her right. The left won't get toe-blisters or broken foot-bones, the tendons won't tear, the knee won't give, and the ankle has no chance of buckling. The only difference that *she* can see between the cyborged leg and the natural one is that the cyborg is a little heavier — not enough to make any difference to her if she can change the choreography — and it's a lot sturdier."

A few more of Doctor Kenny's patients came up on the screen, but neither of them were paying attention.

"There have to be some problems," Tia said, finally. "I mean, nothing is perfect."

"We don't have *full* duplication of sensory input. In Lila's case, we have it in the entire foot and the ankle and knee-joints, and we've pretty much ignored the stretches of leg in between. Weight is the other problem. The more sensory nerves we duplicate, the higher the weight. A ten-kilo hand is going to give someone a lot of trouble, for instance." Kenny shifted a little in his chair. "But all of this is coming *straight* out of what's going on in the Lab Schools, Tia! And most of it is from the brainship program — the same thing that gives you sensory input from the ships' systems are what became the sensory linkups for those artificial limbs."

"That's wonderful!" Tia said, very pleased for him. "You're quite something, Doctor Kennet!"

"Oh, there's a lot more to be done," he said modestly. "I haven't heard any of Lila's fellow dancers clamoring to have double-amputations and new legs installed. She has her problems, and there's some pain involved, even after healing is completed. In a way, it's a good thing for us that our first leg-installation was for a dancer, because Lila was used to living with pain — all dancers are. And it's *very* expensive; she was lucky, because the insurance company involved judged that compensating her for a lost — very lucrative — career was more expensive than an artificial limb. Although — given the life expectancy of you shellpersons, and compare it to those of us still in our designed-by-genetics containers — well, I can foresee a day when we'll all have our brains tucked into minishells when the old envelope starts to decay, and instead of deciding what clothes we want to wear, we have to decide what body to put on."

"Oh, I don't think it'll come to that, really," Tia said decisively. "For one thing, if it's expensive for one limb, a whole body would be impossible."

"It is that," Kenny agreed. "But to tell you the truth, right now the problem besides expense isn't technical — we could put the fully-functioning body together — and do it today. It's actually easier to do that than just one limb. Oh, by that, I mean one with full sensory inputs."

He didn't say anything, but he winked, and grinned wickedly. "And by 'full sensory input,' I mean exactly what you're thinking, you naughty young lady."

"Me?" she said, with completely feigned indignation. "I have *no* idea what you're talking about! I am as innocent as — as — "

"As I am," Kenny said. "You were the one who was asking about me and Anna."

She remained silent, pretending dignity. He continued to grin, and she knew he wasn't fooled in the least.

"Well, anyway, the problem is having a life-support

system for a naked brain." He shrugged. "Can't quite manage that — putting a whole body into a life-support shell is still the only way to deal with trauma like yours. And we can't fit *that* into a human-sized body."

"Oh, you could make us great *big* bodies and create a whole race of giants," she joked. "That should actually be easier, from what you've told me."

He cast his eyes upwards, surprising her somewhat with his sudden flare of exasperation. "Believe it or not, there's a fellow who wants to do something like that, for the holos. He wants to create giant full-sensory bodies of — oh, dinosaurs, monsters, whatever — hire a shellperson actor, and use the whole setup in his epics."

"No!" she exclaimed.

"I swear," he said, placing his hand over his heart. "True, every word of it. And believe it or not, he *has* the money. Holostars make more than you do, my love. I think the next time some brain wants to retire from active ship-service, especially one that's bought out his contract, this fellow just might tempt them into the holos."

"Amazing. Virtual headshaking here." She thought for a moment. "What would the chances be of creating a life-sized body with some kind of brainstem link to the shell?"

"Like a radio?" he hazarded. "Hmm. Good question. A real problem; there is a *lot* of information carried by these nerves — you'd need separated channels for everything, but — well, the effective range would be very, very short, otherwise you run the risk of signal breakup. That turned out to be the problem with this rig," he finished, nodding at his armored legs. "It has to stay in the same room with me, otherwise — Greek frieze time."

She laughed.

"Anyway, the whole rig would probably cost as much

as a brainship, so it's not exactly practical," he concluded. "Not even for me, and they pay me very well."

Not exactly practical for me, either, she thought, and dismissed the whole idea. Practical, for a brainship, meant buying out her contract. After all, if she wanted to be free to join the Institute as an active researcher and go chasing the EsKays on her own, she was going to have to buy herself out.

"Well, money — that's the other reason I wanted to talk to you," she said.

"And the bane of the BB program rears its ugly head," he intoned, and grinned. "Oh, they're going to hate you. You're just like all the rest of the really good ones. You want to buy that contract out, don't you?"

"I don't think there are too many CS ships that *don't* plan on doing it someday," she countered. "We're people, not AI drones. We like to have a choice of where we go. So, do you have any ideas of how I can start raising my credit balance? Moira has kind of cornered the market on spotting possible new sites from orbit and entry."

"Gave her the idea, did you?" Kenny shook his finger at you. "Don't you know you should never give ideas away to the competition?"

"She wasn't competition, then," Tia pointed out.

"Well, you have a modest bonus from the Zombie Bug run, right?" he said, scratching his eyebrow as he thought. "What about investing it?"

"In what?" she countered. "I don't know anything about investing money."

"Operating on my own modest success in putting my own money into Moto-Prosthetics — and not in paper stock, my dear, but in shares in the company itself — if you use your own knowledge to choose where to invest, the results can be substantial." He tapped his fingers on the side of his chair. "It's not insider trading, if you're thinking that. I would consider putting your money where your interest and expertise is."

"Virtual headshaking," she replied. "I have *no* idea what you're getting at. What do *I* know?"

"Look — " he said, leaning forward, his eyes bright with intensity. "The one thing an archeologist is *always* cognizant of is the long term — especially long-term patterns. And the one thing that most often trips up the sophonts of any race is that they are *not* thinking in the long term. Look for what a friend of mine called 'disasters waiting to happen,' and invest in the companies that will be helping to recover from that disaster."

"Well, that sounds good in theory," she said doubtfully. "But in practice? How am I going to find situations like that? I'm only one person, and I've already got a job."

"Tia, you have the computing power of an entire brainship at your disposal," Kenny told her firmly. "And you have access to Institute records for every inhabited planet that also holds ruins. Use both. Look for problems the ancients had, then see if they'll happen again at current colonies."

Well, nothing sprung immediately to mind, but it *would* while away some time. And Kenny had a point.

He glanced at his wrist-chrono. "Well, my shuttle should be hailing you right about — "

"Now," she finished. "It's about to dock: four slots from me, to your right as you exit the lock. Thanks for coming, Kenny."

He directed his Chair to the lift. "Thank you for having me, Tia. As always, it's been a pleasure."

He turned to look back over his shoulder as he reached the lift, and grinned. "By the way, don't bother to check my med records. Anna has never complained about my performance yet."

If she could have blushed . . .

While Alex spent his time with some of his old

classmates — presumably living up to what he had told her was the class motto, "The Party Never Ends" — she dove headlong into Institute records. The Institute gave her free, no-charge access to anything she wanted; perhaps because they counted her as a kind of member-researcher, perhaps because of her part in the Zombie Bug rescue — or perhaps because brainship access was one hole in their access system they'd never plugged because they never thought of it. Normally they charged for every record downloaded from the main archives. It didn't matter to her; there was plenty there to look into.

But first — her own peculiar quest. She caught up on everything having to do with the old EsKay investigations in fairly short order. There wasn't much of anything new from existing digs, so she checked to see what Pota and Braddon were doing, then went on to postings on brand new EsKay finds.

It was there that she came across something quite by accident.

It was actually rather amusing, when it came down to it. It was the report from a Class Two dig, from the group taking over a site that had initially gotten a lot of excitement from the Exploration team. *They* had reported it as an EsKay site — the first ever to be uncovered on a non-Marslike world. And an EsKay Evaluation team was sent post-haste.

It turned out to be a case of misidentification; not Es-Kays at all, but another race entirely, the Megalt Tresepts, one of nowhere near as much interest to the Institute. Virtually everything was known about the Megalts; they had sent out FTL ships in the far distant past, and some of the colonies they had established still existed. Some of their artifacts looked like EsKay work, and if there was no notion that the Megalts had been in the neighborhood, it was fairly easy to make the mistake.

The world was surprisingly Terran — which would have made an EsKay site all the more valuable *if* it really had been there.

Although it was not an EsKay site after all, Tia continued reading the report out of curiosity. Largo Draconis was an odd little planet — with an eccentric orbit that made for one really miserable decade every century or so. Other than that, it was quite habitable; really pleasant, in fact, with two growing seasons in every year. The current settlements were ready for that dismal decade, according to the report — but also according to the report, the Megalts had been, too.

Yet the Megalt sites had been abandoned, completely. Not typical of the logical, systematic race.

During the first year of that wretched ten years, every Megalt settlement on the planet (all two of them) had been abandoned. And not because they ran out of food, either, which was her first thought. They had stockpiled more than enough to carry them through, even with no harvests at all.

No; not because the *settlers* ran out of food — but because the native rodents did.

Curious about what had happened, the Evaluation team had found the settlement records, which outlined the entire story, inscribed on the thin metal sheets the Megalts used for their permanent hardcopy storage. The settlements had been abandoned so quickly that no one had bothered to find and take them.

It was a good thing the Megalts used metal for their records; nothing else would have survived what had happened to the settlement. The rodents had swarmed both colonies; a trickle at first, hardly more than a nuisance. But then, out of nowhere, a swarm, a flood, a *torrent* of rodents had poured down over the settlement. They overwhelmed the protections in place — electric fences — and literally ate their way into the buildings. Nothing had stopped them. Killing them in hordes had done nothing. They merely ate the bodies and kept moving in.

The evidence all pointed to a periodic change in the rodents' digestive systems that enabled them to eat *anything* with a cellulose or petrochemical base, up to and including plastic.

The report concluded with the Evaluation team's final words on the attitude of the current government of Largo Draconis, in a personal note that had been attached to the report.

"Fred: I am just glad we are getting *out* of here. We told the Settlement Governor about all this, and they're ignoring us. They think that just because I'm an archeologist, I have my nose so firmly in the past that I have no grasp on the present. They told me in the governor's office that their ward-off fields should be more than enough to hold off the rats. Not a chance. We're talking about a feeding-frenzy here, furry locusts, and I don't think they're going to give a ward-off field a second thought. I'm telling you, Fred, these people are going to be in trouble in a year. The Megalts threw in the towel, and they weren't anywhere near as backward as the governor thinks they were. *Maybe* this wonder ward-off field of his will keep the rats off, but I don't think so. And I don't want to find out that he was wrong by waking up under a blanket of rats. They didn't eat the Megalts — but they ate their *clothes*. I don't fancy piling into a shuttle with my derriere bared to the gentle breezes — which by that time should be, oh, around fifty kilometers per hour, and minus twenty Celsius. So I may even beat this report home. Keep the beer cold and the fireplace warm for me."

Well. If ever there was something that matched what Doctor Kenny had suggested, this was it.

Just to be certain, she checked several other sources — not for the veracity of the report, but to see just how prepared the colony was for the "rats" as well as the worsening weather.

Everything she found bore out what the unknown writer had told "Fred." Ward-off generators were standard issue, not heavy-duty. Warehouses had metal doors — and many had plastic or wooden siding. Homes were made of native stone and well-insulated against the cold, but had plastic or wooden doors. Food had been stockpiled, but what would the colonists do when the "rats" ate through the warehouse sides to get at the stockpiled rations? The colony had been depending on food grown on-planet for the past twenty years. There were no provisions for importing food and no synthesizers of any real size. They had protein farms — but what if the "rats" got into them and ate the yeast-stock along with everything else? What would they do when the stockpiled food was gone? Or if they managed to save the food, what would they do when — as Fred had suggested — the "rats" ate through their doors and made a meal off their clothing, their blankets, their furniture. . . .

So much for official records. Was there *anyone* on-planet that could pull these people out of their disaster?

It took a full day of searching business-directories before she had her answer. An on-planet manufacturer of specialized protection equipment, including heavy-duty ward-off and protection-field generators, could provide protection once the planetary governor admitted there was a problem. Governmental resources might not be able to pay for all the protection the colonists needed — but over eighty percent of the inhabitants carried hazard insurance, and the insurance companies should pay for protection for their clients.

That was half of the answer. The other half?

Another firm with multi-planet outlets, and a load of old-fashioned synthesizers in a warehouse within shipping distance. They didn't produce much in the way of variety, but load them up with raw materials, carbon from coal or oil, minerals, protein from yeast and fiber from other vat-grown products, and you had something basic to eat — or wear — or make into furnishings. . . .

She set her scheme in motion. But *not* through Beta, her supervisor, but through Lars and his.

Before Alex returned, she had made all the arrangements; and she had included carefully worded letters to the two companies she had chosen — plus all of the publicly available records. She tried to convey a warning without sounding like some kind of crazed hysteric.

Of course, the fact that she was investing in their firms should at least convey the idea that she was an hysteric with money. . . .

If they had any sense, they would be able to put the story together for themselves from the records, and they would believe her. Hopefully, they would be ready.

She transmitted the last of the messages, just as Alex arrived at her airlock.

"Permission to come aboard, ma'am," he called cheerfully, as she opened the lock for him. He ran up the stairs two at a time, and when he burst into the main cabin, she told herself that fashions would surely change, soon — he was dressed in a chrome yellow tunic with neon-red piping, and neon-red trousers with chrome-yellow piping. Both bright enough to hurt the eyes and dazzle the pickups, and she was grateful she could tune down the intensity of her visual receptors.

"How was your reunion?" she asked, once his clothes weren't blinding her.

"There weren't more than a half dozen of them," he told her, continuing through the hall and down to his own cabin. He pitched both his bags on his bed, and returned. "We just missed Chria by a hair. But we had a good time."

"I'm surprised you didn't come back with a hang-over."

He widened his eyes with surprise. "Not me! I'm the Academy designated driver — or at any rate, I make sure people get on the right shuttles. Never touch the stuff, myself, or almost never. Clogs the synapses."

Tia felt irrationally pleased to hear that.

"So, did you miss me? I missed you. Did you have enough to do?" He flung himself down in his chair and put his feet up on the console. "I hope you didn't spend all your time reading Institute papers."

"Oh," she replied lightly, "I found a few other things to occupy my time...."

The comlink was live, and Alex was on his very best behavior — including a fresh, and only marginally rumpled, uniform. He sat quietly in his chair, the very picture of a sober Academy graduate and responsible CS brawn.

Tia reflected that it was just as well she'd bullied him into that uniform. The transmission was shared by Professor Barton Glasov y Verona-Gras, head of the Institute, and a gray-haired, dark-tunicked man the professor identified as Central Systems Sector Administrator Joshua Elliot-Rosen y Sinor. Very high in administration. And just now, very concerned about something, although he hid his concern well. Alex had snapped to a kind of seated "attention" the moment his face appeared on the screen.

"Alexander, Hypatia — we're going to be sending you a long file of stills and holos," Professor Barton began. "But for now, the object you see here on my desk is representative of our problem."

The "object" in question was a perfectly lovely little vase. The style was distinctive; skewed, but with a very sensuous sinuousity, as if someone had fused Art Nouveau with Salvador Dali. It seemed — as nearly as

Tia could tell from the transmission — to be made of multiple layers of opalescent glass or ceramic.

It also had the patina that only something that has been buried for a very long time achieves.

Or something with a chemically faked patina. But would the professor himself have called them if all he was worried about were fake antiquities? Not likely.

The only problem with the vase — if it was a genuine artifact — was that it did not match the style of any known artifact in any of Tia's files.

"You know that smuggling and site-robbing has always been a big problem for us," Professor Barton continued. "It's very frustrating to come on a site and find it's already been looted. But this — this is doubly frustrating. Because, as I'm sure Hypatia has already realized, the style of this piece does not match that of any known civilization."

"A few weeks ago, hundreds of artifacts in this style flooded the black market," Sinor said smoothly. "Analysis showed them to be quite ancient — this piece for instance was made some time when Ramses the Second was Pharaoh."

The professor was not wringing his hands, but his distress was fairly obvious. "There are *hundreds* of these objects!" he blurted. "Everything from cups to votive offerings, from jewelry to statuary! We not only don't know where they've come from, but we don't even know anything *about* the people that made them!"

"Most of the objects are not as well-preserved as this one, of course," Sinor continued, sitting with that incredible stillness that only a professional politician or actor achieves. "But besides being incredibly valuable, and not incidentally, funneling money into the criminal subculture, there is something else rather distressing associated with these artifacts."

Tia knew what it *had* to be as soon as the words were out of the man's mouth. Plague.

"Plague," he said solemnly. "So far, this has not been a fatal disease, at least, not to the folk who bought these little trinkets. *They* have private physicians and in-house medicomps, obviously."

High Families, Tia surmised. *So the High Families are mixed up in this.*

"The objects really aren't dangerous, once they've been through proper decontam procedures," the professor added hastily. "But whoever is digging these things up isn't even bothering with a run under the UV gun. He's just cleaning them up —"

Tia winced inwardly, and *saw* Alex wince. To tell an archeologist that a smuggler had "cleaned up" an artifact, was like telling a coin collector that his nephew Joey had gotten out the wire brush and shined up his collection for him.

" — cleaning them up, putting them in cases, and selling them." Professor Barton sighed. "I have no idea why his helpers aren't coming down with this. Maybe they're immune. Whatever the reason, the receivers of these pieces *are,* they are not happy about it, and they want something done."

His expression told Tia more than his words did. The High Families who had bought artifacts they must have known were smuggled and possibly stolen, and some members of their circle, had gotten sick. And because the Institute was the official organization in charge of ancient relics, they expected the Institute to find the smuggler and deal with him.

Not that any of them would tell us how and where they found out about these treasures. Nor would they ever admit that they knew they were gray market, if not black. And if they'd stop buying smuggled artifacts, they wouldn't get sick.

But none of that meant anything when it came to the High Families, of course. They were too wealthy and too powerful to ever find themselves dealing with such simple concepts as *cause* and *effect.*

Hmm. Except once in a great while — like now — when it rises up and bites them.

"In spite of the threat of disease associated with these pieces, they are still in very high demand," Sinor said.

Because someone in the High Families spread the word that you'd better run the thing through decontamination after you buy it, so you can have your pretty without penalty. But there was something wrong with this story. Something that didn't quite fit. But she couldn't figure out what it was.

Meanwhile, the transmission continued. "But I don't have to tell either of you how dangerous it is to have these things out there," Professor Barton added. "It's fairly obvious that the smugglers are not taking even the barest of precautions with the artifacts. It becomes increasingly likely with every piece sold at a high price that someone will steal one, or find out where the source is, or take one to a disadvantaged area to sell it."

A slum, you mean, Professor. Was he putting too much emphasis on this?

Tia decided to show that both she and her brawn *were* paying attention. "I can see what could happen then, gentlemen," she countered. "Disease spreads very quickly in areas of that sort, and what might not be particularly dangerous for someone of means will *kill* the impoverished."

And then we have a full-scale epidemic and a panic on our hands. But he had to know how she felt about this. *He* knew who she was — there weren't too many "Hypatias" in the world, and he had been the immediate boss of Pota and Braddon's superior. He had to know the story. He was probably trading on it.

"Precisely, Hypatia," said Sinor, in an eerie "answer" to her own thoughts.

"I hope you aren't planning on using us as smuggler hunters," Alex replied, slowly. "I couldn't pass as High Family in a million years, so I couldn't be in on the purchasing end. And we aren't allowed to be armed — I know I don't want to take on the smuggling end without a locker full of artillery!"

In other words, gentlemen, "we ain't stupid, we ain't expendable, and we ain't goin'." But this was all sounding a little too pat, a little too contrived. If Sinor told them that they *weren't* expected to catch the smugglers themselves . . .

"No — " Sinor said soothingly — and a little too hastily. "No, we have some teams in the Enforcement Division going at both ends. *However,* it is entirely possible that the source for these artifacts is someone — or rather, several someones — working on Exploration or Evaluation teams. Since the artifacts showed up in this sector first, it is logical to assume that they originate here."

Too smooth. Too pat. This is *all a story. But why?*

"So you want us to keep our eyes peeled when we make our deliveries," Alex filled in.

"You two are uniquely suited," Professor Barton pointed out. "You both have backgrounds in archeology. Hypatia, you know how digs work, intimately. Once you know how to identify these artifacts, if you see even a hint of them — shards, perhaps, or broken bits of jewelry — you'll know what they are and where they came from."

"We can do that," Tia replied, carefully. "We can be a little snoopy, I think, without arousing any suspicions."

"Good. That was what we needed." Professor Barton sounded very relieved. "I suppose I don't need to add that there is a bonus in this for you."

"I can live with a bonus," Alex responded cheerfully.

The two VIPs signed off, and Alex turned immediately to Tia.

"Did that sound as phony to you as it did to me?" he demanded.

"Well, the objects they want are certainly real enough," she replied, playing back her internal recording of the conversation and analyzing every word. "But whether they really are artifacts is another question. There's definitely more going on than they're willing to tell us."

Alex leaned back in his chair and put his hands behind his head. "Are these things financing espionage or insurrection?" he hazarded. "Or buying weapons?"

She stopped her recording; there was something about the artifact that bothered her. She enhanced the picture and threw it up on the screen.

"What's wrong with this?" she demanded. Alex leaned forward to have a look.

"Is that a hole bored in the base?" he said. "Bored in, then patched over?"

"Could be." She enhanced her picture again. "Does it seem to you that the base is awfully thick?"

"Could be," he replied. "You know . . . we have only *their* word that these are 'alien artifacts.' What if they are nothing of the sort?"

"They wouldn't be worth much of anything then — unless — "

The answer came to her so quickly that it brought its own fireworks display with it. "Got it!" she exclaimed, and quickly accessed the Institute library for a certain old news program.

She remembered this one from her own childhood; both for the fact that it had been an ingenious way to smuggle and because Pota had caught her watching it, realized what the story was about, and shut it off. But not before Tia had gotten the gist of it.

One of the Institute archeologists had been subverted by a major drug-smuggler who wanted a way to get his supply to Central. In another case where there were small digs on the same planets as colonies, the archeologist had himself become addicted to the mood-altering drug called "Paradise," and had made himself open to blackmail.

The blackmail came from the supplier-producer himself. Out there in the fringe, it was easy enough to hide his smuggled supplies in ordinary shipments of agri-goods, but the nearer one got to civilization, the harder it became. Publicly available transport was out of the question.

But there were other shipments going straight to the heart of civilization. Shipments that were so innocent, and so fragile, they never saw a custom's inspector. Such as . . . Institute artifacts.

So the drug-dealer molded his product in the likeness of pottery shards. And the archeologist on-site made sure they got packed like any other artifacts and shipped — although they were never cataloged. Once the shipment arrived at the Institute, a worker inside the receiving area would set the crates with particular marks aside and leave them on the loading dock overnight. They would, of course, disappear, but since they had never been cataloged, they were never missed.

The only reason the archeologist in question had been caught was because an overzealous graduate student *had* cataloged the phony shards, and when they came up missing at the Institute, the police became involved.

Tia ran the news clip for Alex, who watched it attentively. "What do you think?" she asked, when it was over.

"I think our friend in the dull blue-striped tunic had a strangely fit look about him. The look that says 'police' to yours truly." Alex nodded. "I think you're right. I think someone is trying the artifact-switch again, except that this time they're coming in on the black market."

She did a quick access to the nets, and began searching for a politician named Sinor. She found one — but he did *not* match the man she had seen on the transmission.

"The trick is probably that if someone sees a crate full of smuggled glassware, they don't think of drugs." Tia felt very smug over her deduction, and her identification of Sinor as a ringer. Of course, there was no way of knowing if her guess was right or wrong, but still. . . . "The worst that is likely to happen to an artifact-smuggler is a fine and a slap on the wrist. They aren't taken very seriously, even though there's serious money in it and the smugglers may have killed to get them."

"That's assuming inspectors even find the artifacts. So where were *we* supposed to fit in to all this?" Alex ran his hand through his hair. "Do they think we're going to find this guy?"

"I think that they think he's working with one of the small-dig people again. By the way, you were right about Sinor. Or rather, the Sinor we saw is not the one of record." Another thought occurred to her. "You know — their story may very well have been genuine. There's not a lot of room in jewelry to hide drugs. Whoever is doing this may have *started* by smuggling out the artifacts, freelance — got tangled up with some crime syndicate, and now he's been forced to deal the fake, drug-carrying artifacts along with the real ones."

"Now *that* makes sense!" Alex exclaimed. "That fits all the parameters. Do we still play along?"

"Ye-es," she replied slowly. "But in a severely limited sense, I'd say. We aren't trained in law enforcement, and we don't carry weapons. If we see something, we report it, and get the heck out."

"Sounds good to me, lady," Alex replied, with patent relief. "I'm not a coward — but I'm not stupid. And I didn't sign up with the BB program to get ventilated by some low-down punk. If I wanted to do *that,* all I have to do is stroll into certain neighborhoods and flash some glitter. Tia — why all that nonsense about plague?"

"Partially to hook us in, I think," she said, after a moment. "They know we were the team that got the Zombie Bug — we'll feel strongly about plague. And partially to keep us from touching these objects. If we don't mess with them, we won't know about the drug link."

He made a sound of disgust. "You'd think they'd have trusted us with the real story. I'm half tempted to blow this whole thing off, just because they didn't. I won't — " he added hastily, "but I'm tempted."

He began warming up the boards, preparatory to taking off. Tia opened a channel to traffic control — but while she did so, she was silently wondering if there was even more to the story than *she* had guessed.

There was something bothering Alex, and as they continued on their rounds, he tried to put his finger on it. It was only *after* he replayed the recorded transmission of Professor Barton and the bogus "Sinor" that he realized what it was.

Tia had known that Professor Barton was genuine — without checking. And *Barton* had said things that indicated he knew who she was.

Alex had never really wondered about her background. He'd always assumed that she was just like every other shellperson he'd ever known; popped into her shell at birth, because of fatal birth-defects, with parents who rather would forget she had ever been born. Who were just as pleased that she was someone else's problem.

What was it that the professor had said, though? *You both have backgrounds in archeology. Hypatia, you know how digs work, intimately.*

From everything that Jon Chernov had said, the shellperson program was so learning-intensive that there *was* no time for hobbies. A shellperson only acquired hobbies after he got out in the real world and had leisure time for them. The Lab Schools' program was so intensive that even play was scheduled and games were choreographed, planned, and taught just like classes. There was no room to foster an "interest" in archeology. And it was not on the normal course curriculum.

The only way you knew how digs worked "intimately" was to work on them yourself.

Or be the child of archeologists who kept you on-site with them.

That was when it hit him; something Tia had said. *The Cades met while they were recovering from Henderson's Chorea.* That kind of information would not be the sort of thing someone who made a hobby of archeology would know. Details of archeologists' lives were of interest only to people who knew them.

Under cover of running a search on EsKay digs, he pulled up the information on the personnel — backtracking to the last EsKay dig the Cades had been on.

And there it was. C-121. Active personnel, Braddon Maartens-Cade, Pota Andropolous-Cade. Dependent, *Hypatia* Cade, age seven.

Hypatia Cade; evacuated to station-hospital *Pride of Albion* by MedService AI-drone. Victim of some unknown disease. Braddon and Pota put in isolation — Hypatia never heard from again. Perhaps she died — but that wasn't likely.

There could not be very many girls named "Hypatia" in the galaxy. The odds of two of them being evacuated to the same hospital-ship were tiny; the odds that *his* Tia's best friend, Doctor Kennet Uhua-Sorg — who was chief of Neurology and Neurosurgery — would have been the same doctor in charge of that other Tia's case were so minuscule he wasn't prepared to try to calculate them.

He replaced the file and logged off the boards feeling as if he had just been hit in the back of the head with a board.

Oh, spirits of space. When she took me as brawn, I made a toast to our partnership — "may it be as long and fruitful as the Cades'." Oh, decom it. I'm surprised she didn't bounce me out the airlock right then and there.

"Tia," he said carefully into the silent cabin. "I — uh — I'd like to apologize —"

"So, you found me out, did you?" To his surprise and profound relief, she sounded *amused.* "Yes, I'm Hypatia Cade. I'd thought about telling you, but then I was afraid you'd feel really badly about verbally falling over your own feet. You do realize that you can't access any data without my being aware of it, don't you?"

"Well, heck, and I thought I was being so sneaky." He managed a weak grin. "I thought I'd really been covering my tracks well enough that you wouldn't notice. I — uh — really am sorry if I made you feel badly."

"Oh, Alex, it would only have been tacky and tasteless — or stupid and insensitive — if you'd done it on purpose." She laughed; he'd come to like her laugh, it was a deep, rich one. He'd often told her BB jokes just so he could hear it. "So it's neither; it's just one of those things. I assume that you're curious now. What is it you want to know about me?"

"Everything!" he blurted, and then flushed with embarrassment. "Unless you'd rather not talk about it."

"Alex, I don't mind at all! I had a very *happy* childhood, and frankly, it will be a lot more comfortable being able to talk about Mum and Dad — or *with* Mum and Dad — without trying to hide them from you." She giggled this time, instead of laughing. "Sometimes I felt as if I was trying to hide a secret lover, only in reverse!"

"So you still stay in contact with your parents?" Alex was fascinated; this went against *everything* he'd been told about shellpersons, either at the academy or directly from Jon Chernov. Shellpersons didn't have families; their supervisors and their classmates were their families.

"Of course I still stay in contact with them. I'm their biggest fan. If archeologists can have fans." Her center screen came up; on it was a shot of Pota and Braddon, proudly displaying an ornate set of body-armor. "Here's something from their latest letter; they just uncovered the armory, and what they found is going to set the scholastic world on its collective ears. That's iron plates you see on Bronze Age armor."

"No — " He stared in fascination, and not just at the armor. At Pota and Braddon, smiling and waving like any other parents for their child. Pota pointed to something on the armor, while Braddon's mouth moved, explaining something. Tia had the sound off, and the definition wasn't good enough for Alex to lip-read.

"That's not *my* real interest though," she continued. "I was telling you the truth. I'm after the EsKay homeworld, but I want it because I want to *find* the bug that got me." The two side-screens came up, both with older pictures. "Before you ask, dear, there I am. The one on the right is my seventh birthday party, the one on the left, as you can see, is a picture of me with Theodore Bear and Moira's brawn Tomas — Ted was a present from both of them." She paused for a moment. "Just checking. Yes, that's the last good picture that was taken of me. The rest are all in the hospital, and I wouldn't inflict them on anyone but a neurologist."

Alex studied the two pictures, each of which showed the same bright-eyed, elfin child. An incredibly *pretty* child, dark-haired, blue-eyed, with a thin, delicate face and a smile that wouldn't stop. "How did you get into the shellperson program?" he asked. "I thought they didn't take anyone after the age of one!"

"They didn't, until me," she replied. "That was Doctor Kenny's doing, and Lars, the systems manager for the hospital; they were convinced that I was flexible enough to make the transition — since I was intelligent enough to *understand* what had happened to me, and what it meant. Which was — " she added, " — complete life-support. No mobility."

He shuddered. "I can see why you wouldn't want that to happen to anyone else ever again."

"Precisely." She blanked the screens before he had a chance to study the pictures further. "After I turned out so well, Lab Schools started considering older children on a case-by-case basis. They've taken three, so far, but none as old as me."

"Well, my lady — as remarkable as you are now, you must have been just as remarkable a child," he told her, meaning every word.

"Flatterer," she said, but she sounded pleased.

"I mean it," he insisted. "I interviewed with two other ships, you know. None of them had your personality. I was looking for someone like Jon Chernov; *they* were more like AI drones."

"You've mentioned Jon before — " she replied, puzzled. "Just what does *he* have to do with us?"

"Didn't I tell you?" he blurted — then hit himself in the forehead with his hand. "*Decom* it, I didn't! Jon's a shell-person too; he was the supervisor and systems manager on the research station where my parents worked!"

"Oh!" she exclaimed. "So *that's* why — "

"Why what?"

"Why you treat me like you do — facing my column, asking permission to come aboard, asking me what kind of music I want in the main cabin — "

"Oh, you bet!" he said with a grin. "Jon made darn sure I had good shell-soft manners before he let me go off to the Academy. He'd have verbally blistered my hide if I *ever* forgot you're here — and that you're the part of the team that can't go off to her own cabin to be alone."

"Tell me about him," she urged.

He had to think hard to remember the first time he ever started talking to Jon. "I think I first realized that he was around when I was about three, maybe two. My folks are chemtechs at one of the Lily-Baer research stations — there weren't a lot of kids around at the time, because it was a new station and most of the personnel were unattached. There weren't a lot of facilities for kids, and I guess what must have happened was that Jon volunteered to sort of babysit while my parents were at work. Wasn't that hard — basically all he had to do was make sure that the door to my room stayed locked except when he sent in servos to feed me and so forth. But I guess I kind of fascinated him, and he started talking to me, telling me stories — then directing the servos in playing with me." He laughed. "For a while my folks thought I was going through the 'invisible friend' stage. Then they got worried, because I didn't grow out of it, and were going to send me to a headshrinker. That was when Jon interrupted while they were trying to make the appointment and told them that *he* was the invisible friend."

Tia laughed. "You already knew that Moira and I have known each other for a long time — well, she was the CS ship that always serviced my folks' digs, that was how I got to know her."

"Gets you used to having a friend that you can't see, but can talk to," he agreed. "Well, once I started preschool, Jon lost interest for a while, until I started learning to play chess. He is *quite* a player himself; when he saw that I was beating the computer regularly, he remembered who I was and stepped in, right in the middle of a game. I *was* winning until he took over," he recalled, still a little aggrieved.

"What can I say?" she asked rhetorically.

"I suppose I shouldn't complain. He became my best friend. He was the one that encouraged my interest in archeology — and when it became obvious my parents weren't going to be able to afford all the university courses that would take, he helped get me into the Academy. Did you know that a recommendation from a shellperson counts twice as much as a recommendation from anyone but a PTA and up?"

"No, I didn't!" She sounded surprised and amused. "Evidently they trust our judgment."

"Well, you've heard his messages. He's probably as pleased with how things turned out as I am." He spread his hands wide. "And that's all there is to know about me."

"Hardly," she retorted dryly. "But it does clear up a few mysteries."

When Alex hit his bunk that night, he found he was having a hard time getting to sleep. He'd always thought of Tia as a person — but now he had a face to put with the name.

Jon Chernov had shown him, once, what Jon would have looked like if he could have survived outside the shell. Alex had known that it was going to be hideous, and had managed not to shudder or turn away, but it had taken a major effort of will. After that it had just been easier not to put a face with the voice. There were completely non-human races that looked more human than poor Jon.

But Tia had been a captivatingly pretty child. She would have grown up into a stunning adult. *Shoot, inside that shell, she probably is a stunning adult. A stunning, lifeless adult. Like a puppet with no strings; a sex-companion android with no hookups.* He had no desire to crack her column; he was not the sort to be attracted by anything lifeless. Feelie-porn had given him the creeps, and his one adolescent try with a sex-droid had sent him away feeling dirty and used.

But it made the tragedy of what had happened to her all the more poignant. Jon's defects were such that it was a relief for everyone that he was in the shell. Tia, though...

But she was happy. She was as happy as any of his classmates in the Academy. So where was the tragedy? Only in his mind.

Only in his mind. . . .

• CHAPTER SIX

Alex would have been perfectly happy if the past twelve hours had never happened.

He and Tia returned to Diogenes Base after an uneventful trip expecting to be sent out on another series of message-runs, only to learn that on *this* run, they would be carrying passengers. Those passengers were on the way from Central and the Institute by way of commercial liner and would not arrive for another couple of days.

That had given him a window of opportunity for a little shore leave, in a base-town that catered to some fairly heavy space-going traffic, and he had taken it.

Now he was sorry he had . . . oh, not for any serious reasons. He hadn't gotten drunk, or mugged, or into trouble. No, he'd only made a fool out of himself.

Only.

He'd gone out looking for company in the spaceport section, hanging around in the pubs and food-bars. He'd gotten more than one invitation, too, but the one he had followed up on was from a dark-haired, blue-eyed, elfin little creature with an infectious laugh and a nonstop smile. "Bet" was her name, and she was a fourth-generation spacer, following in her family's footloose tradition.

He hadn't wondered what had prompted his choice — hadn't even wondered why he had so deviated from his normal "type" of brown-haired, brown-eyed and athletic. He and the girl — who it turned out was the crew chief of an AI-freighter — had a good time together. They hit a show, had some dinner — and by mutual agreement, wound up in the same hotel room.

He *still* hadn't thought about his choice of company; then came the moment of revelation.

When, in the midst of intimacy, he called her "Tia."

He could have died, right then and there. Fortunately the young lady was understanding; Bet just giggled, called him "Giorgi" back, and they went on from there. And when they parted, she kissed him, and told him that his "Tia" was a lucky wench, and to give her Bet's regards.

Thank the spirits of space he didn't have to tell her the truth. All she'd seen was the CS uniform and the spacer habits and speech patterns; he could have been anything. She certainly wasn't thinking "brawn" when she had picked him up, and he hadn't told her what he did for the Courier Service.

Instead of going straight back to the ship, he dawdled; visited a multi-virtual amusement park, and took five of the wildest adventures it offered. It took all five to wash the embarrassment of his slip out of his recent memory, to put it into perspective.

But nothing would erase the meaning of what he had done. And it was just his good fortune — and Tia's — that his partner hadn't known who Tia was. Brawns had undergone Counseling for a lot less. CS had a nasty reputation for dealing with slips like that one. They wouldn't risk one of their precious shellpersons in the hands of someone who might become so obsessed with her that he would try to get at the physical body.

He returned to the docks in a decidedly mixed state of mind, and with no ideas at all about what — if anything — he could do about it.

Tia greeted her brawn cheerfully as soon as he came aboard, but she left him alone for a little while he got himself organized — or as organized as Alex ever got.

"I've got the passenger roster," she said, once he'd stowed his gear. "Want to see them, see what we're getting for the next couple of weeks?"

"Sure," Alex replied, perking up visibly. He had looked tired when he came in; Tia reckoned shrewdly that he had been celebrating his shore leave a little too heavily. He wasn't suffering from a hangover, but it looked to her as if he'd done his two-day pass to the max, squeezing twenty-two hours of fun into every twenty-four hour period. He dropped down into his chair and she brought up her screens for him.

"Here's our team leader, Doctor Izak Hollister-Aspen." The Evaluation team leader was an elderly man; a quad-doc, as thin as a grass stem, clean-shaven, silver-haired, and so frail-looking Tia was half-afraid he might break in the first high wind. "He's got four doctorates, he's published twelve books and about two hundred papers, and he's been head of twenty-odd teams already. He also seems to have a pretty good sense of humor. Listen."

She let the file-fragment run. "I must admit," Aspen said, in a cracked and quavery voice, "there are any number of my colleagues who would say that I should sit behind my desk and let younger bodies take over this dig. Well," he continued, cracking a smile. "I am going to do something like that. I'm going to sit behind my desk in my dome, and let the younger bodies of my team members take over the digging. Seems to me that's close enough to count."

Alex chuckled. "I like him already. I was afraid this trip was going to be a bore."

"Not likely, with him around. Well, this is our second-in-command, double-doc Siegfried Haakon-Fritz. And if this lad had been in charge, I think it might have been a truly dismal trip." She brought up the image of Fritz, who was a square-jawed, steely-eyed, stern-faced monument. He could have been used as the model for any ortho-Communist memorial statue to The Glorious Worker In Service To The State. Or maybe the Self-Righteous In Search Of A Convert. There was nothing like humor anywhere in the man's expression. It looked to her as if his head might crack in half if he ever smiled. "This is all I have, five minutes of silent watching. He didn't say a word. But maybe he doesn't believe in talking when it's being recorded."

"Why not?" Alex asked curiously. "Is he paranoid about being recorded or something?"

"He's a Practical Darwinist," she told him.

"Oh, *brother,*" Alex replied with disgust. The Practical Darwinists had their own sort of notoriety, and Tia was frankly surprised to find one in the Institute at all. They were generally concentrated in the soft sciences — when they were in the sciences at all. Personally, Tia did not consider political science to be particularly scientific. . . .

"His political background is kind of dubious," she continued, "but since there's nothing anyone can hang on him, it simply says in the file that his politics have not always been those of the Institute. That's bureaucratic double-talk for someone they would rather not trust, but have no reason to keep them out of positions of authority."

"Got you." Alec nodded. "So, we'll just not mention politics around him, and we'll make sure it's one of the forbidden subjects in the main cabin. Who's next?"

"These are our post-docs; they have their hard science doctorates, and now they're working on their archeology doctorates." She split her center screen and installed them both on it at once. "On the right, Les Dimand-Taylor, human; on the right, Treel rish-Yr nal-Leert, Rayanthan. Treel is female. Les has a Bio Doc, and Treel Xenology."

"Hmm, for Treel wouldn't Xenology be the study of *humans*?" Alex pointed out. Les was a very intense fellow, thin, heavily tanned, very fit-looking, but with haunted eyes. Treel's base-type seemed to be cold-weather mammalian, as she had a pelt of very fine, dense brown fur that extended down onto her cheek-bones. Her round, black eyes stared directly into the lens, seeing everything, and giving the viewer the impression that she was cataloging it all.

"No audio on the post-docs, just static file pictures," she continued. "They're attached to Aspen."

"Not to Old Stone Face?" Alex asked. "Never mind. Any grad student or post-doc he'd have would be a clonal copy of himself. I can't imagine any other type staying with him for long."

"And here are our grad students." Again she split the screen. "Still working on the first doctorate. Both male. Aldon Reese-Tambuto, human; and Fred, from Dushayne."

"*Fred?*" Alex spluttered. Understandably. The Dushaynese could not possibly have looked *less* human; he had a square, flat head — literally. Flat on top, flat face, flattened sides. He was bright green and had no mouth, just a tiny hole below his nostril slits. Dushaynese were vegetarian to an extreme; on their homeworld they lived on tree sap and fruit juice. Out in the larger galaxy they did very well on sucrose-water and other liquids. They had, as a whole, very good senses of humor.

"*Fred?*" Alex repeated.

"Fred," she said firmly. "Very few humans would be able to reproduce his real name. His vocal organ is a vibrating membrane in the top of his head. He does human speech just fine, but we can't manage his." She blanked her screens. "I'll spare you their speeches; they are very eager, very typical young grad students and this will be their first dig."

"Save me — " Alex moaned.

"Be nice," she said firmly. "Don't disillusion them. Let the next two years take care of that."

He waved his hands vigorously. "Far be it from me to let them know what gruesome fate awaits them. What was the chance of death on a dig? Twenty percent? And there's six of them?"

"The chance of catching something non-fatal is a lot higher," she pointed out. "Actually, the honor of being the fatality usually goes to the post-docs or the second-in-command; they're the ones doing the major explorations when a dig hits something like a tomb. The grad students usually are put to sifting sand and cataloging pottery shards."

Alex didn't get a chance to respond to that, for the first members of the team arrived at the lock at that moment, and he went down the lift to welcome them aboard, while Tia directed the servos in storing most of their baggage in the one remaining empty hold. As they came up the lift, both the young "men" were chattering away at high speed, with Alex in the middle, nodding sagely from time to time and clearly not catching more than half of what they said. Tia decided to rescue him.

"Welcome aboard, Fred, Aldon," she said, cutting through the chatter with her own, higher-pitched voice.

Silence, as both the grad students looked around for the speaker.

Fred caught on first, and while his face remained completely without expression, he had already learned the knack of displaying human-type emotions with his voice. "My word!" he exclaimed with delight, "you are a brainship, are you not, dear lady?"

As a final incongruity, he had adopted a clipped British accent to go along with his voice.

"Precisely, sir," she replied. "AH One-Oh-Three-Three at your service, so to speak."

"Wow," Aldon responded, clearly awestruck. "We get to ride in a brainship? They've actually put us on a brainship? Wow, PTAs don't even get rides from brain-ships! I've never even seen a brainship before — Uh, hi, what's your real name?" He turned slowly, trying to figure out which way to face.

"Hypatia, Tia for short," she replied, tickled by the young beings' responses. "Don't worry about where to look, just assume I'm the whole ship. I am, you know. I even have eyes in your quarters — " she chuckled at Aldon's flush of embarrassment " — but don't worry, I won't use them. Your complete privacy is important to us."

"I can show you the cabins, and you can pick the ones you want," Alex offered. "They're all the same; I'm just reserving the one nearest the main cabin for Doctor Hollister-Aspen."

"Stellar!" Aldon enthused. "Wow, this is better than the liner coming in! I had to share a cabin with Fred and two other guys."

"Quite correct," Fred seconded. "I enjoyed Aldon's company, but the other two were — dare I say — spoiled young reprobates? High Family affectations without the style, the connections, or the Family. Deadly bores, I assure you, and a spot of privacy will be welcome. Shall we, then?"

The two grad students were unpacking their carry-on baggage when the two post-docs arrived, this time singly. Treel arrived first, accepted the greetings with the calm, intense demeanor of a Zen Master, and took the first cabin she was offered.

Les Dimand-Taylor was another case altogether. It was obvious to Tia the moment he came aboard — *without* the automatic salute he made to her column — that he was ex-military. He confirmed her assumption as soon as Alex offered him a cabin.

"Anything will do, old man," he said, with a kind of nervous cheer. "Better than barracks, that's for sure. Unless — lady Tia, you don't have anything that makes an unexpected noise in the middle of the night, do you? I'm afraid—" he laughed a little shakily "—I'm afraid I'm just a little twitchy about noises when I'm asleep. What they euphemistically call 'unfortunate experiences.' I'll keep my door locked so I don't disturb anyone but—"

"Give him the cabin next to Treel, Alex," she said firmly. "Doctor Dimand-Taylor—"

"Les, my dear," he replied, with a thin smile. "Les to you and your colleagues, always. Pulled me out of a tight spot, one of you BB teams did. Besides, when people hear my title they tend to start telling me about their backs and innards. Hate to have to tell them that I'd only care about their backs if the too, too solid flesh had been melted off the bones for the past thousand years or so."

"Les, then," she said. "I assume you know Treel?"

"Very well. A kind and considerate lady. If you have her assigned as my neighbor, she's so quiet I never know she's there." He seemed relieved that Tia didn't press him for details on the "tight spot" he'd been in.

"That cabin and hers are buried in the sound-proofing around the holds," Tia told him. "You shouldn't hear anything — and I can generate white-noise for you at night, if you'd like."

He relaxed visibly. "That would be charming of you, thanks awfully. My superior, Doc Aspen, told the others about my little eccentricities, so they know not to startle me. So we should be fine."

He went about his unpacking, and Alex returned to the main cabin.

"Commando," Tia said succinctly.

"That in his records?" Alex asked. "I'm surprised they left that there. Not saying where, though, are they?"

"If you know where to look and what to look at, the fact that he was a commando *is* in his records," she told her brawn. "But where — that's not in the Institute file. It's probably logged somewhere. Remember not to walk quietly, my dear."

"Since I'd rather not get karate-chopped across the

throat, that sounds like a good idea." He thought for a moment and went off to his cabin, returning with what looked like a bracelet with a bell on it. "These things went into fashion a couple of months ago, and I bought one, but I didn't like it." He bent over to fasten it around his boot. "There. Now he'll hear me coming, in case I forget to stamp." The bell was not a loud one, but it was definitely producing an audible sound.

"Good idea — ah, here's the Man himself — Alex, he's going to need some help."

Alex hurried down to the lift area and gave Doctor Aspen a hand with his luggage. There wasn't much of it, but Doctor Aspen was not capable of carrying much for long. Tia wondered what could have possessed the Institute to permit this man to go out into the field again.

She found out, once he was aboard. His staff immediately clustered around him, fired with enthusiasm, as soon as he was settled in his cabin. He asked permission of Tia and Alex to move the convocation into the main cabin and use one of her screens.

"Certainly," Tia answered, when Alex deferred to her. She was quite charmed by Doctor Aspen, who called her "my lady," and accorded to her all the attention and politeness he gave his students and underlings.

As they moved into main room, Doctor Aspen turned toward her column. "I am told that you have some interest and education in archeology, my lady Tia," he said, as he settled into a seat near one of the side screens. "And you, too, Alex. Please, since you'll be on-site with us, feel free to participate. And if you know something we should, or notice something we miss, feel free to contribute."

Alex was obviously surprised; Tia wasn't. She had gleaned some of this from the records. Aspen's students stayed with him, went to enormous lengths to go on-site with him, went on to careers of their own full of warm praise for their mentor. Aspen was evidently that rarest of birds: the exceptional, inspirational teacher who was also a solid researcher and scientist.

Within moments, Aspen had drawn them all into his charmed circle, calling up the first team's records, drawing his students — and even Alex — into making observations. Tia kept a sharp eye out for the missing member of the party, however, for she had the feeling that Haakon-Fritz had deliberately timed his entrance to coincide with the gathering of Aspen's students. Tia figured that he wanted an excuse to feel slighted. She wasn't going to give it to him.

She could — and did — hook herself into the spaceport surveillance system, and she spotted Haakon-Fritz coming long before he was in range of her own sensors. Plenty of time to interrupt the animated discussion with a subtle, "Gentlebeings, Doctor Haakon-Fritz is crossing the tarmac."

Treel and Les exchanged a wordless look, but said nothing. Aspen simply smiled, and rose from his chair, as Tia froze the recording they had been watching. Alex hurried down the stairs to intercept Haakon-Fritz at the lift.

So instead of being greeted by the backs of those deep in discussion, the man found himself greeted by the Courier Service brawn, met at the top of the lift by the rest of his party, and given an especially hearty greeting by his superior.

His expression did not change so much as a hair, but Tia had the distinct feeling that he was disgruntled. "Welcome aboard, Doctor Haakon-Fritz," Tia said, as he shook hands briefly with the other members of his party. "We have a choice of five cabins for you, if you'd care — "

"If you have more than one cabin available," Haakon-Fritz interrupted rudely, speaking not to Tia, who he ignored, but to Alex, "I would like to see them all before I make a choice."

Tia knew Alex well enough by now to know that he was angry, but he covered it beautifully. "Certainly, Professor," he said, giving Haakon-Fritz the lesser of his titles. "If you'll follow me —"

He led the way back into the cabin section, leaving Haakon-Fritz to carry his own bags.

Treel made a little growl that sounded like disgust; Fred rolled his eyes, which was the closest he could come to a facial expression. "My word," Fred said, his voice ripe with surprise. *"That* was certainly rude!"

"He ees a Practical Darweeneest," Treel replied, with a curl to her lip. "Your pardon, seer," she said to Aspen. "I know that you feel he ees a good scienteest, but I am glad he ees not the one in scharge."

Fred was still baffled. "Practical Darwinist?" he said. "Does someone want to explain to a baffled young veggie just what that might be and *why* he was so rude to lady Tia?"

Les took up the gauntlet with a sigh. "A Practical Darwinist is one who believes that Darwin's Law applies to *everything*. If someone is in an accident, they shouldn't be helped, if an earthquake levels a city, no aid should be sent, if a plague breaks out, only the currently healthy should be inoculated; the victims should be isolated and live or die as the case may be."

Fred's uneasy glance toward her column made Tia decide to spare Les the embarrassment of stating the obvious. "And as you have doubtless surmised, the fanatical Practical Darwinists find the existence of shellpersons to be *horribly* offensive. They won't even acknowledge that we exist, given the option."

Professor Aspen shook his head sadly. "A brilliant scientist, but tragically flawed by fanaticism," he said, as he took his seat again. "Which is why he has gotten as far as he will ever go. He had a chance — was given a solo Exploration dig — and refused to consider any evidence that did not support his own peculiar party-line. Now he is left to be the chief clerk of digs like ours." He looked soberly into the faces of his four students. "Let this be a lesson to you, gentlebeings. Never let fanatic devotion blind you to truth."

"Or, in other words," Tia put in blithely, "the problem with a fanatic is that their brains turn to tofu and they accept nothing as truth except what conforms to their ideas. What makes them dangerous is not that *they'll* die to prove their truth, but that they'll let *you* die — or take you with them — to prove it."

"Well put, my lady." Doctor Aspen turned his attention back to the screen. "Now since I know from past experience that Haakon-Fritz will spend the time until takeoff sulking in his cabin — shall we continue with our discussion?"

The Exploration team had left the site in good shape; equipment stowed, domes inflated but sealed, open trenches covered to protect them. The Evaluation team erected two new living domes and a second laboratory dome in short order, and settled down to their work.

Everything seemed to be under control; now that the team was on-site, even the sulky Haakon-Fritz fell to and took on his share of the duties. There would seem to have been no need for AH One-Oh-Three-Three to remain on-planet when they could have been making the rounds of "their" established digs.

But that was not what regulations called for, and both Tia and Alex knew why, even if the members of the team didn't. Regulations for a CS ship attached to Institute duty hid a carefully concealed second agenda, when the ship placed a new Exploration or Evaluation team.

Archeological teams were put together with great

care; not only because of the limited number of personnel, but because of their isolation. They were going to be in danger from any number of things — all of the hazards that Tia had listed to Alex on their first mission. There was no point in exposing them to danger from within.

So the prospective members of a given team were probed, tested, and Psyched to a fair-thee-well, both for individual stability and for interactive stability with the rest of the team. Still, mistakes could be made, and had been in the past. Sometimes those mistakes had led to a murder, or at least, an attempted murder.

When a psychological problem surfaced, it was usually right at the beginning of the stint, after the initial settling in period was over, and once a routine had been established and the stresses of the dig started to take their toll. About that time, if something was going to go wrong, it did. The team had several weeks in cramped quarters in transit to establish interpersonal relations; ideal conditions for cabin fever. Ideal conditions for stress to surface, and that stress could lead to severe interpersonal problems.

So regulations were that the courier, whether BB or fully-manned, was to manufacture some excuse to stay for several days, with the ship personnel staying inside and out of sight, but with the site being fully monitored from inside the ship. The things they were to look for were obvious personality conflicts, new behavioral quirks, or old ones going from "quirk" to "psychosis." Making sure there was nothing that might give rise to a midnight axe murder. It would not have been the first time that someone snapped under stress.

Alex was most worried about Les, muttering things about post-trauma syndrome and the fragility of combat veterans. Tia had her own picks for trouble, *if* trouble came — either Fred or Aldon, for neither one of them had ever been on-site in a small dig before, and until he went to the Institute, Aldon had never even been off-planet. Despite his unpleasantness to *her*, Haakon-Fritz was brilliant and capable, and he had been on several digs before without any trouble surfacing. And now that they were all on-site, while he was distant, he was also completely cooperative, and his behavior in no way differed from his behavior on previous digs. There was no indication that he was likely to take his fanatic beliefs into his professional life. Fred and Aldon had only been part of a crew of hundreds with an Excavation team — where there were more people to interact with, fewer chances for personality stress, and no real trials to face but the day to day boredom of repetitive work.

For the first couple of days, everything seemed to be just fine, not only as far as the personnel were concerned, but as far as the conditions. Both Tia and Alex breathed a sigh of relief.

Too soon by half.

For that night, the winter rains began.

Tia had been sifting through some of the records she'd copied at the base, looking for another potential investment prospect like Largo Draconis. It was late; very late — the site was quiet and dark, and Alex had called it a night. He was in his cabin, just about at the dreaming stage, and Tia was considering shutting down for her mandated three hours of DeepSleep — when the storm struck.

"Struck" was the operative word, for a wall of wind and rain hit her skin hard enough to rattle her for a moment, and that was followed by a blast of lightning and thunder that shook Alex out of bed.

"What?" he yelped, coming up out of sleep with a shout. "How? Who?"

He shook his head to clear it, as another peal of thunder made Tia's walls vibrate. "What's going on?"

he asked, as Tia sank landing-spikes from her feet into the ground beneath her, to stabilize her position. "Are we under attack or something?"

"No, it's a storm, Alex," she replied absently, making certain that everything was locked down and all her servos were inside. "One incredible thunderstorm. I've never experienced anything like it!"

She turned on her external cameras and fed them to her screens so he could watch, while she made certain that *she* was well-insulated against lightning strikes and that all was still well at the site. Alex wandered out into the main cabin and sat in his chair, awestruck by the display of raw power going on around them.

Multiple lightning strikes were going on all around them; not only was the area as bright as day, it was often brighter. Thunder boomed continuously, the wind howled, and sheets — no, entire linen-closets — of rain pounded the ground, not only baffling any attempt at a visual scan of the site, but destroying any hope of any other kind of check. With this much lightning in the air, there was no point even in trying a radio call.

"What's happening down at the site?" Alex asked anxiously.

"No way of telling," she said reluctantly. "The Exploration team went through these rains once already, so I guess we can assume that the site itself isn't going to wash away, or float away. For the rest — the domes are insulated against lightning, but who knows what's likely to happen to the equipment? Especially in all this lightning."

Her words proved only too prophetic; for although the rain lasted less than an hour, the deluge marked a forty-degree drop in temperature, and the effects of the lightning were permanent.

When the storm cleared, the news from the site was bad. Lightning had not only struck the ward-off field generator, it had slagged it. There was nothing left but a half-melted pile of plasteel and duraloy. Tia didn't see how one strike could have done that much damage; the generator must have been hit over and over. The backup was corroded beyond any repair, though Haakon-Fritz and Les labored over it for most of the night. Too many parts had been ruined — probably while it sat in its crate through who-knew-how-many transfers. Never once uncrated and checked — and now Doctor Aspen's team paid the price for that neglect.

Tia consulted with Doctor Aspen in person the next morning. There was little sign of the damage from where they sat, but the results were undeniable. No ward-off generator. No protection from native fauna, from insectoids to the big canids. And if the huge grazers, the size of moose, were to become aggressive, there would be no way to keep them out of the camp. Ordinary fences would not hold against a herd of determined grazers; the last team had proved that.

"I don't have a spare in the holds," Tia told the team leader. "I don't have even half the parts you need for the corroded generator. There were no storms like the one last night mentioned in the records of the previous team, but we should assume there are going to be more. How many of them can you handle? Winter is coming on, and I can't predict what the native animals are going to do. Do you want to pull the team out?"

Doctor Aspen pursed his lips thoughtfully. "I can't think of any reason why we should, my lady," he replied. "The only exterior equipment that had no protection was the ward-off generator. The first team stayed here without incident all winter — there's nothing large enough to be a real threat to us, so far as I can tell. We'll have a few insects, perhaps, until first hard frost — I imagine those jackal-like beasts will lurk about and make a nuisance of themselves. But they're hardly a threat."

Alex, feet up on the console as usual, agreed with the

archeologist. "I don't see any big threat here, either. Unless lightning takes out something a lot more vital."

Tia didn't like it, but she didn't challenge them, either. "If that's the way you want it," she agreed. "But we'll stay until the rains are over, just in case."

Stay they did; but that was the first and the last of the major storms. After the single, spectacular downpour, the rains came gently, between midnight and dawn, with hardly a peal of thunder to wake Alex. She had to conclude that the first storm had been a freak occurrence, something no one could have predicted, and lost a little of her ire over the lack of warning from the previous team.

But that still didn't excuse the corroded generator.

Still, the weather stayed cold, and the rain left coatings of ice on everything. It would be gone by midmorning, but the difficulty in walking around the site meant that the team changed their working hours — beginning around ten-hundred and finishing about twenty-two-hundred. Despite his recorded disclaimer, Doctor Aspen insisted on working alongside his students, and no one, not even Haakon-Fritz, wanted him to risk a fall on the ice.

Meanwhile, Tia made note of a disturbing development. The sudden cold had sent most of the small game and pest animals into hiding or hibernation. That left the normally solitary jackal-dogs without their usual prey, and in what appeared to be seasonal behavior, they began to pack up for the winter, so that they could take down the larger grazers.

The disturbing part was that a very large pack began lurking around the camp.

Now Tia regretted her choice of landing areas. The site was between her and the camp; that was all very well, especially for observing the team at work, but the dogs were lurking in the hills around the *camp*. And with no ward-off generator to keep them out of it —

She mentioned her worry to Alex, who pointed out

that the beasts always scattered at any sign of aggression on the part of a human. She mentioned it again to Doctor Aspen, who said the animals were probably just looking for something to scavenge and would leave the camp alone once they realized there was nothing to eat there.

She never had a chance to mention it again.

With two moons, both in different phases, the nights were never dark unless it was raining. But the floodlights at the site made certain that the darkness was driven away. And lately, the nights were never silent either; the pack of jackal-dogs wailed from the moment the sun went down to the moment the rains began. Tia quickly became an expert on what those howls meant; the yipping social-howl, the long, drawn-out rally-cry, and most ominous, the deep-chested hunting call. She was able to tell, just by the sounds, where they were, whether they were in pursuit, and when the quarry had won the chase, or lost it.

Tia wasn't too happy about them; the pack numbered about sixty now, and they weren't looking too prosperous. Evidently the activity at the site had driven away the larger grazers they normally preyed on; that had the effect of making all the smaller packs join up into one mega-pack — so there was always some food, but none of them got very much of it. They weren't at the bony stage yet, but there was a certain desperate gauntness about them. The grazers they did chase were escaping five times out of six — and they weren't getting in more than two hunts in a night.

Should I suggest that the team feed them? Perhaps take a grav-sled and go shoot something and drag it in once every couple of days? But would that cause problems later? That would be giving the pack the habit of dependence on humans, and that wouldn't be good. Could they lure the pack into another territory that way, though? Or — would feeding them make them lose their fear of

humans? She couldn't quite make up her mind about
that, but the few glimpses she'd had of the pack before
sunset had put her in mind of certain Russian folk-
tales — troikas in the snow, horses foaming with panic,
and wolves snapping at the runners. Meanwhile, the
pack got a little closer each night before they faded into
the darkness.

At least it was just about time for the team to break off for
the night. Once they were in their domes, they'd be safe.

As if in answer to her thought, the huge lights
pivoted up and away from the site, as they were
programmed to do, lighting a clear path for the team
from the site to the camp. When everyone was safely in
the domes, Les would turn them off remotely. So far,
the lights alone had kept the jackal-dogs at bay. They
lurked just outside the path carved by the lights, but
would not venture inside.

As if to answer that thought, the pack howled just as
the first of the team members emerged from the
covered excavation area. It sounded awfully close —

Tia ran a quick infrared scan.

The pack *was* awfully close — right on the top of the
hill to the right of the site!

The beasts stared down at the team — and the leader
howled again. There was *no* mistaking that howl, not
when all the rest answered it. It was the hunt-call.
Quarry sighted; time to begin the chase.

And the leader was staring right at the archeologists.
The team stared back, sensing that there was something different tonight. No one stirred; not
archeologists, nor jackal-dogs. The beasts' eyes glared
red in the darkness, reflection from the work lights, but
no less disturbing for having a known scientific
explanation.

"Alex," she said tightly. "Front and center. We have a
situation."

He emerged from his cabin as if shot from a gun,

took one look at the screen, and pelted for the hold where they kept the HA grav-sled.

Then the pack poured down the hillside in a furry avalanche.

Haakon-Fritz took off like a world-class sprinter, leaving the rest behind. For all the attention that he paid them, the rest of his team might just as well have not existed.

Shellcrack! Aspen can't run —

But Les and Treel were not about to leave Aspen to become the à la carte special; as if they had rehearsed the move, they each grabbed one arm and literally picked him up off his feet between them and started running. Fred and Aldon grabbed shovels to act as some kind of flank-guard. With the jackal-dogs closing on them with every passing moment, the entire group pelted off for the shelters.

They were barely a quarter of the way there, with the jackals halfway down the hill and gaining momentum, when Haakon-Fritz reached the nearest shelter. He hit the side of the dome with a crash and pawed the door open. He flung himself inside —

And slammed it shut; the red light coming on over the frame indicating that he had locked it.

"Alex!" Tia cried in anguish, as the jackal-dogs bore down upon their prey. "Alex, *do* something!" She had never felt so horribly helpless.

Grav-sleds made no noise — but they had hedra-players and powerful speakers, meant both to entertain their drivers and to broadcast prerecorded messages on the fly. A blast of raucous hard-wire shatter-rock blared out from beneath her — she got her underbelly cameras on just as Alex peeled out in the sled at top speed, music screaming at top volume.

The unfamiliar shrieks and howls behind them startled the pack for a moment, and they hesitated, then came to a dead halt, peering over their shoulders.

The rock music was so unlike anything they had ever heard before that they didn't know how to react; Alex plowed straight through the middle of them and they shied away to either side.

He was never going to be able to make a pickup on the five still running for their lives without the pack being on all of them — but while he was on the move with music caterwauling, the jackal-dogs hesitated to attack him. And while he was harassing them, their attention was on him, not on their quarry.

That must have been what he had figured in the first place — that he would startle them enough to give the rest of the team a chance to get to safety inside that second dome. While the archeologists ignored what was going on behind them and kept right on to the second shelter, Alex kept making dives at the pack — scattering them when he could, keeping the sled between them and the team. It was tricky flying — stunt-flying with a grav-sled, pulling crazy maneuvers less than a meter from the ground. Not a lot of margin for error.

He cornered wildly; rocking the sled up on one side, skewing it over in flat spins, feinting at the pack leader and gunning away before the beast had a chance to jump into the sled. Over the sound of the wild music, the warning signals and overrides screamed objection for what Alex was doing. Alex challenged the jackal-dogs with the only weapon he had; the sled. Tia longed for her ethological pack; still not approved for the Institute ships. With a stun-needler, they could have at least knocked some of the pack out.

The animals assumed that the attack was meant to drive them off or kill them. They must have been hungrier than any of them had guessed, for when nothing happened to hurt or kill any of the pack, they began making attempts to mob the sled, and they seemed to be trying to think of ways to pull it down.

Tia knew why, then, in a flash of insight. Alex had just gone from "fellow predator" to "prey"; the jackal-dogs were used to grazer-bulls charging them aggressively to try to drive them away. Alex was imitating the behavior of the bulls, though he did not know it — and in better times, the pack probably *would* have responded by moving to easier prey. But these were lean times, and any imitation of prey-behavior meant they would try to catch and kill what was taunting them.

Alex was now in real danger.

But Alex was a better flyer than Tia had ever thought; he kept the sled just out of reach of a strong jump, kept it moving in unpredictable turns and spins.

Then, one of the biggest beasts in the pack leapt — and landed, feet scrabbling on the back bumper of the sled.

"Alex!" Tia shrieked again. He glanced back over his shoulder and saw his danger.

He sent the sled into a spin; the sled's protection overrides objected strenuously, whining as they fought him. The jackal-dog fought, too, hind-claws skidding against the duraloy of the bumper. Alex watched desperately over his shoulder as the beast's claws found a hold, and it began hauling itself over the bumper toward him.

In what was either a burst of inspiration or insanity, he jammed on the braking motors. The sled stopped dead in mid-spin, flinging him sideways against his safety-belts —

And flinging the jackal-dog off the back of the sled entirely, sending it flying into the pack, and tumbling at least a dozen of them nose-over-tail.

At that moment the team reached the second dome.

The flash of light as they opened the door told Alex they were safe, and he no longer had to make a target of himself. Alex burned air back towards Tia; she dropped open a cargo-bay, activated restraint-fields and hoped he'd be able to brake in time to keep from hitting the back wall. At the speed he was coming — the restraint-fields, meant to keep the sled from banging around too much in rough flight, wouldn't do much.

He didn't even slow down as he hit the bay door, which she slammed down behind him. Instead, he killed the power and skidded to a halt on the sled's belly in a shower of sparks. The sled skewed sideways and crashed into the back wall — but between Alex's own maneuver and the restraint-fields, the impact wasn't bad enough to do more than dent her hold-wall. Once again, Alex was hurled sideways against his seat-belts. There were a half-dozen impacts on the cargo door, indicating the leaders of the pack hitting it, unable to stop.

He sat there for a moment, then sagged over the steering wheel, breathing heavily. Nothing on Tia's pickups made her think he was hurt, so she waited for him to catch his breath.

When his breathing slowed, and he looked up, she focused on his face. He was flushed, but showed no shock, and no sign of pain.

"Well," she said, keeping her voice calm and light, "you certainly know how to make an entrance."

He blinked — then leaned back in his seat, and began laughing.

It was no laughing matter the next day, when Haakon-Fritz emerged from his shelter and was confronted by the remainder of his team. He had no choice; Tia had threatened to hole his dome if he didn't, giving the beasts a way inside. It was an empty threat, but he didn't know that; like any other fanatic Practical Darwinist, he had never bothered to learn the capabilities of brainships.

Les took charge of him before he had a chance to say anything; using some kind of commando-tactics to get a hold on the man that immobilized him, then frog-marching him into the ship.

By common consent, everyone else waited until Les and Tia had secured Haakon-Fritz in one of her cabins, with access to what was going on in the main cabin, but no way of interrupting the proceedings. Any time he started in on one of his speeches, she could cut him off, and he'd be preaching to the bare walls.

As the others gathered in the cabin, Doctor Aspen looking particularly shaken and worn, Tia prepared to give them the news. It wasn't completely bad . . . but they weren't going to like part of it.

"We aren't pulling you out," she said, "although we've got that authority. We understand your concern about leaving this dig and losing essentially two years, and we share it."

As she watched four of the five faces register their mix of relief and anticipation, she wished she could give them unmixed orders.

"That's the good news," Alex said, before anyone could respond. "Here's the bad news. In order to stay here, we're going to order you to stay in your domes until the next courier shows up with your new generator and parts for the old one. We ordered one for you when the old one slagged; the courier should arrive in about a month or two with the new one."

"But —" Doctor Aspen started to object.

"Doctor, it's that, or we pull you right this moment," Tia said firmly. "We *will not* leave you with those canids on the prowl unless you, each of you, pledge us that. You didn't see how those beasts attacked Alex in his sled. They have no fear of humans now, and they're hungry. They'll attack you without hesitation, and I wouldn't bet on them waiting until dark to do it."

"What's better?" Alex asked shrewdly. "Lose two months of work, or two years?"

With a sigh, Doctor Aspen gave his word, as did the

rest — although Fred and Aldon did so with visible relief.

"If they'd just supply us with damned guns . . . " Les muttered under his breath.

"There are sophonts on the other continent. I didn't make the rules, Les," Tia replied, and he flushed. "I didn't make them, but I *will* enforce them. And by the letter of those rules, I should be ordering you to pack right now."

"Speaking of packing — " Alex picked up the cue. "We need you to bundle Haakon-Fritz' things and stow them in the hold. He's coming back with us."

Now Les made no attempt to hide his pleasure, but Doctor Aspen looked troubled. "I don't see any reason — " he began.

"Sorry, Doctor, but we do," Alex interrupted. "Haakon-Fritz finally broke the rules. It's pretty obvious to both of us that he attempted to turn his politics into reality."

In his cabin, the subject of discussion got over his shock and began a shouted tirade. As she had threatened, Tia cut him off — but she kept the recorders going. At the moment, they couldn't *prove* what had been on the man's mind when he locked his colleagues out. With any luck, his own words might condemn him.

"Doctor, no matter what his motivations were, he abandoned us," Les said firmly. "One more fighter might have made a difference to the pack — and the fact remains that when he reached shelter, instead of doing anything helpful, he ran inside and *locked the door.* The former might only have been cowardice — but the latter is criminal."

"That's probably the way the Board of Inquiry will see it," Tia agreed. "We'll see to it that he has justice, but he can't be permitted to endanger anyone else's life this way again."

After a bit more argument, Doctor Aspen agreed.

The team left the shelter of the ship, gathered what they could from the dig, and returned to the domes. Well before sunset, Les and Fred returned with a grav-ed laden with Haakon-Fritz' belongings stowed in crates — and by the rattling they were making, the goods hadn't been stowed any too carefully.

Tia didn't intend to expend too much effort in stow-ng the crates either.

"You'll keep everyone in the domes for us, won't you?" Tia asked Les anxiously. "You're the one I'm really counting on. I don't trust Doctor Aspen's com-mon sense to hold his curiosity at bay for too long."

"You read him right there, dear lady," Les replied, tossing the last of the crates off the sled for the servo to pick up. "But the rest of us have already agreed. Treel was the most likely hold-out, but even she agrees with you on your reading of the way those jackal-dogs were acting."

"What will happen to the unfortunate Haakon-Fritz?" Fred asked curiously.

"That's going to depend on the board," she told him. "I've got a recording of him ranting in his cabin about survival and obsolescence, and pretty much spouting the extremist version of the Practical Darwinism party line. That isn't going to help him any, but how much of this admissible, I don't know."

"Probably none of it to a court," Les admitted after thought. "But the board won't like it."

"All of it's been sent on ahead," she told him. "He'll probably be met by police, even if, ultimately, there's nothing he can be charged with."

"At the very least, after this little debacle, he'll be dropped from the list of possible workers for anything less than a Class Three dig," Fred observed cheerfully. "They'll take away his seniority, if they have any sense, and demote him back to general worker. He'll spend the rest of his life with us undergrads, sorting pot-shards."

"Assuming he can *find* anyone who is willing to take a chance on him," Alex responded. "Which I would make no bets on."

He patted Tia's side. "Just be grateful you're not having to go back with us," he concluded. "If you thought the trip out was bad with Haakon-Fritz sulking, imagine what it's going to be like returning."

CHAPTER SEVEN

There was a message waiting for Tia when they returned to the main base at Central, with Doctor Haakon-Fritz still confined to quarters. A completely mysterious message. Just the words, "Call this number," a voice-line number for somewhere in the L-5 colonies, and an ID-code she recognized as being from Lars.

Now what was Lars up to?

Puzzled, she left the message in storage until Alex completed the complicated transfer of their not-quite-prisoner, and accompanied him and duplicate copies of the records involving him down to the surface. Only then, when she was alone, did she make the call.

"Friesner, Sherman, Stirling and Huff," said a secretary on the first ring. There was no delay, so Tia assumed that the office was somewhere in one of the half-dozen stations or L-5 colonies nearby. "Investment brokers."

"I was told to call this number," Tia said cautiously. "I — my name is Hypatia Cade — " She hesitated as she almost gave her ship-numbers instead of her name.

"Ah, Miz Cade, of course," the secretary said, sounding pleased. "We've been waiting for you to call. Let me explain the mystery; Friesner, Sherman, Stirling and Huff specialize in investments for shellpersons like yourself. A Mister Lars Mendoza at *Pride of Albion* opened an account for you here to manage the investments you had already made. If you'll hold, I'll see if one of the partners is free — "

Tia *hated* to be put on hold, but it wasn't for more than a microsecond. "Miz Cade," said a hearty-sounding male voice, "I'm Lee Stirling; I'm your broker if you want to keep me on, and I have good news for you. Your investments at Largo Draconis have done *very* well. Probably much better than you expected."

"I don't know about that," she replied, letting a little humor leak through. "My expectations were pretty high." There was something about that voice that sounded familiar, but she couldn't identify it. Was it an accent — or rather, lack of one?

"But did you expect to triple your total investment?" Lee Stirling countered. "Your little seed money grew into quite the mighty oak tree while you were gone!"

"Uh — " she said, taken so much by surprise that she didn't know what to say. "What do you mean by total investment?"

"Oh — your companies split their bonds two times while you were gone; you had the option of cash or bonds, and we judged you wanted the bonds, at least while the value was still increasing." Stirling was trying to sound matter-of-fact, but couldn't keep a trace of gloating out of his voice. "Those bonds are now worth three times what they were after the last split."

"Split?" she said faintly. "I — uh — really don't know what that means. I'm — new at this."

Patiently Stirling walked her through exactly what had happened to her investment. "Now the question you have in front of you is whether you want to sell out now, while the value of the bond is still increasing, or whether you want to wait."

"What's happening on Largo Draconis?" she asked. After all, *her* investment had been based on what was going to happen in the real world, not the strange and unpredictable universe of the stock market. And from the little she had seen, the universe of the stock market seemed to have very little to do with "real" reality.

"I thought you'd ask that. Your companies have pretty much saturated their market," Stirling told her. "The situation has stabilized — just short of disaster, thanks to them. The bond prices are going up, but a lot more slowly. I think they're going to flatten out fairly soon. I'd get out, if I were you."

"Do it," she said flatly. "I'd like you to put everything I earned into Moto-Prosthetics, preferred stock, with voting rights. Hold onto the seed money until I contact you."

"Taking care of it now — there. All logged in, Hypatia. I'm looking forward to seeing what you're going to invest in next." Stirling sounded quite satisfied. "I hope you'll stay with us. We're a new firm, but we're solid, we have a lot of experience, and we intend to service our clients with integrity. Miz Friesner was formerly a senior partner in Weisskopf, Dixon, Friesner and Jacobs, and the rest of us were her handpicked protégés. She's our token softie."

"Token — oh! You're all — "

"Shellpersons, right, all except Miz Friesner. Oh, we all worked on the stock, bond, and commodity exchanges, but as systems managers. We couldn't do any investments while we were systems managers, but Miz Friesner agreed to join us when we bought out our contracts." Stirling chuckled. "We've been planning this for a long time. Now we're relying on grapevine communications within the shell-net for those like us who want to invest, for whatever reasons — and would rather not go through either their Counselors, their Supervisors, or their Advocates." He sent her a complicated burst of emoticons conveying a combination of disgust, weariness, annoyance, and impatience. "We are adults, after all. We can think for ourselves. Just because we're rooted to one spot or one structure, it doesn't follow that all of us need keepers."

She sent back a burst that mirrored his — with the

addition of amusement. "Some of us do — but not anyone who's been out in the world for more than fifty years or so, *I* wouldn't think. Well, I'll tell a couple of friends of mine about you, that's for certain."

"Word of mouth, as I said." Stirling laughed. "I have to tell you, after that phenomenal start, we're all very interested in your next investment choice."

"I'll have it in a couple of days at most," she promised, and signed off.

Well, now it was certainly time to start digging for that second choice, and she couldn't hope to happen on it the way she had the last time.

This time, it was going to take a combination of stupidity on someone's part, and her own computational power. So she concentrated on sorting out those colonies that had been in existence for less than a hundred years. It was probably fair to assume that anything repetitive that *she* would be able to take advantage of would have to take place within that kind of cycle.

That narrowed the field quite a bit — but it meant that she was going to have to concentrate her search by catagories. Floods were the first things that came to mind, so she called up geological and climatological records on all of her candidates and ran a search for flood patterns.

Meanwhile she and Alex were also dealing with the authorities on the Haakon-Fritz case — which looked likely to put the Practical Darwinists out of business, at least with the general public — and the Institute in regards to resupply. Tia was determined not to leave port this time without that ethological tagging kit. *Alex* was tired of dealing with each crisis barehanded.

He demanded a supply of firearms — locked up until authorized if necessary, but he wanted to have *something* to enforce his decisions or to defend himself and others.

"What if Haakon-Fritz had gone berserk?" he asked. "What if those canids had been more aggressive?"

Courier Services was agreeable, but the Institute was fighting him; their long-time policy of absolute pacifism was in direct conflict with any such demand. The ban was clear; on any site where there were near-by sophonts with an Iron Age civilization or above — and "nearby" meant on the same continent — absolutely no arms were to be permitted in association with any Institute personnel, not even those under contract. And since the couriers hit at least one dig on every run that came under the ban, they were not allowed *any* weaponry at any time. Tia backed her brawn, and she was lobbying with CS and the Lab Schools to help. After all, *her* well-being was partially dependent on his. The Institute, on the other hand, was balking because there were those who would take the presence of even small arms on board the courier in the worst possible interpretation.

Tia could see their point — but Institute couriers were the only ones not carrying some kind of hand weaponry. They were likely at any time to run into smugglers, who absolutely *would* be armed. If CS made a ruling on the subject, there would be no way the Institute could get around it.

Meanwhile, on the subject of Haakon-Fritz, things were definitely heating up. The recordings of his Olympic sprint to shelter had somehow gotten leaked to the media — fortunately, long *after* Tia had locked down her copies — along with the following recording of Alex's heroic dash to the rescue via grav-sled. Alex was a minor celebrity for a day — but he successfully avoided the media, and they soon grew tired of his self-deprecating attitude, and his refusal to make himself photogenic. Haakon-Fritz did not avoid the media, he sought them out — and he became everyone's favorite villain. The Institute could not keep the incident quiet.

The Practical Darwinists came to their proponent's rescue, and only made things worse with their public
statements of support and their rhetoric. People did
not care to hear that they were weaklings, failures, and
ought to be done away with for the good of the race. It
began to look as if there was going to be a public trial,
no matter how hard the Institute tried to avoid one.

It was on the eve of that trial that Tia finally found
her next investment project.

In the Azteca system, the third planet — predictably
Terran — known as Quetzecoatl.

Interstellar Teleson, one of the major communications firms in their quadrant with cross-contracts and
reciprocal agreements across known space, had just
relocated their sector corporate headquarters on Quetzecoatl. The location had a great deal to be said for it —
central, in the middle of a stable continental plate, good
climate. That, however, was not why they had relocated
there.

It was one of those secretly negotiated High Family
contracts, and Tia had no doubt that there was a lot
more at stake than just the area. Someone owed someone else a favor — or else someone wanted something
else kept quiet, and this was the price.

She was doubly sure when the location came up red-
flagged on her geological search. According to the survey
records, that lovely, flat plain was a flood basin. Quetzecoatl did not have the kind of eccentric orbit that Largo
Draconis did — just a little tilt. One that didn't affect
anyone in the major settlements at all. But once every
hundred years, that tilt angled the north pole into the solar
plane for a bit longer than usual. The glaciers would start
to melt. The plain below wouldn't exactly "flood" — or at
least, not all at once. It would just get very, very soggy, slowly — then, when the spring rains came, the water would
rise over the course of a week or two. Eventually the entire
plain would be under about two inches of water, and

would remain that way for about three years, gradually drying again for the fourth as the glaciers in the north grew.

But Interstellar Teleson's Corporate Standards dictated that the most sensitive records and delicate instruments, and all their computer equipment, be installed permanently in sub-basements no less than four stories below surface level, to avoid any possibility of damage. Corporate Standards had been set to guard against human interference, not nature's. Corporate Standards evidently did not consider nature to be important.

Whoever was in charge of this project apparently completely disregarded the geological survey. Engineers complained about seepage and warned of flooding; the reaction was to order extra sump pumps. Sump pumps were keeping the sub-basements tolerably dry *now*, but Tia guessed that they were going constantly just to keep up with ordinary groundwater. They were not going to handle the flood.

Especially not when flood waters were seeping in through the ground floor walls and creeping over the doorsills.

According to the meteorological data, the glaciers were melting, and the spring rains were only a couple of months away.

Meanwhile, half a continent away, there was a disaster recovery firm that specialized in data and equipment recovery. They advertised that they could duplicate an existing system in a month, and recover data from devices that had been immersed in saltwater for over a year, or through major fires with extensive smoke damage. Interstellar Teleson was going to need them, and they didn't even know it. Besides, Tia liked the name. Whoever these people were, they had one heck of a sense of humor.

Chuckling to herself, Tia called Lee Stirling and

made her investment — then sent out another carefully worded letter to Crash and Burn Data Recovery,
Limited.

The public trial of Doctor Haakon-Fritz was a ten-
day circus — but by then, Tia and Alex had far more
serious things on their minds and no time to waste on
trivialities.

Tia's recordings — both at the site and in the main
cabin — were a matter of public record now, and that
was the only stake they had in the trial. The Institute
only wanted to keep from looking too foolish. In return
for the supply of small arms Alex demanded, they
asked that he not testify at the trial, since anything he
could say would only corroborate those records. They
both knew what the Institute people were thinking:
records were one thing, but a heroic participant, who
just *might* sound impassioned — no, that was something they didn't want to see. *He* was willing — he
reckoned it was a small price to pay. Besides, there was
little he could add, other than becoming another
source of media attention.

So while the media gathered, the quiet Institute
lawyers and spokesmen tried to downplay the entire
incident, Alex got his arms-locker, and Tia her
ethological kit as the price for their non-participation.
And as they prepared to head out on a new round of
duties, there came an urgent message.

The Institute contract was on hold; CS had another
use for them as the only BB ship on base.

And they suddenly found themselves, not only with
a new agenda — but an entirely new employer.

"Kenny, what *is* all this about?" Tia asked, when the
barrage of orders and follow-up orders concluded,
leaving them with a single destination, an empty flight
plan, and a "wait for briefing" message. So here they

were, docked with the *Pride of Albion,* and the briefing was coming from Doctor Kennet Uhua-Sorg.

"This," Doctor Kennet replied, grimly, sending the live-cam view of one of the isolation rooms.

Alex gasped. Tia didn't blame him.

The view that Doctor Kennet gave them of this, the *Pride of Albion*'s newest isolation patient, was blessedly brief. It had been a human at one point. Now it was a humanoid-shaped mass of suffering. Somewhere in the mass of open sores were eyes, a mouth, a face. Those had been hands, once — and feet.

Tia was the first to recover. "Who is that," she asked sharply, "and what happened to him?"

"Who — we don't know," Kenny replied, his face completely without expression. "He was from a tramp freighter that left him when he didn't get aboard by lift-off time. We don't know if they expected something like this, or if they were just worried because one of their bogus crew turned up missing, but they burned out of Yamahatchi Station with a speed that simply didn't match their rather shabby exterior. He was under false papers, of course — and there isn't enough of his fingers or retinas left to identify him. And unless he's ever been a murder or crime-of-violence suspect, his DNA patterns could take years to match with his birth-records."

Alex nodded. It wouldn't have been too difficult to deduce his ship; anyone logging into a station hostel or hotel had to list his ship-of-origin as well as filing his papers. That information was instantly cross-checked with the ship; the ship had to okay the crewman's ID before he would be allowed to check in. Passengers, of course, used an entirely separate set of hotels.

"That kind of speed probably means a pirate or a smuggler," Alex said.

"I don't think there's much doubt of that," Kenny replied. "Well, when his logged time at the cheap hostel he'd checked into ran out, they opened the door to his room — found *that* — and very wisely slammed the door and reported him."

"What about the hostel personnel?" Tia asked.

"We have them all in isolation, but so far, thank the deity of your choice, none of them are showing any signs of infection."

"For which favor, much thanks," Alex muttered.

"Just what is it that he's got?" Tia asked, keeping her voice even and level.

Kenny shrugged. "Another plague with no name. Symptoms are simple enough. Boils which become superrating sores that seem to heal only to break open again. A complex of viruses and bacteria, reinforced with modified immune deficiency syndrome. So far, no cure. Decontamination sterilized the hostel room completely, and we haven't seen anyone else come down with this thing. And, thank the spirits of space, once he checked into the hostel, door records show he never left his room."

"There is no reason for a pirate to come down with something like that," Tia pointed out, "but an artifact smuggler—"

"Precisely why I asked for you two," Kenny replied, "and precisely why the Institute loaned you to us. Oh, Alex, in case you wondered, I'm in this because, despite my specialty, I seem to have become the expert in diseases associated with archeology."

Alex cast an inquiring glance at her column. Tia knew what he was asking. Could this be the same disease their mysterious "Sinor" had told them about? Could it be that the man had given them a true story, though not his true name?

She printed her answer under Dr. Kenny's image. *It's a coincidence. Not the same as Sinor's phony plague — he would have been frantic if he truly had this to contend with.*

He signaled his question with his eyes. Why?

Immune deficiency. Contact or airborne. Think about it.

His eyes widened, and he nodded, slowly. The nightmare that had haunted the human world since the twentieth century; the specter of an immune deficiency disease communicated by an airborne or simple-contact vector. No one wanted to think about it, yet in the minds of anyone connected to the medical professions, it was an ever-present threat.

"You two are a unique combination that I think has the best chance to track this thing to its source," Kenny said. "Medical Services will have more than one team on this — but you're the only BB team available. The Institute doesn't want any of their people to stumble on the plague the hard way, so they subcontracted you to Medical for the duration. I'm delegating the planning of search patterns to you. Got any ideas on how to start?"

"Right," Alex replied. "Then if that's what you want, let's do this the smart way, instead of the hard way. First off, what's the odds this could have come off a derelict — station *or* ship — out in hard vacuum?"

"Odds? Not likely. Hard vacuum kills all of the bugs involved. That *does* eliminate anything like an asteroid or EsKay situation though, doesn't it?" Kenny looked fairly surprised, as well as pleased. "Let me get Lars in on this, he's been monitoring the poor devil."

It took a few moments for Lars to clear his boards enough to have attention to devote to a vocal circuit. During that time, Tia thought of a few questions she'd like to ask.

"Lars, has he *said* anything?" she asked, as soon as Lars joined the conference call. "Something that could give us clues?"

"Ravings mostly — do you think you can get anything out of that?" Lars sounded fairly dubious. "It's not as if he was an astrogator or anything. Mostly he's been yammering on about the weather, besides the usual; either pain and hallucinations, or about treasure and gold."

"The weather?" Tia responded immediately. "What about it?"

"Here, I'll give you what I've got — cleaned up so you can understand it, of course."

A new voice came over the circuit; harsh, with a guttural accent. "Treasure . . . gold . . . never saw s'much. Piles'n'piles . . . no moon, *frag* it, how c'n a guy see anythin' . . . anythin' out there. No moon. Dark 's a wormhole. Crazy weather. Nothin' but crazy weather . . . snow, rain, snow, sleet, mud — how ya s'pposed t' dig this stuff up in this?"

"That's basically it," Lars said, cutting the recording off. "He talks about treasure, moonless, dark nights, and crazy weather."

"Why not assume he's complaining about where he was? Put that together with an atmosphere and — ?" Tia prompted. "What do you get?"

"Right. Possible eccentric orbit, probably extreme tilt, third-in Terra-type position, and no satellites." Lars sounded pleased. "I'll get Survey on it."

"What about the likely range of the ship that left him?" Tia asked. "Check with CenSec and Military; the docks at Yamahatchi had to have external specs and so forth on that ship. What kind of fuel did they take on, if any? Docks should have external pictures. Military ought to be able to guess at the range, based on that. That should give us a search area."

"Good." Kenny made notes. "I've got another range — how long it probably took for our victim to come down with the disease once he was infected. Combine that one with yours, and we should have a sphere around Yamahatchi."

"Kenny, he couldn't possibly have shown any symptoms while he was *in* space — they'd have pitched him out the airlock," Tia pointed out. "That means he probably went through incubation while they were in FTL and only showed symptoms once they hit port."

"Right. I'll have that calculated for you and get you the survey records for that sphere, then it'll be up to you and the other teams." Kenny signed off, and Alex swiveled his chair to face Tia's column.

"There's an information lag for that area," Alex pointed out. "Yamahatchi is on the edge of known space. Survey is still working out there — except for really critical stuff, it's going to take weeks, months, even years for information to make it here. We need a search *net*, not just a couple of search teams."

"So — how about if we have Kenny call in not just Medical Services, but Decontamination?" she asked. "They don't have any BB teams either, but they do have the AI drones and the med teams assigned to them. They can run the net as well as we can. Slower, but that may not be so bad."

"I'll get on it," Alex replied instantly. "He can be mobilizing every free ship and team they've got while we compute the likely targets."

"And Intelligence!" she added, as Alex got back on the horn with Kenny and his team. "Get Kenny to get in touch with Intel, and have their people inside that sphere be on the watch for more victims, rumors of plague or of plague ships, or ships that have mysteriously lost half their crews!"

That would effectively increase their available eyes and ears a hundred-thousandfold.

"Or of ships that vanish and don't come into port," Alex said grimly. "Somewhere along the line that so-called tramp freighter is going to do just that; go into hyper and never come out again. Or come out and drift with no hand on the helm."

Tia wished she could still shiver; as it was, she felt rather as if her hull temperature had just dropped to absolute zero.

*   *   *

No computer could match the trained mind for being able to identify or discard a prospect with no data other than the basic survey records. Alex and Tia each took cone-shaped segments of the calculated sphere and began running their own kind of analysis on the prospects the computer search came up with.

Some were obvious; geologic instability that would uncover or completely bury the caches unpredictably. Weather that did not include snow, weather that did not include rain. Occupied planets with relatively thick settlements, or planets with no continents, only tiny island chains.

Some were not so obvious. Terrain with no real landmarks or landmarks subject to change. Terrain with snow and rain, but with snow piling up twelve feet thick in the winter; too deep to dig in. The original trove must have been uncovered by accident — perhaps during the construction of a rudimentary base — or by someone just outside, kicking around dirt.

Places with freelance mining operations *were* on the list; agri-colonies weren't. Places marked by the Institute for investigation were, places with full Institute teams weren't. While Tia would not have put it past someone with problems to sell out to smugglers, she didn't think that they'd care to cover up a contagious disease *this* hideous.

As soon as they finished mapping a cone, it went out to a team to cover. They had another plan in mind for themselves: covering free-trade ports, looking for another victim. They could cover the ports a lot faster than any of the AI or softperson-piloted ships; the only one faster would have been someone with a Singularity Drive. Since *those* were all fully occupied — and since, as yet, they had only one victim and not a full-scale plague in progress — there was no chance of getting one reassigned to this duty. So AH One-Oh-Three-Three would be doing what it could — and trying to backtrack the "freighter" to its origin point.

They were running against the clock, and everyone on the project knew it. If this disease got loose in a large, space-going population, the chances of checking it before millions died were slender.

"Alex," Tia called for the third time, raising the volume of her voice a little more. This time he answered, even though he didn't turn his dark-circled eyes away from his work.

"What, m'love?" he said absently, his gaze glued to a topographical map on the screen before him, despite the fact that he could hardly keep his eyes open.

She overrode the screen controls, blanking the one in front of him. He blinked and turned to stare at her with weary accusation.

"Why did you do that?" he asked. "I was right in the middle of studying the geography — "

"Alex!" she said with exasperation. "You hadn't changed the screen in half an hour; you probably hadn't really looked at it in all that time. Alex, you haven't eaten anything in over six hours, you haven't slept in twenty, and you haven't *bathed* or changed your clothes in forty-eight!"

He rubbed his eyes and peered up at the blank screen. "I'm fine," he protested feebly.

"You're not," she countered. "You can hardly hold your head up. Look at your hand shake! Coffee is no substitute for sleep!"

He clenched his fist to stop the trembling of his hand. "I'm fine," he repeated, stubbornly.

She made a rude noise and flashed her screens at him, so that he winced. "There, see? You can't even control your reactions. If you don't eat, you'll get sick, if you don't sleep, you'll miss something vital, and if you don't bathe and change your clothes I'm turning you over to Decontam."

"All right, love, all right," he sighed, reaching over and patting her column. "Heat me up something; I'll be in the galley shortly."

"How shortly?" she asked sharply.

"As long as it takes for a shower and fresh clothes." He pried himself up out of his chair and stumbled for his room. A moment later, she heard the shower running — and when she surreptitiously checked, she discovered that as she had suspected, he was running it on cold.

Trying to wake up, hmm? Not when I want you to relax. She overrode the controls — not bringing it all the way up to blood-heat, but enough that he wasn't standing in something one degree above sleet. It must have worked; when he stumbled out into the galley, freshly clothed, he was yawning.

She fed him food laden with tryptophane; he was too tired to notice. And even though he punched for it, he got no coffee, only relaxing herbal teas.

He patted her auxiliary console — this time as if he were patting someone's hand to get her attention. He'd been doing that a lot, lately — that and touching her column like the arm of an old and dear friend. "Tia, love, don't you realize we're almost through with this? Two cones to go — three if you count the one I'm working on now — "

"Which I can finish," she said firmly. "I don't need to eat, and I only need three hours of DeepSleep in twenty-four. Yes, I knew. But you aren't going to get teams out there any faster by killing yourself — and if you work yourself until you're exhausted, you are going to miss what might be *the* important clue."

"But — " he protested, and was stopped by a yawn.

"No objections," she replied. "I can withhold the data, and I will. No more data for another eight hours. Consider the boards locked, brawn. I'm overriding you, and if I have to, I'll get Medical to second me."

He was too tired to be angry, too tired even to object

In the past several days he had averaged about four hours in each sleep period, with nervous energy waking him long before he should have reawakened. But the strain was taking its toll. She had the feeling he was going to get that eight solid hours this time, whether or not he intended to.

"You aren't going to accomplish anything half-conscious," she reminded him. "You know what they say in the Academy; do it right, or don't do it."

"I give up." He threw his hands up in the air and shook his head. "You're too much for me, lover."

And with that, he wandered back into his cabin and fell onto his bunk, still fully clothed. He was asleep the moment he was prone.

She did something she had never done before; she continued to watch him through her eye in his cabin, brooding over him, trying to understand what had been happening over the past several days.

She had forgotten that she was encased in a column, not once, but for hours at a time. They had talked and acted like — like ordinary people, not like brain and brawn. Somehow, during that time, the unspoken, unconscious barriers between them had disappeared.

And he had called her "love" or "lover" no less than three times in the past ten minutes. He'd been calling her by that particular pet name quite a bit.

He had been patting her console or column quite a bit, these past few days — as if he were touching someone's hand to gain attention, soothe, or emphasize a point.

She didn't think he realized that he was doing either of those things. It seemed very absentminded, and very natural. So she wasn't certain what to make or think of it all. It could simply be healthy affection; some people used pet names very casually. Up until now, Alex hadn't, but perhaps until now he hadn't felt comfortable enough with her to do so. How long had they known each other anyway? Certainly not more than a few months — even though it felt like a lifetime.

No, she told herself firmly. *It doesn't mean a thing. He's just finally gotten to know me well enough to bring all his barriers down.*

But the sooner they completed their searches and got out into space again, the sooner things would go back to normal.

Let's see if I can't do two of those three cones before he wakes up. . . .

Predictably, the port that the mysterious tramp freighter had filed as its next port of call did not have any record of it showing up. Tia hadn't really expected it to; these tramps were subject to extreme changes of flight plan, and if it had been a smuggler, it *certainly* wouldn't log where it expected to go next.

She just hoped that it had failed to show up because the captain had lied — and not because they were drifting out in space somewhere. She let Alex do all the talking; he was developing a remarkable facility for playing a part and very cleverly managed to tell the absolute truth while conveying an impression that was entirely different from the whole truth.

In this case, he left the station manager with the impression that he was an agent for a collection agency — one that meant to collect the entire ship, once he caught up with it.

Alex shut down the com to the station manager, and turned his chair to face her screen and the plots of available destinations.

"How do you do that?" she asked, finally. "How do you make them think something entirely different from the real truth?"

He laughed, while she pulled up the local map and projected it as a holographic image. "I've been in theater groups for as long as I can remember, once I got into school. My *other* hobby, the one I never took too seriously, even though they said I was pretty good. I just try to imagine myself as the person I want to be, and figure out what of the truth fits that image."

"Well," she said, as they studied the ship's possible destinations, "if I were a smuggler, where would I go?"

"Lermontov Station, Presley Station, Korngold Station, Tung Station," he said, ticking them off on his fingers. "They might turn up elsewhere, but the rest all have Intel people on them; we'll know if they hit there."

"Provided whoever Intel has posted there is worth his paycheck. Why Presley Station?" she asked. "That's just an asteroid-mining company headquarters."

"High Family in residence," he replied, leaning back in his chair, and lacing his fingers behind his head. "Money for valuable artifacts. Miners with money — and not all of them are rock-rats."

"I thought miners were all — well, fairly crude," she replied.

He shook his head. "Miners are people, and there are all kinds out there. There are plenty of miners looking to make a stake — and some of them outfit their little tugs in ways that make a High Family yacht look plain. *They* have money for pretties, and they don't much care where the pretty came from. And one more thing; the Presley-Lee y Black consortium will buy ore hauls from anyone, including tramp prospectors, so we have a chance that someone may actually stumble on the trove itself. We can post a reward notice there, and it'll be seen."

"Along with a *danger* warning," she told him. "I only hope these people believe it. Lermontov first, then Tung, then Presley?"

"Your call, love," he replied comfortably, sending a carefully worded notice to the station newsgrid. They didn't want to cause a panic, but they *did* want people to turn in any clue to the whereabouts of the freighter. And they didn't want anyone infected along the way. So the news notice said that the ship in question might have been contaminated with Anthrax Three, a serious, but not fatal, variant of old Terran anthrax.

He finished posting his notice, and turned back to her. "You're the pilot. I'm just along for the ride."

"It's the most efficient vector," she replied, logging her flight plan with Traffic Control. "Three days to Lermontov, one to Tung, a day and a half to Presley."

Despite Alex's disclaimer that he was only along for the ride, the two of them did not spend the three days to Lermontov idle. Instead, they sifted through all the reports they'd gotten so far from the other teams, looking for clues or hints that their mystery ship could have made port anywhere else. Then, when they hit Lermontov, Alex went hunting on-station.

This time his cover was as a shady artifact dealer; looking for entire consignments on the cheap. There were plenty of people like him, traders with negotiable ethics, who would buy up a lot of inexpensive artifacts and forge papers for them, selling them on the open market to middle-class collectors who wanted to have something to impress their friends and bosses with their taste and education. Major pirates wouldn't deal with them — at least, not for the really valuable things. But crewmen, who might pick up a load of pottery or something else not worth the bigger men's time, would be only too happy to see him. In this case, it was fortunate that Tia's hull was that of an older model without a Singularity Drive; she looked completely nondescript and a little shabby, just the sort of thing such a man would lease for a trip to the Fringe.

Lermontov was a typical station for tramp freighters and ships of dubious registration. Not precisely a pirate station, since it *was* near a Singularity, it still had station managers who looked the other way when certain kinds of ships made port, docks that accepted cash in advance and didn't inquire too closely into papers, and a series of bars and restaurants where deals could be made with no fear of recording devices.

That was where Alex went — wearing one of his neon outfits. Tia was terrified that he would be recognized for what he was, but there was nothing she could do about it. He couldn't even wear a contact-button; the anti-surveillance equipment in every one of those dives would short it out as soon as he crossed the threshold. She could only monitor the station newsgrids, look for more clues about "their" ship, and hope his acting ability was as good as he thought it was.

Alex had learned the trick of drinking with someone when you wanted to stay sober a long time ago. All it took was a little sleight of hand. You let the quarry drain his drink, switch his with yours, and let him drain the second, then call for another round. After three rounds, he wouldn't even notice you weren't drinking, particularly not when *you* were buying the drinks.

Thank the spirits of space for a MedService credit account.

He started out in the "Pink Comet," whose neon decorations more than outmatched his jumpsuit. He learned quickly enough there that the commodities *he* wanted weren't being offered — although the rebuff was friendly enough, coming from the bartender after he had already stood the whole house a round. In fact, the commodities being offered were more in the line of quasi-legal services, rather than goods. The bartender didn't know who might have what he wanted — but he knew who would know and sent Alex on to the "Rim-runners."

Several rounds later, he suffered through a comical interlude where he encountered someone who thought he was buying feelie-porn and sex-droids, and another with an old rock-rat who insisted that what he wanted was not artifacts but primitive art. "There's no money in them arty-facts no more," the old boy insisted, banging the table with a gnarled fist. "Them accountants don't want arty-facts, the damn market's got *glutted* with 'em! I'm tellin' ya — primy-tive art is the *next* thing!"

It took Alex getting the old sot drunk to extract himself from the man — which might have been what the rock-rat intended in the first place. By then he discovered that the place he really wanted to be was the "Rockwall."

In the "Rockwall" he hit paydirt, all right — but not precisely what he had been looking for.

The bar had an odd sort of quiet ambience; a nononsense non-human bartender, an unobtrusive bouncer who outweighed Alex by half again his own weight, and a series of little enclosed table-nooks where the acoustics were such that no sound escaped the table area. Lighting was subdued, the place was immaculately clean, the prices not outrageously inflated. Whatever deals went on here, they were discrete.

Alex made it known to the bartender what he was looking for and took a seat at one of the tables. In short order, his credit account had paid for a gross of Betan funeral urns, twenty soapstone figurines of Rg'kedan snake-goddesses, three exquisite little crystal Kanathi skulls that were probably worth enough that the Institute and Medical would forgive him anything else he bought, and — of all bizarre things to see out here — a Hopi kachina figure of Owl Dancer from old Terra herself. The latter was probably stolen from another crewman; Alex made a promise to himself to find the owner and get it back to him — or her. It was not an artifact as such, but it might well represent a precious bit of tribal heritage to someone who was so far from home and tribe that the loss of this kachina could be a devastating blow.

His credit account had paid for these things — but those he did business with were paid in cash. Simply enough done, as he discovered at the first transaction. The seller ordered a "Rock'n'Run" — the bartender came to the table with a cashbox. Alex signed a credit chit for the amount of sale plus ten percent to the bar; the bartender paid the seller. Everyone was happy.

He'd spoken with several more crewmen of various odd ships, prompting, without seeming to, replies concerning rumors of disease or of plague ships. He got old stories he'd heard before, the *Betan Dutchman,* the *Homecoming,* the *Alice Bee.* All ships and tales from previous decades; nothing new.

He stayed until closing, making the bartender stretch his "lips" in a cheerful "smile" at the size of the bills he was paying — and making the wait-beings argue over who got to serve him next with the size of his tips. He had remembered what Jon Chernov had told him once about Intel people: *They have to account for every half-credit they spend, so they're as tightfisted as a corporate accountant at tax time. If you're ever doing Intel work, be a big spender. They'll never suspect you. And better a docked paycheck for overspending than a last look at the business end of a needler.*

Just before closing was when the Quiet Man came in. As unobtrusive as they came, Alex didn't realize the man was in the bar until he caught a glimpse of him talking with the bartender. And he didn't realize that he was coming towards Alex's table until he was standing there.

"I understand you're buying things," the Quiet Man breathed. "I have some — things."

He opened his hand, briefly, to display a miniature vase or bottle, a lovely thing with a rainbow sheen and a style that seemed oddly familiar, although Alex couldn't place it. As if one had fused Art Nouveau with Salvadore Dali, it had a skewed but fascinating sinuousity.

"That's the sort of merchandise I'm interested in, all right," Alex said agreeably, as he racked his brain, trying to place where he had seen a piece like it before. "The trouble is, it looks a little expensive for my pocket."

The Quiet Man slid in opposite Alex at a nod. "Not as expensive as you think," the Quiet Man replied. "The local market's glutted with this stuff." The Quiet Man's exterior matched his speech; gray jumpsuit, pale skin, colorless eyes and hair, features that were utterly average. "I have about a hundred little pieces like this and I haven't been able to unload them, and that's a fact."

"I appreciate your honesty," Alex told him, allowing his surprise to show through.

The Quiet Man shrugged. "You'd find it out sooner or later. The bosses only wanted the big stuff. Some of the other guys took jewelry; I thought they were crazy, since it was only titanium, and the pieces weren't comfortable to wear and a little flimsy. But some of the earlier crews must have brought back these perfume bottles, because I haven't been able to dump even one. I was hoping if you were buying for another sector, you'd be interested. I can give you a good deal on the lot."

"What kind of a good deal?" Alex asked.

The Quiet Man told him, and they began their bargaining. They ended it a good half hour after the bar was officially closed, but since Alex was willingly paying liquor prices for fruit juice — all that was legal after-hours — the bartender was happy to have him there. The staff cleaned up around them, until he and the Quiet Man shook hands on the deal.

"These aren't exactly ancient artifacts," the Quiet Man had admitted under pressure from Alex. "They can be doctored to look like 'em with a little acid-bath, though. They're — oh — maybe eight, nine hundred years old. Come from a place colonized by one of the real early human slowships; colony did all right for a while, then got religion and had themselves a religious war, wiped each other out until there wasn't enough to be self-sustaining. We figured the last of them died out maybe two hundred years ago. Religion. Go figure."

Alex eyed his new acquisition with some surprise. "This's human-made? Doesn't look it!"

The Quiet Man shrugged. "Beats me. Bosses said the colonists were some kind of artsy-craftsy back-to-nature types. Had this kind of offshoot of an earth-religion with sacramental hallucinogenics thrown in to make it interesting, until somebody decided *he* was the next great prophet and half the colony didn't see it that way. I mean, who knows with that kind? Crazies."

"Well, I can make something up that sounds pretty exotic," Alex said cheerfully. "My clients won't give a damn. So, what do you want to do about delivery?"

"You hire a lifter and a kid from SpaceCaps," the Quiet Man said instantly. "I'll do the same. They meet here, tomorrow, at twelve-hundred. Your kid gives mine the credit slip, mine gives yours the box. Make the slip out to the bar, the usual."

Since that was exactly the kind of arrangement Alex had made for the gross of funeral urns, with only the time of delivery differing, he agreed, and he and the Quiet Man left the bar and went their separate ways.

When he returned to the ship, he took the stairs instead of the lift, still trying to remember *where* he had seen the style of the tiny vase.

"You look cheerful!" Tia said, relief at his safe return quite evident in her voice.

"I feel cheerful. I picked up some artifacts on the black market that I'm sure the Institute will be happy to have." He emptied his pockets of everything but the "perfume bottle" and laid out his "loot" where Tia could use her close-up cameras on the objects. "And this, I suspect, is stolen — " He unwrapped the kachina. "See if you can find the owner, will you?"

"No problem," she replied absently. "I've been following your credit chit all over the station; that's how I figured out how to keep track of you. Alex, the two end skulls are forgeries, but the middle one is real, and worth as much as everything you spent tonight."

"Glad to hear it." He chuckled. "I wasn't sure what I was going to say to the Institute and Medical if they found out I'd been overtipping and buying rounds for the house! All right, here's my final find, and I have a load of them coming over tomorrow. Do *you* remember what the devil this is?"

He placed the warped little vase carefully on the console. Tia made a strange little inarticulate gargle.

"Alex!" she exclaimed. "That's one of *Sinor's* artifacts!"

He slapped his forehead with the heel of his hand. "Of course! That's why I couldn't remember what book I'd seen it in! Spirits of space — Tia, I just made a deal with the crewman of the ship that's running these things in for a whole load of them! He said — and I quote — 'the bosses only wanted the bigger stuff.' They're not really artifacts, they're from some failed human art-religious colony."

"I'm calling the contact number Sinor gave us," she said firmly. "Keep your explanations until I get someone on the line."

Tia had been ready to start sending her servos to pick lint out of the carpet with sheer nerves until she figured out that she could trace Alex's whereabouts by watching for his credit number in the station database. She followed him to three different bars that way, winding up in one called "Rockwall," where he settled down and began spending steadily. She called up the drink prices there, and soon knew when he had made an actual artifact purchase by the simple expedient of which numbers didn't match some combination of the drink prices. A couple of times the buys were obvious; no amount of drinking was going to run up numbers like he'd just logged to his expense account.

She had worried a little when he didn't start back as soon as the bar closed — but drinks kept getting logged in, and she figured then, with a little shiver of anticipation, that he must have gotten onto a hot deal.

When he returned, humming a little under his breath, she *knew* he'd hit paydirt of some kind.

The artifacts he'd bought were enough to pacify the Institute — but when he brought out the little vase, she thought her circuits were going to fry.

The thing's identification was so obvious to *her* that she couldn't believe at first that he hadn't made the connection himself. But then she remembered how fallible softperson memory was. . . .

Well, it didn't matter. That was one of the things she was here for, after all. She grabbed a com circuit and coded out the contact number Sinor had given her, hoping it was something without *too* much of a lag time.

She could not be certain where her message went to — but she got an answer so quickly that she suspected it had to come from someone in the same real-space as Lermontov. No visual coming through to them, of course — which, if she still had been entertaining the notion that this was really an Institute directive they were following, would have severely shaken her convictions. But knowing it was probably the Drug Enforcement Arm — she played along with the polite fiction that the visual circuit on their end was malfunctioning, and let Alex repeat the details of the deal he had cut, as she offered only a close-up of the little vase.

"Go through with it," their contact said, when Alex was done. "You've done excellent work, and you'll be getting that bonus. Go ahead and receive the consignment; we'll take care of the rest and clear out the debits on that account for you. And don't worry; they'll never know you weren't an ordinary buyer."

There was no mention of plague or any suggestions that they should take precautions against contamination. Alex gave her a significant look.

"Very well, sir," he only said, with carefully formality. "I hope we've accomplished something here for you."

"You have," the unknown said, and then signed off.

Alex picked up the little vase and turned it around and around in his hands as he sat down in his chair and put his feet up on the console. Tia made the arrangements for the two messengers to come to the ship for the credit chits and then to the bar for the pickups — fortunately, not at the same time. That didn't take more than a moment or two, and she turned her attention back to Alex as soon as she was done.

"Was that stupid, dumb luck, coincidence, or were we set up?" she asked suspiciously. "And where *was* that agent? It sounded like he was in our back pocket!"

"I'm going to make some guesses," Alex said, carefully. "The first guess is that we *did* run into some plain good luck. The Quiet Man had tried all the *approved* outlets for his trinkets — outlets that the Arm doesn't know about — and found them glutted. He was desperate enough to try someone like me. I suspect his ship pulls out tomorrow or the next day."

"Fine — but why go ahead and sell to you if he didn't know you?" Tia asked.

"Because I was in the right bar, making all the right moves, and I didn't act like the Arm or Intel." Alex rubbed his thumb against the sides of the vase. "I was willing to go through the barkeep to pay, which I don't think Intel would do. I had the right 'feel,' and I suspect he was watching to see if any of his buddies got picked up after they sold to me. And lastly, once again, we were lucky. Because *he* doesn't know what his bosses are using the phony artifacts for. He thought the worst

that could happen is a wrist-slap and fine, for importing art objects without paying customs duty on them."

"Maybe *his* bosses aren't using the artifacts for smuggling," she pointed out, thinking out all the
possibilities. "Maybe they are just passing them on to a
second party."

"In this station, that's very possible." Alex put the
vase down carefully. "At any rate, I think the Arm
suspected this cluster of stations all along, and they've
got a ship out here somewhere — which is why we got
an answer so quickly. I *thought* that was a ship-contact
number when I saw it, but I didn't say anything."

"Hmm." Tia ran through all the things *she* would
have done next and came up with a possible answer.
"So now they just find the messenger that goes to
'Rockwall' at noon from a ship that isn't ours, and tags
the ship for watching? Or is that too simple?"

Alex yawned and stretched. "Probably," he said,
plainly bored with the whole game now. "He probably
won't send the messenger from his ship. They'll do
their spy-work somehow; we just gave them what they
didn't have in the first place, a contact point. It's out of
our hands, which is just as well, since I'd rather not get
involved in a smuggler versus Intel shoot-out. I'm
tired."

"Then you should get some rest," she said immediately. "And get that jumpsuit out of my cabin before it
burns out my optics."

He laughed — but he also headed straight for his
bed.

Tia didn't even bother to wake her brawn as she
approached Presley Station and hailed their traffic
control. She expected the usual automated AI most
mining stations had; she got a human. Although it was
audio-only, there was no doubt that this was a real
human being and not an AI-augmented recording.

Because, from the strain in the voice, it was a very nervous and unhappy human.

"AH-One-Oh-Three-Three, be advised we are under a Code Five quarantine," the com officer said, with the kind of hesitation that made her think he wasn't on a microphone very often. "We can let you dock, and we can refuel you with servos, but we can't permit you to open your airlock. And we'd like you to move on to some other station if you have the reserves."

He can't deny us docking under a Code Five, but he's frightened. And he really wants us to go away.

Tia made a quick command decision. "Presley Station, be advised that we are on assignment from CenCom Medical. References coming now." She sent over her credentials in a databurst. "We're coming in, and we'd appreciate Presley Station's cooperation. We'd like to be connected to your Chief Medical Officer while we maneuver for docking, please."

"Uh — I — " There was a brief muttering, as if he was speaking to someone else, then he came back on the mike. "We can do that. Stand by for docking instructions."

At that point the human left the com, and the AI took over; she woke up Alex and briefed him, then gave him a chance to get dressed and gulp some coffee while she dealt with the no longer routine business of docking. As she followed the AI's fairly simple instructions, she wondered just what, exactly, was going on at Presley Station.

Was this the start of the plague, or a false alarm?

Or — was this just one outbreak among many?

She waited, impatiently, for the com officer to return online, while Alex gulped down three cups of coffee and shook himself out of the fog of interrupted sleep. It took forever, or at least it seemed that way.

Finally the com came alive again. "AH-One-Oh-Three-Three, we have the Chief Medical Officer online for you now." It was a different voice; one with more

authority. Before Tia could respond, both voice and
visual channels came alive, and she and Alex found
themselves looking into the face of a seriously
frightened man, a man wearing medical whites and the
insignia of a private physician.

"Hello?" the man said, tentatively. "You — you're
from MedServices? You don't look like a doctor."

"I'm not a doctor," Alex said promptly. "I've been
authorized by CenCom MedServices to investigate a
possible outbreak of a new infectious disease that
involves immune deficiency syndrome. We had reason
to believe that there's an infectious site somewhere in
his sphere, and we've been trying to track the path of
the last known victim."

There was no doubt about it; the doctor paled. "Let
me show you our patient," he whispered, and reached
for something below the screen. A second signal came
on, which Tia routed to her side screen.

The patient displayed suppurating boils virtually
identical to Kenny's victim; the only difference was that
this man was not nearly so far gone as the first one.

"Well, he matches the symptoms of the victim we've
been tracking," Alex said, calmly, while Tia made frantic adjustments to her blood-chemistry levels to get her
heart calmed down. "I trust you have him in full isolation and quarantine."

"Him *and* his ship," the doctor replied, visibly shak-
ing. "We haven't had any new cases, but *decom* it, we
don't know what this is or what the vector is or — "

"I've got a contact number coming over to you right
now," Alex interrupted, typing quickly. "As soon as you
get off the line with me, get onto this line; it's a double-
bounce link up to MedServices and a Doctor Kennet
Jhua-Sorg. He's the man in charge of this; he has the
first case in his custody, and he'll know whatever there
is *to* know. What we'd like is this; we're the team in
charge of tracking this thing to its source. Do you know

anything about where this patient came from, what he was doing — "

"Not much," the doctor said, already looking relieved at the idea that someone at CenCom was "in charge" of this outbreak. Tia didn't have the heart to let him know how little Kenny knew; she only hoped that since they'd left, he'd come up with something more in the way of a treatment. "He's a tramp prospector; he came in here with a load we sealed off, and sick as a dog — crawled into port under his own power, but he collapsed on the dock as soon as he was out of the ship, yelling for a medic. We didn't know he was sick when we let him dock, of course — "

The man was babbling, or he wouldn't have let that slip. Interstellar law decreed that victims of disease be given safe harborage within quarantine, but Tia had no doubt that if traffic control *hadn't* been an AI, the prospector would have never gotten a berth. At best they would have denied him docking privileges; at worst, they'd have sent a fighter out to blast him into noninfectious atoms. She made a mental note to send that information on to Kenny with their initial report.

" — when he collapsed and one of the dockworkers saw the sores, he hit the alarm and we sealed the dock off, sent in a crew in decontam suits to get him and put him into isolation. I sent off a Priority One to our PTA, but it takes so long to get an answer from them — "

"Did he say where he thought he caught this?" Alex said, interrupting him again.

The doctor shook his head. "He just said he was out looking for a good stake when he stumbled across something that looked like an interstellar rummage sale, and he figures that was where he got hit. What he meant by 'interstellar rummage sale' he won't say. Just that it was a lot of 'stuff' he didn't recognize."

Well, that matched their guess as to the last victim.

"Can we talk to him?" Tia asked.

The doctor shrugged. "You can try. I'll give you audiovisual access to the room. He's conscious and coherent, but whether or not he'll be willing to tell you anything, I can't say. He sure won't tell us much."

It was fairly obvious that he was itching to get to a comset and get in contact with MedServices, thus, symbolically at least, passing the problem up the line. If his bosses cared about where the miner had picked up the infection, they hadn't told *him* about it.

Not too surprising. He was a company doctor. He was supposed to be treating execs for indigestion, while his underlings patched up miners after bar fights and set broken bones after industrial accidents. The worst he was ever supposed to see was an epidemic of whatever new influenza was going around. He was *not* supposed to have to be dealing with a plague, at least, not by his way of thinking. Traffic control was supposed to be keeping plague ships from ever coming near the station.

"Thanks for your cooperation, Doctor," Alex said genially. "Get that link set up for us, if you would, and we'll leave you to your work."

The doctor signed off — still without identifying himself, not that Tia was worried. Her recordings were enough for any legal purposes, and at this point, now that he had passed authority on to them, he was a nonentity. They didn't need to talk to him anymore. What they needed was currently incarcerated in an isolation room on that station — and they were going to have to figure out how to get him to talk to them.

"Okay, Alex," she said when the screen was safely blank. "You're a lot closer to being an expert on this than I am. How do we get a rock-rat to tell us what we want to know?"

"Hank, my name's Alex," the brawn said, watching the screen and all the patient-status readouts alongside. "I'm a brawn from CS, on loan to Med-Services; you'll hear another voice in a moment, and that's my brainship, Tia."

"Hello, Hank," she said, very glad that she was safely encased in her column with no reactions for Hank to read. Alex was doing a good job of acting; one she knew she would never be able to match. Just looking at Hank made her feel — twitchy, shivery, and quite uncomfortable; sensations she hadn't known she could still have. "I don't know if anyone bothered to tell you, but we were sent out here because there's someone else with what you've got; it's very contagious, and we're trying to keep it from turning into a plague. Will you help us?"

"Give him the straight story," Alex had said; Kenny had agreed to that when they got hold of him, right after the company doctor had called him. *"There's no point in trying to trick him. If he knows how bad off he is, he just might be willing to cooperate."*

The sores only grew worse when you bandaged them, so Hank was lying in a gel-bed — a big pan full of goo, really, with a waterbed mattress beneath the goo. Right now only the opaque green gel covering him was keeping him from outraging modesty. The gel was a burn-treatment, and something Kenny had come up with for the other man. *He* was still alive, but no better than when they had left. They still had no idea who or what he was, besides horribly unlucky.

Hank peered up at the screen in the corner of his room, through a face grotesquely swollen and broken out. "These company goons won't give me any kind of a straight story," he said hoarsely. "All they do is try and brush me off. How bad off am I?"

"There's no cure," Alex said, flatly. "There's one other known victim. The other man is worse than you, and they haven't found anything to reverse his condition. That's the truth."

Hank cursed helplessly for about four or five minutes straight before he ran out of breath and words. Then he lay back in the gel-bed for another couple of minutes with his eyes closed.

Tia decided to break the silence. "I don't know how you feel about the rest of the universe, Hank, but — we need to know where you came down with this. If this got loose in any kind of population — "

" 'Sall right, lady," he interrupted, eyes still closed. "You're preachin' to the choir. Ain't no percentage in keeping my mouth shut now." He sighed, a sound that sounded perilously close to a sob. "I run across this place by accident, and I ain't sure how I'd find it again — but you guys might be able to. I give you what data I got. I'd surely hate t' see a kid in the shape I'm in right now."

"Thanks, Hank," Alex said, with quiet gratitude. "I wish there was something we could do for you. Can you think of anything you'd like?"

Hank shook his head just a little. "Tell you what; I got some serious hurt here, an' what they're given me ain't doin' much, 'cause they're 'fraid I'm gonna get hooked. You make these bozos give me all the pain meds I ask for — if I ever get cured up, I'll dry out *then*. You think you can do that for me?"

"I'll authorize it," Tia said firmly. At Alex's raised eyebrow, she printed: *Kenny's authorizations include patient treatments. We've got that power, and it seems cruel not to give him that much relief.*

Alex nodded. "Okay, Hank, my partner says she can boss the docs here. So, fire away; we're recording. Unless you want something now."

"Naw. I wanta stay on this planet long enough t' give you what little info I got." Hank coughed. "First off, my boat's an old wreck; falls outa hyper all the time, and the recorder don't always work when she takes a dive. Basically, what happened was she fell out, and there was a Terra-type planet not too far from where she dropped. My holds was pretty empty, so I figured I'd see if there was anything around. Registered somethin' that looked like wrecked buildings in one spot, went down t' take a look-see."

"That was where you caught this thing?" Alex asked.

"I'm gettin' to that. Weren't no signs of life, okay? But there was some buildings there, old and kinda busted up, round, like them flyin' saucers people used to see — I figgered maybe I'd hit some place where the archies hadn't got to, mebbe I could pick up somethin' I could peddle. I went ahead an' landed, okay? Only I found somethin' that looked like somebody else had been there first. Looked like — I dunno, like somebody'd been collectin' and hoardin' for a long, long time, buryin' the stuff in caves by the buildings, stashin' it in the buildings that wasn't busted up. Some of it was dug up already, some of it somebody'd just started t' dig up."

"How do you mean?" Alex asked.

"Like — somebody's kid's idea of a treasure place. Caves, lots of 'em, some of 'em dug up, all of 'em prob'ly had stuff in 'em." Hank's voice started to slur with fatigue, but he seemed willing to continue, so Tia let him.

"Anyway, I got down there, grabbed some of the good stuff, took lots of holos so if I ever figured out where it was, I could stake a legal claim on it." He sighed. "I was keepin' my mouth shut, partly 'cause I don't trust these company goons, partly 'cause I figured on goin' back as soon as I got cured." He coughed, unhappily. "Well, it don't much look like I'm gonna get cured up any time soon, does it?"

"I can't promise anything but the pain meds, Hank," Tia said softly.

"Yeah." He licked cracked and swollen lips with a pale tongue. "Look, you get into my ship. See if the damn recorder was workin' at all. Get them holos, see if you can figure out where the devil I was from 'em. You guys are CS, ev'body knows you can trust CS — if there's anything I can get outa this, see what you can do, okay?" The last was more of a pathetic plea than anything else.

"Hank, I can guarantee you this much — since you've cooperated, there's some kind of reward system with MedService for people who cooperate in closing down plagues," Alex said, after a few moments of checking with regs. "It includes all medical covered — including prosthetics and restorations — and full value of personal possessions confiscated or destroyed. That should include your ship and cargo. We'll itemize the *real* value of your cargo if we can."

Hank just sighed — but it sounded relieved. "Good," he replied, his voice fading with exhaustion. "Knew I could . . . trust CS. Lissen, can I get some'f that pain med now?"

Tia logged the authorization and activated the servo-nurse. "Coming up, Hank," she said. The man turned his head slightly as he heard the whine of the motor, and his eyes followed the hypospray until it touched his arm. "From now on, you just voice-activate the servo — tell it 'DM-Tia' and it will know what to give you." There was a hiss — then for one moment, what was left of his swollen lips curved in something like a smile. Tia closed down the link, after locking in the "on-demand" authorization. It would take someone from CenCom MedServices to override it now.

Meanwhile, Alex had been arguing with Dock Services, and finally had to pull rank on them to get access to the controls for the dock servos and remotes. Once that was established, however, it was a matter of moments for Tia to tie herself in and pick out a servo with a camera still inside the quarantine area to send into the ship.

She selected the most versatile she could find; one with a crawler base, several waldos of various size and strength, and a reasonable optical pickup. "We aren't going to tell them that hard vacuum kills the bugs yet, are we?" she asked, as she activated the servo and sent it crawling towards the abandoned dock.

"Are you kidding?" Alex snorted. "Given the pass-the-credit attitude around here, I may never tell them. Let Kenny do it, if he wants, but I'd be willing to bet that the moment we tell them, they'll seal off the section and blow it, then go in and help themselves to whatever's on Hank's ship before we get a chance to make a record of it."

"I won't take that bet," she replied, steering the crawler up the ramp and into the still-gaping airlock.

Hank hadn't exaggerated when he'd said his ship was a wreck; it had more patches and make-dos on it than she had dreamed possible on a ship still in space and operating. Half the wall-plates were gone on the inside of the lock; the floor-plates were of three different colors. And when she brought the crawler into the control cabin, it was obvious that the patchworking probably extended to the entire ship.

Exposed wiring was everywhere; the original control panels had long ago been replaced by panels salvaged from at least a dozen other places. Small wonder the ship had a tendency to fall out of hyper; she was surprised it ever managed to stay *in* hyper, with all the false signals that should be coming off those boards.

"You think the recorder caught where he went?" Alex asked doubtfully, peering at the view in the screen. The lighting was in just as poor shape as everything else, but Tia had some pretty sophisticated enhancement abilities, and the picture wasn't too bad. The ship's "black box" recorder, that *should* have registered everything this poor old wreck had done, was in no better shape than the rest of the ship.

"Either it did, or it didn't," she said philosophically. "We'll have a pattern of where he was supposed to be going, though, and where he thought he was heading when he left our little plague-spot. We should be able to deduce the general area from that."

"Ah, and since we know the planetary type, if Survey ever found it, we'll know where it is." Alex nodded as his hands raced across the keyboards, helping Tia with the complex servo. "Look, there's the com, I think. Get the servo a little closer, and I'll punch up a link to us."

"Right." She maneuvered the crawler in between two seats with stuffing oozing out of cracks in the upholstery, and got the servo close enough to the panel that Alex could reach it with one of the waldos. While he punched in their access com-code, she activated the black box, plugged the servo into it, and put it on com uplink mode with another waldo. She would have shaken her head, if she could have. Not only was all of this incredibly jury-rigged, it actually looked as if many of the operations that should have been automatic had deliberately been made manual.

"I can't believe this stuff," she said, finally. "It must have taken both hands and feet to fly this wreck!"

"It probably did," Alex observed. "A lot of the old boys are like that. They don't trust AIs, and they'll tell you long stories about how it's because someone who was a friend of a friend had trouble with one and it nearly killed him or wrecked his ship. The longer they stay out here, the odder they get that way."

"And CenCom worries about *us* going loonie," she replied, making a snorting sound. "Seems to me there's a lot more to worry about with one of these old rock-rats — "

"Except that there's never been a case of one of them going around the bend in a way that endangered more than a couple of people," Alex replied. Just about then, one of Tia's incoming lines activated. "There. Have I got you live, lover?"

"Yes, and I'm downlinking now." The black box burped its contents at her in a way that made her suspect more than one gap in its memory-train. *Oh well. Maybe we'll get lucky.* "Should we go check out the holds now?"

"Not the holds, the cabin," Alex corrected. "The holds will probably be half-full of primary-processed metals, or salvage junk. He'll have put his loot from the site in the cabins, if it was anything good."

"Good enough." She backed the servo out, carefully, hoping to avoid tangling it in anything. Somehow she actually succeeded; she wasn't quite sure how. She had no real "feeling" from this servo; no sense of where its limbs were, no feedback from the crawler treads. It made her appreciate her shipbody all that much more. With the kinesthetic input from her skin sensors and the internals, she knew where everything was at all times, exactly as if she had grown this body herself.

There were two cabins off the main one; the first was clearly Hank's own sleeping quarters, and Tia was amazed at how neat and clean they were. Somehow she had expected a rat's nest. But she recalled the pictures of the control room as she turned the servo to the other door, and realized that the control room had been just as neat and clean —

It was only the myriad of jury-rigs and quick-fix repairs that had given the impression of a mess. There wasn't actually any garbage in there — the floor and walls were squeaky-clean. Hank ran as clean a ship as he could, given his circumstances.

The second door was locked; Alex didn't even bother with any kind of finesse. Hank's ship would be destroyed at this point, no matter what they did or didn't do. One of the waldos was a small welding torch; Alex used it to burn out the lock.

The door swung open on its own, when the lock was

no longer holding it. Tia suddenly knew how Lord Carnavon felt, when he peeked through the hole bored into the burial chamber of Tutankhamen.

" 'Wonderful things!'" she breathed, quoting him half-unconsciously.

Hank must have worked like a madman to get everything into that cabin. This *was* treasure, in every sense of the word. There was nothing in that cabin that did not gleam with precious metal or the sleekness of consummate artistry. Or both. The largest piece was a statue about a meter tall, of some kind of stylized winged creature. The smallest was probably one of the rings in the heaps of jewelry piled into the carved stone boxes on the floor — which were themselves works of high art. If Hank could claim even a fraction of this legally, he could buy a new ship and still be a wealthy man.

If he lived to enjoy his wealth, that is.

He had stowed his loot very carefully, Tia saw, with the same kind of neat, methodical care that showed in his own cabin. Every box of jewelry was carefully strapped to the floor; every vase was netted in place. Every statue was lying on the bunk and held down by restraints. The cabin had been crammed as full as possible and still permit the door to open, but every single piece had been neatly stowed and then secured, so that no matter what the ship did, none of it would break loose. And so that none of it would damage anything else.

"Have we got enough pictures?" Alex asked faintly. "I'm being overcome by gold-fever. I'd like to look for those holos before my avarice gets the better of my common sense, and I go running down there to dive into that stuff myself."

"Right!" Tia said hastily, and backed the servo out again. The door swung shut after it, and Alex heaved a very real sigh of relief.

"Sorry, love," he said apologetically. "I never thought I'd ever react like that."

"You've never been confronted with several million credits'-worth of gold alone," she replied soothingly. "I don't even want to think what the real value of all of that is. Do you think he'd keep the holos in his cabin?"

"There's no place to stash them out in the control room," Alex pointed out.

Once again, Hank's neat and methodical nature saved the day for them, and Tia knew why he hadn't bothered to tell them where he'd put his records. Once they entered his cabin, there next to a small terminal was a drawer marked "Records," and in the drawer were the hardcopy claim papers he'd intended to file and the holos he'd taken in a section marked "Possible Claims."

"Luck's on our side today," Alex marveled. Tia agreed. It would have been *far* more likely that they'd have gotten some victim who'd refuse to divulge anything, or one who'd been half-crazed — or one who simply hadn't kept any kind of a record at all.

Luck was further on their side; he'd made datahedron copies of everything, including the holos, and *those* could be uplinked to AH-One-Oh-Three-Three. There would be no need to bring anything out of the quarantined dock area.

It took them several hours to find a way to bring up the reader in the control cabin, then link the reader into the com system, but once they got a good link established, it was a matter of nanoseconds and the precious recordings were theirs.

She guided the servo towards the lock and swiveled the optic back for a last look — and realized that *she* still had control over a number of the ship's functions via the servo.

"Alex," she said slowly, "it would be a terrible thing if the airlock closed and locked, wouldn't it? That would mean even if station ops blew the section to decontaminate it, they wouldn't be able to get into the ship —

or even get it undocked. They'd never know exactly what was on board."

Alex blinked in bewilderment for a moment — then slowly grinned. "That *would* be terrible, wouldn't it?" he agreed. "Well, goodness, Tia, I imagine that they'd probably dither around about it until somebody from CenCom showed up — somebody with authority to confiscate it and hold it for decontamination and evaluation."

"Of course," she continued smoothly, sending a databurst to the servo, programming it to get the airlock to shut and lock up. "And you know, these old ships are *so* unreliable — what if something happened to the ship's systems that made *it* vent to vacuum? Why then, even if the station managers decided to try and short-circuit the lock, they couldn't get it open against a hard vacuum. They'd have to bring in vacuum-welders and cut the locks open — and that would damage their own dock area. That would just be such an inconvenience."

"It certainly would — " Alex said, stifling a laugh.

She sent further instructions to the ship and noted with glee the ship proceeding to vent out the spaceward side. The servo noted hard vacuum on one of its sensors in a fairly reasonable length of time.

Satisfied that no one was going to be able to break into Hank's ship and pilfer his treasure, she sent a last set of instructions to the servo, shutting it down until she sent it an activation key. No one was going to get into that ship without her cooperation.

Hank would get a finder's fee, if nothing else, based on the value of the artifacts he had found. But now it would be based on the *true* value of what he had found, and not just what was left after the owners of Presley Station took their pick of the loot. Assuming they left anything at all.

"Well," she said, when she had finished. "We'd better

get to work. Are *you* any good at deciphering black box recordings?"

"Tolerably," Alex replied. "Tell you what; you analyze the holos while I diddle the black box data, then we'll switch."

"Provided you don't get gold-fever again," she warned him, opening the data on his screens.

The holos showed exactly what Hank had reported; a series of caves — caves that looked to have been artificially cut into the bluffs beside the ruined buildings. The nearest were completely dug up, and plainly emptied, but beyond them, there was another series of caves that were open to the air and still held treasures. But this wasn't like anything Tia had ever seen before. Each one of those caves, rather than being some kind of grave or other archeological entity, was clearly nothing more than a cache — and each one held precious objects from an entirely different culture than the one next to it. The two nearest the camera in the first holo held sacred objects from two cultures that were light-years apart — and from ages when neither civilization had attained even interplanetary flight, much less starflight.

Furthermore, the more Tia studied the holos, the more she came to the conclusion that the original caches were old; never mind who was digging them up now. The kind of weathering of the surface and layering of detritus she saw in the holos took hundreds, perhaps thousands of years to build up. And the buildings in one of the other holos were *very* old.

Nor did she recognize who could have constructed them.

So who could have been responsible for collecting all these treasures in the first place? Why had they buried them? Where did they get it all — and above all, why didn't they come back after it?

There was some evidence around the caves that the

current looters had attempted to rebury their finds. But had they done so in an attempt to hide it again — or had they done it to try and kill the disease? How many of the looters were exposed? From the number of caves that had been broken into, it looked as if there had been quite a few people at work there. . . .

Tia wished she could sit back and chew a nail or something. All she had now were questions and no answers. And the lives of other people might hang in the balance.

There was only one way to answer all those questions. They were going to have to find Hank's mystery planet and find out for themselves.

● CHAPTER EIGHT

Tia didn't entirely trust the integrity of the Presley Station comcenter. She *certainly* expected that whatever she sent out would be monitored by the owners and their underlings. Unfortunately, there had been no provision for the need for secrecy in this mission; she had no codes and no scramblers. There had been no real reason to think that they would ever need such secrecy, so she was forced to send in the clear. Just to be on the safe side, she uplinked on her own and double-sent everything, but she knew that whatever she sent off that way would be subject to delays as it bounced from remote hyperwave relay-station to relay-station, taking the long way "home."

As she had expected, the owners of the station were quick to move on the information that Hank's ship contained treasure, despite the fact that no one should have read her messages back to Kenny and the rest. She was just grateful that the owners' first thought was to grab what they could from the nearby trove, and *not* to try and figure out where Hank came from — or attempt to force him to tell them.

The first intimation that the communications had been leaked was when the station ops tried to claim the ship and all its contents for themselves; filing confiscation papers in the Central Systems Courts. When they discovered that Tia had already tied the ship and its contents up legally on Hank's behalf, they moved on the principle that "possession is nine-tenths of the law, and the fellow arguing the other tenth has to prove it with a lawyer."

They sent crews into the docks, to try and get into the ship to strip it of as much as they could. Tia's cleverness thwarted them, as they worked their way — slowly — through every step she'd expected.

She figured that by the time they were in a position to actually threaten Hank's possessions, the CS authorities would be on the scene in person. Meanwhile, she and Alex had some figuring to do — *where* was Hank's cache-world? Same problem as before, except that this time the possible search area was smaller, and cone-shaped rather than spherical.

Unfortunately, there were some other people who wanted to get their hands on that same information.

And unknown to either of them, those people had decided that Alex and Tia were already privy to it.

Tia kept a careful eye on the activity around her slip just on general principles, even when she wasn't feeling nervous — but given their current circumstances, and the fact that they were the *only* Central Systems ship out here at the moment, she couldn't help but feel a bit, well, paranoid. At the moment, only three people knew for certain that she was a brainship; Hank, the traffic control officer who brought them in, and that doctor. She was pretty certain that the doctor hadn't mentioned it to his superiors; she knew Hank hadn't told anyone, and as jittery as the other man had been, he'd probably forgotten it.

No one addressed *her* when they called, at any rate, and she took pains to make callers think that she was an AI. So far, they seemed to be falling in with the deception. This wasn't a bad state of affairs; no one expected an AI to recognize dangers the way a real sentient could. She could tap into the optical scanners in the dock area around the ship and no one would have any notion that she was keeping watch. She made sure to schedule her three or four hours of DeepSleep while Alex was awake;

normally taking them during his "morning," while he was still rather grumpy and uncommunicative and she'd rather not talk to him anyway. And she scanned the recordings she made while she was under, just to be sure she didn't miss anything.

That was why, a few days after their interview with Hank, she noticed the man in the dock-crew uniform coverall who seemed to be working double shifts. Except that no one else was working double shifts . . . and what was more, there was currently a company prohibition against overtime as a cost-cutting measure.

Something wasn't right, and he never left the immediate area of her slip. What was he doing there? It wasn't as if she was either a freighter with goods to load or unload, or a passenger liner. She didn't need servicing either. He never got close enough that she could see exactly what he was up to — but it seemed to her that he was doing an awful lot of make-work. . . .

She kept a close eye on him as he wandered around the dock area — purposefully, but accomplishing nothing that she could see. Gradually though, he worked his way in closer and closer to *her* slip, and little mental alarms began going off as she watched him and the way he kept glancing at her lock out of the corner of his eye.

Around sixteen-hundred she watched him removing control-panel plates and cleaning in behind them, work too delicate to trust to a servo.

Except that he'd just cleaned that same area two hours ago.

That was senseless; regs stated that the panels only had to be cleaned once every two *weeks*, not every two hours.

Furthermore, there was something not quite right with his uniform. It wasn't exactly the same color of gray as everyone else's; it looked crisply new, and the patches were just a little too bright. There were plenty of dockworkers' uniforms in Presley storage, there was no reason for someone to have had a new one made up unless he was an odd size. And this man was as average as anyone could possibly be. He was so *very* unremarkable that she noticed his uniform long before she noticed him.

That was bad enough — but just as seventeen-hundred passed and everyone else in the dock-crew went on supper break, another man in that too-new uniform showed up, while the first man kept on puttering about.

"Alex?" she said, unhappily. "There's something going on out there I don't like."

He looked up from his perusal of Hank's holos; he had prints made from them spread out all over the floor and was sitting on his heels beside them. "What's up?"

She filled him in quickly, as a third and a fourth person in that same uniform ambled into the dock.

There were now four crewman in the docks during break. All four of them in a dock area where there were no ships loading or unloading and no new ships expected to dock in the next twenty-four hours.

"Tia, I don't like this either," he said, much to her relief, standing up and heading for the main console. "I want you to get the station manager online and see what—"

Abruptly, as if someone had given the four men a signal, they dropped everything they were pretending to do and headed for her docking slip.

Tia made a split-second decision, for within a few seconds they were going to be in her airlock.

She slammed her airlock shut, but one of the men now running for her lock had some kind of black box in his hands; she couldn't trust that he might not be able to override her own lock controls. "Alex!" she cried, as she frantically hot-keyed her engines from cold-start. "They're going to board!"

As Alex flung himself at his acceleration couch, she sent off a databurst to the station manager and hit the emergency override on *her* side of the dock.

The dockside airlock doors slammed shut, *literally* in the faces of the four men approaching. Another databurst to the docking-slip controls gave her an emergency uncouple — there weren't too many pilots who knew about that kind of override, still in place from the bad old days when captains had to worry about pirates and station-raiders. She gave her insystem attitude thrusters a kick and shoved free of the dock altogether, frantically switching to external optics and looking for a clear path out to deep space.

As her adrenaline-level kicked up, her reactions went into overdrive, and what had been real-time became slow motion. Alex sailed ungracefully through the air, lurching for his chair; to her, the high-speed chatter of comlinks between AIs slowed to a drawl. Calculations were going on in her subsystems that she was only minimally aware of; a kind of background murmur as she switched from camera to camera, *looking* for the trouble she knew must be out there.

"The *chair* Alex — " she got out — just in time to spot a bee-craft, the kind made for outside construction work on the station, heading straight for her. Behind it were two men in self-propelled welder-suits. Someone had stolen or requisitioned station equipment, and they were going to get inside her no matter what the consequences were.

Accidents in space were so easy to arrange. . . .

Alex wasn't strapped down yet. She couldn't wait.

She spun around as Alex leapt for his couch, throwing him off-balance, and blasted herself out of station-space with a fine disregard for right of way and inertia as he grabbed and caught the arm of the chair.

Alex slammed face-first into the couch, yelped in pain at the impact, and clung with both hands.

There was another small craft heading for her with the purposeful acceleration of someone who intended to ram. She poured on the speed, all alarms and SOS signals blaring, while Alex squirmed around and fastened himself in, moaning. His nose dripped blood down the side of his face, and his lip poured scarlet where he'd bitten or cut it.

She dove under the bow of a tug, delaying her pursuer.

Who was in on this? Was this something the High Families were behind?

Surely not —

Please, not —

She continued to accelerate, throwing off distress signals even onto the relays, dumping real-time replays into message bursts every few seconds. Another tug loomed up in front of her; she sideslipped at the last moment, skimming by the AI-driven ship so close that it shot attitude thrusters out in all directions, the AI driven into confusion by her wild flying.

The ship behind was still coming on; no longer gaining, but not losing any ground either.

But with all the fuss that Tia was putting up, even Presley Station couldn't ignore the fact that someone was trying to 'jack her. Especially not with Central Systems investigators due any day, and with the way she was dumping her records onto the relays. If "they" were allied with the station, "they" wouldn't be able to catch everything and wipe it. If AH One-Oh-Three-Three disappeared, she was making it very hard for the claim of "accident" to hold any water —

I hope.

As Tia continued to head for deep space, a patrol craft finally put in an appearance, cutting in between her and her pursuer, who belatedly turned to make a run for it.

Tia slowed, and stopped, and held her position, as the adrenaline in her blood slacked off.

I remember panting. I remember shivering. I'd do both right now, if I could. As it was, errant impulses danced along her sensors, ghost-feelings of the *might-have-been* of weapons' fire, tractor beams. . . .

Slow heart. It's all right. Gradually her perception slowed back down to real-time, and the outside world "sped up." That was when the station manager himself hailed her.

"Of *course* I'm sure they were trying to break in," she snapped in reply to his query, re-sending him her recordings, with close-ups on suspicious bulges under the coveralls that were the right size and placement for needlers and other weapons. She followed that with the bee-craft and the two men in the welding-suits — headed straight for her. "And those pursuit-craft certainly were *not* my imagination!" She raised her voice, both in volume and pitch. "I happen to be a fully trained graduate of Lab Schools, you know! I'm not in the habit of imagining things!"

Now her adrenaline kicked in again, but this time from anger. They'd been in real danger — they could have been killed! And this idiot was talking to her as if she was some kind of— of joy-riding tweenie!

"I never said they were, ma'am," the station manager replied, taken somewhat aback. "I — "

"Just what kind of station are you running where a CS craft can be subject to this kind of security breach?" she continued wrathfully, running right over the top of him, now that she had the upper hand and some verbal momentum. "I'm reporting this to the Central Worlds Sector Coordinator on my *own* comlink!"

"You don't need to do that ma— "

"And *furthermore,* I am standing off-station until you can give me a *high-security* slip!" she continued, really getting warmed up and ready to demand all the considerations due a PTA. "My poor brawn is black and blue from head to toe from the knocking around he took, and lucky it wasn't worse! I want you to *catch* these people —"

"We're taking care of that, ma—"

"And I want to know *everything* you learn from them *before* I dock again!" she finished, with a blast of feedback that punctuated her words and made him swear under his breath as the squeal pierced his ears. "Until then, I am going to *sit* out here and clog your approach lanes, and I don't particularly care whether or not you like it!"

And with that, she put him on "record" and let him splutter into a datahedron while she turned her attention to Alex.

He had a wad of tissues at his face, trying to staunch the blood from nose and lip, and his eyes above the tissues were starting to puff and turn dark. He was going to look like a raccoon before too long, with a double set of black eyes.

Obviously the first thing that had impacted with the couch was his face.

"Alex?" she said timidly. "Oh, Alex, I'm so sorry — I didn't mean — there wasn't time —"

"Ith awright," he replied thickly. "You di okay. Din hab mush shoice. Hanneled ev'thing great, hanneled him great. You arn gon moof for wile?"

She correctly interpreted that as praise for her handling of the situation and a query as to whether or not she planned on moving.

"No, I don't *plan* on it," she replied, dryly. "But I hadn't *planned* on any of this in the first place."

He simply grunted, pried himself up painfully out of the acceleration couch and headed for their tiny sickbay to patch himself up.

She sent in a servo, discreetly, to clean up the blood in the sickbay and a second to take care of the mess in the main cabin, thanking her lucky stars that it *hadn't* been worse. If Alex had been standing when she pulled that spin and acceleration instead of heading in the direction of the couch —

She didn't want to think about it. Instead, she ordered the kitchen to make iced gel-packs. Lots of them. And something soft for dinner.

They left as soon as the CS contingent arrived and spent a little time debriefing them. The CS folk showed up in a much fuller force than even Tia had expected. Not only Central Systems Medical and Administrative personnel — but a CenSec Military brainship, the CP-One-Oh-Four-One. Bristling with weaponry —

And with the latest and greatest version of the Singularity Drive, no doubt, she thought, a little bitterly. *Heaven only knows what their version can do. Bring its own Singularity point with it, maybe.*

Whatever the administrators of Presley Station had *thought* they were going to get away with, they were soon dissuaded. The first person off the CenSec ship was a Sector Vice-Admiral; right behind him was an armed escort. He proclaimed the station to be under martial law, marched straight into the station manager's office, and within moments had the entire station swiftly and efficiently secured.

Tia had never been so happy to see anyone in her life. Within the hour all the witnesses and guilty parties had been taken into military custody, and Tia confidently expected someone to call them and take their depositions at any time.

Alex still looked like someone had been interrogating him with rubber hoses, so when the brainship hailed them, she took the call, and let him continue nursing his aching head and bruises.

The ship-number was awfully close to hers, although the military might not use standard CS brainship nomenclature. Still. . . . *One-Oh-Four-One. That's close enough for the brain to have been in my class —*

"Tia, that *is* you, isn't it?" were the first words over the comlink. The "voice" — along with the sharp overtones and aggressive punch behind them — was very familiar.

"Pol?" she replied, wondering wildly what the odds were on *this* little meeting.

"In the shell and ready to kick some tail!" Pol responded cheerfully. "How the heck are you? Heard you had some trouble out here, and the Higher Ups said 'go,' so we came a-running."

"Trouble — you could say so." She sent him over her records of the short — but hair-raising, at least by her standards — flight, in a quick burst. He scanned them just as quickly, and sent a wordless blip of color and sound conveying mingled admiration and surprise. If he had been a softie, he would have whistled.

"Not bad flying, if I do say so myself!" he said. "Like the way you cut right under that tug — maybe you should have opted for CenSec or Military."

"I don't think so," she replied. "That was more than enough excitement for the next decade for me."

"Suit yourself." Pol laughed, as if he didn't believe her. "My brawn wants to talk to your brawn. It's debriefing time."

She called Alex, who had been flat on his back in his bunk with an ice-gel pack on his black eyes. He staggered out to his chair and plopped down into it. For once, she thought, no one was going to notice his rumpled uniform — not with the black-blue-purple and green glory of his bruised face staring out of a screen.

"Line's open," she told Pol, activating the visual circuit.

As she had half-expected, given her impressions of the candidates when she had been picking a brawn, it was Chria Chance who stared out of the screen, with surprise written all over her handsome features. She was still wearing her leather uniforms, Tia noticed — which argued powerfully for "Chria" being High

Family. Little eccentricities like custom-tailored uniforms could be overlooked in someone who was both a High Family scion and had an excellent record of performance. Tia had no doubt that Chria's record was outstanding.

Tia noted also one difference between the Courier Service ships and the CenSec Couriers besides the armament. Directly behind Chria was another console and another comchair; this one held a thin, sharp-featured man in a uniform identical to Chria's, with an ornamental leather band or choker circling his long throat. He looked just as barbaric as she did. More, actually. He had the rangy, take-no-prisoners look of someone from one of the outer systems.

In short, he and Chria probably got along as if they had been made for each other.

"Frigging novas!" Chria exclaimed, after the first few seconds of staring. "Alex, what in blazes happened to *you*? Your dispatches never said anything about — did they — "

"Nobody worked me over, Brunhilde," Alex said tiredly, but with a hint of his customary humor. "So don't get your tights in a knot. This is all my own fault — or maybe just the fault of bad timing. It's the result of my face hitting my chair at — what was that acceleration, Tia?"

"About two gees," she said apologetically.

Chria shook her head in disbelief. "Huh. Well, shoot — here I was getting all ready to go on-station and dent some heads to teach these perps some manners." She sat back in her chair and grinned at him. "Sorry about that, flyboy. Next time, strap in."

"Next time, maybe I'll have some warning," he replied. "Those clowns tried to 'jack us with no advance notice. New regs should require at least twenty-four hours warning before a hijacking. And forms filed in quad."

Chria laughed. "Right. You two have been making my people very happy, did you know that? Their nickname for you is 'Bird-dog,' because you've been flushing so much game out for us."

"No doubt." Alex copied her stance, except that where she steepled her hands in front of her chin, he rubbed his temple. "Do I assume that this is not a social call? As in, 'debriefing time'?"

"Oh, yes and no." She shrugged, but her eyes gleamed. "We don't really need to debrief you, but there's a couple of orders I have to pass. First of all, I've been ordered to tell you that if you've figured out where your rock-rat's treasure trove is, transmit the coordinates to us so we know where you're going, but get on out there as soon as you can move your tail. We'll send a follow-up, but right now we've got some high-level butts to bust here."

"Generous of you," Alex said dryly. "Letting us go in first and catch whatever flack is waiting. Are we still a 'bird-dog,' or have we been elevated to 'self-propelled trouble magnet'?"

Chria only laughed.

"Come on, flyboy, get with the team. There's still a Plague-spot out there, and you're the ones most likely to find it; we don't know what in Tophet we're looking for." She raised an eyebrow at him, and he nodded in grudging agreement. "Then when you find it, *you* know how to handle it. I kind of gather that your people want the plague stopped, but they also want their statues and what-all kept safe, too. What're Neil and I going to do, shoot the bug down? He's hot on the trigger, but he's not up to potting microbes just yet!"

Behind her, the sharp-faced man shrugged in self-deprecation and grinned.

"So, if you've got a probable, let us know so we can keep an eye on you. Otherwise — " she spread her hands " — there's nothing we need you for. Fly free, little birds — the records you so thoughtfully bounced all over the sector are all we need to convict these perps, wrap them up, and stick them where they have to pump in daylight."

"Here's what we have," Tia said before Alex could respond. She sent Pol duplicates of their best guesses. "As you can see, we have narrowed it down to three really good prospects. Only one of those has a record of sentient ruins, so that's the one we think is the most likely — I wish they'd logged something besides just 'presence of structures,' but there it is."

"Survey," Pol said succinctly. "Get lots of burnout cases in Survey. Well, what can you expect, going planet-hopping for months on end, dropping satellites, with nothing but an AI to keep you company? Sometimes surprised they don't go buggy, all things considered. I would."

Pol seemed much more convivial than Tia recalled him ever being, and completely happy with *his* brawn, and Chria had that relaxed look of a brawn with the perfect partner. But still — Chria had been an odd one, and Military and Central Security didn't let their brainships swap brawns without overwhelming reasons. *Was* Pol happy?

"*Pol,*" Tia sent only to him, "*did you get a good one?*"

Pol laughed, replying the same way. "*The best! I wouldn't trade off Chria or Neil for any combo in the Service. We three-up over here, you know — it's a double-brawn and brain setup; it's a fail-safe because we're armed. Chria's the senior officer, and Neil's the gunnery-mate, but Neil's been studying, and now he can double her on anything. Fully qualified. That's not usually the case, from what I hear.*"

"*Why didn't he get his own brainship, then?*" she asked, puzzled. "*If he's fully qualified, shouldn't he get a promotion?*"

"*Who can figure softies?*" Pol said dismissively. "*He and Chria share her cabin. Maybe it's hormonal. How about you —*

you were saying you planned to be pretty picky about your brawns. Did they rush you, or did you get a good one?"

There were a hundred things she could have said — many of which could have gotten her in a world of trouble if she answered as enthusiastically as she would have liked. *"Oh, Alex will do — when he's not shoving his face into chairs,"* she replied as lightly as she could. Pol laughed and made a few softie jokes while Alex and Chria tied up all the loose ends that needed to be dealt with.

They were the only ship permitted to leave Presley space — Chria hadn't been joking when she'd said that there was going to be a thorough examination of everything going on out here. On the other hand, not having to contend with other traffic was rather nice, all things considered.

Now if only they had a Singularity Drive. . . .

Never mind, she told herself, as she accelerated to hyper. *I can manage without it. I just hope we don't have any more "help" from the opposition.*

This place didn't even have a name yet — just a chart designation. Epsilon Delta 177.3.3. Pol had called it right on the nose — whoever had charted this place must have been a burnout case, or he would have at least tried to name it. That was one of the few perks of a Survey mission; most people took advantage of it.

It certainly had all the earmarks of the kind of place they were looking for; eccentric tilt, heavy cloud cover that spoke of rain or snow or both. But as Tia decelerated into the inner system, she suddenly knew that they *had* hit paydirt without ever coming close enough to do a surface scan.

There should have been a Survey satellite in orbit around their hot little prospect. This was a Terra-type planet; even with an eccentric tilt, eventually someone was going to want to claim it. The satellite should have been up there collecting data on planet three, on the entire system, and on random comings and goings within the system, if any. It should have been broadcasting warnings to incoming ships about the system's status — charted but unexplored, under bio-quarantine until checked out, possibly dangerous, native sentients unknown, landing prohibited.

The satellite was either missing or silent.

"Accidents do happen," Alex said cautiously, as Tia came in closer, decelerating steadily, and prepared to make orbit. "Sometimes those babies break."

She made a sound of disbelief. "Not often. And what are the odds? It should at *least* be giving us the navigational bleep, and there's nothing, nothing at all." She scanned for the satellite as she picked her orbital path, hoping to pick something up.

"Oh, Tia — look at that rotation, that orbit! It could have gotten knocked out of the sky by something — " he began.

"Could have, but wasn't. I've got it, Alex," she said with glee. "I found it! And it's deader than a burned-out glow-tube."

She matched orbits with the errant satellite, coming alongside for a closer look. It was about half her size, so there was no question of bringing it inside, but as she circled it like a curious fish, there was one thing quite obvious.

Nothing was externally wrong with it.

"No sign of collision, and it wasn't shot at," Alex observed, and sighed. "No signs of a fire or explosion inside, either. You've tried reactivating it, I suppose?"

"It's not answering," she said firmly. "Guess what? You get to take a walk."

He muttered something under his breath and went after his pressure-suit. After the past few days in transition, his face had begun to heal, turning from black, blue and purple to a kind of dirty green and yellow.

She presumed that the rest of him was in about the same shape — but he was obviously feeling rather sorry for himself.

Do I snap at him, or do I kind of tease him along? she wondered. He hadn't been in a particularly good mood since the call from Chria. Was it that he was still in pain? Or was it something else entirely? There were so many signals of softperson body language that she'd never had a chance to learn, but there had been something going on during that interview — not precisely between Alex and Chria, though. More like, going on *with* Alex, *because* of Chria.

Before she had a chance to make up her mind, he was at the airlock, suited up and tethered, and waiting for her to close the inner lock for him.

She berated herself for wool-gathering and cycled the lock, keeping an anxious eye on him while she scanned the rest of the area for unexpected — and probably unwelcome — visitors.

It would be just our luck for the looters to show up right about now.

He jetted over to the access-hatch of the satellite and popped it without difficulty.

Wait a moment — shouldn't he have had to unlock it?

"Tia, the access hatch was jimmied," he said, his breath rasping in the suit-mike as he worked, heaving the massive door over and locking it down. "You were right, green all the way. The satellite's been sabotaged. Pretty crude work; they just disconnected the solar-cells from the instrument pack. It'll still make orbital corrections, but that's all. Don't know why they didn't just knock it out of the sky, unless they figured Survey has some kind of telltale on it, and they'd show up if it went down."

"What should we do?" she asked, uncertainly. "I know you can repair it, but should you? We need some of the information it can give us, but if you repair it, wouldn't they figure that Survey had been through? Or would they just not notice?"

"I don't want to reconnect the warn-off until we're ready to leave, or they'll definitely know someone's been eating their porridge," he replied slowly, as he floated half-in, half-out of the hatch. "If the satellite's telling them to take a hike as soon as they enter orbit there won't be much doubt that someone from the authorities has been here. But you're right, and I not only want to know if someone shows up in orbit while we're down on the ground, I want the near-space scan it took before they shut it down, and I want it to keep scanning and recording. The question is, am I smart enough to make it do all that?"

"I want the planetary records," she told him. "With luck, the ruins may show up on the scans. We might even see signs of activity where the looters have been digging. As for, are you smart enough — if you can get the solar arrays reconnected, I can reprogram every function it has. I'm CS, remember? We do work for Survey sometimes, so I have the access codes for Survey satellites. Trust me, they're going to work; Survey never seems to think someone might actually want to sabotage one of their satellites, so they never change the codes."

"Good point." He writhed for a moment, upside down, the huge blue-white globe behind him making an impressive backdrop. "Okay, give me a minute or two to splice some cable." Silence for a moment, except for grunts and fast breathing. "Good; it wasn't as awful as I thought. There. Solar array plugged back in. Ah, have the link to the memory established. And — yes, everything is powering up, or at least that's what looks like in here."

She triggered memory-dump, and everything came over in compressed mode, loud and clear. All the near-space scans and all the geophysical records that had been made before the satellite was disabled. Surface-scans in all weathers, made on many passes across the face of the planet.

But then — nothing. Whoever had disabled the satellite had known what he was doing — the memory that should have contained records of visitors was empty. She tried a number of ways of accessing it, only to conclude that the data storage device had been completely reformatted, nonsense had been written over all the memory, and it had been reformatted again. Not even an expert would have been able to get anything out of it now.

"Can you hook in the proximity-alert with our com-system?" she asked.

"I think so." He braced himself against the hatch and shoved himself a little farther inside. "Yes, it's all nodular. I can leave *just* that up and powered, and if they aren't listening on this band, they won't know that there's been anyone up here diddling with it."

A few moments more, and she caught a live signal on one of the high-range insystem comlinks, showing a nearby presence in the same orbit as the satellite. She felt her heart jump and started to panic —

— then she scolded herself for being so jumpy. It was the satellite, registering *her* presence, of course.

Alex closed the hatch and wedged it shut as it had been before, reeling himself back in on the tether. A moment later, her lock cycled, and he came back into the main cabin, pulling off his helmet and peeling off his suit.

Tia spent some time reprogramming the satellite, killing the warn-off broadcast, turning all the near-space scanners on and recording. Then she turned her attention to the recordings it had already made.

"So, what have we got?" he asked, wriggling to get the suit down over his hips. "Had any luck?"

"There's quite a few of those ruins," she said

carefully, noting with a bit of jealousy that the survey satellite array was actually capable of producing sharper and more detailed images than her own. Then again, what it produced was rather limited.

"Well, that's actually kind of promising." He slid out of the suit and into the chair, leaving the pressure-suit in a crumpled heap on the floor. She waited a moment until he was engrossed in the screen, then discretely sent a servo to pick it and the abandoned helmet up.

"I'd say here or here," he said at last, pointing out two of the ruins in or near one of the mountain ranges. "That would give us the rain-snow pattern the first victim raved about. Look, even in the same day you'd get snow in the morning, rain in the afternoon, and snow after dark during some seasons."

She highlighted those — but spotted three more possibilities, all three in areas where the tilt would have had the same effect on the climate. She marked them as well, and was rewarded by his nod of agreement.

"All right. This *has* to be the planet. There's no reason for anyone to have disabled the satellite otherwise. Even if Survey or the Institute were sending someone here for a more detailed look, they'd simply have changed the warn-off message; they wouldn't have taken the satellite off-line." He took a deep breath and some of the tension went out of his shoulders. "Now it's just going to be finding the right place."

This was work the computers could do while Ti slept, comparing their marked areas and looking for changes that were not due to the seasons or the presence or absence of snow. Highest on the priority list was to look for changes that indicated disturbance while there was snow on the ground. Digging and tramping about in the snow would darken it, no matter how carefully the looters tried to hide the signs of their presence. That was a sign that *only* the work of sentient or herd-beasts would produce, and herd-beasts were not likely to search ruins for food.

Within the hour, they had their site — there was no doubt whatsoever that it was being visited and disturbed regularly. Some of the buildings had even been meddled with.

"Now why would they do that?" Tia wondered out loud, as she increased the magnification to show that one of the larger buildings had mysteriously grown a repaired roof. "They can't need that much space — and how did they fix the roof within twenty-four hours?"

"They didn't," Alex said flatly. "That's plastic stretched over the hole. As to *why* — the hole is just about big enough to let a twenty-man ship land inside. Hangar and hiding place all in one."

They changed their position to put them in geosynchronous orbit over their prize — and detailed scans of the spot seemed to indicate that no one had visited it very recently. The snow was still pristine and white, and the building she had noted had a major portion of its roof missing again.

"That's it," Alex said with finality.

Tia groaned. "We know — and we can't prove it. We know for a fact that someone is meddling with the site, but we can't prove the site is the one with the plague. Not without going down."

"Oh, come on, Tia, where's your sense of adventure?" Alex asked, feebly. "We knew we were probably going to have to go down on the surface. All we have to do is go down and get some holos of the area just like the ones Hank took. Then we have our proof."

"My sense of adventure got left back when I was nearly hijacked," she replied firmly. "I can do without adventure, thank you."

And she couldn't help herself; she kept figuratively glancing over her shoulder, watching for a ship —

Would it be armed? She couldn't help but think of

Pol, bristling with weaponry, and picturing those weapons aimed at her.

Unarmed. Unarmored. Not even particularly fast.

On the other hand, she was a *brainship*, wasn't she? The product of extensive training. Surely if she couldn't outrun or outshoot these people, she could out-think them —

Surely.

Well, if she was going to out-think them, the first thing she should do would be to find a way to keep them from spotting her. So it was time to use those enhanced systems on the satellite to their advantage.

"What are you doing?" Alex asked, when she remained silent for several minutes, sending the manual-override signal to the satellite so that she could use the scanners.

"I'm looking for a place to hide," she told him. "Two can play that game. And I'm smaller than their ship; I shouldn't need a building to hide me. I'll warn you, though, I may have to park a fair hike away from the cache sites."

It took a while; several hours of intense searching, while Alex did what he could to get himself prepared for the trip below. That amounted mostly to readying his pressure-suit for a long stay; stocking it with condensed food and water, making certain the suit systems were up to a week-long tour, if it came to that. Recharging the power-cells, triple-checking the seals — putting tape on places that tended to rub and a bit of padding on places that didn't quite fit — everything that could be done to his suit, Alex was doing. They both knew that from the time he left her airlock to the time he returned and she could purge him and the lock with hard vacuum, he was going to have to stay in it.

Finally, in mid-afternoon by the "local" time at the site below them, she found what she was looking for.

"I found my hiding place," she said into the silence, startling him into jumping. "Are you ready?"

"As ready as I'll ever be," he said, a little too jauntily. Was it her imagination, or did he turn a little pale? Well, if she had been capable of it, she'd have done the same. As it was, she was so jittery that she finally had to alter her blood-chemistry a little to deal with it.

"Then strap down," she told him soberly. "We're heading right into a major weather system and there's no getting around it. This is going to be tricky, and the ride is likely to be pretty rough."

Alex took the time to strap down more than himself; he made a circuit of the interior, ensuring that anything loose had been properly stowed before he took his place in the comchair. Only then, when he was double-strapped in, did Tia make the burn that began their descent.

Their entry was fairly smooth until they were on final approach and hit thick atmosphere and the weather that rode the mid-levels. The wild storm winds of a blizzard buffeted her with heavy blows; gusts that came out of nowhere and flung her up, down, in any direction but the one she wanted. She fought her way through them with grim determination, wondering how on earth the looters had gotten this far. Surely with winds like this, the controls would be torn right out of the grip of a softperson's hands!

Of course, they could be coming down under the control of an AI. Once the course had been programmed in, the AI would hold to it. And within limits, it would deal with unexpected conditions all the way to the surface.

Within limits: that was the catch. Throw it too far off the programmed course, and it wouldn't know what to do.

Never mind, she told herself. *You need to get down there yourself!*

A little lower, and it wasn't just wind she was dealing with, it was snow. A howling blizzard, to be precise — one that chilled her skin and caked snow on every surface, throwing off her balance by tiny increments, forcing her to recalculate her descent all the way to the ground. A strange irony — she who had never seen weather as a child was now having to deal with weather at its wildest. . . .

Then suddenly, as she approached the valley she had chosen, the wind died to a mere zephyr. Snow drifted down in picture perfect curtains — totally obscuring visuals, of course, but that was why she was on instruments anyway. She killed forward thrusters and went into null-grav; terribly draining of power, but the only way she could have the control she needed at this point. She inched her way into her chosen valley, using the utmost of care. The spot where she wanted to set down was just big enough to hold her — and right above it, if the readings she'd gotten from above were holding true, there was a big buildup of snow. Just enough to avalanche down and cover her, if she was very careful not to set it off prematurely.

She eased her way into place with the walls of the valley less than a hand-span away from her skin; a brief look at Alex showed him clenching teeth and holding armrests with hands that were white-knuckled. He could read the instruments as well as she could. Well, she'd never set down into a place that was quite this narrow before. And certainly she had never set down under conditions that might change in the next moment. . . .

If that blizzard behind them came howling up this valley, it could catch her and send her right into the valley wall.

There. She tucked herself into the bottom of the valley and felt her "feet" sink through the snow to the rock beneath. Nice, solid rock. Snow-covered rocks on either side.

And above — the snowcrest. Waiting.

Here goes —

She activated an external speaker and blasted the landscape with shatter-rock, bass turned to max.

And the world fell in.

"Are you going to be able to blast free of this?" Alex asked for the tenth time, as another servo came in from the airlock to recharge.

"It's not that bad," she said confidently. She was *much* happier with four meters of snow between her and the naked sky. Avalanches happened all the time; there was nothing about this valley to signal to the looters that they'd been discovered, and that a ship was hiding here. Not only that, but the looters could prance around *on top of her* and never guess she was there unless they found the tunnel her servos were cutting to the surface. And she didn't think any of them would have the temerity to crawl down what *might* be the den-tunnel of a large predator.

"If it's not that bad," Alex said fretfully, "then why is it taking forever to melt a tunnel up and out?"

"Because no one ever intended these little servos to have to do something like that," she replied, as patiently as she could. "They're *welders*, not snow clearers. And they have to reinforce the tunnel with plastic shoring-posts so it doesn't fall in and trap you." He shook his head; she gave up trying to explain it. "They're almost through, anyway," she told him. "It's about time to get into your suit."

That would keep him occupied.

"This thing is getting depressingly familiar," he complained. "I see more of the inside of this suit than I do my cabin."

"No one promised you first-class accommodations on this ride," she teased, trying to keep from showing her own nervousness. "I'll tell you what; how about if I have one of the servos make a nice set of curtains for your helmet?"

"Thanks. I think." He made a face at her. "Well, I'll tell you this much; if I have to keep spending this much time in the blasted thing, I'm going to have some comforts built into it—or demand they get me a better model." He twisted and turned, making sure he still had full mobility. "The sanitary facilities leave a lot to be desired."

"I'll report your complaints to the ship's steward," she told him. "Meanwhile—we have breakout."

"Sounds like my cue." Alex sighed. "I hope this isn't going to be as cold as it looks."

Alex crawled up the long, slanting tunnel to the surface, lighting his way with the work-lamp on the front of his helmet. Not that there was much to see—just a white, shiny tunnel that seemed to go on forever, reaching into the cold darkness . . . as if, with no warning, he would find himself entombed in ice forever. The plastic reinforcements were as white as the snow; invisible unless you were looking for them. Which was the point, he supposed. But he was glad they were there. Without them, tons of snow and ice could come crashing down on him at any moment. . . .

Stop that, he told himself sharply. *Now is not the time to get claustrophobia.*

Still, there didn't seem to be any end to the tunnel—and he was cold, chilled right down to the soul. Not physically cold, or so his readouts claimed. Just chilled by the emptiness, the sterility. The loneliness . . .

You're doing it again. Stop it.

Was the surrounding snow getting *lighter*? He turned off his helmet light—and it was true, there was a kind of cool, blue light filtering down through the ice and snow! And up ahead—yes, there was the mouth of the tunnel, as promised, a round, white "eye" staring down at him!

He picked up his pace, eager to get out of there. The return trip would be *nothing* compared to this long, tedious crawl — just sit down and push away, and he would be able to slide all the way down to the airlock!

He emerged into thickly falling snow and saw that the servos had wrought better than he and Tia had guessed, for the mouth of the tunnel was outside the area of avalanche, just under an overhanging ridge of stone. That must have been what the snow had built up upon; small wonder it buried Tia four meters under when she triggered it! Fortunately, snow could be melted; when they needed to leave, she could fire up her thrusters *and* increase the surface temperature of her skin, and turn it all to water and steam. Well, that was the theory, anyway.

That was assuming it didn't rain and melt away her cover before then.

By Tia's best guess, it was late afternoon, and he should be able to get to the site and look around a little before dark fell. At that point, the best thing he could do would be to get under cover somewhere and curl up for the night. *This* time he had padded all the uncomfortable spots in the suit, and he'd worn soft, old, exercise clothing. It shouldn't be any less comfortable than some of his bunks as a cadet.

He took a bearing from the heads-up display inside his helmet and headed for the site.

"Tia," he called. "Tia, come in."

"Reading you loud and clear, Alex," she responded immediately. Funny how easy it was to think of her as a person sitting back in that ship, eyes glued to the screens that showed his location, hands steady on the com controls —

Stop that. Maybe it's a nice picture, but it's one that can get you in more trouble than you already have. "Tia, we have the right place, all right." He toggled his external suit-camera and gave her a panoramic sweep from his vantage point above the valley holding the site. It was fairly obvious that this place was subject to some pretty heavy-duty windstorms; the buildings were all built into the lee of the hills, and the hills themselves had been sculpted by the prevailing winds until they looked like cresting waves. No doubt either why the entities who built this place used rounded forms; less for the winds to catch on.

"Does this look like any architecture in your banks?" he asked, panning across the buildings. "I sure as heck don't recognize it."

"Nothing here," she replied, fascination evident in her voice. "This is amazing! That's not metal, I don't think — could it be ceramic?"

"Maybe some kind of synthetic," Alex hazarded. "Plague or not, there are going to be murders done over the right to excavate this place. How in the name of the spirits of space did that Survey tech just dismiss this with 'presence of structures'?"

"We'll never know," Tia responded. "Well, since there can't be two sites like this in this area, and since these buildings match the ones in Hank's holos, we can at least assume that we have the right planet. Now — about the caches — "

"I'm going down," he said, feeling for footholds in the snow. It crunched under his feet as he eased down sideways, one careful step at a time. Now that he was out of Tia's valley, there were signs everywhere of freeze-thaw cycles. Under the most recent layer of snow, the stuff was dirty and covered with a crust of granular ice. It made for perilous walking. "The wind is picking up, by the way. I think that blizzard followed us in."

"That certainly figures," she said with resignation.

As he eased over the lip of the valley, he saw the caves — or rather, storage areas — cut into the protected side of the face of a lower level canyon cutting through the middle of the valley. There were more buildings down there, too, and some kind of strange pylons — but it was the "caves" that interested him most. Regular, ovoid holes cut into the earth and rock that were then plugged with something rather like cement, a substance slightly different in color from the surrounding earth and stone. Those nearest him were still sealed; those nearest the building with the appearing-disappearing roof were open.

He worked his way down the valley to the buildings and found to his relief that there was actually a kind of staircase cut into the rock, going down to the second level. Protected from the worst of the weather by the building in front of it, while it was a bit slippery, it wasn't as hazardous as his descent into the valley had been.

It was a good thing that the contents of Hank's cabin and the holos the man had taken had prepared him for what he saw.

The wall of the valley where the storage caves had been opened looked like the inside of Ali Baba's cave. The storage caches proved to be much smaller than Alex had thought; the "window" slits in the nearby building were tiny, as might have been expected in a place with the kind of punishing weather this planet had. That had made the caches themselves appear much larger in the holos. In reality, they were about as tall as his waist and no deeper than two or three meters. That was more than enough to hold a king's ransom in treasure....

Much hadn't even been taken. In one of the nearest, ceramic statuary and pottery had been left behind as worthless — some had been broken by careless handling, and Alex winced.

There were dozens of caches that had been opened and cleaned out; perhaps a dozen more with less-desirable objects still inside. There were dozens more, still sealed, running down the length of the canyon wall —

And one whose entrance had been sealed with some kind of a heat-weapon, a weapon that had been turned on the entrance until the rock slagged and melted metal ran with it, mingling and forming a new, permanent plug.

"Do you think that's where the plague bug came from?" Tia asked in his ear.

"I think it's a good bet, anyway," he said absently. "I sure hope so, anyway."

Suddenly, with the prospect of contamination looming large in his mind, the shine of metal and sheen of priceless ceramic lost its allure. *Whether it is or isn't, there is no way I am going to crack this suit, I don't care what is out there.* Hank and the other man drifted in his memory like grisly ghosts. The suit, no longer a prison, had just become the most desirable place in the universe.

Oh, I just love this suit. . . .

Nevertheless, he moved forward towards the already-opened caches, augmenting the fading light with his suit-lamp. The caches themselves were very old; that much was evident from the weathering and buildup of debris and dirt along the side of the canyon wall. The looters must have opened up one of the caches out of sheer curiosity or by accident while looking for something else. Perhaps they had been exploring the area with an eye to a safe haven. Whatever had led them to uncover the first, they had then cleared away the buildup all along the wall, exposing the rest. And it looked as if the loot of a thousand worlds had been tucked away here.

He began taking careful holos of everything that had been left behind, Tia recording the tiniest details as he covered every angle, every millimeter. At least this way if anything more was smashed there would be a record of it. Some things he picked up and stashed in his pack to bring back with him — a curious metal book, for instance —

Alex moved forward again, reaching out for a discarded ceramic statue of some kind of winged biped —

"*Alex!*" Tia exclaimed urgently. He started back, his hand closing on empty air.

"What?" he snapped. "I — "

"Alex, you have to get back here *now*," she interrupted. "The alarms just went off. They're back, and they're heading in to land right now!"

"Alex!" Tia cried, as her readouts showed the pirates making their descent burn and Alex moving *away* from her, not back in. "Alex, what are you doing?"

Dusk was already making it hard to see out there, even for her. She couldn't imagine what it was like for him.

"I'm going to hide out in the upper level of one of these buildings and watch these clowns," Alex replied calmly. "There's a place up on this one where I can get in at about the second-story level — see?"

He was right; the structure of the building gave him easy hand- and foot-holds up to the window-slits on the second floor. Once there, since the building had fallen in at that point, he would be able to hide himself up above eye-level. And with the way that the blizzard was kicking up, his tracks would be hidden in a matter of moments.

"But — " she protested. "You're all alone out there!" She tried to keep her mind clear, but a thousand horrible possibilities ran around and around inside her thoughts, making her frantic. "There's no way I can help you if you're caught!"

"I won't be caught," he said confidently, finding handholds and beginning his climb.

It was already too late anyway; the pirates had begun entry. Even if he left now, he'd never make it back to the safety of the tunnel before they landed. If they had heat-sensors, they couldn't help but notice him, scrambling across the snow.

She poured relaxants into her blood and tried to stay as calm as he obviously felt, but it wasn't working. As the looters passed behind the planet's opposite side, he reached the top of the first tier of window-slits, moving slowly and deliberately — so deliberately that she wanted to scream at him to hurry.

As they hit the edge of the blizzard, Alex reached the broken place in the second story. And just as he tumbled over the edge into the relatively safe darkness behind the wall, they slowed for descent, playing searchlights all over the entire valley, cutting pathways of brightness across the gloom and thickly falling snow.

Alex took advantage of the lights, moving only after they had passed so that he had a chance to see exactly what lay in the room he had fallen into.

Nothing, actually; it was an empty section with a curved inner and outer wall, one door in the inner wall, and a wall at either end. Roughly half of the curving roof had fallen in; not much, really. Dirt and snow mounded under the break, near the join of end wall and outer wall the windows were still intact, and the floor was relatively clean. That was where Alex went.

From there he had a superb view of both the caches and the building that the looters were slowly lowering their ship into. Tia watched carefully and decided that her guess about an AI in-system pilot was probably correct; the movements of the ship had the jerkiness she associated with AIs. She kept expecting the looters to pick up Alex's signal, but evidently they were not expecting anyone to find this place — they seemed to be taking no precautions whatsoever. They didn't set any telltales or any alerts, and once they landed the ship and began disembarking from it, they made no effort to maintain silence.

On the other hand, given the truly appalling weather, perhaps they had no reason to be cautious. The worst of the blizzard was moving in, and not even the best of AIs could have landed in *that* kind of buffeting wind. She was just glad that Alex was under cover.

The storm didn't stop the looters from sending out crews to open up a new cache, however. . . .

She could hardly believe her sensors when she saw, via Alex's camera, a half-dozen lights bobbing down the canyon floor coming towards his hiding place. She switched to IR scan and saw that there were three times that many men, three to a light. None of them were wearing pressure-suits, although they were bundled up in cold weather survival gear.

"I don't believe they're doing that," Alex muttered.

"Neither do I," she replied softly. "That storm is going to be a killing blizzard in a moment. They're out of their minds."

She scanned up and down the radio wavelengths, looking for the one the looters were using. She found it soon enough; unmistakable by the paint-peeling language being used. While Alex huddled in his shelter, the men below him broke open yet another cache and began shoveling what were probably priceless artifacts into sacks as if they were so many rocks. Tia winced, and thought it likely that Alex was doing the same.

The looters were obviously aware that they were working against time; their haste alone showed the fact that they knew the worst of the storm was yet to come. Whoever was manning the radio back at the ship kept them appraised of their situation, and before long, he began warning them that it was time to start back, before the blizzard got so bad they would never be able to make it the few hundred meters back to their ship.

They would not be able to take the full fury of the storm — but Alex, in his pressure-suit, would be able to handle just about anything. With his heads-up helmet

displays, he didn't need to be able to see where he was
going. Was it possible that he would be able to sneak
back to her under the cover of the blizzard?

It was certainly worth a try.

The leader of the looters finally growled an acknow-
ledgement to the radio operator. "We're comin' in,
keep yer boots on," he snarled, as the lights turned
away from the cache and moved slowly back up the
canyon. The operator shut up; a moment later a signal
beacon shone wanly through the thickening snow at
the other end of the tiny valley. Soon the lights of the
looters had been swallowed up by darkness and heavy
snowfall — then the beacon faded as the snow and
wind picked up still more.

"Alex," she said urgently, "do you think you can
make it back to me?"

"Did you record me coming in?" he asked.

"Yes," she assured him. "Every step. I ought to be
able to guide you pretty well. You won't get a better
chance. Without the storm to cover you, they'll spot
you before you've gone a meter."

He peered out his window again, her camera
"seeing" what he saw — there was nothing out there.
Wind and snow made a solid wall just outside the building. Even Tia's IR scan couldn't penetrate it.

"I'll try it," he said. "You're right. There won't ever
be a better chance."

Alex ignored the darkness outside his helmet and
concentrated on the HUD projected on the inner surface. This was a lot like fly-by-wire training — or virtual
reality. Ignore what your eyes and senses wanted you
to do and concentrate on what the instruments are telling you.

Right now, they said he was near the entrance to the
valley hiding Tia.

It had been a long, frightening walk. The pressure

suit was protection against anything that the blizzard flung at him, but if he made a wrong step — well, it wouldn't save him from a long fall. And it wouldn't save him from being crushed by an avalanche if something triggered another one. Snow built up quickly under conditions like this.

It helped to think of Tia as he imagined her; made him feel warm inside. She kept a cheerful monologue going in his left ear, telling him what she had identified from the holos they'd made before the looters arrived. Sometimes he answered her, mostly he just listened. She was warmth and life in a world of darkness and cold, and as long as he could think of her sitting in the pilot's seat, with her sparkling eyes and puckish smile, he could muster the strength to keep his feet moving against the increasingly heavy weight of the snow.

Tired — he was getting so tired. It was tempting to lie down and let the snow cover him for a while as he took a little rest.

"Alex — you're here — " she said suddenly, breaking off in the middle of the sentence.

"I'm where?" he said stupidly. He was so tired —

"You're here — the entrance to the tunnel is somewhere around there — " The urgency in her voice woke him out of the kind of stupor he had been in. "Feel around for the rock face — the tunnel may be covered with snow, but you should be able to find it."

That was something he hadn't even thought of! What if the entrance to the tunnel had filled in? He'd be stuck out here in the blizzard, nowhere to go, out alone in the cold!

Stop that! he told himself sternly. *Just stop that! You'll be all right. The suit heaters won't give out in this — they're made for space, a little cold blizzard isn't going to balk them!*

Unless the cold snow clogged them somehow . . . or the wind was too much for them to compensate for . . . or they just plain gave up and died. . . .

He stumbled to his right, hands out, feeling frantically in the darkness for the rock face. He stumbled into it, cracking his faceplate against the stone. Fortunately the plate was made of sterner stuff than simple polyglas; although his head rang, the plate was fine.

Well, there was the rock. Now *where* —

The ground gave away beneath his feet, and he yelled with fear as he fell — the back of his head smacked against something and he kept falling —

No —

No, he wasn't falling, he was sliding. He'd fallen into the tunnel!

Quickly he spread hands and feet against the wall of the tunnel to slow himself and toggled his headlamp on; it had been useless in the blizzard. Now it was still pretty useless, but the light reflecting from the white ice above his face made him want to laugh with pleasure. Light! At last!

Light — and more of it down below his feet. The opposite end of the tunnel glowed with warm, white light as Tia opened the airlock and turned on the light inside it. He shot down the long dark tunnel and into the brightness, no longer caring if he hit hard when he landed. Caring only that he was coming home.

Coming home. . . .

• CHAPTER NINE

The whisper of a sensor-sweep across the landscape — like the brush of silk across Tia's skin, when she'd had skin. Like something not-quite-heard in the distance.

Tia stayed quiet and concentrated on keeping all of her outputs as low as possible. *We aren't here. You can't find us. Why don't you just fill your holds and go away?*

What had been a good hiding place was now a trap. Tia had shut down every system she could; Alex moved as little as possible. She had no way of knowing how sophisticated the pirates' systems were, so they were both operating on the assumption that anything out of the ordinary would alert the enemy to their presence, if not their location.

Whether or not the looters' initial carelessness had been because of the storm or because of greed — or whether they had been alerted by something she or Alex had done — now they were displaying all the caution Tia had expected of them. Telltales and alarms were in place; irregular sensor sweeps made it impossible for Alex to make a second trip to the ruins without being caught.

And now there were two more ships in orbit that had arrived while the blizzard still raged. One of those two ships had checked the satellite. Had they found Alex's handiwork, or were they simply following a procedure they had always followed? She had no way of knowing.

Whatever the case, those two ships kept her from taking off — and she wasn't going to transmit *anything* to the satellite. It was still broadcasting, and they only hoped it was because the pirates hadn't checked that closely. But it could have been because the pirates wanted them lulled into thinking they were safe.

So Tia had shut off all nonessential systems, and they used no active sensors, relying entirely on passive receptors. Knowing that sound could carry even past her blanket of snow, especially percussive sounds, Alex padded about in stocking feet when he walked at all. Three days of this now — and no sign that the looters were ready to leave yet.

Mostly he and Tia studied holos and the few artifacts that he had brought out of the cache area — once Tia had vacuum-purged them and sterilized them to a fair-thee-well.

After all, she kept telling herself, the pirates couldn't stay up there forever. Could they?

Unless they had some idea that Tia was already here. *Someone* had leaked what they knew about Hank and his cargo when they were on Presley Station. The leak could have gone beyond the station.

She was frightened and could not tell him; strung as tightly as piano strings with anxiety, with no way to work off the tension.

She knew that the same thoughts troubled Alex, although he never voiced them. Instead, he concentrated his attention completely on the enigmatic book of metal plates he had brought out of the cache.

There were glyphs of some kind etched into it, along the right edge of each plate, and a peculiarly matte-finished strip along the left edge of each. But most importantly, the middle of each page was covered with the pinprick patterns of what could only be stellar configurations. Having spent so much time studying stellar maps, both of them had recognized that they *were* nav-guides immediately. But to what — and far more importantly, what was the reference point? There was no way of knowing that she could see.

And who had made the book in the first place? The glyphs had an odd sort of familiarity about them, but nothing she was able to put a figurative finger on.

It was enough of a puzzle to keep Alex busy, but not enough to occupy her. It was very easy to spend a lot of time brooding over her brawn. Slumped in his chair, peculiarly handsome face intent, with a single light shining down on his head and the artifact, with the rest of the room in darkness — or staring into a screen full of data —

Like a scene out of a thriller-holo. The hero, biding his time, ready to crack under the strain but not going to show his vulnerability; the enemies waiting above. Priceless data in their hands, data that they dared not allow the enemy to have. The hero, thinking about the lover he had left behind, wondering if he will ever see her again —

Shellcrack. This was getting her nowhere.

She couldn't pace, she couldn't bite her nails, she couldn't even read to distract herself. Finally she activated a single servo and sent it discretely into his cabin to clean it. It hadn't *been* cleaned since they'd left the base; mostly Alex had just shoved things into drawers and closets and locked the doors down. She couldn't clean his clothing now — but as soon as they shook the hounds off their trail —

If they shook the hounds off their trail — if the second avalanche and the blizzard hadn't piled too much snow on top of them to clear away. There were eight meters of snow up there now, not four. Much more, and she might not be able to blast free.

Stop that. We'll get out of this.

Carefully she cleaned each drawer and closet, replacing what wasn't dirty and having the servo kidnap what was. Carefully, because there were lots of loose objects shoved in with the clothing.

But she never expected the one she found tumbled in among the bedcoverings.

A holocube — of her.

She turned the cube over and over in the servo's pinchers, changing the pictures, finding all of them familiar. Scenes of her from before her illness; the birthday party, posing with Theodore Bear —

Standing in her brand new pressure-suit in front of a fragment of wall covered with EsKay glyphs — that was a funny one; Mum had teased Dad about it because he'd focused on the glyphs out of habit. She'd come out half out of the picture, but the glyphs had been nice and sharp.

It hit her like a jolt of current. The glyphs. *That* was where she had seen them before! Oh, these were carved rather than inscribed, and time and sandstorms had worn them down to mere suggestions. They were formed in a kind of cursive style, where the ones on the book were angular — but —

She ran a quick comparison and got another jolt, this time of elation. "Alex!" she whispered excitedly. "Look!"

She popped the glyphs from the old holo up on her screen as he looked up, took the graphic of the third page of the book, and superimposed the one over the other. Aside from the differences in style, they were a perfect match.

"EsKays," he murmured, his tone awestruck. "Spirits of space — this book was made by the EsKays!"

"I think these caches and buildings must have been made by some race that knew the EsKays," she replied. "But even if they weren't — Alex, how much will you wager that this little set of charts shows the EsKay homeworld, once you figure out how to decipher it?"

"It would make sense," he said, after a moment. "Look at this smooth area on every page — always in the same place along the edge. I bet this is some kind of recording medium, like a datahedron — maybe optical —"

"Let me look at it," she demanded. "Put it in the lab."

Now she had something to keep *her* attention.

And something to keep her mind off him.

Alex had nothing more to do but read and brood. While Tia bent all the resources at her disposal on the artifact, he was left staring at screens and hoping the pirates didn't think to scan for large masses of metal under the snow.

Reading palled after too long; music was out because it could be detected, even if he were wearing headphones, and he hated headphones. He'd never been much of a one for entertainment holos, and they made at least as much noise as music.

That left him alone in the dark with his thoughts, which kept turning back towards Tia. He knew her childhood very well now — accessing the data available publicly and then doing the unthinkable, at least for anyone in the BB program: contacting Doctor Kennet and Doctor Anna and pumping them for information. Not with any great subtlety, he feared, but they hadn't taken it amiss. Of course, if anyone in CS found out what he'd been doing, he would be in major trouble. There was an ugly name for his feeling about Tia.

Fixation.

After that single attempt at finding a temporary companion in port, Alex had left the women alone — because he kept picking ones who looked like Tia. He had thought it would all wear off after a while; that sooner or later, since nothing could be done about it, the fascination would fade away.

And meanwhile, or so he'd told himself, it only made sense to learn as much about Tia as he could. She was unique; the oldest child ever to have been put into a shell. He had to be very careful with someone like that; the normal parameters of a brain-brawn relationship simply would not apply.

So now he knew what she had looked like — and, thanks to computer-projection, what she would have looked like if she had never caught that hideous disease and had grown up normally. Why, she might even have wound up at the Academy, if she hadn't chosen to follow in her famous parents' footsteps. He knew most of the details, not only of her pre-shell life, but of her life at Lab Schools. He knew as much about her as he would have if she had been his own sibling — except that his feelings about her had been anything but brotherly.

But he had told himself that they *were* brotherly, that he was not falling in love with a kind of ghost, that everything would be fine. He'd believed it, too.

That is, up until he ran into Chria Chance and her gunner.

There was *no* doubt in his mind from the moment the screen lit up that Chria and Neil were an item. The signs were there for anyone who knew how to read body language, especially for someone who knew Chria as well as Alex did. And his initial reaction to the relationship caught him completely by surprise.

Envy. Sheer, raw, uncomplicated envy. Not jealousy, for he wasn't at all interested in Chria and never had been. In some ways, he was very happy for her; she had been truly the poor little rich girl — High Family with four very proper brothers and sisters who were making the Family even more prestige and money. She alone had been the rebel; she of all of them had wanted something more than a proper position, a place on a board of directors, and a bloodless, loveless, high-status spouse. After she threatened to bring disgrace on all of them, blackmailing them by swearing she would join a shatter-rock synthocom band under her real name, they had permitted her the Academy under an assumed one.

No, he was happy for Chria; she had found exactly the life and partners that she had longed for.

But he *wanted* what she had — only he wanted it to be Tia sitting back there in the second seat. Or Tia in the front and himself in the back; it didn't much matter who was the one in command, if he could have had her *there*.

The strength of his feelings had been so unexpected that he had not known what to do with them — so he had attempted, clumsily, to cover them. Fortunately, everyone involved seemed to put his surliness down to a combination of pain from his injuries and wooziness due to the pain-pills he'd gulped.

If only it had been . . .

I'm in love with someone I can't touch, can't hold, can't even tell that I love her, he thought with despair, clenching his hand tightly on the armrest of his chair. *I —*

"Alex?" Tia whispered, her voice sounding unnaturally loud in the silence of the ship, for she had turned even the ventilation system down to a minimum. "Alex, I've decoded the storage-mode. It's old-fashioned hard-etched binary storage and I think that it's nav directions that relate to the stellar map on the page. Once I find a reference point I recognize, I'm pretty sure I can decode it all eventually. I got some ideas, though, since I was able to match some place-name glyphs — and we were right — I'm positive that these are directions to all the EsKay bases from the homeworld! So if we could just find a base — "

"And trace it back!" This was what she'd been looking for from the beginning, and excitement *for* her shoved aside all other feelings for the moment. "What's the deal — why the primitive navcharts? Not that it isn't a break for us, but if they were space-going, why limit ourself to a crawl?"

"Well, the storage medium is pretty hard to damage; you wouldn't believe how strong it is. So I can see why they chose it over something like a datahedron that a strong magnetic field can wipe. As for why the charts

themselves are so primitive, near as I can make out,
they didn't have Singularity Drive and they could or
would only warp *between* stars, using them as navigational stepping-stones. I don't know why; there may be
something there that would give the reason, but I can't
decode it." There was something odd and subdued
about her voice —

"What, hopping like a Survey ship?" he asked
incredulously. "You could spend years getting across
space that way!"

"Maybe they didn't care. Maybe hyper made them
sick." Now he recognized what the odd tone in her
voice was; she didn't seem terribly excited, now that she
had what she was looking for.

"Well, *we* don't have to do that," he pointed out.
"Once we get out of here, we can backtrack to the
EsKay homeworld, make a couple of jumps, and we'll
be stellar celebs! All we have to do is — "

"Is forget about our responsibilities," she said,
sharply. "Or else 'forget' to turn in this book with the
rest of the loot until we get a long leave. Or turn it in
and hope no one else beats us to the punch."

Keeping the book was out of the question, and he
dismissed it out of hand. "They won't," he replied positively. "No one else has spent as much time staring at
star-charts as we have. You've said as much yourself
the archeologists at the Institute get very specialized
and see things in a very narrow way. I don't think that
there's the slightest chance that anyone will figure out
what this book means within the next four or five years.
But you're right about having responsibilities; we are
under a hard contract to the Institute. We'll have to
wait until we can buy or earn a long leave — "

"That's not what's bothering me," she interrupted
in a very soft voice. "It's — the ethics of it. If we hold
back this information, how are we any better than
those pirates out there?"

"How do you mean?" he asked, startled.

"Withholding information — that's like data piracy, in a way. We're holding back, not only the data, but the career of whoever is the EsKay specialist right now — Doctor Lana Courtney-Rai, I think. In fact, if we keep this to ourselves, we'll be *stealing* her career advancement. I mean, we aren't even *real* archeologists!" There was no mistaking the distress in her voice.

"I think I see what you mean." And he did; he could understand it all too well. He'd seen both his parents passed over for promotions in favor of someone who hadn't earned the advancement but who "knew the right people." He'd seen the same thing happen at the Academy. It wasn't fair or right. "We can't do everything, can we?" he said slowly. "Not like in the holos, where the heroes can fight off pirates while performing brain surgery."

Tia made a sad little chuckle. "I'm beginning to think it's all we can do just to get our real job done right."

He leaned back in his chair and stared at the ceiling. "Funny. When this quest of ours was all theoretical, it was one thing — but we really can't go shooting off by ourselves and still do our duty, the duty that people are expecting us to do."

She didn't sigh, but her voice was heavy with regret. "It's not only a question of ethics, but of priorities. We can simply go on doing what we do best — and Chria Chance really put her finger on it, when she pointed out that she and Neil and Pol wouldn't know how to recognize our plague spot, and we would. *She* knows when she should let the experts take over. I hate to give up on the dream — but in this case, that dream was the kind of thing a kid could have, but — "

"But it's time to grow up — and let someone else play," Alex said firmly.

"Maybe we could go pretend to be archeologists," Tia added, "but we'd steal someone else's career in the process. Become second-rate — but very, very lucky amateur pot-hunters."

He sighed for both of them. "They'd hate us, you know. Everyone we respected would hate us. And we'd be celebrities, but we wouldn't be real archeologists."

"Alex?" she said, after a long silence. "I think we should just seal that book up with our findings and what we've deduced about it. Then we should lock it up with the rest of the loot and go on being a stellar CS team. Even if it does get awfully boring running mail and supplies, sometimes."

"It's not boring now," he said ruefully, without thinking. "I kind of wish it was."

Silence for a long time, then she made a tiny sound that he would have identified as a whimper in a softperson. "I wish you hadn't reminded me," she said.

"Why?"

"Because — because it seems as if we're never going to get out of here — that they're going to find us eventually."

"Stop that," he replied sharply, reacting to the note of panic in her voice. "They can't hover up there forever. They'll run out of supplies, for one thing."

"So will we," she countered.

"And they'll run out of patience! Tia, think — these are pirates, and they don't even know there's anyone else here, not for certain, anyway! When they don't find anything, they'll give up and take their loot off to sell!" He wanted, badly, to pace — but that would make noise. "We can leave when they're gone!"

"If — we can get out."

"What?" he said, startled.

"I didn't want you to worry — but there's been two avalanches since you got back, and all the snow the blizzard dropped."

He stared at her column in numbed shock, but she wasn't finished.

"There's about eleven meters of snow above us. I don't know if I can get out. And even if CenSec shows up, I don't know if they'll hear a hail under all this ice. I lost the signals from the surface right after that last avalanche, and the satellite signals are getting too faint to read clearly."

He said the first thing that came into his head, trying to lighten the mood, but without running it past his internal censor first. "Well, at least if I'm going to be frozen into a glacier for all eternity, I've got my love to keep me warm."

He stopped himself, but not in time. *Oh, brilliant. Now she thinks she's locked in an iceberg with a fixated madman!*

"Do — " Her voice sounded choked, probably with shock. "Do you mean that?"

He could have shot himself. "Tia," he began babbling, "it's all right, really, I mean I'm not going to go crazy and try to crack your column or anything, I really am all right, I — "

"Did you *mean* that?" she persisted.

"I — " *Oh well. It's on the record. You can't make it worse.* "Yes. I don't know, it just sort of — happened." He shrugged helplessly. "It's not anything crazy, like a fixation. But, well — I just don't want any partner of *any* kind but you. If that's love, then I guess I love you. And I really, really love you a lot." He sighed and rubbed his temples. "So there it is, out in the open at last. I hope I don't offend or frighten you, but you're the best thing that ever happened to me, and that's a fact. I'd rather be with you than anyone else I know, or know of." He managed a faint grin. "Holostars and stellar celebs included."

The plexy cover to Ted Bear's little "shrine" popped open, and he jumped.

"I can't touch you, and you can't touch me, but — would you like to hug Theodore?" she replied softly. "I love you, too, Alex. I think I have ever since you went out to face the Zombie Bug. You're the bravest, cleverest, most wonderful brawn I could ever imagine, and I wouldn't want to be anyone's partner but yours."

The offer of her childhood friend was the closest she could come to intimacy — and he knew it.

He got up, carefully, and took the little fellow down out of his wall-home, hugging the soft little bear once, hard, before he restored him again and closed the door.

"You have a magnificent lady, Theodore Bear," he told the solemn-faced little toy. "And I'm going to do my best to make her happy."

He turned back to her column and cleared his throat, carefully. Time, and more than time, to change the subject. "Right," he said. "Now that we've both established why we've been touchy — let's see if we can figure out what our options are."

"Options?" she replied, confused.

"Certainly." He raised his chin defiantly. "I intend to spend the rest of my life with you — and I don't intend *that* to be restricted to how long it takes before the pirates find us or we freeze to death! So let's figure out some *options*, hang it all!"

To his great joy and relief, she actually laughed. And if there was an edge of hysteria in it, he chose to ignore that little nuance.

"Right," she said. "Options. Well, we can start with the servos, I guess. . . ."

Tia snuggled down into his arms, and turned into a big blue toy bear. The bear looked at him reproachfully.

He started to get up, but the bedcovers had turned to snowdrifts, and he was frozen in place. The bear tried to chip him out, but its blunt arms were too soft to make an impression on the ice-covered drifts.

Then he heard rumbling — and looked up, to see an avalanche poised to crash down on him like some kind of slow-motion wave —

The avalanche rumbled, and Tia-the-bear growled back, interposing herself between him and the tumbling snow —

"Alex, wake up!"

He floundered awake, flailing at the bedclothes, hitting the light button more by accident than anything else. He blinked as the light came up full, blinding him, his legs trapped in a tangle of sheets and blankets. "What?" he said, his tongue too thick for his mouth. "Who? Where?"

"Alex," Tia said, her voice strained, but excited. "Alex, I have been trying to get you to wake up for fifteen minutes! There's a CenSec ship Upstairs, and it's beating the tail off those two pirates!"

CenSec? Spirits of space —

"What happened?" he asked, grabbing for clothing and pulling it on. "From the beginning —"

"The first I knew of it was when one of the pirates sent a warning down to the ship here to stay under cover and quiet. I got the impression that they thought it was just an ordinary Survey ship, until it locked onto one of them and started blasting." Tia had brought up all of her systems again; fresher air was moving briskly through the ventilator, all the lights and boards were up and active in the main cabin. "That was when all the scans stopped — and I started breaking loose. I ran that freeze-thaw cycle you suggested, and a couple of minutes ago, I fired the engines. I can definitely move, and I'm pretty sure I can pull out of here without too much trouble. I might lose some paint and some bits of things on my surface, but nothing that can't be repaired."

"What about Upstairs?" he asked, running for his chair without stopping for shoes or even socks, and strapping himself down.

"Good news and bad news. The CenSec ship looks like its going to take both the pirates," she replied. "The bad news is that while I can receive, I can't seem to broadcast. The ice might have jammed something, I can't tell."

"All right; we can move, and the ambush Upstairs is being taken care of." Alex clipped the last of his restraint belts in place; when Tia moved, it could be abruptly, and with little warning. "But if we can't broadcast, we can't warn CenSec that there's another ship down here — we can't even identify ourselves as a friend. And we'll be a sitting duck for the pirates if we try to rise. They can just hide in their blinds and ambush the CenSec ship, then wait to see if we come out of hiding — as soon as we clear their horizon they can pot us."

Alex considered the problem as dispassionately as he could. "Can we stay below their horizon until we're out of range?"

Tia threw up a map as an answer. If the pirate chose to pursue them, there was no way that she could stay out of range of medium guns, and they had to assume that was what the pirate had.

"There has to be a way to keep them on the ground, somehow," Alex muttered, chewing a hangnail, aware that with every second that passed their window of opportunity was closing. "What's going on Upstairs?"

"The first ship is heavily damaged. If I'm reading the tactics right, the CenSec ship is going to move in for the kill — provided the other pirate gives him a chance."

Alex turned his attention back to their own problem. "If we could just cripple them — throw enough rocks down on them or — wait a minute. Bring up the views of the building they're hiding in — the ones you got from my camera."

Tia obeyed, and Alex studied the situation carefully, matching pictures with memory. "Interesting thing about those hills — see how some of them look broken-off, as if those tips get too heavy to support after a while? I bet that's because the winds come in from different directions and scour out under the crests once in a while. Can you give me a better shot of the hills overhanging those buildings?"

"No problem." The viewpoint pulled back, displaying one of those wave-crest hills overshadowing the building with the partial roof. "Alex!" she exclaimed.

"You see it too," he said with satisfaction. "All right girl, think we can pull this off?"

For answer, she revved her engines. "Be a nice change to hit back, for once!"

"Then let's lift!"

The engines built from a quiet purr to a bone-deep, bass rumble, more felt than heard. Tia pulled in her landing gear, then began rocking herself by engaging null-grav, first on the starboard, then on the port side, each time rolling a little more. Alex did what he could, playing with the attitude jets, trying to undercut some of the ice.

Her nose rose, until Alex tilted back in his chair at about a forty-five degree angle. That was when Tia cut loose with the full power of her rear thrusters.

"We're moving!" she shouted over the roar of her own engines, engines normally reserved only for in-atmosphere flight. There was no sensation of movement, but Alex clearly heard the scrape of ice along her hull, and winced, knowing that without a long stint in dry dock, Tia would look worse than Hank's old tramp-freighter. . . .

Suddenly, they were free —

Tia killed the engines and engaged full null-gee drive, hovering just above the surface of the snow in eerie silence.

"CenSec got the first ship; the other one jumped them. It looks pretty even," Tia said shortly, as Alex heard the whine of the landing gear being dropped again. "So far, no one has noticed us. Are you braced?"

"Go for it," he replied. "Is there anything I can do?"

"Hold on," she said shortly.

She shot skyward, going for altitude. She knew the capabilities of her hull better than Alex did; he was going to leave this in her hands. The hill they wanted was less than a kilometer away — when they'd gotten high enough, Tia nosed over and dove for it. She aimed straight for the crest, as if it were a target and she a projectile.

Sudden fear clutched at his throat, his heart going a million beats per second. *She can't mean to ram* —

Alex froze, his hands clutching the armrests.

At the last minute, Tia rolled her nose up, hitting the crest of the hill with her landing gear instead of her nose.

The shriek and crunch of agonized metal told Alex that they were not going to make port anywhere but a space station now. The impact rammed him back into his chair, the lights flickered and went out, and crash systems deployed, cushioning him from worse shock. Even so, he blacked out for a moment.

When he came to again, the lights were back on, and Tia hovered, tilted slightly askew, above the alien city.

Below and to their right was what was left of the roofless building — now buried beneath a pile of ice, earth and rock.

"Are you all right?" he managed, though it hurt to move his jaw.

"Space-worthy," she said, and there was no mistaking the shakiness in her voice. "Barely. I'll be as leaky as a sieve in anything but the main cabin and the passenger section, though. And I don't know about my drives — hang on, we're being hailed."

The screen flickered and filled with the image of Neil, with Chria Chance in the background. "AH One

Oh-Three-Three, is that you? I assume you had a good reason for playing 'chicken' with a mountain?"

"It's us," Alex replied, feeling all of his energy drain out as his adrenaline level dropped. "There's another one of your playmates under that rockpile."

"Ah." Neil said nothing more, simply nodded. "All right, then. Can you come up to us?"

"We aren't going to be making any landings," Tia pointed out. "But I don't know about the state of our drives."

Chria leaned over her partner's shoulder. "I wouldn't trust them if I were you," she said. "But if you can get up here, we can take you in tow and hold you in orbit until one of the transports shows up. Then you can ride home in their bay."

"It's a deal," Alex told her — then, with a lift of an eyebrow, "I didn't know you could do that."

"There's a lot you don't know," she told him. "Is that all right with you, Tia?"

"At this point, just about anything would be all right with me," she replied. "We're on the way."

Tia was still a little dizzy from the call she'd gotten from the Institute. *When you're refitted, we'd like you to take the first Team into what we think is the EsKay homeworld. You and Alexander have the most experience in situations where plague is a possibility of any other courier on contract to us.* It had only made sense; to this day no one knew what had paralyzed *her*. She had a vested interest in making sure the team stayed healthy, and an even bigger one in helping to find the bug.

Of course, they knew that. And they knew she would never buy out her contract until *this* assignment was over. Blackmail? Assuredly. But it was a form of blackmail she could live with.

Besides, if her plan worked, she would soon be digging *with* the Prime Team, not just watching them. It might take a while, but sooner or later, she'd have enough money made from her investments—

Once she paid for the repairs, that is. From the remarks of the techs working on her hull, they would not be cheap.

Then Stirling stunned her again, presenting her with the figures in her account.

"So, my dear lady," said Stirling, "between an unspecified reward from the Drug Enforcement Arm, the bonus for decoding the purpose of the EsKay navbook, the fine return from your last investment, and the finders' fee for that impressive treasure trove, you are *quite* a wealthy shellperson."

"So I see," Tia replied, more than a little dazed. "But what about the bill for repairs—"

"Covered by CenSec." Stirling wasn't precisely gloating, but he was certainly enjoying himself. "And if you don't mind my saying so, that was *my* work. I merely repeated what you had told me about the situation— pointed out that your damages were due entirely to a civilian aiding in the apprehension of dangerous criminals — and CenSec seemed positively eager to have the bills transferred over. When I mentioned how you had kept *their* ship from ambush from the ground, they decided you needed that Singularity Drive you've always wanted."

She suspected he had done more than merely mention it . . . perhaps she ought to see if she could get Lee Stirling as her Advocate, instead of the softperson she had, who had done *nothing* about the repairs or the drive! So, she would not have to spend a single penny of all those bonuses on her own repairs! "What about my investments in the prosthetics firm? And what if I take my bonus money and plow it back into Moto-Prosthetics?"

"Doing brilliantly. And if you do that — hmm — do you realize you'll have a controlling interest?" Stirling sounded quite amazed. "Is this something you wanted? You *could* buy out your contract with all this. Or get yourself an entire new refit internally and externally."

"Yes," she replied firmly. She was glad that Alex wasn't aboard at the moment, even though she felt achingly lonely without the sounds of his footsteps or his tuneless whistling. This was something she needed absolute privacy for. "In fact, I am going to need a softperson proxy to go to the Board of Directors for me."

"Now?" Stirling asked.

"As soon as I have controlling interest," she replied. "The sooner the better."

And it can't be soon enough to suit me.

Alex looked deeply into the bottom of his glass and decided that this one was going to be his last. He had achieved the state of floating that passed for euphoria; any more and he would pass it, and become disgustingly drunk. Probably a weepy drunk, too, all things considered. That would be a bad thing; despite his civilian clothing, someone might recognize him as a CS brawn, and that would be trouble. Besides, this was a high-class bar as spaceport bars went; human bartender, subdued, restful lighting, comfortable booths and stools, good music that was not too loud. They didn't need a maudlin drunk; they really didn't need any drunk. No point in ruining other people's evening just because his life was a mess. . . .

He felt the lump in his throat and knew one more drink would make it spill over into an outpouring of emotion. The bartender leaned over and said, confidingly, "Buddy, if I were you, I'd cut off about now."

Alex nodded, a little surprised, and swallowed back the lump. Had liability laws gotten to the point where barenders were watching their customers for risky behavior? "Yeah. What I figured." He sniffed a bit and told himself to straighten up before he became an annoyance.

The bartender — a human, which was why Alex had chosen to drink away his troubles here, if such a thing was possible — did not leave. Instead, he polished the slick pseudo-wooden bar beside Alex with a spotless cloth, and said, casually, "If you don't mind my saying so, buddy, you look like a man with a problem or two."

Alex laughed, mirthlessly. The man had no idea. "Yeah. Guess so."

"You want to talk about it?" the bartender persisted. "That's what they hire me for. That's why you're paying so much for the drinks."

Alex squinted up at the man, who was perfectly ordinary in a way that seemed very familiar. Conservative haircut, conservative, casual clothing. Nothing about the face or the expression to mark him except a certain air of friendly concern. It was that "air" that tipped him off — it was very polished, very professional. "Counselor?" he asked, finally.

The bartender nodded to a framed certificate over the three shelves of antique and exotic bottles behind the bar. "Licensed. Confidential. Freelance. Been in the business for five years. You probably can't tell me anything I haven't heard a hundred times before."

Freelance and confidential meant that whatever Alex told him would stay with him, and would not be reported back to his superiors. Alex was both surprised and unsurprised — the Counselor-attended bars had been gaining in popularity when he had graduated. He just hadn't known they'd gotten *that* popular. He certainly hadn't expected to find one out here, at a refit station. People tended to pour out their problems when they'd been drinking; someone back on old Terra had figured out that it might be a good idea to give them someone to talk to who *might* be able to tender some reasonable advice. Now, so he'd heard there were more Counselors behind bars than there were in offices, and a large number of bartenders were going back to school to get Counselor's licenses.

Suddenly the need to unburden himself to *someone* was too much to withstand. "Ever been in love?" he asked, staring back down at the empty glass and shoving it back and forth a little between his index fingers.

The bartender took the glass away and replaced it with a cup of coffee. "Not personally, but I've seen a lot of people who are — or think they are."

"Ah." Alex transferred his gaze to the cup, which steamed very nicely. "I wouldn't advise it."

"Yeah. A lot of them say that. Personal troubles with your significant?" the bartender-*cum*-Counselor prompted. "Maybe it's something I can help out with."

Alex sighed. "Only that I'm in love with someone that — isn't exactly reachable." He scratched his head for a moment, trying to think of a way to phrase it without giving too much away. "Our — uh — professions are going to keep us apart, no matter what, and there's some physical problems, too."

The habit of caution was ingrained too deeply. Freelance Counselor or no, he couldn't bring himself to tell the whole truth to this man. Not when telling it could lose him access to Tia altogether, if the wrong people heard all this.

"Can't you change jobs?" the Counselor asked, reasonably. "Surely a job isn't worth putting yourself through misery. From everything I've ever seen or heard, it's better to have a low-paying job that makes you happy than a high-paying one that's driving you into bars."

Alex shook his head, sorrowfully. "That won't help," he sighed hopelessly. "It's not just the job, and changing it will only make things worse. Think of us as — as a Delphin and an Avithran. She can't swim, I can't fly. Completely incompatible lives."

And that puts it mildly.

The Counselor shook his head. "That doesn't sound promising, my friend. Romeo and Juliet romances are all very well for the holos, but they're hell on your insides. I'd see if I couldn't shake my emotional attachment, if I was you. No matter how much you think you love someone, you can always turn the heat down if you decide that's what you want to do about it."

"I'm trying," Alex told him, moving the focus of his concentration from the coffee cup to the bartender's face. "Believe me, I'm *trying*. I've got a couple of weeks extended leave coming, and I'm going to use every minute of it in trying. I've got dates lined up; I've got parties I'm hitting — and a friend from CenSec is planning on taking me on an extended shore leave crawl."

The bartender nodded, slowly. "I understand, and seeing a lot of attractive new people is one way to try and shake an emotional attachment. But friend — you are not going to find your answer in the bottom of a bottle."

"Maybe not," Alex replied sadly. "But at least I can find a little forgetfulness there."

And as the bartender shook his head, he pushed away from his seat, turned, took a tight grip on his dubious equilibrium, and walked out the door, looking for a little more of that forgetfulness.

Angelica Guon-Stirling bint Chad slid into her leather-upholstered seat and smiled politely at the man seated next to her at the foot of the huge, black marble table. He nodded back and returned his attention to the stock market report he was reading on the screen of his datalink. Other men and women, dressed in conservative suits and the subdued hues of management filed in and took the remaining places around the table. She refrained from chuckling. In a few more moments, he might well be more interested in her than in anything that datalink could supply. She'd gotten entry to the meeting on the pretext of representing her uncle's firm on some unspecified business — they represented enough fluid wealth that the secretary had added her to the agenda and granted her entry to the sacred boardroom. It was a very well-appointed sacred boardroom; rich with the scent of expensive leather and hushed as only a room ringed with high-priced anti-surveillance equipment could be. The lights were set at exactly the perfect psychological hue and intensity for the maximum amount of alertness, the chair cradled her with unobtrusive comfort. The colors of warm white, cool black, and gray created an air of efficiency and importance, without being sterile.

None of this intimidated Angelica in the least. She had seen a hundred such board rooms in the past, and would probably see a thousand more before her career had advanced to the point that she was too busy to be sent out on such missions. Her uncle had not only chosen her to be Ms. Cade's proxy because they were related; he had chosen her because she was the best proxy in the firm. And this particular venture was going to need a very delicate touch, for what Ms. Cade wanted was not anything the board of directors of Moto-Prosthetics was going to be ready for. *They* thought in terms of hostile takeovers, poison pills, golden parachutes. Ms. Cade had an entirely different agenda. If this were not handled well and professionally, the board might well fight, and that would waste precious time.

Though it might seem archaic, board meetings still took place in person. It was too easy to fake holos, to create a computer-generated simulacrum of someone who was dead or in cold sleep. That was why she was here now, with proxy papers in order and properly filed with all the appropriate authorities. Not that she minded. This was exciting work, and every once in a while there was a client like Hypatia Cade, who wanted something so different that it made everything else she had done up to now seem like a training exercise.

The meeting was called to order — and Angelica stood up before the chairman of the board could bring up normal business. Now was the time. If she waited until her scheduled turn, she could be lost or buried in nonsense — and as of this moment, the board's business was no longer what had been scheduled anyway. It was hers, Angelica's, to dictate. It was a heady brew, power, and Angelica drank it to the dregs as all eyes centered on her, most affronted that she had "barged in" on their business.

"Gentlemen," she said smoothly, catching all their attentions. "Ladies. I believe you should all check your datalinks. If you do, you will see that my client, a Miz Hypatia Cade, has just this moment purchased a controlling interest in your preferred stock. As of this moment, Hypatia Cade *is* Moto-Prosthetics. As her proxy, she directs me to put the normal business before the board on hold for a moment."

There was a sudden, shocked moment of silence — then a rustle as cuffs were pushed back — followed by another moment of silence as the members of the board took in the reality of her statement, verified that it was true, wondered how it had happened without them noticing, then waited for the axe to fall. All eyes were on Angelica; some of them desperate. Most of the desperate were those who backed risky ventures within the company, and were wondering if their risk-taking had made them into liabilities for the new majority owner.

Ah, power. I could disband the entire board and bring in my own people, and you all know it. These were the moments that she lived for; the feeling of having the steel hand within the velvet glove — knowing that she held immense power, and choosing not to exercise it.

Angelica slid back down into her seat and smiled —

smoothly, coolly, but encouragingly. "Be at ease, ladies and gentlemen. The very first thing that my client wishes to assure you of is that she intends no shakeups. She is satisfied with the way this company is performing, and she does not intend to interfere in the way you are running it."

Once again, the faces around the table changed. Disbelief in some eyes, calculation in others. Then understanding. It would be business as usual. Nothing would change. These men and women still had *their* lives, *their* power, undisturbed.

She waited for the relief to set in, then pounced, leaning forward, putting her elbows down in the table, and steepling her hands before her. "But I must tell you that this will be the case only so long as Miz Cade is satisfied. And Miz Cade *does* have a private agenda for this company."

Another pause, to let the words sink in. She saw the questions behind the eyes — what kind of private agenda? Was it something that this Cade person wanted them to do — or to make? Or was it something else altogether?

"It's something that she wants you to construct; nothing you are not already capable of carrying off," Angelica continued, relishing every moment. "In fact, I would venture to say that it is something you *could* be doing now, if you had the inclination. It's just a little personal project, shall we say. . . . "

Alex's mouth tasted like an old rug; his eyes were scratchy and puffed, and his head pounded. Every joint ached, his stomach churned unhappily, and he was not at all enjoying the way the room had a tendency to roll whenever he moved.

The wages of sin were counted out in hangovers, and this one was one of monumental proportions.

Well, that's what happens when you go on a two-week drunk.

He closed his eyes, but that didn't help. It hadn't

exactly been a two-week drunk, but he had never once in the entire span been precisely sober. He had chosen, quite successfully, to glaze his problems over with the fuzz and blurring of alcohol.

It was *all* that had happened. He had not shaken his fixation with Tia. He was just as hopelessly in love with her as he had been before he started his binge. And he had tried everything short of brain-wipe to get rid of the emotion; he'd made contact with some of his old classmates, he'd gone along with Neil and Chria on a celebratory spree, he'd talked to more bartender-Counselors, he'd picked up girl after girl. . . .

To no avail whatsoever.

Tia Cade it was who was lodged so completely in his mind and heart, and Tia Cade it would remain.

So, besides being hung over, he was still torn up inside. And without that blur of alcohol to take the edge off it, his pain was just as bad as before.

There was only one thing for it: he and Tia would have to work it all out, somehow. One way or another.

He opened his eyes again; his tiny rented cubicle spun slowly around, and he groaned as his stomach protested.

First things first; deal with the hangover. . . .

It was just past the end of the second shift when he made his way down the docks to the refit berth where CenSec had installed Tia for her repair work. It had taken that long before he felt like a human being again. One thing was certain; that was *not* something he intended to indulge in ever again. One long binge in his life was enough.

I just hope I haven't fried too many brain cells with stupidity. I don't have any to spare.

He found the lock closed, but there were no more workers swarming about, either inside the bay or out. That was a good sign, since it probably meant all the repairs were over. He'd used the day-and-night nois as an excuse to get away, assuming Tia would contact him if she needed to.

As he hit the lock controls and gave them his palm to read, it suddenly occurred to him that she hadn't made any attempt at all to contact him in all the time he'd been gone.

Had he frightened her?

Had she reported him?

The lock cycled quickly, and he stepped onto a ship that was uncannily silent.

The lights had been dimmed down; the only sounds were of the ventilation system. Tia did not greet him; nothing did. He might as well have been on an empty, untenanted ship, without even an AI.

Something was wrong.

His heart pounding, his mouth dry with apprehension, he went to the main cabin. The boards were all dark, with no signs of activity.

Tia wasn't sulking; Tia didn't sulk. There was nothing functioning that could not be handled by the stand-alone redundant micros.

He dropped his bag on the deck, from fingers that had gone suddenly nerveless.

There could be only one cause for this silence, this absence of activity. Tia was gone.

Either the BB authorities had found out about how he felt, or Tia herself had complained. They had come and taken her away, and he would never see or talk to her again.

As if to confirm his worst fears, a glint of light on an open plexy window caught his eye. Theodore Edward Bear was gone, his tiny shrine empty.

No —

But the evidence was inescapable.

Numb with shock, he found himself walking towards his own cabin. Perhaps there would be a note there, in his personal database. Perhaps there would be a message waiting from CS, ordering him to report for official Counseling.

Perhaps both. It didn't matter. Tia was gone, and very little mattered anymore.

Black despair washed into him, a despair so deep that not even tears would relieve it. Tia was gone. . . .

He opened the door to his cabin, and the light from the corridor shone inside, making the person sitting on his bunk blink.

Person sitting on my —

Female. It was definitely female. And she wasn't wearing anything like a CS uniform, Counselor, Advocate, or anything else. In fact, she wasn't wearing very much at all — a little neon-red Skandex unitard that left nothing to imagine.

He turned on the light, an automatic reflex. His visitor stared up at him, lips creasing in a shy smile. She was tiny, smaller than he had first thought; dark and elfin, with big blue eyes, the image of a Victorian fairy — and oddly familiar.

In her hands, she gently cradled the missing Teddy Bear. It was the bear that suddenly shook his brain out of inactive and into overdrive.

He stared; he gripped the side of the door. "T-T-Tia," he stammered.

She smiled again, with less shyness. "Hi," she said — and it was Tia's voice, sounding a bit — odd — coming from a mouth and not a speaker. "I'm sorry I had to shut so much down, I can't run *this* and the ship, too."

It was Tia — *Tia!* — sitting there in a body, a human body, like the realization of his dream!

"This?" he replied cleverly.

"I hope you don't mind if I don't get up," she continued, a little ruefully. "I'm not very good at walking yet. They just delivered this today, and I haven't had much practice in it yet."

"It?" he said, sitting heavily down on his bunk and staring at her. "How — what — "

"Do you like it?" she asked, pathetically eager for his approval. He wasn't sure what he was supposed to approve of — the body?

"How could I *not* like it — you — " His head was spinning as badly as it had a few hours ago. "Tia, what on earth *is* this?"

She blinked, and giggled. "I keep forgetting. You know all that bonus money we've been getting? I kept investing it, then reinvesting the profits in Moto-Prosthetics. But when we got back here, I was thinking about something Doctor Kenny told me, that they had the capability to make a body like this, but that there was no way to put a naked brain in it, and there was so *much* data-transfer needed to run it that the link could only be done at very short distances."

"Oh." He couldn't help but stare at her; this was his dream, his daydream — his —

Never mind.

"Anyway," she continued, blithely unaware that she had stunned him into complete silence, "it seemed to me that the body would be perfect for a brainship, I mean, we've got all the links already, and it wouldn't be any harder to control a body from inside than a servo. But he was already an investor, and he told me it wasn't likely they'd ever build a body like that, since there was no market for it, because it would cost as much as a brainship contract buy-out."

"But how — "

She laughed aloud. "That was why I took all my share of the bonuses and bought more stock! I bought a controlling interest, then I told them to build me a body! I don't need a buy-out — I don't really want a buy-out — not since the Institute decided to give us the EsKay homeworld assignment."

He shook his head. "That simple? It hardly seems possible . . . didn't they argue?"

"They were too happy that I was letting them keep their old jobs," she told him cynically. "After all, as controlling stockholder, I had the right to fire them all and set up my own Board of Directors. But I have to tell you the funniest thing!"

"What's that?" he asked.

Her hands caressed Theodore's soft fur. "Word of what I was doing leaked out, and now there *is* a market! Did you have any idea how many shellpersons there are who've earned a buy-out, but didn't have any place to go with it, because they were happy with their current jobs?"

He shook his head, dumbly.

"Not too many ships," she told him, "but a lot of shellpersons running installations. Lots of them. And there were a lot of inquiries from brainships, too — some of them saying that they'd be willing to skip a buy-out to have a body! Moto-Prosthetics even got a letter of protest from some of the Advocates!"

"Why?" he asked, bewildered. "Why on earth would they care?"

"They said that we were the tools of the BB program, that we had purposely put this 'mechanical monster' together to tempt brainships out of their buy-out money." She tilted her head to one side, charmingly, and frowned. "I must admit that angle had never occurred to me. I hope that really isn't a problem. Maybe I should have Lars and Lee Stirling look into it for me."

"Tia," he managed, around the daze surrounding his thoughts, "what *is* this 'mechanical monster' of yours?"

"It's a cybernetic body, with a wide-band comlink in the extreme shortwave area up here." She tapped her forehead. "What's different about it is that it's using shellperson tech to give me full sensory input from the skin as well as output to the rest. My range isn't much outside the ship, but my techs at Moto are working on that. After all, when we take the Prime Team out to the EsKay homeworld, I'm going to want to join the dig, if they'll let me. What with alloys and silicates and carbon-fibers and all, it's not much heavier than you are, even though it outmasses a softperson female of this type by a few kilos. *Everything* works, though, full sensory and well — everything. Like a softperson again, except that I don't get muscle fatigue and I can shut off the pain-sensors if I'm damaged. That was why I took Ted out; I wanted to feel him, to hug him again."

She just sat there and beamed at him, and he shook his head. "But why?" he asked, finally.

She blinked, and then dropped her eyes to the bear. "I — probably would have gone for a buy-out, if it hadn't been for you," she said shyly. "Or maybe a Sin-gularity Drive, except that CenSec decided that maybe they'd better give me one and threw it in with the repairs. But — I told you, Alex. You're the most special person in my life. How could I know this was possible, and *not* do it for — for both of us?"

He dared to touch her then, just one finger along her cheek, then under her chin, raising her eyes to meet his. There was nothing about those lucent eyes that looked mechanical or cold; nothing about the warmth and resiliency of the skin under his hand that said "cybernetic."

"You gave up your chance of a buy-out for me — for us?" he asked.

She shrugged. "Someone very wise once said that the chance for happiness was worth giving up a little freedom for. And really, between the Advocates and everybody, they really can't *make* us do anything we don't want to."

"I guess not." He smiled, and she smiled back. "You do realize that you've actually done the BB program two favors, don't you?"

"I have?" She blinked again, clearly bewildered.

"You've given shellpersons something *else* to do with

their buy-out money. If they don't have Singularity Drives, they'll *want* those first — and *then* they'll want one of these." He let go of her chin and tapped her cheek playfully. "Maybe more than one. Maybe one of each sex, or in different body types. Some brainships may never buy out. But the other problem — you've solved fixation, my clever lady."

She nodded after a moment. "I never thought of that. But you're right! If you have a *body*, someone to be with and — ah — everything — you won't endanger the shellperson. And if it's just an infatuation based on the dream instead of the reality — well — "

"Well, after a few rounds with the body, it will cool off to something manageable." He chuckled. "Watch out, or they'll give you a bonus for that one, too!"

She laughed. "Well, I won't take it as a buy-out! Maybe I'll just build myself a second body! After all, if we aren't going to be exploring the universe like a couple of holo-heroes, we have the time to explore things a little — closer to hand. Right?"

She posed, coyly, looking at him flirtatiously over her shoulder. He wondered how many of her entertain-ment holos she'd watched to find *that* pose. "So, what would you like, Alex? A big, blond Valkyrie? An Egyp-tian queen? A Nubian warrior-maid? How about a Chinese princess or — "

"Let's learn about what we have at hand, shall we?" he interrupted, sliding closer to her and taking her in his arms. Her head tilted up towards his, her eyes shin-ing with anticipation. Carefully, gently, he took the bear out of her hands and placed him on the shelf above the foot of the bed, as her arms slid around his waist, cautiously, but eagerly.

"Now," he breathed, "about that exploration . . . "

– End –

MERCEDES LACKEY

The Hottest Fantasy Writer Today!

URBAN FANTASY

Knight of Ghosts and Shadows with Ellen Guon

Elves in L.A.? It would explain a lot, wouldn't it? Eric Banyon is a musician with a lot of talent but very little ambition—and his lady just left him lovelorn in a deserted corner of the Renaissance Fairegrounds, singing the blues and playing his flute. He couldn't have known the desperate sadness of his music would free Korendil a young elven noble, from the magical prison he had been languishing in for centuries. Eric really needed a good cause to get his life in gear—now he's got one. With Korendil he must raise an army to fight against the evil lord who seeks to conquer all of California. And Eric's music will show the way....

Summoned to Tourney with Ellen Guon

Elves in San Francisco? Where else would an elf go when L.A. got too hot? All is well there with our elf-lord his human companion and the mage who brought them all together—until it turns out that San Francisco doomed to fall off the face of the continent. Doomed that is, unless our mage can summon the Nightflyers, the soul-devouring shadow creatures from the dreaming world—creatures no one on Earth could possibly control....

Born to Run with Larry Dixon

There are elves out there. And more are coming. But even elves need money to survive in the "real" world. The good elves in South Carolina, intrigued by the thrill of stock car racing, are manufacturing new, light-weight engines (with, incidentally, very little "cold" iron); the bad elves run a kiddie-porn and snuff-film ring, with occasional forays into drugs. *Children in Peril—Elves to the Rescue.* (Part of the SERRAted Edge series.)

HIGH FANTASY

Bardic Voices: The Lark & The Wren

Rune could be one of the greatest bards of her world, but the daughter of a tavern wench can't get much in the way of formal training. So one night she goes up to play for the Ghost of Skull Hill. She'll either fiddle till dawn to prove her skill as a bard—or die trying....

Also by Mercedes Lackey:

Reap the Whirlwind with C.J. Cherryh
Part of the Sword of Knowledge series.

Castle of Deception with Josepha Sherman
Based on the bestselling computer game, *The Bard's Tale*. (Available July 1992.)

The Ship Who Searched with Anne McCaffrey
The Ship Who Sang is not alone! (Available August 1992.)

And watch for *Wheels of Fire*, Book II of the SERRAted Edge series, with Mark Shepherd, coming in October 1992.
